Dear Reader,

This book includes both *Wedding at Cardwell Ranch* and an earlier favorite, *The Cowgirl in Question*.

It is always fun to visit the Cardwell Ranch. *Wedding at Cardwell Ranch* introduces the second Cardwell cousin, Jackson, and his five-year-old son, Ford. They leave Texas for Montana to attend Tag Cardwell's wedding to Lily McCabe.

After an ugly divorce and worse custody battle, Jackson isn't a fan of weddings, though, so he just wants this one to be over. What he didn't plan on was the wedding planner, Allie Taylor, and her five-year-old daughter, Natalie. Allie is struggling after losing her husband eight months before. Or is someone trying to make her think she's crazy?

Meanwhile, back at the Sundown Ranch, I enjoyed spending time with the McCall family. Of course bad-boy Rourke is a favorite hero. Framed for a murder he didn't commit, Rourke is heading home to prove his innocence and even the score with Cassidy Miller, the woman who helped send him to prison for eleven years. Can Cassidy convince him he's wrong about her? Or is he?

I hope you enjoy visiting both the Cardwells and the McCalls. The trip will take you first to Big Sky, Montana, and the Cardwell Ranch before traveling across the state to Antelope Flats and the Tongue River area. Saddle up.

B.J. Daniels

www.BJDaniels.com
www.Facebook.com/pages/BJ-Daniels

ABOUT THE AUTHOR

New York Times bestselling author B.J. Daniels wrote her first book after a career as an award-winning newspaper journalist and author of thirty-seven published short stories. That first book, *Odd Man Out*, received a four-and-a-half-star review from *RT Book Reviews* and went on to be nominated for Best Intrigue that year. Since then, she has won numerous awards, including a career achievement award for romantic suspense and many nominations and awards for best book.

Daniels lives in Montana with her husband, Parker, and two springer spaniels, Spot and Jem. When she isn't writing, she snowboards, camps, boats and plays tennis. Daniels is a member of Mystery Writers of America, Sisters in Crime, International Thriller Writers, Kiss of Death and Romance Writers of America.

To contact her, write to B.J. Daniels, P.O. Box 1173, Malta, MT 59538, or email her at bjdaniels@mtintouch.net. Check out her website, www.bjdaniels.com.

Books by B.J. Daniels

HARLEQUIN INTRIGUE

897—CRIME SCENE AT CARDWELL RANCH
996—SECRET OF DEADMAN'S COULEE*
1002—THE NEW DEPUTY IN TOWN*
1024—THE MYSTERY MAN OF WHITEHORSE*
1030—CLASSIFIED CHRISTMAS*
1053—MATCHMAKING WITH A MISSION*
1059—SECOND CHANCE COWBOY*
1083—MONTANA ROYALTY*
1125—SHOTGUN BRIDE§
1131—HUNTING DOWN THE HORSEMAN§
1137—BIG SKY DYNASTY§
1155—SMOKIN' SIX-SHOOTER§
1161—ONE HOT FORTY-FIVE§
1198—GUN-SHY BRIDE**
1204—HITCHED!**
1210—TWELVE-GAUGE GUARDIAN**
1234—BOOTS AND BULLETS^
1240—HIGH-CALIBER CHRISTMAS^
1246—WINCHESTER CHRISTMAS WEDDING^
1276—BRANDED‡
1282—LASSOED‡
1288—RUSTLED‡
1294—STAMPEDED‡
1335—CORRALLED‡
1353—WRANGLED‡
1377—JUSTICE AT CARDWELL RANCH
1413—CARDWELL RANCH TRESPASSER
1455—CHRISTMAS AT CARDWELL RANCH

1497—RESCUE AT
         CARDWELL RANCH
1500—WEDDING AT
         CARDWELL RANCH

*Whitehorse, Montana
§Whitehorse, Montana:
   The Corbetts
**Whitehorse, Montana:
   Winchester Ranch
^Whitehorse, Montana:
   Winchester Ranch Reloaded
‡Whitehorse, Montana:
   Chisholm Cattle Company

Other titles by this author
available in ebook format.

WEDDING AT CARDWELL RANCH

& THE COWGIRL IN QUESTION

New York Times Bestselling Author

B.J. DANIELS

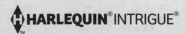

ISBN-13: 978-0-373-83800-4

WEDDING AT CARDWELL RANCH &
THE COWGIRL IN QUESTION

Copyright © 2014 by Harlequin Books S.A.

The publisher acknowledges the copyright holder of the individual works as follows:

WEDDING AT CARDWELL RANCH
Copyright © 2014 by Barbara Heinlein

THE COWGIRL IN QUESTION
Copyright © 2004 by Barbara Heinlein

Recycling programs for this product may not exist in your area.

www.Harlequin.com

Printed in U.S.A.

CONTENTS

WEDDING AT CARDWELL RANCH   7

THE COWGIRL IN QUESTION   229

This is dedicated to my readers and my Facebook friends who shared their "gaslighting" ideas and proved that they think as creepy me.

If you haven't already, come say hello on my author Facebook page at www.facebook.com/pages/BJ-Daniels/127936587217837

Thanks for stopping by Cardwell Ranch!

WEDDING AT CARDWELL RANCH

CHAPTER ONE

ALLISON TAYLOR BRUSHED back a lock of her hair and willed herself not to scream.

"Is something wrong?" her brother-in-law asked from the kitchen doorway, startling her and making her jump.

She dropped the heavy covered pot she'd taken from the pantry a little too hard onto the counter. The lid shifted, but not enough that she could see inside.

"Didn't mean to scare you," Drew Taylor said with a laugh as he lounged against the kitchen door frame. "I was cravin' some of your famous chili, but I think maybe we should go out."

"I just need a minute. If you could see to Natalie…"

"She's still asleep. I just checked." Drew studied her for a long moment. Like his brother, he had russet-brown hair and dark brown eyes and classic good looks. His mother had assured both of her sons that they were wonderful. Fortunately Drew had taken it with a grain of salt—unlike his brother Nick.

"Are you okay, Allie? I've been so worried about you since Nick…"

"I'm fine." She didn't want to talk about her presumed-dead husband. She really just wanted her brother-in-law to go into the other room and leave her alone for a moment.

Drew had been a godsend. She didn't know what she would have done without him, she thought as she pulled a band from her jeans pocket and secured her long, blond hair in a single tail at the back of her head.

When she'd mentioned how nice his brother was to Nick shortly after they married, he'd scoffed.

"Just be glad he likes you. He's about the only one in my family," he had added with a laugh.

"Why don't you let me help you with that," Drew said now as he took a step toward her. He frowned as his gaze went to the pot and the pile of ingredients she'd already stacked up on the counter. The chili pot was the last thing she'd brought into the kitchen from the porch of the small cabin. "You kept the pot?"

So his mother had told him about the incident.

He must think I'm losing my mind just like his mother and sister do.

The worst part was she feared they were right.

Allie looked down at the heavy cast-iron pot with its equally heavy cast-iron lid. Her hand trembled as she reached for the handle. The memory of the last time she'd lifted that lid—and what she'd found inside—sent a shudder through her.

The covered cast-iron casserole pot, enameled white inside and the color of fresh blood on the outside, had been a wedding present from her in-laws.

"She does know how to cook, doesn't she?" her mother-in-law, Mildred, had asked all those years ago as if Allie hadn't been standing there. Mildred was a twig-thin woman who took pride in these things: her petite, slim, fifty-eight-year-old body, her sons and her standing in the community. Her daughter, Sarah, was just the opposite of her mother, overweight and dumpy by comparison. And Mildred was always making that comparison to anyone who would listen, including Sarah.

Mildred was on her fourth husband and lived in one of

the more modest mansions at Big Sky. Of her two sons, Nick had been the baby—and clearly her favorite.

Nick had laughed that day when his mother had asked if his new wife could cook. "She makes pretty good chili, I'll give her that," he told Mildred. "But that's not why I married her." He'd given Allie a side hug, grinning like a fool and making her blush to the roots of her hair.

Nick had liked to say he had the prettiest wife in town. "Just make sure you stay that way," he'd always add. "You start looking like my sister and you can pack your bags."

The red, cast-iron, covered pot she was now reaching for had become her chili pot.

"Allie, I thought you'd thrown that pot away!" Drew reached to stop her, knocking the lid off in the effort. It clattered to the counter.

Allie lunged back, her arm going up protectively to shield her face. But this time the pot was empty. No half-dead squirrel inside it.

"I'm throwing this pot in the trash," Drew announced. "If just the sight of it upsets you—"

"No, your mother will have a fit."

"Let her." He swept pot and lid off the counter and carried it out to the garbage can.

When he came back into the room, he looked at her and shook his head. "Allie, you've got to pull it together. Maybe you should go back to the doctor and see if there is something else he can give you. You're strung like a piano wire."

She shook her head. "I don't need a doctor." She just needed for whatever was happening to her to stop.

His gaze moved past her, his expression going from a concerned frown to a smile. "Hey, girl," he said as his five-year-old niece came into the kitchen. He stepped past Allie to swing Nat into his arms. "I came over to check on the two of you. Mama was going to cook us some dinner but I think we should go out to eat. What do you say?"

Allie started to argue that she couldn't let Drew do any more for them and she sure couldn't afford to go out to eat, but stopped as her daughter said, "Are you sick, Mama?" Her precious daughter looked to her with concern. Allie saw the worry in Nat's angelic face. She'd seen it too much lately. It was bad enough that Natalie had recently lost her father. Now more than ever she needed her mother to be sane.

"I'm fine, sweetie. It's too hot for chili, anyway. So let's go out, why not?" Allie said, relieved and thankful for Drew. Not just for coming by to check on them, but for throwing out the pot. She hadn't because her mother-in-law was upset enough and the Taylors were the only family she had, especially now.

"Just let me freshen up and change," she said as Drew took Nat to look for her shoes.

In the bathroom, Allie locked the door, turned on the shower and stripped off her clothes. She was still sweating from fear, her heart beating hard against her chest.

"You found a what in the chili pot?" her mother-in-law had asked in disbelief when Allie had called her—a huge mistake in retrospect. But at the time, she'd hoped her mother-in-law would understand why she couldn't keep the pot. Why she didn't want it in her house.

"I found a squirrel in that cast-iron pot you gave me. When I picked up the lid—"

"No way would a squirrel get into your cabin, let alone climb under a heavy lid like that. Why would it? You must have imagined it. Are you still on those drugs the doctor gave you after my Nicky died?"

Allie's husband had always been "my Nicky" to his

mother while Mildred had insisted Allie call *her* "Mother Taylor."

"No, Mother Taylor, I told you." Allie's own mother had died when she was nineteen. Her father had moved, remarried and started a new family. They'd lost touch. "I quit taking the pills a long time ago."

"I think it's those pills," Mildred had said as if Allie hadn't spoken. "You said they had you seeing things that weren't there."

"The squirrel *was* there. I had to take it out back and—"

"If I were you, I'd talk to your doctor. Why do you need the pills, anyway? It isn't like you're still grieving over my Nicky. Charlotte Reynolds told me she saw you having lunch the other day, you and Natalie, and you were *laughing.*"

Allie had closed her eyes, remembering the lunch in question. "I am trying to make things more normal for Nat."

"Well, it looks bad, you having a good time while your poor husband is barely cold in his grave."

She wanted to mention that Nick wasn't in his grave, but knew better than to bring that up. "It's been eight months."

"Like you have to tell me that!" Mildred sniffed and blew her nose. She'd cried constantly over the death of her favorite son and couldn't understand why Allie wasn't still doing the same.

"We all grieve in our own way and I have a young daughter to raise," Allie had said more times than she wanted to recall.

The phone call had ended with Mildred crying and talking about what a wonderful man her Nicky had been. A lie at best. He'd been a lousy husband and an even worse father, but now that he was dead, he would always be the wonderful man Mildred remembered.

After that, she'd learned her lesson. She kept the other crazy things that had been happening to herself. If Mildred knew, she would have her in a straitjacket. And little Nat…? She couldn't bear to think about Mildred having anything to do with raising her daughter.

"So," Drew said as she and Nat sat across from him in a booth at a local café later that evening. "Did I hear you've gone back to work?"

It was impossible to keep anything a secret in this canyon, Allie thought. She had hoped to keep it from the Taylor family as long as possible.

"Dana Savage called me about doing a Western wedding up at her ranch for her cousin Tag and his soon-to-be wife, Lily." She didn't mention that she'd accepted the job several months ago. Or how badly she needed the money. With the investigation into Nick's presumed death still unresolved, the insurance company was holding off paying her. Not that it would last long if she didn't get back to work.

Her mother-in-law kept mentioning "that big insurance check my Nicky left you," but the insurance money would barely cover a couple years of Natalie's college, if that. And Allie hoped to invest it for that very use.

"I've been doing some work at Cardwell Ranch. Nice people to work for. But are you sure you're up to it?" Drew asked quietly, real concern in his tone. "Mother mentioned that she was worried about you. She said you were still taking the pills and they were making you see things?"

Of course Mildred told Drew and his sister, Sarah, everything. Allie tried not to show her irritation. She had no appetite, but she attempted to eat what she could. She didn't want Drew mentioning to his mother, even accidentally, that she wasn't eating much. Mildred would make it into her not taking care of herself.

"I'm fine. I'm *not* taking the pills. I told your mother—"

He held up his hand. "You don't have to tell me about my mother. She hears only what she wants to hear. I'm on your side. I think going back to work might be the best thing for you. So what do you plan to do with Natalie? I don't have to tell you what Mother is going to say."

"Nat's going with me," Allie said emphatically. "Dana has children she can play with. As a matter of fact, Dana is going to teach Nat to ride a horse."

Natalie grinned and clapped her small hands excitedly. She was the spitting image of Allie at that age: straight, pale blond hair cut in a bob, green eyes with a pert little nose and deep dimples. Allie got the blond hair from her Scandinavian mother and the green eyes from her Irish father.

There was no sign of the Taylor family in her daughter, something that had caused a lot of speculation from not only Nick, but his mother.

Nat quickly told her uncle that it would be a very gentle horse and Dana's kids Hank and Mary were riding before they were even her age. "The twins are too young to ride yet," she announced.

"Dana wouldn't let Nat do it if she thought it wasn't all right," Allie added.

"I'm sure it will be fine," Drew said, but she could tell that he already knew what her mother-in-law was going to have to say about it. "Cardwell Ranch is where the wedding is going to be, I take it?"

"The wedding will be in a meadow on the ranch with the reception and a lot of other events in the large, old barn."

"You know that we've been invited," Drew said almost in warning.

The canyon was its own little community, with many of the older families—like Dana's—that dated back to the eighteen hundreds before there was even a paved road through it. Mildred Taylor must be delighted to be invited to a wedding of a family that was like old canyon royalty. Mother Taylor might resent the Cardwell clan, say things behind their back, but she would never outright defy them since everyone loved Dana Cardwell Savage and had held great respect for her mother, Mary Justice.

"How are things with you?" Allie asked.

"Everything's fine." He smiled but she'd seen the lines around his eyes and had heard that his construction company was struggling without Nick.

He'd been so generous with her and Natalie that she feared he was giving away money he didn't have.

She was just thankful when the meal was over and Drew dropped her and Nat off at the small cabin in the Gallatin Canyon where she'd lived with Nick until his disappearance. *The canyon* as it was known, ran from the mouth just south of Gallatin Gateway almost to West Yellowstone, fifty miles of winding road that trailed the river in a deep cut through the mountains.

The drive along the Gallatin River was breathtaking, a winding strip of highway that followed the blue-ribbon trout stream up over the Continental Divide. In the summer as it was now, the Gallatin ran crystal clear over tinted green boulders. Pine trees grew dark and thick along its edge and against the steep mountains. Aspens, their leaves bright green, grew among the pines.

Sheer rock cliffs overlooked the highway and river, with small areas of open land. The canyon had been mostly cattle and dude ranches, a few summer cabins and homes—that was until Big Sky resort and the small town that followed developed at the foot of Lone Mountain.

Luxury houses had sprouted up all around the resort, with Mother Taylor's being one of them. Fortunately, some of the original cabins still remained and the majority of the canyon was National Forest so it would always remain undeveloped.

Allie's was one of the older cabins. Because it was small and not in great shape, Nick had gotten a good deal on it. Being in construction, he'd promised to enlarge it and fix all the things wrong with it. That hadn't happened.

After Drew left, Allie didn't hurry inside the cabin. It was a nice summer night, the stars overhead glittering brightly and a cool breeze coming up from the river.

She had begun to hate the cabin—and her fear of what might be waiting for her inside it. Nick had been such a force of nature to deal with that his presence seemed to have soaked into the walls. Sometimes she swore she could hear his voice. Often she found items of his clothing lying around the house as if he was still there—even though she'd boxed up his things and taken them to the local charity shop months ago.

Just the thought of what might be waiting for her inside the cabin this time made her shudder as she opened the door and stepped in, Nat at her side.

She hadn't heard Nick's voice since she'd quit taking the drugs. Until last night. When she'd come into the living room, half-asleep, she'd found his favorite shirt lying on the floor by the couch. She'd actually thought she smelled his aftershave even though she'd thrown the bottle away.

The cabin looked just as she'd left it. Letting out a sigh of relief, she put Nat to bed and tried to convince herself she hadn't heard Nick's voice last night. Even the shirt that she'd remembered picking up and thinking it felt warm and smelled of Nick before she'd dropped it over the back of the couch was gone this morning, proving the whole incident had been nothing but a bad dream.

"Good night, sweetheart," she said and kissed her daughter's forehead.

"Night," Nat said sleepily and closed her eyes.

Allie felt as if her heart was going to burst when she looked at her precious daughter. She couldn't let Mildred get her hands on Nat. But if the woman thought for a moment that Allie was incapable of raising her daughter...

She quickly turned out the light and tiptoed out of the room. For a moment, she stood in the small living area. Nick's shirt wasn't over the back of the couch so that was a relief.

So many times she had stood here and wished her life could be different. Nick had been so sweet while they were dating. She'd really thought she'd met her Prince Charming—until after the wedding and she met the real Nick Taylor.

She sighed, remembering her decision soon after the wedding to leave him and have the marriage annulled, but then she'd realized she was pregnant. Had she really been so naive as to think a baby would change Nick into the man she'd thought she'd married?

Shaking her head now, she looked around the cabin, remembering all the ideas she had to fix the place up and make it a home. Nick had hated them all and they had ended up doing nothing to the cabin.

Well, she could do what she wanted now, couldn't she? But she knew, even if she had the money, she didn't have the heart for it. She would never be able to exorcize Nick's ghost from this house. What she really wanted was to sell the cabin and move. She promised herself she would— once everything with Nick's death was settled.

Stepping into her bedroom, she was startled to see a pile of her clothes on her bed. Had she taken them out of the closet earlier when she'd changed to go to dinner? Her heart began to pound. She'd been upset earlier but she wouldn't have just thrown her clothes on the bed like that.

Then how had they gotten there? She'd locked the cabin when she'd left.

Panicked, she raced through the house to see if anything was missing or if any of the doors or windows had been broken into. Everything was just as she'd left it—except for the clothes on her bed.

Reluctantly, she walked back into her bedroom half-afraid the clothes wouldn't still be on the bed. Another hallucination?

The clothes were there. Unfortunately, that didn't come as a complete relief. Tonight at dinner, she'd worn capris, a blouse and sandals since it was June in Montana. Why would she have pulled out what appeared to be almost everything she owned from the closet? No, she realized, not *everything*. These were only the clothes that Nick had bought her.

Tears blurred her eyes as she started to pick up one of the dresses. Like the others, she hated this dress because it reminded her of the times he'd made her wear it and how the night had ended. It was very low cut in the front. She'd felt cheap in it and told him so but he'd only laughed.

"When you've got it, flaunt it," he'd said. "That's what I say."

Why hadn't she gotten rid of these clothes? For the same reason she hadn't thrown out the chili pot after the squirrel incident. She hadn't wanted to upset her mother-in-law. Placating Mother Taylor had begun right after Allie had married her son. It was just so much easier than arguing with the woman.

"Nick said you don't like the dresses he buys you," Mildred had said disapprovingly one day when she'd stopped by the cabin and asked Allie why she wasn't wearing the new dress. "There is nothing wrong with looking nice for your husband."

"The dresses he buys me are just more revealing than I feel comfortable with."

Her mother-in-law had mugged a face. "You'd better loosen up and give my son what he wants or he'll find someone who will."

Now as she reached for the dress on the top of the pile, she told herself she would throw them out, Mother Taylor be damned.

But the moment she touched the dress, she let out a cry of surprise and panic. The fabric had jagged cuts down the front. She stared in horror as she saw other deep, angry-looking slices in the fabric. *Who had done this?*

Her heart in her throat, she picked up another of the dresses Nick had made her wear. Her sewing scissors clattered to the bedroom floor. She stared down at the scissors in horror, then at the pile of destroyed clothing. All of the dresses Nick had bought her had been ruined.

Allie shook her head as she dropped the dress in her hand and took a step back from the bed. Banging into the closed closet doors, she fought to breathe, her heart hammering in her chest. *Who did this?* Who *would* do this? She remembered her brother-in-law calling from out in the hall earlier, asking what was taking her so long before they'd gone to dinner. But that was because she'd taken a shower to get the smell of her own fear off her. It wasn't because she was in here cutting up the clothes her dead husband had made her wear.

Tears welled in her eyes, making the room blur. She shoved that bitter thought away and wiped at her tears. She wouldn't have done this. She *couldn't* have.

Suddenly, she turned and stared at the closed closet door with mounting fear. Slowly, she reached for the knob, her hand trembling. As the closet door came open, she froze. Her eyes widened in new alarm.

A half dozen new outfits hung in the otherwise nearly empty closet, the price tags still on them. As if sleepwalking, Allie reached for one of the tags and stared in shock at the price. Hurriedly, she checked the others. She couldn't afford any of them. So where had they come from?

Not only that, the clothes were what she would call "classic," the type of clothes she'd worn when she'd met Nick. The kind of clothes she'd pleaded with him to let her wear.

"I want other men to look at you and wish they were me," Nick had said, getting angry.

But when she and Nick went out and she wore the clothes and other men did look, Nick had blamed her.

"You must have given him the eye," Nick would say as they argued on the way home. "Probably flipped your hair like an invitation. Who knows what you do while I'm at work all day."

"I take care of your daughter and your house."

Nick hadn't let her work after they'd gotten married, even though he knew how much she loved her wedding planning business. "Women who work get too uppity. They think they don't need a man. No wife of mine is going to work."

Allie had only the clothes he bought her. She'd purchased little since his death because the money had been so tight. Nick had wanted to know about every cent she'd spent, so she hadn't been able to save any money, either. Nick paid the bills and gave her a grocery allowance. He said he'd buy her whatever she needed.

Now she stared at the beautiful clothes hanging in her closet. Beautiful blouses and tops. Amazing skirts and pants and dresses. Clothes Nick would have taken out in the yard and burned. But Nick was gone.

Or was he? He still hadn't been declared legally dead. That thought scared her more than she wanted to admit. What if he suddenly turned up at her door one night?

Was that what was making her crazy? Maybe she *had* done this. She had yearned for clothing like this and hated the clothes Nick had bought her, so had she subconsciously...

Allie stumbled away from the closet, bumped into the corner of the bed and sat down hard on the floor next to it. Her hand shook as she covered her mouth to keep from screaming. Had she shoplifted these clothes? She couldn't have purchased them. Just as she couldn't have cut up the dresses and not remembered. There had to be another explanation. Someone was playing a horrible trick on her.

But even as she pondered it, more rational thoughts came on its heels. Did she really believe that someone had come into the cabin and done this? Who in their right mind would believe that?

Pushing herself up, she crawled over to where she'd dropped her purse as she tried to remember even the last time she'd written a check. Her checkbook wasn't in her purse. She frowned and realized she must have left it in the desk when she'd paid bills.

Getting up she walked on wobbly legs to the desk in the corner, opened the drawer and took out her checkbook. Her fingers shook with such a tremor that she could barely read what was written in it.

But there it was. A check for more than eight hundred dollars! The handwriting was scrawled, but she knew it had to be hers. She saw the date of the check. *Yesterday?*

She had dropped Nat off for a playdate and then gone into Bozeman... Could she account for the entire afternoon? Her heart pounded as she tried to remember everything she'd done and when she might have bought these clothes. She'd been wandering around in a daze since Nick's death. She couldn't account for every minute of yesterday, but what did that matter? The proof was staring her in the face.

Allie shoved the checkbook into the drawer and tried to pull herself together. She had to think about her daughter.

"You're fine," she whispered to herself. "Once you get back to work…" She couldn't have been more thankful that she had the Cardwell Ranch wedding. More than the money, she needed to do what she loved—planning weddings—and get her mind off everything else.

Once she was out of this house she'd shared with Nick… Yes, then she would be fine. She wouldn't be so…forgetful. What woman wouldn't feel she was losing her mind, considering what she'd been going through?

CHAPTER TWO

"WHO'S THAT SINGING?" five-year-old Ford Cardwell asked as he and his father followed the sound.

Jackson Cardwell had parked the rental SUV down by his cousin Dana's ranch house when they'd arrived, but finding no one at home, they'd headed up the hill toward the barn and the van parked in front of it.

"I have no idea, son," Jackson said, but couldn't help smiling. The voice was young and sweet, the song beautiful. "It sounds like an angel."

"It *is* an angel," Ford cried and pointed past the barn to the corrals.

The girl was about his son's age, but while Ford had taken after the Cardwell side of the family with his dark hair and eyes, this child had pale blond hair and huge green eyes.

When she saw them, she smiled, exposing two deep dimples. Both children were adorable, but this little girl was hands down more angelic-looking and—Jackson would bet—*acting* than Ford.

She wore cowboy boots with a pale green-and-white-polka-dotted, one-piece, short jumpsuit that brought out the emerald-green of her eyes. Jackson saw that the girl was singing to several horses that had come up to the edge of the corral fence.

The girl finished the last of the lyrics before she seemed

to notice them and came running over. "If you're looking for my mother, she's in the barn working."

Next to him, Jackson saw that his son had apparently been struck dumb.

"I'm Nat," the girl announced. "My name is really Natalie, though." She shifted her gaze to the mute Ford. "Everyone calls me Nat, so you can if you want to."

"This is my son, Ford."

Nat eyed Ford for a moment before she stepped forward and took his hand. "Come on, Ford. You'll probably want to see the rest of the animals. There are chickens and rabbits and several mules along with all the horses. Don't worry," she added before Jackson could voice his concern. "We won't get too close. We'll just pet them through the corral fence and feed the horses apples. It's okay. Mrs. Savage showed me how."

"Don't go far," Jackson said as the precocious Nat led his son toward several low-slung buildings. The girl was busy talking as they left. Ford, as far as Jackson could tell, hadn't uttered a word yet.

As he turned back toward the barn, he saw the logo on the side of the van: Weddings by Allie Knight. The logo looked old as did the van.

The girl had said her mother was working in the barn. That must be where the wedding was going to be held. His brother Tag had mentioned something about his wedding to Lily McCabe being very *Western*.

"You mean like Texas meets Montana?" Jackson had joked.

"Something like that. Don't worry. You'll feel right at home."

His brother's wedding wasn't what had him worried. After talking to Tag for a few moments on the phone, he'd known his brother had fallen head over heels for Lily. He was happy for him.

No, what worried Jackson was nailing down the last of the plans before the wedding for the opening of a Texas Boys Barbecue joint in Big Sky, Montana. He had hoped that all of the brothers would be here by now. Laramie and Austin hadn't even flown up to see the space Tag had found, let alone signed off on the deal.

From the time the five brothers had opened their first restaurant in an old house in Houston, they'd sworn they would never venture outside of Texas with their barbecue. Even as their business had grown and they'd opened more restaurants and finally started their own franchise, they had stayed in the state where they'd been raised.

Jackson understood why Tag wanted to open one here. But he feared it had nothing to do with business and everything to do with love and not wanting to leave Montana, where they had all been born.

Before the wedding had seemed the perfect time for all of them to get together and finalize the deal. Hayes had come here last month to see if the restaurant was even feasible. Unfortunately, Hayes had gotten sidetracked, so now it was up to the rest of them to make sure Tag was doing the best thing for the business—and before the wedding, which was only four days away.

He hoped all his brothers arrived soon so they could get this over with. They led such busy lives in Texas that they hardly ever saw each other. Tag had said on the phone he was anxious to show him the building he'd found for the new restaurant. Tag and Hayes had already made arrangements to buy the building without the final okay from the other brothers, something else that made Jackson nervous.

Jackson didn't want this move to cause problems among

the five of them. So his mind was miles away as he started to step into the dim darkness inside the barn.

The cool air inside was suddenly filled with a terrified scream. An instant later, a black cat streaked past him and out the barn door.

JACKSON RACED INTO the barn not sure what he was going to find. What he found was a blond-haired woman who shared a striking resemblance to the little girl who'd been singing outside by the corrals.

While Nat had been angelic, this woman was as beautiful as any he'd ever seen. Her long, straight, blond hair was the color of sunshine. It rippled down her slim back. Her eyes, a tantalizing emerald-green, were huge with fear in a face that could stop traffic.

She stood against the barn wall, a box of wedding decorations open at her feet. Her eyes widened in even more alarm when she saw him. She threw a hand over her mouth, cutting off the scream.

"Are you all right?" he asked. She didn't appear to be hurt, just scared. No, not scared, *terrified.* Had she seen a mouse? Or maybe something larger? In Texas it might have been an armadillo. He wasn't sure what kind of critters they had this far north, but something had definitely set her off.

"It was nothing," she said, removing her hand from her mouth. Some of the color slowly returned to her face but he could see that she was still trembling.

"It was *something,*" he assured her.

She shook her head and ventured a look at the large box of decorations at her feet. The lid had been thrown to the side, some of the decorations spilling onto the floor.

He laughed. "Let me guess. That black cat I just saw

hightailing it out of here… I'm betting he came out of that box."

Her eyes widened further. *"You saw it?"*

"Raced right past me." He laughed. "You didn't think you imagined it, did you?"

"It happened so fast. I couldn't be sure."

"Must have given you quite a fright."

She let out a nervous laugh and tried to smile, exposing deep dimples. He understood now why his son had gone mute. He felt the same way looking at Natalie's mother. There was an innocence about her, a vulnerability that would make a man feel protective.

Just the thought made him balk. He'd fallen once and wasn't about to get lured into that trap again. Not that there was any chance of that happening. In a few days he would be on a plane back to Texas with his son.

"You know cats," he said, just being polite. "They'll climb into just about anything. They're attracted by pretty things." Just like some cowboys. Not him, though.

"Yes," she said, but didn't sound convinced as she stepped away from the box. She didn't look all that steady on her feet. He started to reach out to her, but stopped himself as she found her footing.

He couldn't help noticing that her eyes were a darker shade of green than her daughter's. "Just a cat. A black one at that," he said, wondering why he felt the need to fill the silence. "You aren't superstitious, are you?"

She shook her head and those emerald eyes brightened. That with the color returning to her cheeks made her even more striking.

This was how he'd fallen for Ford's mother—a pretty face and what had seemed like a sweet disposition in a woman who'd needed him—and look how that had turned out. No, it took more than a pretty face to turn his head after the beating he'd taken from the last one.

"You must be one of Tag's brothers," she said as she wiped her palms on her jeans before extending a hand. Along with jeans, she wore a checked navy shirt, the sleeves rolled up, and cowboy boots. "I'm Allie Taylor, the wedding planner."

Jackson quickly removed his hat, wondering where he'd left his manners. His mother had raised him better than this. But even as he started to shake her hand, he felt himself hesitate as if he were afraid to touch her.

Ridiculous, he thought as he grasped her small, ice-cold hand in his larger, much warmer one. "Jackson Cardwell. I saw your van outside. But I thought the name on the side—"

"Taylor is my married name." When his gaze went to her empty ring finger, she quickly added, "I'm a widow." She pulled back her hand to rub the spot where her wedding band had resided not that long ago. There was a thin, white line indicating that she hadn't been widowed long. Or she hadn't taken the band off until recently.

"I believe I met your daughter as my son and I were coming in. Natalie?"

"Yes, my baby girl." Her dimpled smile told him everything he needed to know about her relationship with her daughter. He knew that smile and suspected he had one much like it when he talked about Ford.

He felt himself relax a little. There was nothing dangerous about this woman. She was a single parent, just like him. Only she'd lost her husband and he wished he could get rid of his ex indefinitely.

"Your daughter took my son to see the horses. I should probably check on him."

"Don't worry. Nat has a healthy respect for the horses

and knows the rules. Also Warren Fitzpatrick, their hired man, is never far away. He's Dana's semi-retired ranch manager. She says he's a fixture around here and loves the kids. That seems to be his job now, to make sure the kids are safe. Not that there aren't others on the ranch watching out for them, as well. Sorry, I talk too much when I'm... nervous." She took a deep breath and let it out slowly. "I want this wedding to be perfect."

He could tell she was still shaken by the black cat episode. "My brother Tag mentioned that Dana and the kids had almost been killed by some crazy woman. It's good she has someone she trusts keeping an eye on the children, even with everyone else on the ranch watching out for them. Don't worry," he said, looking around the barn. "I'm sure the wedding will be perfect."

The barn was huge and yet this felt almost too intimate standing here talking to her. "I was just about to get Ford and go down to the house. Dana told me she was baking a huge batch of chocolate chip cookies and to help ourselves. I believe she said there would also be homemade lemonade when we got here."

Allie smiled and he realized she'd thought it was an invitation. "I really need to get these decorations—"

"Sorry. I'm keeping you from your work." He took a step back. "Those decorations aren't going to put themselves up."

She looked as if she wasn't so sure of that. The cat had definitely put a scare into her, he thought. She didn't seem sure of anything right now. Allie looked again at the box of decorations, no doubt imagining the cat flying out of it at her.

Glancing at her watch, she said, "Oh, I didn't realize it was so late. Nat and I are meeting a friend for lunch. We need to get going."

Jackson was suddenly aware that he'd been holding his hat since shaking Allie's hand. He quickly put it back on as they walked out of the barn door into the bright sunshine. "My son is quite taken with your daughter," he said, again feeling an unusual need to fill the silence.

"How old is he?"

"Ford's five."

"Same age as Nat."

As they emerged into the beautiful late-June day, Jackson saw the two children and waved. As they came running, Nat was chattering away and Ford was hanging on her every word.

"They do seem to have hit it off." Allie sounded surprised and pleased. "Nat's had a hard time lately. I'm glad to see her making a new friend."

Jackson could see that Allie Taylor had been having a hard time, as well. He realized she must have loved her husband very much. He knew he should say something, but for the life of him he couldn't think of what. He couldn't even imagine a happy marriage. As a vehicle came roaring up the road, they both turned, the moment lost.

"Hey, bro," Tanner "Tag" Cardwell called from the rolled down window of his pickup as he swung into the ranch yard. "I see you made it," he said, getting out to come over and shake his brother's hand before he pulled Jackson into a hug. Tag glanced over at Ford and Natalie and added with a laugh, "Like father like son. If there's a pretty female around, you two will find them."

Jackson shook his head. That had been true when he'd met Ford's mother. But since the divorce and the custody battle, he'd been too busy single-handedly raising his son to even think about women. That's why red flags had gone up when he'd met Allie. There was something about her that had pulled at him, something more than her obvious beauty.

"Dana's right behind me with the kids," Tag said. "Why don't I show you and Ford to your cabin, then you can meet everyone." He pointed up in the pines that covered the mountainside. "Let's grab your bags. It's just a short walk."

Jackson turned to say goodbye to Allie, but she and her daughter had already headed for the old van.

"COME ON, NAT, we're meeting Belinda for lunch," Allie said as the Cardwell men headed for the cabins on the mountain behind the barn. Working here had been a godsend. Nat was having a wonderful time. She loved Dana's children. Hank was a year older than Nat, with Mary being the same age. Dana's twin boys, Angus and Brick, were just over a year and her sister Stacy's daughter, Ella, was a year and a half. Dana had her hands full but Stacy helped out with the younger ones. All of them loved the animals, especially the horses.

True to her word, Dana had made sure Nat had begun her horseback riding lessons. Nat was a natural, Dana had said, and Allie could see it was true.

Their few days here so far had been perfect.

Until the cat, there hadn't been any other incidents.

Her friend Belinda Andrews was waiting for them at a little Mexican food place near Meadow Village at Big Sky. While other friends had gone by the wayside since she'd married Nick six years ago, Belinda hadn't let Nick run her off. Allie suspected that, like her, she didn't have a lot of friends and Nick, while he'd made it clear he didn't like Belinda, had grudgingly put up with her the times they'd crossed paths.

"I hope we didn't keep you waiting," Allie said as she and Nat met Belinda on the patio. "You didn't have any trouble getting off work for the wedding shoot?" Belinda worked for a local photographer, but freelanced weddings. It was how they'd met back when Allie had her own wedding planning business.

Belinda grinned. "All set for the Tag Cardwell and Lily McCabe wedding. I took Dana up on her offer. I'm moving into one of the guest cabins later today!"

Allie wasn't all that surprised. Dana had offered her a cabin, as well, while she was preparing everything for the wedding. But since she lived just down the highway a few miles, Allie thought it best to remain at home for Nat's sake. Her daughter had had enough changes in her life recently.

"You really are excited about this," Allie said, noticing how nice Belinda looked. Her friend was dressed in a crop top and cut-off jeans, her skin tanned. Her dark hair was piled haphazardly up on her head, silver dangly earrings tinkled from her earlobes and, while she looked makeup free, Allie could tell she wasn't.

Belinda looked enchanting, a trick Allie wished she could pull off, she thought. On the way here, she'd pulled her hair up in a ponytail and even though she'd showered this morning, she'd forgone makeup. Nick was always suspicious when she wore it when he wasn't around so she'd gotten out of the habit.

Inside the café, Nat asked if she could play in the nearby area for kids and Allie said she could as long as she didn't argue about coming back to eat when her meal came.

"You look…pale," Belinda said, studying her after they were seated outside on the patio under an umbrella so they could see Nat. "You haven't had anymore of those… incidents, have you?"

Allie almost laughed at that. "I just need to get more sun," she said and picked up her menu to hide behind.

"I know you too well," Belinda said, dragging down the menu so she could look into her eyes. "What's happened *now?*"

"A black cat jumped out of one of my decoration boxes and scared me just before I came over here. And guess what? Someone else saw it." *So there,* she wanted to say, *I don't need my head examined.*

Belinda nodded, studying her. "A *black* cat?"

"Yes, a *black* cat and I didn't imagine it. One of the Cardwell brothers saw it, as well." She couldn't even voice how much of a relief that had been.

"That's all that's happened?"

"That's it." She had to look down at the menu to pull off the lie and was just glad when Belinda didn't question her further. She hadn't told *anyone* about the shredded dresses from her closet or the new clothes she'd taken back. The sales associate hadn't remembered her, but said the afternoon when the clothing was purchased had been a busy one. None of the other sales associates remembered her, but agreed they'd been too busy to say for sure. She'd ended up keeping two of the outfits to wear while working the rehearsal dinner and the wedding.

"I already moved some of my things into the cabin," Belinda said.

Allie couldn't help being surprised. "Already? Why didn't you stop by the barn and say hello?" Allie had suggested Belinda as the wedding photographer and felt responsible and anxious since this was her first wedding in five years.

"You were busy," her friend said. "We can't keep each other from our jobs, right?"

"Right." She loved that Belinda understood that. In truth, Allie had been hesitant to suggest her friend. She didn't want to have to worry about Belinda, not with everything else that she had going on in her life right now. While her friend was a great photographer, sometimes she got sidetracked if a handsome man was around. But when she'd broached the subject with the bride-to-be, Lily had been delighted that it was one other thing she didn't have to worry about.

Dana had been kind enough to offer Belinda a cabin on the ranch for the five-day affair. "It will make it easier for you to get great shots if you're staying up here and experiencing all the wedding festivities," Dana had said. "And any friend of Allie's is a friend of ours."

She and Belinda had been friends since grade school. Lately they hadn't been as close, probably Allie's fault. Belinda was in between men right now, and much wilder, freer and more outspoken than Allie had ever been. But Belinda didn't have a five-year-old daughter, either.

"You have no idea what this means to me," Belinda said now. "I've been dying to photograph a Western wedding for my portfolio."

"Your portfolio?"

Belinda looked embarrassed as if she'd let the cat out of the bag, so to speak. "I'm thinking about opening my own studio."

"That's great." Allie was happy for her friend, although she'd wondered if Belinda had come into some money because it wouldn't be cheap and as far as she knew Belinda lived from paycheck to paycheck like everyone else she knew.

The waitress came and took their orders. A light breeze stirred the new leaves on the nearby trees. The smell of summer mixed with that of corn tortillas, the most wonderful smell of all, Allie thought. They sipped Mexican Cokes, munched on chips and salsa to the sound of Latin music playing in the background and Allie felt herself begin to relax.

"I wasn't going to bring this up," Belinda said, "but you know that psychic that I've seen off and on?"

Allie fought not to roll her eyes.

"I know you say you don't believe in this stuff, but she said something interesting when I mentioned you."

"You told her about *me?*" Allie hadn't meant for her voice to rise so high. Her daughter looked over. She smiled at Nat and quickly changed her tone. "I really don't want you talking to anyone about me, let alone a…" She tried to come up with a word other than *charlatan.*

Belinda leaned forward, unfazed. "She thinks what's happening to you is because of guilt. Simply put, you feel guilty and it is manifesting itself into these…*incidents.*"

Allie stared at her. Leave it to Belinda to get right to the heart of it.

Her friend lowered her voice as if afraid Nat might be listening. "It makes sense, if you think about it. Nick didn't know you were—" she glanced at Nat "—leaving him and going to file for custody of you-know-who, but *you* did know your plan. Then he goes and gets himself…" She grimaced in place of the word *killed.* "Something like that has to mess with your mind."

"Yes, losing your husband does mess with your mind no matter what kind of marriage you had." Fortunately, the waitress brought their food. Allie called Nat up to the table and, for a few moments, they ate in silence.

"The thing is…" Belinda said between bites.

"Can't we just enjoy our meal?" Allie pleaded.

Her friend waved that suggestion away, but didn't say more until they had finished and Nat had gone back to the play area.

"The psychic thinks there is more to it," Belinda said. "What if Nick *knew* about your…plan?"

"What are you saying?"

"Come on. You've been over Nick for a long time. His death wouldn't make you crazy—"

"I'm not crazy," she protested weakly.

"But what if he *did* know or at least suspected? Come on, Allie. We both know it was so not like Nick to go hunting up into the mountains alone, knowing that the grizzlies were eating everything they could get their paws on before hibernation." She didn't seem to notice Allie wince. "Didn't the ranger say Nick had food in his backpack?"

"He didn't take food to attract a bear, if that's what you're saying. He planned to stay a few days so of course he had food in his backpack."

"I'm not trying to upset you. But if he went up there to end it all, that was his choice. You can't go crazy because you feel guilty."

Her stomach turned at the thought of the backpack she'd been asked to identify. It had been shredded by the grizzly's claws. She'd been horrified to think of what the bear had done to Nick. She would never forget the officer who'd brought her the news.

"From what we've been able to assess at the scene, your husband was attacked by a grizzly and given the tracks and other signs—"

"Signs?"

"Blood, ma'am."

She'd had to sit down. "You're telling me he's…dead?"

"It certainly looks that way," the ranger said. Four days later, the search for Nick Taylor was called off because a winter storm had come in and it was believed that there was little chance he could have survived such an attack without immediate medical attention.

"Nick wouldn't," she managed to say now. In her heart of hearts, the man she knew so well, the man she'd been married to for more than six years, wouldn't purposely go into the woods with a plan to be killed by a grizzly.

But Nick had always been unpredictable. Moody and often depressed, too. The construction business hadn't been doing well even before Nick's death. What would he have done if he'd known she was leaving him and taking his daughter? Hadn't she been suspicious when Nick told her of his plan to go hunting alone? She'd actually thought he might be having an affair and wanted to spend a few days with his mistress. She'd actually hoped that was the case.

"You're going by yourself?" she'd asked. Nick couldn't even watch football by himself.

"I know things haven't been great with us lately," he'd said. That alone had surprised her. She really thought Nick hadn't noticed or cared. "I think a few days apart is just what we both need. I can tell you aren't happy. I promise you there will be changes when I get back and maybe I'll even come home with a nice buck." He'd cupped her face in his hands. "I don't think you know what you mean to me, but I promise to show you when I get back." He'd kissed her then, softly, sweetly, and for a moment, she'd wondered if Nick could change.

"You're wrong about Nick," she said now to Belinda. "If he was going to end it, he would have chosen the least painful way to do it. Not one—" she looked at Nat, who was swinging nearby, humming to herself and seemingly oblivious to their conversation "—that chose him. He had a gun with him he could have used."

"Maybe he didn't get the chance, but you're probably right," Belinda said and grabbed the check. "Let me get this. I didn't mean to upset you. It's just that you need to get a handle on whatever's been going on with you for you-know-who's sake." She cut her eyes to Nat, who headed toward them as they stood to leave.

"You're right about the guilt, though," Allie said, giving her friend that. She'd known as she'd watched Nick leave that day to go up into the mountains that nothing could change him enough to make her stay. She was going to ask him for a divorce when he came back.

Belinda changed the subject. "I saw your brother-in-law, Drew, earlier on the ranch."

Allie nodded. "He mentioned he was working up there. His construction company built the guest cabins."

"I'd forgotten that." Belinda frowned. "I was talking to Lily about photos at the rehearsal dinner. Did you know that Sarah is one of her bridesmaids?"

"My sister-in-law worked with Lily one season at her brother James's Canyon Bar." Allie had the impression that Lily didn't have a lot of female friends. Most of the math professors she knew were male, apparently. "I think James feels sorry for Sarah and you know Lily, she is so sweet."

"I have to hand it to Sarah, putting up with her mother day in and day out," Belinda said.

Allie didn't want to think about it. Along with fewer incidents the past few days, she'd also been blessed with no visits from her mother-in-law and Sarah.

"Sarah's a saint, especially—" Belinda lowered her voice "—the way Mildred treats her. She is constantly bugging her about her weight and how she is never going to get a husband... It's awful."

Allie agreed.

"I don't understand why she doesn't leave."

"Where would she go and what would she do?" Allie said. "Sarah was in college when Mildred broke her leg. She quit to come home and take care of her mother. Mildred has milked it ever since. It used to annoy Nick, Sarah living in the guesthouse. He thought Sarah was taking advantage of his mother."

"Ha, it's the other way around. Sarah is on twenty-four-hour call. She told me that her mother got her out of bed at 2:00 a.m. one time to heat her some milk because she couldn't sleep. I would have put a pillow over the old nag's face."

Allie laughed and changed the subject. "You look especially nice today," she commented, realizing that her friend had seemed happier lately. It dawned on her why. "There's someone new in your life."

Belinda shrugged. She didn't like to talk about the men she dated because she thought it would jinx things for her. Not talking about them didn't seem to work, either, though. Belinda was so superstitious. Why else would she see a psychic to find out her future?

"This is going to be so much fun, the two of us working together again. Don't worry. I won't get in your way." Belinda took her hand. "I'm sorry I upset you. Sometimes I don't have the brains God gave a rock."

She didn't think that was the way the expression went, but said nothing. Belinda could be so...annoying and yet so sweet. Allie didn't know what she would have done without her the past few years. Belinda had been the only person she would talk freely to about Nick and the trouble between them.

"I'm just worried about you, honey," Belinda said, squeezing her hand. "I really think you should see someone—"

"I don't need a shrink."

"Not a shrink. Someone more...spiritual who can help you make sense of the things that you say keep happening."

"Things *do* keep happening," she snapped. "I'm not making them up."

"So talk to this woman," Belinda said just as adamantly. She pressed a business card into Allie's hand.

She glanced at it and groaned. "Your psychic friend?"

"She might be the *only* person who can help you," Belinda said cryptically. She gripped Allie's hand tighter. "She says she can get you in touch with Nick so you can get past this."

Allie stared at her for a moment before laughing out loud. "You have got to be kidding. What does she use? A Ouija board?"

"Don't laugh. This woman can tell you things that will make the hair on your head stand straight up."

That's all I need, she thought, reminded of Jackson Cardwell asking her if she was superstitious.

"Call her," Belinda said, closing Allie's fingers around the woman's business card. "You need closure, Allie. This woman can give it to you. She's expecting your call."

"I've been expecting your call, as well," said a sharp, older voice.

They both turned to see Mildred and her daughter. From the looks on their faces, they'd been standing there for some time.

CHAPTER THREE

"WANT TO SEE the building for Montana's first Texas Boys Barbecue?" Tag asked after they'd dropped Jackson and Ford's luggage off at the small cabin on the side of the mountain and gone down to meet cousin Dana and her brood.

Dana Cardwell Savage was just as Tag had described her. Adorable and sweet and delighted that everyone was coming for the wedding.

"How is your cabin?" she asked after introducing him to her children with husband, Marshal Hud Savage. Hank was the spitting image of his father, Dana said, and six now. Mary was five and looked just like her mom. Then there were the twins, Angus and Brick, just a year and a half old with the same dark hair and eyes as all the Cardwells.

"The cabin is great," Jackson said as Ford instantly bonded with his second cousins. "Thank you so much for letting me stay there."

"Family is why we had them built," Dana said. "My Texas cousins will always have a place to stay when you visit. Or until you find a place to live in Montana when you realize you want to live up here," she added with a wink. "Isn't that right, Tag?"

"I would love to visit, but I'm never leaving Texas," Jackson said.

"Never say never," Tag commented under his breath.

"I was just about to take him down to see the restaurant location."

Ford took off with the other kids into a room full of toys and didn't even look back as his father left. Jackson almost felt as if he were losing his son to Montana and the Cardwell clan.

"Are you sure you don't want to wait until everyone gets here?" he asked as they left.

"Hayes and Laramie are flying in tomorrow. I was hoping you would pick them up at the airport. Austin is apparently on a case tying up some loose ends." He shrugged. Of the five of them, Austin was the loner. He was dedicated to his job and being tied up on a case was nothing new. "Anyway, it's your opinion I want. You're better at this than all three of them put together."

"So you haven't heard from Austin on the deal," Jackson guessed.

Tag shook his head. "You know how he is. He'll go along with whatever everyone else says. Come on," he said with a laugh when Jackson groaned. "I really do want your opinion."

"*Honest* opinion?" Jackson asked.

"Of course."

Jackson glanced around as they drove out of the ranch and down the highway to the turnoff to Big Sky. Being the youngest, he didn't remember anything about Montana. He'd been a baby when his mother had packed up her five sons and taken them to Texas.

Big Sky looked more like a wide spot in the road rather than a town. There were clusters of buildings broken only by sagebrush or golf greens.

"This is the lower Meadow Village," Tag told him. "There is also the Mountain Village higher up the mountain where the ski resort is. You really have to see this place in the winter. It's crazy busy around the holidays. There are a lot of second homes here so the residents fly in and spend a few weeks generally in the summer and the holidays. More and more people, though, are starting to live here year-round. There is opportunity here, Jackson."

Jackson wanted to tell his brother that he didn't need to sell him. He'd go along with whatever the others decided. In fact, he'd already spoken to Hayes about it. Once Hayes got on board, it was clear to Jackson that this was probably a done deal. The holdout, if there was one, would be Austin and only because he wouldn't be available to sign off on the deal. Even Laramie sounded as if he thought the restaurant was a good idea.

"Where does Harlan live?" Jackson asked as they drove past mansions, condos and some tiny old cabins that must have been there before anyone even dreamed of a Big Sky. He had only a vague recollection of his father from those few times Harlan had visited Texas when he was growing up.

"He lives in one of those cabins back there, the older ones. We can stop by his place if you like. More than likely he and Uncle Angus are down at the Corral Bar. It's their favorite watering hole. Maybe we could have a beer with them later."

"I'm sure I'll see him soon enough." Harlan was a stranger who hadn't even made Jackson's wedding, not that the marriage had lasted long, anyway. But he felt no tie to the man who'd fathered him and doubted he ever would. It was only when he thought about Ford that he had regrets. It would have been nice for Ford to have a grandfather. His ex-wife's family had no interest in Ford. So the only family his son had in Texas was Jackson's mother, Rosalee Cardwell and his brother Laramie. Tag had already moved to Montana and Hayes would be moving here soon.

"I'm getting to know Dad," Tag said. "He's pretty remarkable."

"Tell me about your wedding planner," Jackson said, changing the subject then regretting the topic he'd picked when his brother grinned over at him. "I'm just curious about her." He hadn't told anyone about the cat or the terrified woman he'd found in the barn earlier. Her reaction seemed over the top given it had only been a cat. Though it *had* been a black one. Maybe she *was* superstitious.

"Allie's great. Dana suggested her. That's our Dana, always trying to help those in need. Allie lost her husband eight months ago. Terrible thing. He was hunting in the mountains and apparently killed by a grizzly bear."

"Apparently?"

"They never found his body. They think the bear dragged the body off somewhere. Won't be the first time remains have turned up years later in the mountains—if they turn up at all. They found his backpack and enough blood that he can be declared legally dead but I guess the insurance company has been dragging its feet."

Jackson thought of Allie and her little girl, Nat. "How horrible for them."

"Yeah, she's been having a hard time both emotionally and financially according to Dana, who suggested her for our wedding planner because of it. But Lily loves Allie and, of course, Natalie. That little girl is so darned bright."

"Yeah, Ford is definitely taken with her." But his thoughts were on Allie and her reaction to the cat flying out of that box of wedding decorations. It must have scared her half out of her wits in the emotional state she was in. "That was nice of Dana to hire her."

"Allie worked as a wedding planner before she married Nick Taylor. Dana offered Allie and Nat one of the new guest ranch cabins where we're staying. But I guess she thinks it would be better for Natalie to stay in their own home."

"Where do Allie and her daughter live now?"

"An old cabin down by the river. I'll show you on the way back." Tag swung into a small complex and turned off the engine. "Welcome to the site of the next Texas Boys Barbecue joint."

"I THOUGHT YOU HAD A JOB," Mildred said to Allie over the sound of brass horns playing cantina music at the Mexican café.

"They allow lunch breaks," she said. "But I really need to get back." She excused herself to go to the ladies' room.

Mildred turned to Natalie, leaned down and pinched her cheek. "How is my sweetie today? Grandma misses you. When are you coming to my house?"

In the restroom, Allie splashed cold water on her face and tried to calm down. How much had they heard?

Enough that they had been looking at her strangely. Or was that all in her mind, as well? But if they heard Belinda trying to get her to see a psychic so she could reach Nick on the other side... Allie could well imagine what they would think.

She hurried, not wanting to leave Natalie with her grandmother for long. She hated it, but Mildred seemed to nag the child all the time about not spending enough time with her.

Leaving the restroom, she saw that Sarah and her mother hadn't taken a seat. Instead, they were standing at the takeout counter. There was no avoiding talking to them again.

"I couldn't help but overhear your...friend suggesting you see a...psychic?" Mother Taylor said, leaving no doubt that they had been listening. "Surely she meant a psychiatrist, which indicates that you are still having those hallucinations." She quirked an eyebrow, waiting for an answer.

"Belinda was only joking. I'm feeling much better, thank you."

Mildred's expression said she wasn't buying a minute of it. "Sarah, I left my sweater in the car."

"I'll get it, Mother." Sarah turned and headed for their vehicle parked out front.

"How is this…job of yours going?" Mildred asked. "I've never understood what wedding planners do."

Allie had actually told her once, listing about fifty things she did but Mildred clearly hadn't been listening.

"I'll have to tell you sometime," she said now. "But I need to get back to it. Come on, Natalie."

"You should let me have her for the rest of the day," Mildred said. "In fact, she can spend the night at my house."

"I'm sorry, but Natalie is getting horseback riding lessons this afternoon," Allie lied. "She's having a wonderful time with Dana's children."

"Well, she can still—"

"Not only that, I also prefer to have Nat with me right now. It's hard enough without Nick." Another lie followed by the biggest truth of all, "I need my daughter right now."

Mildred looked surprised. "That's the first time I've heard you mention my Nicky in months." She seemed about to cry. Sarah returned with her sweater, slipping it around her shoulders without even a thank-you from Mildred.

Nearby, Belinda was finishing up their bill.

"I really should get back to work." Allie tried to step past her mother-in-law, but the older woman grabbed her arm. "I worry that you are ill-equipped to take care of yourself, let alone a child. I need Natalie more than you do. I—"

Allie jerked her arm free. "Natalie would be heartbroken if she was late to her horseback riding lesson." She hurried to her daughter, picked up her purse off the table and, taking Nat's hand, left the restaurant, trying hard not to run.

She told herself to calm down. Any sign of her being upset and her in-laws would view it as her being unable to take care of Nat. But all she wanted was to get away and as quickly as possible.

But as she and Nat reached her van and she dug in her purse for her keys, she realized they weren't there. Her heart began to pound. Since Nick's death, she was constantly losing her keys, her purse, her sunglasses… her mind.

"Forgetfulness is very common after a traumatic event," the doctor had told her when she'd gotten an appointment at her in-laws' insistence.

"It scares me. I try to remind myself where I put things so this doesn't happen, but when I go back to get whatever it was…I'm always so positive that's where I left it. Instead, I find it in some…strange place I could never imagine."

The doctor had chuckled and pulled out his prescription pad. "How are you sleeping?" He didn't even wait for her to answer. "I think once you start sleeping through the night, you're going to find that these instances of forgetfulness will go away."

The pills had only made it worse, though, she thought now as she frantically searched for her van keys. She could feel Nat watching her, looking worried. Sometimes it felt as if her five-year-old was taking care of her instead of the other way around.

"It's okay, sweetheart. Mama just misplaced her keys. I'm sure they're in here…."

"Looking for these?" The young waitress from the café came out the door, holding up her keys.

"Where did you find them?" Allie asked, thinking they must have fallen out of her purse at the table and ended up on the floor. That could happen to anyone.

"In the bathroom sink."

Allie stared at her.

"You must have dropped them while you were washing your hands," the young woman said with a shrug as she handed them over.

As if that was likely. She hadn't even taken her purse to the restroom, had she? But she had it now and she couldn't remember. She'd been so upset to see Sarah and Mildred.

"Nat, what was Grandmother saying to you in the restaurant?"

"She wanted me to go to her house but I told her I couldn't. I'm going horseback riding when we get to the ranch," Nat announced. "Dana is taking me and the other kids." Her lower lip came out for a moment. "Grandma said she was really sad I wasn't going with her."

"Yes," Allie said as, with trembling fingers, she opened the van door. Tears stung her eyes. "But today is a happy day so *we* aren't going to be sad, right? There are lots of other days that you can spend with your grandmother." Nat brightened as she strapped her into her seat.

Just a few more minutes and she and Nat would be out of here. But as she started the van, she looked up to find Mother Taylor watching her from beside Sarah's pearl-white SUV. It was clear from her expression that she'd witnessed the lost-key episode.

From the front steps of the restaurant, Belinda waved then made the universal sign to telephone.

Allie knew Belinda didn't mean call her. Reaching in her pocket, she half expected the psychic's business card to be missing. But it was still there, she realized with sagging relief. As crazy as the idea of reaching Nick beyond the grave was, she'd do *anything* to make this stop.

WHEN ALLIE AND HER daughter returned, Jackson was watching her from inside his cousin's two-story ranch house.

"She lost her husband some months back," Dana said, joining him at the window.

"I wasn't—"

"He went up into the mountains during hunting season," she continued, ignoring his attempt to deny he'd been wondering about Allie. "They found his backpack and his rifle and grizzly tracks."

"Tag mentioned it." Tag had pointed out Allie's small, old cabin by the river on their way back to the ranch. It looked as if it needed work. Hadn't Tag mentioned that her husband was in construction? "Tag said they never found her husband's body."

Dana shook her head. "But Nick's backpack was shredded and his rifle was half-buried in the dirt with grizzly tracks all around it. When he didn't show up after a few days and they had no luck finding him…"

"His remains will probably turn up someday," Hud said as he came in from the kitchen. Dana's husband, Hud, was the marshal in the canyon—just as his father had been before him. "About thirty years ago now, a hiker found a human skeleton of a man. He still hasn't been identified so who knows how long he'd been out there in the mountains."

"That must make it even harder for her," Jackson said.

"It was one reason I was so glad when she decided to take the job as wedding planner."

He watched Allie reappear to get a box out of the van. She seemed nervous, even upset. He wondered if something had happened at lunch. Now at least he understood why she had overreacted with the black cat.

Hud kissed his wife, saying he had to get back to work, leaving Dana and Jackson alone.

"Our fathers are setting up their equipment on the bandstand in the barn," Dana said. "Have you seen Harlan yet?"

"No," Jackson admitted. "Guess there is no time like the present, huh?"

Jackson hadn't seen his father in several years, and even then Harlan hadn't seemed to know how to act around him—or his other sons, for that matter. As they entered the barn, Tag joining them, he saw his father and uncle standing on the makeshift stage, guitars in their hands, and was surprised when he remembered a song his father had once sung to him.

He didn't know how old he'd been at the time, but he recalled Harlan coming into his bedroom one night in Texas and playing a song on his guitar for him He remembered being touched by the music and his father's voice.

On stage, the two brothers began playing their guitars in earnest. His father began singing. It was the voice Jackson remembered and it was like being transported back to his childhood. It rattled him more than he wanted to admit. He'd thought he and his father had no connection. But just hearing Harlan sing made him realize that he'd been lying to himself about not only the lack of connection, but also his need for it.

Harlan suddenly broke off at the sight of his sons. He stared through the dim barn for a moment, then put down his guitar to bound off the stage and come toward Jackson. He seemed young and very handsome, belying his age, Jackson thought. A man in his prime.

"Jackson," he said, holding out his hand. His father's

hand was large and strong, the skin dry, callused and warm. "Glad you made it. So where are the rest of your brothers?"

"They're supposed to fly in tomorrow. At least Laramie and Hayes are," Tag said. "Austin... Well, he said he would do his best to make it. He's tied up on a case, but I'm sure you know how that goes." At Christmas, Tag had found out what their father did besides drink beer and play guitar—and shared that amazing news with them. Both Harlan and his brother Angus had worked undercover as government agents and still might, even though they were reportedly retired.

"Duty calls sometimes," Harlan agreed. "I'm glad I'm retired."

"Until the next time someone gets into trouble and needs help," Tag said.

Harlan merely smiled in answer.

Jackson was glad to see that his brother and their father could joke. Tag, being the oldest, remembered the years living in Montana and their father more than his brothers.

"The old man isn't so bad," Tag had told them after his visit at Christmas. "He's starting to grow on me."

Jackson had laughed, but he'd been a little jealous. He would love for his son to have a grandfather. He couldn't imagine, though, how Harlan could be a part of his only grandson's life, even if he wanted to. Texas and Montana were just too far apart. And Harlan probably had no interest, anyway.

"Where's that bride-to-be?" Uncle Angus asked Tag as he hopped off the stage and came toward them.

"Last minute preparations for the wedding," Tag said. "You can't believe the lists she's made. It's the mathematician in her. She's so much more organized than I am. Which reminds me, Jackson and I have to drive down to Bozeman to pick up the rings."

"It took a wedding to get you Cardwell boys to Montana, I see." Uncle Angus threw an arm around Jackson. "So how are you liking it up here? I saw that boy of yours. Dana's got him riding horses already. You're going to have one devil of a time getting him to go back to Texas after this."

Didn't Jackson know it. He'd hardly seen his son all day. Even now Ford had been too busy to give Jackson more than a quick wave from the corral where he'd been with the kids and the hired man, Walker.

"Ford is going to sleep like a baby tonight after all this fresh air, sunshine and high altitude," Jackson said. "He's not the only one," he added with a laugh.

"It's good for him," Harlan said. "I was talking to him earlier. He's taken with that little girl."

"Like father like son," Tag said under his breath as Allie came in from the back of the barn.

Jackson saw her expression. "I think I'd better go check on my son," he said as he walked toward Allie. He didn't have time to think about what he was about to do. He moved to her, taking her arm and leading her back out of the barn. "What's wrong?"

For a moment she looked as if she were going to deny anything was. But then tears filled her eyes. He walked her around the far side of the barn. He could hear Dana out by the corral instructing the kids in horseback riding lessons. Inside the barn, his father and uncle struck up another tune.

"It's nothing, really," she said and brushed at her tears. "I've been so forgetful lately. I didn't remember that the band would be setting up this afternoon."

He saw that she held a date book in her trembling hand.

"It wasn't written down in your date book?"

She glanced at her book. "It was but for some reason I marked it out."

"No big deal, right?"

"It's just that I don't remember doing it."

He could see that she was still upset and wondered if there wasn't something more going on. He reminded himself that Allie had lost her husband only months ago. Who knew what kind of emotional roller coaster that had left her on.

"You need to cut yourself more slack," he said. "We all forget things."

She nodded, but he could see she was still worried. No, not worried, scared. He thought of the black cat and had a feeling it hadn't been her first scare like that.

"I feel like such a fool," she said.

Instinctively, he put his arm around her. "Give yourself time. It's going to be all right."

She looked so forlorn that taking her in his arms seemed not only the natural thing to do at that moment, but the only thing to do under the circumstances. At first she felt board-stiff in his arms, then after a moment she seemed to melt into him. She buried her face into his chest as if he were an anchor in a fierce storm.

Suddenly, she broke the embrace and stepped back. He followed her gaze to one of the cabins on the mountainside behind him and the man standing there.

"Who is that?" he asked, instantly put off by the scowling man.

"My brother-in-law, Drew. He's doing some repairs on the ranch. He and Nick owned a construction company together. They built the guest cabins."

The man's scowl had turned into a cold stare. Jackson saw Allie's reaction. "We weren't doing anything wrong."

She shook her head as the man headed down the mountainside to his pickup parked in the pines. "He's just very

protective." Allie looked as if she had the weight of the
world on her shoulders again.

Jackson watched her brother-in-law slowly drive out of
the ranch. Allie wasn't the only one the man was glaring at.

"I need to get back inside," she said and turned away.

He wanted to go after her. He also wanted to put his
fist into her brother-in-law's face. Protective my butt,
he thought. He wanted to tell Allie to ignore all of it.
Wanted… Hell, that was just it. He didn't know what he
wanted at the moment. Even if he did, he couldn't have
it. He warned himself to stay away from Allie Taylor. Far
away. He was only here for the wedding. While he felt for
the woman, he couldn't help her.

"There you are," Tag said as he came up behind them.
"Ready to go with me to Bozeman to get the rings?"

Jackson glanced toward the barn door Allie was stepping through. "Ready."

CHAPTER FOUR

As JACKSON STARTED to leave with his brother, he turned to look back at the barn. Just inside the door he saw Allie. All his survival instincts told him to keep going, but his mother had raised a Texas cowboy with a code of honor. Or at least she'd tried. Something was wrong and he couldn't walk away.

"Give me just a minute," he said and ran back. As he entered the barn, he saw Allie frantically searching for something in the corner of the barn. His father and brother were still playing at the far end, completely unaware of them.

"What are you looking for?"

She seemed embarrassed that he'd caught her. He noticed that she'd gone pale and looked upset. "I know I put my purse right there with my keys in it."

He glanced at the empty table. "Maybe it fell under it." He bent down to look under the red-and-white-checked tablecloth. "The barn is looking great, by the way. You've done a beautiful job."

She didn't seem to hear him. She was moving from table to table, searching for her purse. He could see that she was getting more anxious by the moment. "I know I put it right there so I wouldn't forget it when I left."

"Here it is," Jackson said as he spied what he assumed had to be her purse not on a table, but in one of the empty boxes that had held the decorations.

She rushed to him and took the purse and hurriedly looked inside, pulling out her keys with obvious relief.

"You would have found it the moment you started loading the boxes into your van," he said, seeing that she was still shaken.

She nodded. "Thank you. I'm not usually like this."

"No need to apologize. I hate losing things. It drives me crazy."

She let out a humorless laugh. "Crazy, yes." She took a deep breath and let it out slowly. Tears welled in her eyes.

"Hey, it's okay."

He wanted to comfort her, but kept his distance after what had happened earlier. "It really is okay."

She shook her head as the music stopped and quickly wiped her eyes, apologizing again. She looked embarrassed and he wished there was something he could say to put her at ease.

"Earlier, I was just trying to comfort you. It was just a hug," he said.

She met his gaze. "One I definitely needed. You have been so kind…."

"I'm not kind."

She laughed and shook her head. "Are you always so self-deprecating?"

"No, just truthful."

"Well, thank you." She clutched the keys in her hand as if afraid she would lose them if she let them out of her sight.

At the sound of people approaching, she stepped away from him.

"Let me load those boxes in your van. I insist," he said before she could protest.

As Dana, Lily and the kids came through the barn door they stopped to admire what Allie had accomplished.

There were lots of oohs and ahhs. But it was Lily whose face lit up as she took in the way the barn was being transformed.

Jackson shifted his gaze to Allie's face as she humbly accepted their praise. Dana introduced Jackson to Lily. He could see right away why his brother had fallen for the woman.

"Please come stay at one of the guest cabins for the rest of the wedding festivities," Dana was saying to Allie.

"It is so generous of you to offer the cabin," Allie said, looking shocked at the offer.

"Not at all. It will make it easier for you so you don't have to drive back and forth. Also I'm being selfish. The kids adore Natalie. It will make the wedding a lot more fun for them."

Allie, clearly fighting tears of gratitude, said she would think about it. Jackson felt his heartstrings pulled just watching. "I'll work hard to make this wedding as perfect as it can be. I won't let you down."

Lily gave her a hug. "Allie, it's already perfect!"

Jackson was surprised that Lily McCabe had agreed to a Western wedding. According to the lowdown he'd heard, Lily taught mathematics at Montana State University. She'd spent her younger years at expensive boarding schools after having been born into money.

Jackson wondered if the woman had ever even been on a horse—before she met the Cardwells. Apparently, Allie was worried that a Western wedding was the last thing a woman like Lily McCabe would want.

"Are you sure this is what *you* want?" Allie asked Lily. "After all, it is *your* wedding."

Lily laughed. "Just to see the look on my parents' faces will make it all worthwhile." At Allie's horrified look, she quickly added, "I'm kidding. Though that is part of it. But when you marry into the Cardwell family, you marry into ranching and all that it comes with. I want this wedding to be a celebration of that.

"This is going to be the best wedding ever," Lily said as she looked around the barn. "Look at me," she said, holding out her hands. "I'm actually shaking I'm so excited." She stepped to Allie and gave her another hug. "Thank you so much."

Allie appeared taken aback for a moment by Lily's sudden show of affection. The woman really was becoming more like the Cardwells every day. Or at least Dana Cardwell. That wasn't a bad thing, he thought.

"We should probably talk about the other arrangements. When is your final dress fitting?"

"Tomorrow. The dress is absolutely perfect, and the boots!" Lily laughed. "I'm so glad Dana suggested red boots. I love them!"

This was going to be like no wedding Allie had ever planned, Jackson thought. The Cardwells went all out, that was for sure.

He looked around the barn, seeing through the eyes of the guests who would be arriving for the wedding. Allie had found a wonderful wedding cake topper of a cowboy and his bride dancing that was engraved with the words: *For the rest of my life.* Tag had said that Lily had cried when she'd seen it.

The cake was a little harder to nail, according to Tag. Jackson mentally shook his head at even the memory of his brother discussing wedding cakes with him. Apparently, there were cake designs resembling hats and boots, covered wagons and cowhide, lassoes and lariats, spurs and belt buckles and horses and saddles. Some cakes had a version of all of them, which he could just imagine would have thrown his brother for a loop, he thought now, grinning to himself.

"I like simple better," Lily had said when faced with all the options. "It's the mathematician in me."

Allie had apparently kept looking until she found what she thought might be the perfect one. It was an elegant white, frosted, tiered cake with white roses and ribbons in a similar design as Lily's Western wedding dress.

"I love it," Lily had gushed. "It's perfect."

They decided on white roses and daisies for her bouquet. Bouquets of daisies would be on each of the tables, the vases old boots, with the tables covered with red-checked cloths and matching napkins.

Jackson's gaze returned to Allie. She seemed to glow under the compliments, giving him a glimpse of the self-assured woman he suspected she'd been before the tragedy.

"Jackson?"

He turned to find Tag standing next to him, grinning.

"I guess you didn't hear me. Must have had your mind somewhere else." Tag glanced in Allie's direction and then wisely jumped back as Jackson took a playful swing at him as they left the barn.

"You sure waited until the last minute," Jackson said to his brother as they headed for Tag's vehicle. "Putting off the rings…" He shook his head. "You sure you want to go through with this?"

His brother laughed. "More sure than I have been about anything in my life. Come on, let's go."

"I'll see if Ford wants to come along," Jackson said. "I think that's enough cowboy-ing for one day."

But when he reached the corral, he found his son wearing a straw Western hat and atop a huge horse. Jackson felt his pulse jump at the sight and his first instinct was to insist Ford get down from there right away.

But when he got a good look at his son's face, his words died on a breath. He'd never seen Ford this happy. His cheeks were flushed, his eyes bright. He looked…proud.

"Look at me," he called to his father.

All Jackson could do was nod as his son rode past him. He was incapable of words at that moment.

"Don't worry about your son," his father said as he joined him at the corral fence. "I'll look after him until you get back."

ALLIE LISTENED TO Jackson and Tag joking with each other as they left the barn. Jackson Cardwell must think her the most foolish woman ever, screaming over nothing more than a cat, messing up her date book and panicking because she'd misplaced her purse.

But what had her still upset was the hug. It had felt so good to be in Jackson's arms. It had been so long since anyone had held her like that. She'd felt such an overwhelming need…

And then Drew had seen them. She'd been surprised by the look on his face. He'd seemed…angry and upset as if she was cheating on Nick. Once this investigation was over, maybe they could all put Nick to rest. In the meantime, she just hoped Drew didn't go to his mother with this.

Instinctively, she knew that Jackson wouldn't say anything. Not about her incidents or about the hug.

Dana announced she was taking the kids down to the house for naptime. Allie could tell that Nat had wanted to go down to the house—but for lemonade and cookies. Nat probably needed a nap, as well, but Allie couldn't take her up to the cabin right now. She had work to do if she hoped to have the barn ready for the rehearsal dinner tomorrow night.

"I really need your help," she told her daughter. Nat was

always ready to give a helping hand. Well, she was before the Cardwell Ranch and all the animals, not to mention other kids to play with.

"Okay, Mama." She glanced back at the barn door wistfully, though. Nat had always wanted brothers and sisters, but they hadn't been in Allie's plans. She knew she could take care of one child without any help from Nick. He'd wanted a boy and insisted they try for another child soon after Nat was born.

Allie almost laughed. Guilt? She had so much of it where Nick and his family were concerned. She had wanted to enjoy her baby girl so she'd gone on the pill behind Nick's back. It had been more than dishonest. He would have killed her if he had found out. The more time that went by, the less she wanted another child with her husband so she'd stayed on the pill. Even Nick's tantrums about her not getting pregnant were easier to take than having another child with him.

She hadn't even told Belinda, which was good since her friend was shocked when she told her she was leaving Nick and moving far away.

"Divorcing him is one thing," Belinda had said. "But I don't see how you can keep his kid from him or keep Nat from his family."

"Nick wanted a son. He barely takes notice of Nat. The only time he notices her is when other people are around and then he plays too rough with her. When she cries, he tells her to toughen up."

"So you're going to ask for sole custody? Isn't Nick going to fight you?"

Allie knew it would be just like Nick to fight for Nat out of meanness and his family would back him up. "I'm going to move to Florida. I've already lined up a couple of jobs down there. They pay a lot more than here. I really doubt Nick will bother flying that far to see Nat—at least more than a few times."

"You really are going to leave him," Belinda had said. "When?"

"Soon." That had been late summer. She'd desperately wanted a new start. Nick would be occupied with hunting season in the fall so maybe he wouldn't put up much of a fight.

Had Belinda said something to Nick? Or had he just seen something in Allie that told him he had lost her?

"How can I help you, Mama?" Nat asked, dragging her from her thoughts.

Allie handed her daughter one end of a rope garland adorned with tiny lights in the shape of boots. "Let's string this up," she suggested. "And see how pretty it looks along the wall."

Nat's eyes lit up. "It's going to be beautiful," she said. *Beautiful* was her latest favorite word. To her, most everything was beautiful.

Allie yearned for that kind of innocence again—if she'd ever had it. But maybe she could find it for her daughter. She had options. She could find work anywhere as a wedding planner, but did she want to uproot her daughter from what little family she had? Nat loved her Uncle Drew and Sarah could be very sweet. Mildred, even as ungrandmotherly as she was, was Nat's only grandmother.

Allie tried to concentrate on her work. The barn was taking shape. She'd found tiny cowboy boot lights to put over the bar area. Saddles on milk cans had been pulled up to the bar for extra seating.

Beverages would be chilling in a metal trough filled with ice. Drinks would be served in Mason jars and lanterns would hang from the rafters for light. A few bales of hay would be brought in around the bandstand.

When they'd finished, Allie plugged in the last of the lights and Nat squealed with delight.

She checked her watch. "Come on," she told her daughter. "We've done enough today. We need to go into town for a few things. Tomorrow your aunt Megan will be coming to help." Nat clapped in response. She loved her auntie Megan, Allie's half sister.

After Allie's mother died, her father had moved away, remarried and had other children. Allie had lost touch with her father, as well as his new family. But about a year ago, her stepsister Megan had found her. Ten years younger, Megan was now twenty-three and a recent graduate in design. When she'd shown an interest in working on the Cardwell Ranch wedding, Allie had jumped at it.

"I really could use the help, but when can you come down?" Megan lived in Missoula and had just given her two weeks' notice at her job.

"Go ahead and start without me. I'll be there within a few days of the wedding. That should be enough time, shouldn't it?"

"Perfect," Allie had told her. "Natalie and I will start. I'll save the fun stuff for you." Natalie loved Megan, who was cute and young and always up for doing something fun with her niece.

The thought of Megan's arrival tomorrow had brightened Natalie for a moment, but Allie now saw her looking longingly at the Savage house.

"How about we have something to eat while we're in Bozeman?" Allie suggested.

Nat's eyes widened with new interest as she asked if they could go to her favorite fast-food burger place. The Taylors had introduced her daughter to fast food, something Allie had tried to keep at a minimum.

But this evening, she decided to make an exception. She

loved seeing how happy her daughter was. Nat's cheeks were pink from the fresh air and sunshine.

All the way into town, she talked excitely about the horses and the other kids. This wedding planner job at Cardwell Ranch was turning out to be a good thing for both of them, Allie thought as they drove home.

By the time they reached the cabin Nat had fallen asleep in her car seat and didn't even wake up when Allie parked out front. Deciding to take in the items she'd purchased first, then bring in her daughter, Allie stepped into the cabin and stopped dead.

At the end of the hall, light flickered. A candle. She hadn't lit a candle. Not since Nick. He liked her in candlelight. The smell of the candle and the light reminded her of the last time they'd had sex. Not made love. They hadn't made love since before Natalie was born.

As she started down the hallway, she told herself that she'd thrown all the candles away. Even if she'd missed one, she wouldn't have left a candle burning.

She stopped in the bedroom doorway. Nick's shirt was back, spread on the bed as if he were in it, lying there waiting for her. The smell of the sweet-scented candle made her nauseous. She fought the panicked need to run.

"Mama?" Nat's sleepy voice wavered with concern. "Did Daddy come back?" Not just concern. Anxiety. Nick scared her with his moodiness and surly behavior. Nat was smart. She had picked up on the tension between her parents.

Allie turned to wrap her arms around her daughter. The warmth of her five-year-old, Nat's breath on her neck, the solid feel of the ground under her feet, those were the things she concentrated on as she carried Natalie down the hallway to her room.

Her daughter's room had always been her haven. It was

the only room in the house that Nick hadn't cared what she did with. So she'd painted it sky-blue, adding white floating clouds, then trees and finally a river as green and sunlit as the one out Nat's window.

Nick had stuck his head in the door while she was painting it. She'd seen his expression. He'd been impressed— and he hadn't wanted to be—before he snapped, "You going to cook dinner or what?" He seemed to avoid the room after that, which was fine with her.

Now, she lay down on the bed with Nat. It had been her daughter's idea to put stars on the ceiling, the kind that shone only at night with the lights out.

"I like horses," Nat said with a sigh. "Ms. Savage says a horse can tell your mood and that if you aren't in a good one, you'll get bucked off." She looked at her mother. "Do you think that's true?"

"I think if Ms. Savage says it is, then it is."

Nat smiled as if she liked the answer.

Allie could tell she was dog-tired, but fighting sleep.

"I'm going to ride Rocket tomorrow," Natalie said.

"Rocket? That sounds like an awfully fast horse." She saw that Nat's eyelids had closed. She watched her daughter sleep for a few moments, then eased out of bed.

After covering her, she opened the window a few inches to let the cool summer night air into the stuffy room. Spending time with her daughter made her feel better, but also reminded her how important it was that she not let anyone know about the things that had been happening to her.

She thought of Jackson Cardwell and the black cat that had somehow gotten into her box of decorations. She hadn't imagined that. She smiled to herself. Such a small thing and yet...

This time, she went straight to her bedroom, snuffed

out the candle and opened the window, thankful for the breeze that quickly replaced the sweet, cloying scent with the fresh night air.

On the way out of the room, she grabbed Nick's shirt and took both the shirt and the candle to the trash, but changed her mind. Dropping only the candle in the trash, she took the shirt over to the fireplace. Would burning Nick's favorite shirt mean she was crazy?

Too bad, she thought as she dropped the shirt on the grate and added several pieces of kindling and some newspaper. Allie hesitated for only a moment before lighting the paper with a match. It caught fire, crackling to life and forcing her to step back. She watched the blaze destroy the shirt and reached for the poker, determined that not a scrap of it would be left.

She had to get control of her life. She thought of Jackson Cardwell and his kindness. He had no idea how much it meant to her.

As she watched the flames take the last of Nick's shirt, she told herself at least this would be the last she'd see of that blamed shirt.

CHAPTER FIVE

JACKSON MET HAYES and Laramie at the airport, but while it was good to see them, he was distracted.

They talked about the barbecue restaurant and Harlan and the wedding before McKenzie showed up while they were waiting for their luggage to pick up Hayes. Hayes had been in Texas tying up things with the sale of his business.

Jackson had heard their relationship was serious, but seeing McKenzie and Hayes together, he saw just how serious. Another brother falling in love in Montana, he thought with a shake of his head. Hayes and McKenzie would be joining them later tonight at the ranch for dinner.

He and Laramie ended up making the drive to Cardwell Ranch alone. Laramie talked about the financial benefits of the new barbecue restaurant and Jackson tuned him out. He couldn't get his mind off Allie Taylor.

Maybe it was because he'd been through so much with his ex, but he felt like a kindred spirit. The woman was going through her own private hell. He wished there was something he could do.

"Are you listening?" Laramie asked.

"Sure."

"I forget how little interest my brothers have in the actual running of this corporation."

"Don't let it hurt your feelings. I just have something else on my mind."

"A woman."

"Why would you say that, knowing me?"

Laramie looked over at him. "I was joking. You swore off women after Juliet, right? At least that's what you… Wait a minute, has something changed?"

"Nothing." He said it too sharply, making his brother's eyebrow shoot up.

Laramie fell silent for a moment, but Jackson could feel him watching him out of the corner of his eye.

"Is this your first wedding since…you and Juliet split?" Laramie asked carefully.

Jackson shook his head at his brother's attempt at diplomacy. "It's not the wedding. There's this…person I met who I'm worried about."

"Ah. Is this person—"

"It's a woman, all right? But it isn't like that."

"Hey," Laramie said, holding up his hands. "I just walked in. If you don't want to tell me—"

"She lost her husband some months ago and she has a little girl the same age as Ford and she's struggling."

Laramie nodded. "Okay."

"She's the wedding planner."

His brother's eyebrow shot up again.

"I'll just be glad when this wedding is over," Jackson said and thought he meant it. "By the way, when is Mom flying in?" At his brother's hesitation, he demanded, "What's going on with Mom?"

ALLIE HAD UNPACKED more boxes of decorations by the time she heard a vehicle pull up the next morning. Natalie, who had been coloring quietly while her mother worked, went running when she spotted her aunt Megan. Allie smiled as Megan picked Nat up and swung her around, both of them laughing. It was a wonderful sound. Megan had a way with Natalie. Clearly, she loved kids.

"Sorry I'm so late, but I'm here and ready to go to work." Megan was dressed in a T-shirt, jeans and athletic shoes. She had taken after their father and had the Irish green eyes with the dark hair and complexion. She was nothing short of adorable, sweet and cute. "Wow, the barn is already looking great," she exclaimed as she walked around, Natalie holding her hand and beaming up at her.

"I helped Mama with the lights," Nat said.

"I knew it," Megan said. "I can see your handiwork." She grinned down at her niece. "Did I hear you can now ride a horse?"

Natalie quickly told her all about the horses, naming each as she explained how to ride a horse. "You have to hang on to the reins."

"I would imagine you do," Megan agreed.

"Maybe you can ride with us," Nat suggested.

"Maybe I can. But right now I need to help your mom."

Just then Dana stuck her head in the barn doorway and called to Natalie. Allie introduced Dana to her stepsister, then watched as her daughter scurried off for an afternoon ride with her friends. She gave a thankful smile to Dana as they left.

"Just tell me what to do," Megan said and Allie did, even more thankful for the help. They went to work on the small details Allie knew Megan would enjoy.

Belinda stopped by to say hello to Megan and give Allie an update on the photos. She'd met with Lily that morning, had made out a list of photo ideas and sounded excited.

Allie was surprised when she overheard Belinda and Megan discussing a recent lunch. While the three of them had spent some time together since Megan had come back into Allie's life, she hadn't known that Belinda and Megan had become friends.

She felt jealous. She knew it was silly. They were both

single and probably had more in common than with Allie, who felt as if she'd been married forever.

"How are you doing?" Megan asked after Belinda left.

"Fine."

"No, really."

Allie studied her stepsister for a moment. They'd become close, but she hadn't wanted to share what was going on. It was embarrassing and the fewer people who knew she was losing her mind the better, right?

"It's been rough." Megan didn't know that she had been planning to leave Nick. As far as her sister had known, Allie had been happily married. Now Allie regretted that she hadn't been more honest with Megan.

"But I'm doing okay now," she said as she handed Megan another gift bag to fill. "It's good to be working again. I love doing this." She glanced around the barn feeling a sense of satisfaction.

"Well, I'm glad I'm here now," Megan said. "This is good for Natalie, too."

Good for all of us, Allie thought.

JACKSON LOOKED AT his brother aghast. "Mom's dating?" He should have known that if their mom confided in anyone it would be Laramie. The sensible one, was what she called him, and swore that out of all her sons, Laramie was the only one who she could depend on to be honest with her.

Laramie cleared his throat. "It's a little more than dating. She's on her honeymoon."

"Her *what?*"

"She wanted it to be a surprise."

"Well, it sure as hell is that. Who did she marry?"

"His name is Franklin Wellington the Fourth. He's wealthy, handsome, very nice guy, actually."

"*You've* met him?"

"He and Mom are flying in just before the wedding on his private jet. It's bigger than ours."

"Laramie, I can't believe you would keep this from the rest of us, let alone that Mom would."

"She didn't want to take away from Tag's wedding but they had already scheduled theirs before Tag announced his." Laramie shrugged. "Hey, she's deliriously happy and hoping we will all be happy for her."

Jackson couldn't believe this. Rosalee Cardwell hadn't just started dating after all these years, she'd gotten married?

"I wonder how Dad will take it?" Laramie said. "We all thought Mom had been pining away for him all these years...."

"Maybe she was."

"Well, not anymore."

"BUT YOU *HAVE* TO GO on the horseback ride," Natalie cried.

As he stepped into the cool shade, Jackson saw Allie look around the barn for help, finding none. Hayes was off somewhere with his girlfriend, McKenzie, Tag was down by the river writing his vows, Lily was picking her parents up at the airport, Laramie had restaurant business and Hud was at the marshal's office, working. There had still been no word from Austin. Or their mother.

Wanting to spend some time with his son, Jackson had agreed to go on the short horseback ride with Dana and the kids that would include lunch on the mountain.

"Dana promised she would find you a very gentle horse, in other words, a really *old* one," Megan joked.

Natalie was doing her "please-Mama-please" face.

"Even my dad is going to ride," Ford said, making everyone laugh.

Allie looked at the boy. "Your dad is a cowboy."

Ford shook his head. "He can't even rope a cow. He tried once at our neighbor's place and he was really bad at it. So it's okay if you're really bad at riding a horse."

Jackson smiled and ruffled his son's hair. "You really should come along, Allie."

"I have too much work to—"

"I will stay here and get things organized for tomorrow," Megan said. "No more arguments. Go on the ride with your daughter. Go." She shooed her toward the barn door.

"I guess I'm going on the horseback ride," Allie said. The kids cheered. She met Jackson's gaze as they walked toward the corral where Dana and her ranch hand, Walker, were saddling horses. "I've never been on a horse," she whispered confidentially to Jackson.

"Neither had your daughter and look at her now," he said as he watched Ford and Natalie saddle up. They both had to climb up the fence to get on their horses, but they now sat eagerly waiting in their saddles.

"I'll help you," Jackson said as he took Allie's horse's reins from Dana. He demonstrated how to get into the saddle then gave her a boost.

"It's so high up here," she said as she put her boot toes into the stirrups.

"Enjoy the view," Jackson said and swung up onto his horse.

They rode up the mountain, the kids chattering away, Dana giving instructions to them as they went.

After a short while, Jackson noticed that Allie seemed to have relaxed a little. She was looking around as if enjoying the ride and when they stopped in a wide meadow, he saw her patting her horse's neck and talking softly to it.

"I'm afraid to ask what you just said to your horse," he joked as he moved closer. Her horse had wandered over to some tall grass away from the others.

"Just thanking him for not bucking me off," she admitted shyly.

"Probably a good idea, but your horse is a she. A mare."

"Oh, hopefully, she wasn't insulted." Allie actually smiled. The afternoon sun lit her face along with the smile.

He felt his heart do a loop-de-loop. He tried to rein it back in as he looked into her eyes. That tantalizing green was deep and dark, inviting, and yet he knew a man could drown in those eyes.

Suddenly, Allie's horse shied. In the next second it took off as if it had been shot from a cannon. To her credit, she hadn't let go of her reins, but she grabbed the saddlehorn and let out a cry as the mare raced out of the meadow headed for the road.

Jackson spurred his horse and raced after her. He could hear the startled cries of the others behind him. He'd been riding since he was a boy, so he knew how to handle his horse. But Allie, he could see, was having trouble staying in the saddle with her horse at a full gallop.

He pushed his harder and managed to catch her, riding alongside until he could reach over and grab her reins. The horses lunged along for a moment. Next to him Allie started to fall. He grabbed for her, pulling her from her saddle and into his arms as he released her reins and brought his own horse up short.

Allie slid down his horse to the ground. He dismounted and dropped beside her. "Are you all right?"

"I think so. What happened?"

He didn't know. One minute her horse was munching on grass, the next it had taken off like a shot.

Jackson could see that she was shaken. She sat down on the ground as if her legs would no longer hold her. He could hear the others riding toward them. When Allie heard her daughter calling to her, she hurriedly got to her feet, clearly wanting to reassure Natalie.

"Wow, that was some ride," Allie said as her daughter came up.

"Are you all right?" Dana asked, dismounting and joining her.

"I'm fine, really," she assured her and moved to her daughter, still in the saddle, to smile up at her.

"What happened?" Dana asked Jackson.

"I don't know."

"This is a good spot to have lunch," Dana announced more cheerfully than Jackson knew she felt.

"I'll go catch the horse." He swung back up into the saddle and took off after the mare. "I'll be right back for lunch. Don't let Ford eat all the sandwiches."

ALLIE HAD NO IDEA why the horse had reacted like that. She hated that she was the one who'd upset everyone.

"Are you sure you didn't spur your horse?" Natalie asked, still upset.

"She isn't wearing spurs," Ford pointed out.

"Maybe a bee stung your horse," Natalie suggested.

Dana felt bad. "I wanted your first horseback riding experience to be a pleasant one," she lamented.

"It was. It is," Allie reassured her although in truth, she wasn't looking forward to getting back on the horse. But she knew she had to for Natalie's sake. The kids had been scared enough as it was.

Dana had spread out the lunch on a large blanket with the kids all helping when Jackson rode up, trailing her horse. The mare looked calm now, but Allie wasn't sure she would ever trust it again.

Jackson met her gaze as he dismounted. Dana was already on her feet, heading for him. Allie left the kids to join them.

"What is it?" Dana asked, keeping her voice down.

Jackson looked to Allie as if he didn't want to say in front of her.

"Did I do something to the horse to make her do that?" she asked, fearing that she had.

His expression softened as he shook his head. "You didn't do *anything*." He looked at Dana. "Someone shot the mare." He moved so Dana could see the bloody spot on the horse. "Looks like a small caliber. Probably a .22. Fortunately, the shooter must have been some distance away or it could have been worse. The bullet barely broke the horse's hide. Just enough to spook the mare."

"We've had teenagers on four-wheelers using the old logging roads on the ranch," Dana said. "I heard shots a few days ago." Suddenly, all the color drained from Dana's face. "Allie could have been killed," she whispered. "Or one of the kids. When we get back, I'll call Hud."

JACKSON INSISTED ON riding right beside Allie on the way back down the mountain. He could tell that Allie had been happy to get off the horse once they reached the corral.

"Thank you for saving me," she said. "It seems like you keep doing that, doesn't it?" He must have looked panicked by the thought because she quickly added, "I'm fine now. I will try not to need saving again." She flashed him a smile and disappeared into the barn.

"Ready?" Tag said soon after Jackson had finished helping unsaddle the horses and put the tack away.

Dana had taken the kids down to the house to play, saying they all needed some downtime. He could tell that she was still upset and anxious to call Hud. "Don't forget the barbecue and dance tonight," she reminded him. "Then tomorrow is the bachelor party, right?"

Jackson groaned. He'd forgotten that Tag had been waiting for them all to arrive so they could have the party. The last thing he needed was a party. Allie's horse taking off like that… It had left him shaken, as well. Dana was convinced it had been teenagers who'd shot the horse. He hoped that was all it had been.

"Glad you're back," Tag said. "We're all going down to the Corral for a beer. Come on. At least four of us are here. We'll be back in time for dinner."

Ford was busy with the kids and Dana. "Are you sure he isn't too much?" Jackson asked his cousin. "I feel like I've been dumping him on you since we got here."

She laughed. "Are you kidding? My children adore having their cousin around. They've actually all been getting along better than usual. Go have a drink with your brothers. Enjoy yourself, Jackson. I suspect you get little time without Ford."

It was true. And yet he missed his son. He told himself again that he would be glad when they got back to Texas. But seeing how much fun Ford was having on the ranch, he doubted his son would feel the same.

ALLIE STARED AT her date book, heart racing. She'd been feeling off balance since her near-death experience on the horse. When she'd told Megan and Belinda about it on her return to the barn, they'd been aghast.

She'd recounted her tale right up to where Jackson had returned with the mare and the news that it had been shot.

"That's horrible," Megan said. "I'm so glad you didn't get bucked off. Was the mare all right?"

Belinda's response was, "So Jackson saved you? Wow, how romantic is that?"

Needing to work, Allie had shooed Belinda out of the barn and she and Megan had worked quietly for several hours before she'd glanced at her watch and realized something was wrong.

"The caterer," Allie said. "Did she happen to call?"

Megan shook her head. "No, why?"

"Her crew should have been here by now. I had no idea it was so late." Allie could feel the panic growing. "And when I checked my date book…"

"What?" Megan asked.

"I wouldn't have canceled." But even as she was saying it, she was dialing the caterer's number.

A woman answered and Allie quickly asked about the dinner that was to be served at Cardwell Ranch tonight.

"We have you down for the reception in a few days, but… Wait a minute. It looks as if you did book it."

Allie felt relief wash through her, though it did nothing to relieve the panic. She had a ranch full of people to be fed and no caterer for the barbecue.

"I'm sorry. It says here that you called to cancel it yesterday."

"That's not possible. It couldn't have been me."

"Is your name Allie Taylor?"

She felt her heart drop. "Yes."

"It says here that you personally called."

Allie dropped into one of the chairs. She wanted to argue with the woman, but what good would it do? The damage was done. And anyway, she couldn't be sure she hadn't called. She couldn't be sure of anything.

"Just make sure that the caterers will be here on the Fourth of July for the wedding reception and that no one, and I mean not even me, can cancel it. Can you do that for me?" Her voice broke and she saw Megan looking at her with concern.

As she disconnected, she fought tears. "What am I going to do?"

"What's wrong?"

Her head snapped up at the sound of Jackson's voice. "I thought you were having beers with your brothers?"

"A couple beers is all I can handle. So come on, what's going on?"

She wiped at her eyes, standing to turn her back to him until she could gain control. What the man must think of her.

"The caterer accidentally got canceled. Looks like we might have to try to find a restaurant tonight," Megan said, reaching for her phone.

"Don't be ridiculous," Jackson said, turning Allie to look at him. "You have some of the best barbecue experts in the country right here on the ranch. I'll run down to the market and get some ribs while my brothers get the fire going. It's going to be fine."

This last statement Allie could tell was directed at her. She met his gaze, all her gratitude in that one look.

Jackson tipped his hat and gave her a smile. "It's going to be better than fine. You'll see."

"I HOPE YOU DON'T MIND," Allie heard Jackson tell Dana and Lily. "I changed Allie's plans. I thought it would be fun if the Cardwell boys barbecued."

Dana was delighted and so was Lily. They insisted she, Natalie, Megan and Belinda stay and Allie soon found herself getting caught up in the revelry.

The Texas Boys Barbecue brothers went to work making dinner. Allie felt awful that they had to cook, but soon saw how much fun they were having.

They joked and played around while their father and Dana's provided the music. All the ranch hands and neighbors ended up being invited and pretty soon it had turned into a party. She noticed that even Drew, who'd been working at one of the cabins, had been invited to join them.

The barbecue was amazing and a lot more fun than the one Allie had originally planned. Everyone complimented the food and the new restaurant was toasted as a welcome addition to Big Sky.

Allie did her best to stay in the background. The day had left her feeling beaten up from her wild horseback ride to the foul-up with the caterer, along with her other misadventures. She was just happy to sit on the sidelines. Megan and Belinda were having a ball dancing with some of the ranch hands. All the kids were dancing, as well. At one point, she saw Jackson showing Ford how to do the swing with Natalie.

Someone stepped in front of her, blocking her view of the dance floor. She looked up to see Drew.

"I don't believe you've danced all night," he said.

"I'm really not—"

"What? You won't dance with your own brother-in-law? I guess you don't need me anymore now that you have the Cardwells. Or is it just one Cardwell?"

She realized he'd had too much to drink. "Drew, that isn't—"

"Excuse me," Jackson said, suddenly appearing beside her. "I believe this dance is mine." He reached for Allie's hand.

Drew started to argue, but Jackson didn't give him a chance before he pulled Allie out onto the dance floor. The song was a slow one. He took her in his arms and pulled her close.

"You really have to quit saving me," she said only half joking.

"Sorry, but I could see you needed help," Jackson said. "Your brother-in-law is more than a little protective, Allie."

She didn't want to talk about Drew. She closed her eyes for a moment. It felt good in the cowboy's arms. She couldn't remember the last time she'd danced, but that felt good, too, moving to the slow country song. "You saved my life earlier and then saved my bacon tonight. Natalie thinks you're a cowboy superhero. I'm beginning to wonder myself."

He gave her a grin and a shrug. "It weren't nothin', ma'am," he said, heavy on the Texas drawl. "Actually, I don't know why my brothers and I hadn't thought of it before. You did me a favor. I'd missed cooking with them. It was fun."

"Did I hear there is a bachelor party tomorrow night?"

Jackson groaned. "Hayes is in charge. I hate to think." He laughed softly. "Then the rehearsal and dinner the next night and finally the wedding." He shook his head as if he couldn't wait for it to be over.

Allie had felt the same way—before she'd met Jackson Cardwell.

Drew appeared just then. "Cuttin' in," he said, slurring his words as he pried himself between the two of them.

Jackson seemed to hesitate, but Allie didn't want trouble. She stepped into Drew's arms and let him dance her away from the Texas cowboy.

"What the hell do you think you're doing?" Drew demanded as he pulled her closer. "My brother is barely cold in his grave and here you are actin' like—"

"The wedding planner?" She broke away from him as the song ended. "Sorry, but I'm calling it a night. I have a lot of work to do tomorrow." With that she went to get Natalie. It was time to go home.

CHAPTER SIX

ALLIE WAS GETTING ready to go to the ranch the next morning when she heard a vehicle pull up. She glanced out groaning when she saw it was Drew. Even more disturbing, he had his mother with him. As she watched them climb out, she braced herself for the worst. Drew had been acting strangely since he'd seen her with Jackson that first time.

"Hi," she said opening the door before either of them could knock. "You just caught me heading out."

"We *hoped* to catch you," Mildred said. "We're taking Natalie for the day so you can get some work done."

Not may we, but *we're taking*. "I'm sorry but Natalie already has plans."

Mildred's eyebrow shot up. "Natalie is five. Her plans can change."

"Natalie is going with the Cardwells—"

"The Cardwells aren't family," Mildred spat.

No, Allie thought, *but I wish they were.* "If you had just called—"

"I'm sure Nat would rather spend the day with her grandmother than whatever you have planned for—" Mildred broke off at the sound of a vehicle coming up the road toward them.

Who now? Allie wondered, fearing she was about to lose this battle with her in-laws—and break her daughter's heart. Her pulse did a little leap as she recognized the SUV as the one Jackson Cardwell had been driving yesterday. But what was he doing here? Allie had said she would bring Nat to the ranch.

Jackson parked and got out, Ford right behind him. He seemed to take in the scene before he asked, "Is there a problem?"

"Nothing to do with you," Drew said.

"Jackson Cardwell," he said and held out his hand. "I don't believe we've been formally introduced."

Drew was slow to take it. "Drew Taylor." Allie could see her brother-in-law sizing up Jackson. While they were both a few inches over six feet and both strong-looking, Jackson had the broader shoulders and looked as if he could take Drew in a fair fight.

Mildred crossed her arms over her chest and said, "We're here to pick up my granddaughter."

"That's why *I'm* here," Jackson said. Just then Natalie came to the door. She was dressed for the rodeo in her Western shirt, jeans and new red cowboy boots. Allie had braided her hair into two plaits that trailed down her back. A straw cowboy hat was perched on her head, her smile huge.

"I'm going to the rodeo with Ford and Hank and Mary," Nat announced excitedly. Oblivious to what was going on, she added, "I've never been to a rodeo before."

"Hop into the rig with Ford. I borrowed a carseat from Dana," Jackson said before either Drew or Mildred could argue otherwise.

With a wave, Nat hurried past her grandmother and uncle and taking Ford's hand, the two ran toward the SUV.

Allie held her breath as she saw Drew ball his hands into fists. She'd never seen him like this and realized Jackson was right. This was more than him being protective.

Jackson looked as if he expected Drew to take a swing—and was almost daring him to. The tension between the two men was thick as fresh-churned butter. Surely it wouldn't come to blows.

"Are you ready?" Jackson said to her, making her blink in surprise. "Dana gave me your ticket for the rodeo."

He *knew* she wasn't planning to go. This wedding had to be perfect and let's face it, she hadn't been herself for some time now.

"Going to a rodeo is part of this so-called wedding planning?" Mildred demanded. She lifted a brow. "I heard it also entails dancing with the guests."

"All in a day's work," Jackson said and met Allie's gaze. "We should get going. Don't want to be late." He looked to Drew. "Nice to meet you." Then turned to Mildred. "You must be Allie's mother-in-law."

"Mildred." Her lips were pursed so tightly that the word barely came out.

"I just need to grab my purse," Allie said, taking advantage of Jackson's rescue, even though she knew it would cost her.

When she came back out, Jackson was waiting for her. He tipped his hat to Drew and Mildred as Allie locked the cabin door behind her. She noticed that Mother Taylor and Drew were still standing where she'd left them, both looking infuriated.

She hated antagonizing them for fear what could happen if they ever decided to try to take Natalive from her. If they knew about just a few of the so-called incidents…

Like Nat, Allie slipped past them out to the SUV and didn't let out the breath she'd been holding until she was seated in the passenger seat.

"That looked like an ambush back there," Jackson said as they drove away.

She glanced back knowing she might have escaped this time, but there would be retribution. "They mean well."

JACKSON GLANCED OVER at her. "Do they?"

She looked away. "With Nick gone... Well, we're all adjusting to it. I'm sure they feel all they have left of him is Nat. They just want to see more of her."

He could see that she felt guilty. His ex and her family had used guilt on him like a club. He remembered that beat-up, rotten feeling and hated to see her going through it.

In the backseat, Natalie was telling Ford about something her horse had done yesterday during her ride. They both started laughing the way only kids can do. He loved the sound.

"Thank you for the rescue, but I really can't go to the rodeo. You can drop me at the ranch," Allie said, clearly nervous. "I need to check on things."

"You've done a great job. A few hours away at the rodeo is your reward. Dana's orders. She's the one who sent me to get you, knowing you wouldn't come unless I did."

"I really should be working."

"When was the last time you were at a rodeo?" he asked.

She chewed at her lower lip for a moment. "I think I went with some friends when I was in the fifth grade."

He smiled over at her. "Well, then it is high time you went again."

"I want an elephant ear!" Ford cried from the backseat.

"An elephant ear?" Nat repeated and began to giggle.

"So Nat's never been to a rodeo, either?" Jackson asked.

"No, I guess she hasn't."

"Well, she is going today and she and her mother are going to have elephant ears!" he announced. The kids laughed happily. He was glad to hear Ford explaining that an elephant ear really was just fried bread with sugar and cinnamon on it, but that it was really good.

Allie seemed to relax, but he saw her checking her side

mirror. Did she think her in-laws would chase her down? He wouldn't have been surprised. They'd been more than overbearing. He had seen how they dominated Allie. It made him wonder what her husband had been like.

When they reached the rodeo grounds, Dana and Hud were waiting along with the kids and Tag and Lily and Hayes and McKenzie and Laramie.

"Oh, I'm so glad you decided to come along," Dana said when she saw Allie. "Jackson said he wasn't sure he could convince you, but he was darned sure going to try." She glanced at her cousin. "He must be pretty persuasive."

"Yes, he is," Allie said and smiled.

Jackson felt a little piece of his heart float up at that smile.

Easy, Texas cowboy, he warned himself.

But even as he thought it, he had to admit that he was getting into the habit of rescuing this woman—and enjoying it. Allie needed protecting. How badly she needed it, he didn't yet know.

It was the least he could do—until the wedding. And then he and Ford were headed back to Texas. Allie Taylor would be on her own.

Just the thought made him scared for her.

ALLIE COULDN'T REMEMBER the last time she'd had so much fun. The rodeo was thrilling, the elephant ear delicious and the Cardwells a very fun family. She'd ended up sitting next to Jackson, their children in front of them.

"I want to be a barrel racer," Natalie announced.

"We'll have to set up some barrels at the ranch," Dana said. "Natalie's a natural in the saddle. She'd make a great barrel racer."

"Well, I'm not riding the bulls," Ford said and everyone laughed.

"Glad you came along?" Jackson asked Allie as he offered some of his popcorn.

She'd already eaten a huge elephant ear and loved every bite, but she still took a handful of popcorn and smiled. "I am. This is fun."

"You deserve some fun."

Allie wasn't so sure about that. She wasn't sure what she deserved, wasn't that the problem? She leaned back against the bleachers, breathing in the summer day and wishing this would never end.

But it did end and the crowd began to make their way to the parking lot in a swell of people. That's when she saw him.

Nick. He was moving through the crowd. She'd seen him because he was going in the wrong direction—in their direction. He wore a dark-colored baseball cap, his features lost in the shadow of the cap's bill. She got only a glimpse— Suddenly, he turned as if headed for the parking lot, as well. She sat up, telling herself her eyes were deceiving her. Nick was dead and yet—

"Allie, what it is?" Jackson asked.

In the past when she'd caught glimpses of him, she'd frozen, too shocked to move. She sprang to her feet and pushed her way down the grandstand steps until she reached the ground. Forcing her way through the crowd, she kept Nick in sight ahead of her. He was moving fast as if he wanted to get away.

Not this time, she thought, as she felt herself gaining on him. She could see the back of his head. He was wearing his MSU Bobcat navy ball cap, just like the one he'd been wearing the day he left to go up into the mountains—and his favorite shirt, the one she'd burned.

Her heart pounded harder against her ribs. She told herself she wasn't losing her mind. She couldn't explain any of this, but she knew what she was seeing. Nick. She was within yards of him, only a few people between them. She could almost reach out and grab his sleeve—

Suddenly, someone grabbed her arm, spinning her around. She stumbled over backward, falling against the person in front of her, tripping on her own feet before hitting the ground. The fall knocked the air from her lungs and skinned her elbow, worse, her pride. The crowd opened a little around her as several people stopped to see if she was all right.

But it was Jackson who rushed to help her up. "Allie, are you all right?"

All she could do was shake her head as the man she thought was Nick disappeared into the crowd.

"WHAT'S GOING ON?" Jackson asked, seeing how upset she was. Had he said or done something that would make her take off like that?

She shook her head again as if unable to speak. He could tell *something* had happened. Drawing her aside, he asked her again. The kids had gone on ahead with Dana and her children.

"Allie, talk to me."

She looked up at him, those green eyes filling with tears. "I saw my husband, Nick. At least I think I saw him." She looked shocked as she darted a glance at the crowd, clearly expecting to see her dead husband again.

"You must think I'm crazy. *I* think I'm crazy. But I saw Nick. I know it couldn't be him, but it looked so much like him...." She shivered, even though the July day was hot. "He was wearing his new ball cap and his favorite shirt, the one I burned..." She began to cry.

"Hey," he said, taking her shoulders in his hands to turn

her toward him. "I don't think you're crazy. I think you've had a horrible loss that—"

"I didn't *love* him. I was *leaving* him." The words tumbled out in a rush. "I...I...*hated* him. I *wanted* him gone, not dead!"

Jackson started to pull her into his arms, but she bolted and was quickly swept up in the exiting crowd. He stood for a moment, letting her words sink in. Now, more than ever, he thought he understood why she was letting little things upset her. Guilt was a powerful thing. It explained a lot, especially with her relationship with her in-laws that he'd glimpsed that morning. How long had they been browbeating her? he wondered. Maybe her whole marriage.

He found himself more curious about her husband, Nick Taylor. And even more about Allie. Common sense told him to keep his distance. The wedding was only days away, then he and Ford would be flying back to Houston.

Maybe it was because he'd gone through a bad marriage, but he felt for her even more now. Like her, he was raising his child alone. Like her, he was disillusioned and he'd certainly gone through a time with his ex when he thought he was losing his mind. He'd also wished his ex dead more than once.

ALLIE CAUGHT UP to Dana as she was loading all the kids into her Suburban. Hud had brought his own rig since he had to stop by the marshal's office.

"Mind if I catch a ride with you?" Allie asked. "Jackson had some errands to run in town." The truth was that after her outburst, she was embarrassed and knew Dana had room for her and Nat in the Suburban.

"Of course not."

Allie had stopped long enough to go into the ladies' room and wash her face and calm down. She knew everyone had seen her take off like a crazy woman. She felt embarrassed and sick at heart, but mostly she was bone-deep scared.

When she'd seen Jackson heading for the parking lot, she'd motioned that she and Nat were going with Dana. He'd merely nodded, probably glad.

Dana didn't comment on Allie's red eyes or her impromptu exit earlier, though as she joined them at the Suburban. Instead, Dana made small talk about the rodeo, the weather, the upcoming wedding.

They were almost back to the ranch before Dana asked, "How are things going?" over the chatter of the kids in the back of the SUV.

Allie could tell that she wasn't just making conversation anymore. She really wanted to know. "It's been hard. I guess it's no secret that I've been struggling."

Dana reached over and squeezed her hand. "I know. I feel so bad about yesterday. I'm just so glad you weren't hurt." She smiled. "You did a great job of staying on that horse, though. I told Natalie how proud I was of you."

Allie thought of Jackson. He'd saved her life yesterday. She remembered the feel of his arms as he'd pulled her from the horse—and again on the dance floor last night. Shoving away the memory, she reminded herself that once the wedding was over, he and Ford would be leaving. She was going to have to start saving herself.

"Did Hud find out anything about who might have shot the horse?" she asked, remembering Hud talking to the vet when he'd stopped by to make sure the mare was all right.

"Nothing yet, but he is going to start gating the roads on the ranch. We can't keep people from the forest service property that borders the ranch, but we can keep them at a distance by closing off the ranch property. In the meantime, if there is anything I can do to help you…"

"Dana, you've already done so much. Letting Natalie come to the ranch and teaching her to ride…" Allie felt overwhelmed at Dana's generosity.

"Let's see if you thank me when she's constantly bugging you about buying her a horse," Dana joked. "Seriously, she can always come up to the ranch and ride. And if someday you do want a horse for her…"

"Thank you. For everything."

"I love what you've done to the barn," Dana said, changing the subject. "It is beyond my expectations and Lily can't say enough about it. I'm getting so excited, but then I'm a sucker for weddings."

"Me, too," Allie admitted. "They are so beautiful. There is so much hope and love in the air. It's all like a wonderful dream."

"Or fantasy," Dana joked. "Nothing about the wedding day is like marriage, especially four children later."

No, Allie thought, but then she'd had a small wedding in Mother Taylor's backyard. She should have known then how the marriage was going to go.

"Have you given any more thought to moving up to a guest cabin?" Dana asked.

"I have. Like I said, I'm touched by the offer. But Natalie has been through so many changes with Nick's death, I think staying at the cabin in her own bed might be best. We'll see, though. She is having such a great time at the ranch and as the wedding gets closer…"

"Just know that I saved a cabin for you and Natalie," Dana said. "And don't worry about your daughter. We have already adopted her into the family. The kids love her and Ford…." She laughed and lowered her voice, even though the kids weren't paying any attention behind them. "Have you noticed how tongue-tied he gets around her?"

They both laughed, Allie feeling blessed because she

felt as if she, too, had been adopted into the family. The Cardwells were so different from the Taylors. She pushed that thought away. Just as she did the memory of that instant when she would have sworn she saw Nick at the rodeo.

Every time she thought she was getting better, stronger, something would happen to make her afraid she really was losing her mind.

"Hey," Belinda said, seeming surprised when Allie and Nat walked into the barn that afternoon. "Where have you been? I thought you'd be here working."

"We went to the rodeo!" Natalie said. "And now I'm going to go ride a horse!" With that she ran out of the barn to join the other kids and Dana.

"You went to the rodeo?"

"You sound like my in-laws," Allie said. "Yes, I was invited, I went and now I will do the last-minute arrangements for the rehearsal dinner tomorrow and it will all be fine."

Belinda lifted a brow. "Wow, what a change from the woman who was panicking because she couldn't find her keys the other day. Have you been drinking?"

"I'm taking my life back." She told her friend about the candle, Nick's shirt and what she did with it. Also about chasing the man she thought was Nick at the rodeo. "I almost caught him. If someone hadn't grabbed my arm…"

Belinda's eyes widened in alarm. "Sorry, but doesn't that sound a little…"

"Crazy? Believe me, I know. But I was sick of just taking it and doing nothing."

"I can see you thinking you saw someone who looked like Nick at the rodeo…."

"He was wearing his favorite shirt and his new ball cap."

Belinda stared at her. "The shirt you'd burned a few nights ago, right?"

Allie regretted telling her friend. "I know it doesn't make any sense. But all these things that have been happening? I'm not imagining them." From her friend's expression, she was glad she hadn't told her about the dresses or the new clothes she'd found in her closet.

"Sweetie," Belinda asked tentatively. "Did you give any more thought to making that call I suggested?"

"No and right now I have work to do."

"Don't we all. Some of us didn't spend the day at the rodeo."

Her friend actually sounded jealous. Allie put it out of her mind. She had to concentrate on the wedding. The barn looked beautiful. After the rehearsal dinner tomorrow night, she would get ready for the wedding. All she had to do was hold it together until then.

Megan came in with her list of last-minute things that needed to be tended to before the wedding rehearsal.

"I'll meet you down in the meadow in a few minutes." Left alone, Allie looked around the barn. She was a little sad it would be over. Jackson and Ford would be returning to Texas. Nat was really going to miss them.

And so are you.

ALLIE WASN'T SURE what awakened her. Dana had insisted she take the rest of the day off and spend it with Natalie.

"You have accomplished so much," Dana had argued. "Tomorrow is another day. The men are all going with Tag for his bachelor party tonight. I plan to turn in early with the kids. Trust me. We all need some downtime before the wedding."

Emotionally exhausted, Allie had agreed. She and Nat had come back to the cabin and gone down to the river until dinner. Nat loved building rock dams and playing in the water.

After dinner even Natalie was exhausted from the full day. After Allie had put her down to sleep, she'd turned in herself with a book. But only a few pages in, she had turned out the light and gone to sleep.

Now, startled awake, she lay listening to the wind that had come up during the night. It was groaning in the boughs of the pine trees next to the cabin. Through the window, she could see the pines swaying and smell the nearby river. She caught only glimpses of the moon in a sky filled with stars as she lay listening.

Since Nick's death she didn't sleep well. The cabin often woke her with its creaks and groans. Sometimes she would hear a thump as if something had fallen and yet when she'd gone to investigate, she would find nothing.

One time, she'd found the front door standing open. She had stared at it in shock, chilled by the cold air rushing in—and the knowledge that she distinctly remembered locking it before going to bed. Only a crazy woman would leave the front door wide open.

Now, though, all she heard was the wind in the pines, a pleasant sound, a safe sound. She tried to reassure herself that everything was fine. She thought of her day with the Cardwell family and remembered how Jackson had saved her by having the Cardwell brothers make their famous Texas barbecue for supper. She smiled at the memory of the brothers in their Texas Boys Barbecue aprons joking around as they cooked.

She'd overheard one of the brothers say he was glad to see Jackson loosening up a little. Allie found herself watching him earlier at the rodeo, wondering how he was doing as a single father. She didn't feel as if she'd done very well so far as a single mother.

Ford was having a sleepover at the main house at the ranch again tonight. Allie knew if Nat had known about it, she would have wanted to stay, as well. But she suspected that Dana had realized that she needed her daughter with her tonight. What a day! First a run-in earlier with Mildred and Drew... Allie felt a chill at the memory. They had both been so furious and no doubt hurt, as well. Then thinking she saw Nick. She shook her head and, closing her eyes, tried to will herself to go back to sleep. If she got to thinking about any of that—

A small thump made her freeze. She heard it again and quickly swung her legs over the side of the bed. The sound had come from down the hall toward the bedroom where Natalie was sleeping.

Allie didn't bother with her slippers or her robe; she was too anxious as she heard another thump. She snapped on the hall light as she rushed down the short, narrow hallway to her daughter's room. The door she'd left open was now closed. She stopped in front of it, her heart pounding. The wind. It must have blown it shut. But surely she hadn't left Nat's window open that much.

She grabbed the knob and turned, shoving the door open with a force that sent her stumbling into the small room. The moon and starlight poured in through the gaping open window to paint the bedroom in silver as the wind slammed a loose shutter against the side of the cabin with a thump.

Allie felt her eyes widen as a scream climbed her throat.

Nat's bed was empty.

CHAPTER SEVEN

JACKSON FELT AT LOOSE ENDS after the bachelor party. Part of the reason, he told himself, was because he'd spent so little time with his son. Back in Texas on their small ranch, he and Ford were inseparable. It was good to see his son having so much fun with other children, but he missed him.

Tonight Ford was having a sleepover at the main house with Dana's brood. He'd wanted to say no when Dana had asked, but he had seen that Ford had his heart set and Jackson had no choice but to attend Tag's bachelor party.

Fortunately, it had been a mild one, bar-hopping from the Corral to Lily's brother's bar at Big Sky, The Canyon Bar. They'd laughed and joked about their childhoods growing up in Texas and talked about Tag's upcoming wedding and bugged Hayes about his plans with McKenzie. Hayes only grinned in answer.

Hud, as designated driver, got them all home just after midnight, where they parted company and headed to their respective cabins. That was hours ago. Jackson had slept for a while before the wind had awakened him.

Now, alone with only his thoughts, he kept circling back to Allie. She'd had fun at the rodeo—until she'd thought she'd seen her dead husband. He blamed her in-laws. He figured they'd been laying a guilt trip on her ever since Nick Taylor had been presumed dead. Her run-in with them that morning must have made her think she saw Nick. He wanted to throttle them for the way they treated Allie and shuddered at the thought of them having anything to do with raising Natalie.

Allie was too nice. Did she really believe they meant well? Like hell, he thought now. They'd been in the wrong and yet they'd made her feel badly. It reminded him too much of the way his ex had done him.

It had been fun cooking with his brothers again—just as they had when they'd started their first barbecue restaurant. Allie'd had fun at the barbecue, too. He'd seen her laughing and smiling with the family. He'd enjoyed himself, as well. Of course Austin still hadn't arrived. But it was nice being with the others.

As much as he'd enjoyed the day, he felt too antsy to sleep and admitted it wasn't just Ford who was the problem. He tried to go back to sleep, but knew it was impossible. He had too much on his mind. Except for the wind in the pines, the ranch was quiet as he decided to go for a walk.

Overhead the Montana sky was a dazzling glitter of starlight with the moon peeking in and out of the clouds. The mountains rose on each side of the canyon, blacker than midnight. A breeze stirred the dark pines, sending a whisper through the night.

As he neared his rental SUV, he decided to go for a ride. He hadn't had that much to drink earlier and, after sleeping for a few hours, felt fine to drive.

But not far down the road, he found himself slowing as he neared Allie's cabin. The cabin was small and sat back from the highway on the river.

He would have driven on past, if a light hadn't come on inside the cabin.

Something about that light coming on in the wee hours of the morning sent a shiver through him. He would have said he had a premonition, if he believed in them. Instead, he didn't question what made him turn down her road.

Just as he pulled up to the cabin, Allie came running out.

At first he thought she'd seen him turn into her yard and that was why she'd come running out with a flashlight. But one look at her wild expression, her bare feet and her clothed in nothing but her nightgown, and he knew why he'd turned into her cabin.

"Allie?" he called to her as he jumped out. "Allie, what's wrong?"

She didn't seem to hear him. She ran toward the side of the cabin as if searching furiously as her flashlight beam darted into the darkness. He had to run after her as she headed around the back of the cabin. He grabbed her arm, thinking she might be having a nightmare and was walking in her sleep.

"Allie, what's wrong?"

"Nat! She's gone!"

He instantly thought of the fast-moving river not many yards out the back door. His gaze went to Allie's feet. "Get some shoes on. I'll check behind the house."

Taking her flashlight, he pushed her toward the front door before running around to the back of the cabin. He could hear and smell the river on the other side of a stand of pines. The July night was cool, almost cold this close to the river. Through the dark boughs, he caught glimpses of the Gallatin River. It shone in the moon and starlight, a ribbon of silver that had spent eons carving its way through the granite canyon walls.

As he reached the dense pines, his mind was racing. Had Natalie gotten up in the night and come outside? Maybe half-asleep, would she head for the river?

"Natalie!" he called. The only answer was the rush

of the river and moan of the wind in the pine boughs overhead.

At the edge of the river, he shone the flashlight beam along the edge of the bank. No tracks in the soft earth. He flicked the light up and down the area between the pines, then out over the water. Exposed boulders shone in the light as the fast water rushed over and around them.

If Natalie had come down here and gone into the swift current...

At the sound of a vehicle engine starting up, he swung his flashlight beam in time to see a dark-colored pickup take off out of the pines. Had someone kidnapped Natalie? His first thought was the Taylors.

As he ran back toward the cabin, he tried to tell himself it had probably been teenagers parked down by the river making out. Once inside, he found Allie. She'd pulled on sandals and a robe and had just been heading out again. She looked panicked, her cheeks wet with tears.

"You're sure she isn't somewhere in the house," he said, thinking about a time that he'd fallen asleep under his bed while his mother had turned the house upside down looking for him.

The cabin was small. It took only a moment to search everywhere except Nat's room. As he neared the door to the child's bedroom, he felt the cool air and knew before he pushed open the door that her window was wide open, the wind billowing the curtains.

He could see the river and pines through the open window next to the bed. No screen. What looked like fresh soil and several dried pine needles were on the floor next to the bed. As he started to step into the room, a sound came from under the covers on the bed.

Jackson was at the bed in two long strides, pulling back the covers to find a sleeping Natalie Taylor curled there.

Had she been there the whole time and Allie had somehow missed her?

Allie stumbled into the room and fell to her knees next to her daughter's bed. She pulled Nat to her, snuggling her face into the sleeping child.

Jackson stepped out of the room to leave them alone for a moment. His heart was still racing, his fear now for Allie rather than Nat.

A few minutes later, Allie came out of her daughter's room. He could see that she'd been crying again.

"She's such a sound sleeper. I called for her. I swear she wasn't in her bed."

"I believe you."

"I checked her room. I looked under her bed...." The tears began to fall again. "I looked in her closet. I called her name. *She wasn't there.* She wasn't anywhere in the cabin."

"It's all right," Jackson said as he stepped to her and put his arms around her.

Her voice broke as she tried to speak again. "What if she was there the whole time?" she whispered against his chest. He could feel her trembling and crying with both relief and this new fear. "She can sleep through anything. Maybe—"

"Did you leave the window open?"

"I cracked it just a little so she could get fresh air...."

"Natalie isn't strong enough to open that old window all the way like that."

Allie pulled back to look up at him, tears welling in her green eyes. "I *must* have opened it. I *must* have—"

He thought of the pickup he'd seen leaving. "There's something I need to check," he said, picking up the flashlight from where he'd laid it down just moments before. "Stay here with Natalie."

Outside he moved along the side of the house to the

back, shining the flashlight ahead of him. He suspected what he would find so he wasn't all that surprised to discover the boot prints in the soft dirt outside Nat's window.

Jackson knelt down next to the prints. A man-size boot. He shone the light a few feet away. The tracks had come up to the window, the print a partial as if the man had sneaked up on the toes of his boots. But when the prints retreated from the child's window, the prints were full boot tracks, deep in the dirt as if he'd been carrying something. The tracks disappeared into the dried needles of the pines, then reappeared, this time headed back to the house. When the man had returned Natalie to her bed—and left dried pine needles and dirt on the bedroom floor.

ALLIE SAT ON THE EDGE of her daughter's bed. She'd always loved watching Natalie sleep. There was something so incredibly sweet about her that was heightened when she slept. The sleep of angels, she thought as she watched the rise and fall of her daughter's chest.

Outside the now closed window, Jackson's shadow appeared and disappeared. A few minutes later, she heard him come back into the cabin. He came directly down the hall, stopping in Nat's bedroom doorway as if he knew she would be sitting on the side of the bed, watching her daughter sleep. That was where he would have been if it had been his son who'd gone missing, he thought.

She was still so shaken and scared. Not for Natalie, who was safe in her bed, but for herself. How could she have thought her daughter was missing? She really was losing her mind. Tucking Nat in, she checked to make sure the window was locked and left the room, propping the door open.

Jackson followed her into the small living room. She held her breath as she met his gaze. He was the one person who had made her feel as if she was going to be all right. He'd seen the black cat. He'd sympathized with her when she'd told him about misplacing her car keys and messing up her date book.

But earlier he'd looked at her as if she were a hysterical woman half out of her mind. She *had* been. Maybe she *was* unstable. When she'd found Nat's bed empty— Just the thought made her blood run cold again.

"I swear to you she wasn't in her bed." She could hear how close she was to breaking down again.

He must have, too, because he reached over and gripped her arm. "You didn't imagine it any more than you did the black cat."

She stared at him. "How can you say that?"

"Someone was outside Natalie's window tonight. There were fresh tracks where he'd stood. He took Natalie."

Her heart began to thunder in her ears. "Someone tried to…" She couldn't bring herself to say the words as she imagined a shadowed man taking her baby girl out through the window. "But why…?"

"He must have heard me coming and changed his mind," Jackson said.

"Changed his mind?" This all felt too surreal. First Nick's death then all the insane incidents, now someone had tried to take her child?

"Why don't you sit down," Jackson suggested.

She nodded and sank into the closest chair. He took one and pulled it next to hers.

"Is there someone who would want to take your daughter?" he asked.

Again she stared at him, unable to speak for a moment. "Why would anyone want to kidnap Natalie? I don't have any money."

He seemed to hesitate. "What about your husband's family?"

JACKSON SAW THAT HE'D voiced her fear. He'd seen the way her in-laws had been just that morning. It wasn't much of a stretch that they would try to take Natalie. But through an open window in the middle of the night?

"They've made no secret that they want to see her more, but to steal her from her bed and scare me like this?"

Scare her. He saw her eyes widen in alarm and he took a guess. "There have been other instances when something happened that scared you?"

Her wide, green eyes filled with tears. "It was nothing. Probably just my imagination. I haven't been myself since…"

"Tell me about the incidents."

She swallowed and seemed to brace herself. "I found a squirrel in my cast-iron pot that has a lid."

"A live squirrel?"

"Half dead. I know it sounds crazy. How could a squirrel get under a heavy lid like that?"

"It couldn't. What else?"

She blinked as if stunned that he believed her, but it seemed to free her voice. "My husband used to buy me clothes I didn't like. I found them all cut up but I don't remember doing it. My brother-in-law took Nat and me out for dinner and when I got back they were lying on the bed and there were new clothes in the closet, eight hundred dollars' worth, like I would have bought if…"

"If you had bought them. Did you?"

She hesitated. "I don't think so but there was a check missing from my checkbook and when I took them back to the store, the clerks didn't remember who'd purchased them."

"No one was ever around when any of these things happened?"

She shook her head. "When I told my mother-in-law about the squirrel in the pot…she thought I was still taking the drugs the doctor gave me right after Nick's death. The drugs did make me see things that weren't there...." Her words fell away as if she'd just then realized something. "Unless the things *had* been there."

Allie looked up at him, tears shimmering in her eyes. "Like the black cat.... I wasn't sure I'd even seen it until you..."

It broke his heart. For months after her husband's death, she'd been going through this with no one who believed her.

"I don't think you imagined any of these things that have been happening to you," he said, reaching for her hand. "I think someone wants you to *believe* you are losing your mind. What would happen if you were?"

She didn't hesitate an instant. "I would lose Natalie."

As RELIEVED AS SHE WAS, Allie had trouble believing what he was saying. She got up and started to make a fire.

"Let me do that," Jackson said, taking a handful of kindling from her.

Allie moved restlessly around the room as he got the blaze going. "You think it's someone in Nick's family?"

"That would be my guess. It's clear they want Natalie, especially your mother-in-law. Would her son, Drew, help her?"

She shook her head. "Nick would do whatever his mother wanted. But Drew..." She didn't want to believe it, but he seemed to have turned against her lately. She felt sick at the thought that she might have been wrong about him all this time.

"You must think I'm such a fool."

"My mother said be careful what family you're marrying into. I didn't listen. I didn't even *know* the woman

I was really marrying. But then she hid it well—until we were married."

"I know exactly what you're saying."

His chuckle held no humor. "I learned the hard way."

"So did I. I would have left Nick, if he hadn't disappeared.... I suppose you heard that he went hiking up in the mountains late last fall and was believed killed by a grizzly."

He nodded. "I'm sorry. You must have all kinds of conflicting emotions under the circumstances."

Allie let out a sigh. "You have no idea. Or maybe you do. My friend Belinda says my so-called incidents are brought on by my guilt. She's even suggested that I see a psychic to try to contact Nick on the other side to make the guilt go away."

He shook his head. "I think there is a very sane explanation that has nothing to do with guilt, and the last thing you need is some charlatan who'll only take your money."

She laughed. "That was exactly what I thought." She couldn't believe how much better she felt. She hadn't felt strong for so long. Fear had weakened her, but Jackson's words brought out some of the old Allie, that strong young woman who'd foolishly married Nick Taylor.

He hadn't broken her at first. It had taken a few years before she'd realized what he'd done to her. She no longer had her own ideas—if they didn't agree with his. He dressed her, told her what friends he liked and which ones he didn't.

He'd basically taken over her life, but always making it seem as if he were doing her a favor since he knew best. And she had loved him. At least at first so she'd gone along because she hadn't wanted to upset him. Nick could be scary when he was mad. She'd learned not to set him off.

When Nick had been nice, he'd been so sweet that she

had been lulled into thinking that if she was just a little more accommodating he would be sweet all the time.

"Belinda thinks Nick knew that I was leaving him and went up in the mountains to…"

"Kill himself? What do you think?" Jackson asked.

"Nick did say he wanted to change and that he was sorry about the way he'd acted, but…"

"You didn't believe it?"

She shook her head. "The Nick I knew couldn't change even if he'd wanted to."

So why had Nick Taylor gone up into the mountains last fall and never come back? Jackson wondered.

The fact that his body hadn't been found made Jackson more than a little suspicious. If the man had purposely gone to the mountains intending to die and leave his wife and child alone, then he was a coward. If he set the whole thing up and was now trying to have his wife committed…

The timing bothered him. His stomach roiled with anger at the thought. "Is there any chance he knew of your plans?"

"I didn't think so. For months I'd been picking up any change he left lying around. I also had been skimping on groceries so I could save a little. He might have noticed." She looked away guiltily. "I also took money out of his wallet if he'd been drinking. I figured he wouldn't know how much he spent. He never said anything."

Jackson hoped this bastard was alive because he planned to punch him before the man went to prison for what he was doing to this woman. Not letting her have her own money was a sin in any marriage, no matter what some head-of-the household types said.

"I hate to even ask this, but is there any chance—"

"Nick is still alive?" She stood and paced around the

room. "That would explain it, wouldn't it? Why I think I see him or why I smell his aftershave in the house, even though I threw out the bottle months ago. Why when I start feeling better, he shows up."

"Like at the rodeo?" Jackson asked, feeling his skin crawl at the thought of the bastard. "This only happens when there is no one else around who sees him, right?"

She nodded. "It all happens in a split second so I can't be sure. At the rodeo, though, I almost caught him. Just a few more yards..." Allie's eyes suddenly widened. "I remember now. Someone grabbed my arm and spun me around. That's why I fell."

"You think it was someone who didn't want you to catch him."

"Did you see anyone you recognized in the crowd before you found me?"

He thought for a moment. "I wasn't looking for anyone but you, I'm sorry. Allie, all of this is classic gaslighting. Someone wants to unnerve you, to make you think you're imagining things, to make you doubt your own reality and ultimately make you doubt your own sanity."

She met his gaze. Her eyes filled with tears. "You think it's Nick?"

"I think it's a possibility. If he suspected you were going to leave him and take Natalie...he might have staged his death. He had the most to lose if you left him and with his body never being found..."

NICK ALIVE? Allie felt a chill move through her. Her husband had been a ghost, haunting her from his mountain grave for months. Now he had taken on an even more malevolent spirit.

She got up and threw another log on the fire. But not even the hot flames could chase away the icy cold that had filled her at the thought of Nick still alive. Not just alive but stalking her, trying to make her think she was crazy. Still, why—

"You think he's after Natalie," she said and frowned. "He's never cared that much about her. He wanted a son and when he didn't get one…"

"Believe me. I know what it's like to have a vindictive spouse who would do anything to hurt me—including taking a child she didn't really want."

"Oh, Jackson, I'm so sorry."

"If your husband is alive, you can bet he is behind all of this."

If Nick really was alive, then Drew would know. It would also explain why Drew was being so protective and acting jealous over Jackson.

Jackson stepped to her. "There is one thing you can count on. It's going to get worse. Nick will have to escalate his plan. He probably has a story already planned for when he comes stumbling out of the mountains after being attacked and having no memory for months. But that story won't hold up if it goes on much longer. I don't want to scare you, but if whoever is behind this can't drive you crazy, they might get desperate and decide the best way to get Natalie is to get rid of her mother for good."

She shuddered.

"Sorry," he said. "I know it seems like a leap…"

Jackson looked to the dark window before returning his gaze to her. "But if your husband is alive, then you have to assume he is watching your every move."

If Nick wasn't, then Drew was doing it for him, she realized. "You really think it's possible?" she asked in a whisper as if not only was he watching but he was listening, as well.

"Given what has been happening to you and the fact

that his body was never found?" Jackson nodded. "But if he is alive, we can't let him know that we're on to him."

We. That had such a wonderful sound. She had felt so alone in all this. Suddenly, she wasn't. Jackson believed her. He didn't think she was crazy. Far from it. He thought all of this was happening because someone wanted her to *believe* she was crazy. Maybe not just *someone,* but the man she'd married.

She swallowed back the bile that rose in her throat at the thought of how far her husband had gone and to what end? "He must have known I was leaving him and taking Natalie."

"That would be my guess. With you in the nuthouse, he could reappear and take your daughter."

The thought of Natalie with a man who would do something like that turned her blood to ice.

"But if he is alive, then—" Jackson seemed to hesitate "—then I really can't see how he could have pulled this off without help."

Allie knew what he was saying. Not just Drew but Mildred and Sarah might be in on this. "His brother, Drew, has been around a lot since Nick…disappeared and has helped out financially until the investigation is over. His mother's never liked me and didn't believe me when I've told her about only some of the things that have been happening. Or at least she pretended not to. "

Jackson nodded. "What about Drew's sister, Sarah?"

"She's afraid of Mother Taylor, not that I can blame her."

He looked away for a moment. "What about the two women working with you on the wedding?"

"*Belinda and Megan?* Belinda's the only friend who stuck with me after I married Nick. He tried to run her off but she wasn't having any of it." Allie didn't want to believe it. Refused to. She shook her head. "She's been on my side against them. And Megan? She's my *stepsister* I never knew until..."

"Until?" he prompted.

"I guess it was right before Nick died. Megan contacted me. She was just finishing up her college degree at the University of Montana in Missoula. After my mother died, my father remarried several times and had more children. He moved away and I lost track of him and my step-siblings. Megan was like a gift coming into our lives when she did. Nat adores her. I adore her. You can't think she is somehow involved in any of this."

Jackson didn't say anything. He didn't have to. His skepticism was written all over his face. "It's the timing that bothers me."

She nodded. He thought she was naive. She'd always been too trusting. Isn't that what Nick had told her time and time again?

Allie quickly turned away as she felt hot tears scald her eyes. All of this was just too much. She thought of her daughter and hurriedly wiped at her tears. Straightening her back, she felt a surge of anger and turned back to face Jackson.

"Whoever is doing this, they aren't going to win. What do we do?" she asked.

"We catch them. Do you have a photograph of Nick?"

As she left the room, she noticed that the sun had come up. She came back with a snapshot. "This is the only one I could find. It's one of Nick and his brother, Drew. Nick is the one on the right."

Jackson looked down at the photo. "They look alike."

"Do they?" she said, looking at the snapshot he was holding. "I guess they do a little," she said, surprised that she hadn't noticed it because their personalities were so different. "Drew was always the quiet one. Nick was his mother's favorite. I'm sure that had something to do with why he was so cocky and smart-mouthed. Drew was the one always standing back watching."

"Did Drew resent that?" Jackson asked.

Allie frowned. "I don't know. He didn't seem to. Just the other day he was telling me how hard it was to keep the business going without Nick."

Jackson turned thoughtful for a moment. "You mentioned something about Belinda wanting you to see some psychic so you could reach Nick on the other side? I think you should do it."

Allie blinked in surprise. "Seriously? You don't think I'm messed up enough?"

"It's Belinda's idea, right? If she is involved, then this séance with the psychic is a trap. But since we are on to them now, it would help to know what they have planned for you. I suspect it won't be pleasant, though. I'm sure it is supposed to push you over the edge, if you aren't already dangling there. Do you think you can handle it?"

She raised her chin, her eyes dry, resolve burning in her like a blazing fire. She thought of the people who had been tricking her for months. Anger boiled up inside her along with a steely determination. She hadn't felt this strong in years. "I can handle it."

Jackson smiled at her. "Good." He checked his watch. "Give the psychic a call. Calling this early she will think you are desperate to see her, exactly what we want her to think."

Allie dug the card out, glad now that she'd saved it. She took a breath, let it out and dialed the number. Jackson stepped closer so he could hear.

She was surprised when a young-sounding woman answered after three rings.

"I'm sorry to call so early but I need your help. My

friend Belinda suggested I call you." Jackson gave her a thumbs-up.

"You must be Allie. I was hoping you'd call. You're in danger—and so is your daughter. I need to see you as soon as possible."

"Is today too soon, then?" Allie asked.

"Why don't you come this evening, say about eight? Will that work for you?"

Allie met Jackson's gaze. He nodded. "That would be fine. I hope you can help me."

"I will do my best but ultimately it will be up to the spirits."

Jackson swore softly as Allie disconnected. "Spirits my ass. Between now and then, I will try to find out everything I can about the people with access to you." He reached over and took her hand. "Don't worry. We're going to catch these bastards."

CHAPTER EIGHT

WHEN JACKSON RETURNED to the ranch, he found his brothers, told them what he thought was going on and asked for their help. He no longer kidded himself that he wasn't involved.

"I can talk to the cops about what they found in the mountains," Hayes said. "You say Nick Taylor's body still hasn't been found? Isn't that odd? He died late last fall and even with hikers in the area, no remains have turned up?"

"No, that's what makes me suspicious," Jackson said. "His claw-shredded backpack and rifle were discovered at the scene with grizzly prints in the dirt and enough blood to make them believe he was killed there. But still no remains of any kind."

Hayes nodded. "I'll get right on it."

"What can I do?" Laramie asked.

"Financials on everyone involved including Allie's friend Belinda Andrews and her stepsister, Megan Knight, as well as all of the Taylor family. Nick and his brother, Drew, were partners in a construction company called Gallatin Canyon Specialty Construction."

"You got it," Laramie said. "What about Allie herself?"

"Sure, and Nick, just in case he had something going on that she didn't know about," Jackson said.

"Wait a minute," Tag said. "What about me?"

"You, brother dear, are getting married. You just concentrate on your lovely bride-to-be," Jackson told him. Tag started to object. "If you're going to be hanging around the ranch here, then do me a favor. Keep an eye on Drew Taylor. He's apparently doing some repairs here."

Jackson stopped by the barn to find Allie and Megan hard at work putting together centerpieces for the tables. Allie pretended she needed something from her van and got up to go outside with him.

"No more trouble last night?" he asked, seeing worry in her gaze.

"None. I'm just having a hard time believing any of that happened last night." She glanced around as if she expected Nick to materialize before her gaze came back to him. Or maybe she was worried about her brother-in-law, Drew, seeing them together again. "I can't believe Belinda or Megan—"

"Have you seen Belinda?"

"She had to go into Bozeman. She left about twenty minutes ago, why?"

He shook his head. "You better get back inside. Try not to let on that you're suspicious."

She sighed. "You don't know how hard that is."

"I can imagine." He gave her an encouraging smile. "Just be your usual sweet self." He loved it when she returned his smile and those gorgeous dimples of hers showed.

As she went back into the barn and rejoined Megan, he headed up the hillside. Belinda was staying in the last guesthouse to the east. Each cabin was set away from the others in the dense pines for the most privacy.

A cool pine-scented breeze restlessly moved the boughs over his head as he walked on the bed of dried needles toward Belinda's cabin. He could hear the roar of the river and occasionally the sound of a semi shifting down on the highway far below. A squirrel chattered at him as he passed, breaking the tranquility.

He was almost to her cabin when he heard the crack of a twig behind him and spun around in surprise.

His brother Hayes grinned. "I would imagine the cabin will be locked," he said as he stepped on past to climb the steps to the small porch and try the door. "Yep, I know your lock-picking skills are rusty at best." He pulled out his tool set.

Jackson climbed the steps and elbowed his brother out of the way. "I told Dana I was locked out. She gave me the master key." He laughed and opened the door.

"You know I do this for a living, right?" his brother asked.

"I'd heard that. But are you any good?"

Hayes shot him a grin and headed for the log dresser in the room with the unmade bed.

Jackson glanced around the main room of the cabin and spotted Belinda's camera bag. He could hear his brother searching the bedroom as he carefully unzipped the bag. There were the usual items found in a professional photographer's large bag. He carefully took out the camera, lens and plastic filter containers and was about to put everything back, thinking there was nothing to find when he saw the corner of a photo protruding from one of the lower pockets.

"What did you find?" Hayes asked as he returned after searching both bedrooms.

Jackson drew out the photos and thumbed through them. They were shots taken with apparent friends. Each photo had Belinda smiling at the camera with her arm around different friends, all women. He was thinking how there wasn't one of her and Allie, when he came to the last photo and caught his breath.

"Who is that?" Hayes asked.

"Allie's husband, Nick, and her best friend Belinda Andrews. Allie said that Nick never liked Belinda." The snapshot had been taken in the woods along a trail. There was a sign in the distance that said Grouse Creek Trail. Nick had his arm possessively around Belinda. Both were smiling at each other rather than the camera the way lovers do.

"Apparently, they liked each other a lot more than Allie knew," Hayes said. "But you know what is really interesting about that photo? That trailhead sign behind them."

"Let me guess. Up that trail is where Nick Taylor was believed to have been killed."

WHEN THEY'D FINISHED the centerpieces, Allie sent Megan into Bozeman for an order of wedding items that had been delayed. It had been difficult working with her and suspecting her of horrible things. Allie was relieved when she was finally alone in the barn.

Everything was coming along on schedule. It had been Dana's idea to start days early. "I don't want you to feel any pressure and if you need extra help, you just let me know," Dana had said.

"No, I'm sure that will be fine."

"I want you to have some free time to go for a horseback ride or just spend it on the ranch with your daughter."

"You are so thoughtful," Allie had said.

"Not at all. I just know what it's like with a little one, even though Natalie isn't so little anymore," she said with a laugh. "I promise I will keep your daughter busy so you can work and not have to worry about her having a good time."

Dana had been good to her word. Allie stepped outside the barn now to check on Natalie only to find her on the back of a horse about to take a short ride up the road for another picnic with Dana and the other children.

"Come along," Dana encouraged. "Warren would be

happy to saddle you a horse. You know what they say about almost falling off a horse, don't you?" she asked with a smile. "You have to get back on."

Allie laughed, thinking that was exactly what she was doing with her life, thanks to Jackson. She was tempted to go on the ride until she saw him headed her way. "Next time."

"We're going to hold you to it," Dana said. "In fact, we're all going on a ride tomorrow before the rehearsal dinner. Plan on coming along." With that they rode off, the kids waving and cheering as they disappeared into the pines.

Jackson waved to his son, making the same promise before he continued on down the mountainside toward her.

When she saw his expression, her heart fell. He'd discovered something and whatever it was, it wasn't good.

"Let's go up to my cabin," Jackson said as he glanced around. "We can talk there."

They made the short hike up the mountainside. His cabin faced the river, sheltered in the pines and was several dozen yards from the closest cabin where his brothers were staying together.

"What is it?" Allie asked the moment they were inside.

Jackson handed her a snapshot in answer.

She looked down at her smiling husband and her best friend. There was no doubt what she was looking at but still she was shocked and found it hard to believe. For more than six years Belinda and Nick had acted as if they couldn't stand each other. Had it been a lie the entire time?

"When was this taken?" she asked.

Jackson shook his head. "There isn't a date. I found it in her camera bag with a lot of other photos of her with friends."

Allie raised an eyebrow. "You aren't going to try to convince me that they are just friends."

He shook his head. "You weren't at all suspicious?"

She laughed as she made her way to the couch and sat down. The ground under her feet no longer felt stable. "Nick always said I was too trusting. Belinda was the only friend who could put up with Nick. So I guess a part of me suspected that Nick liked her more than he let on."

"I'm sorry."

"Don't be. I stopped loving Nick Taylor the year we got married. If I hadn't gotten pregnant with Nat…" She tossed the photo on the coffee table in front of her.

"She was the only one you told about your plans to leave Nick?" he asked as he took a seat across from her.

Allie let out a laugh. "So of course she told him."

"More than likely," he agreed. "There's more." He took a breath and let it out as he studied her. "You sure you want to hear all of this?"

She sat up straighter. "Let me have it."

"I got my brothers to help me. They have the expertise in their chosen fields that we needed. Hayes talked to the cops who had a copy of Nick's file with reports from the hiker who found the backpack and rifle to the warden who investigated the initial scene. He reported that there was sufficient evidence to assume that Nick was dead based on the shredded backpack and the amount of blood soaked into the pine needles."

"So…he's dead?"

"Or he made it look that way," Jackson said. "No DNA was tested at the scene because there didn't appear to be a need to do so. But there are still a lot of questions. No shots were fired from the rifle, leading the investigators to believe he didn't have time to get off a shot before he was attacked by the bear. Or he could have staged the whole thing. But the incidents you've been having with things disappearing and reappearing, those can't be Nick. If he's alive, he has to keep his head down."

"So we're back to my in-laws and Belinda and Megan."

"I'm afraid so. Belinda, if involved with Nick, would be the obvious one. Was she around before any of the incidents happened?"

Allie thought back to when her keys had ended up in the bathroom sink at the Mexican restaurant. She'd left her purse at the table, but then Sarah and her mother had been there, too. She sighed, still refusing to believe it, even after seeing the photo. "Yes, but Belinda wouldn't—"

"Wouldn't have an affair with your husband behind your back?"

"She's been so *worried* about me."

Jackson raised a brow.

Allie hugged herself against the thought of what he was saying. Belinda *had* apparently betrayed her with Nick. Maybe Jackson was right. Then she remembered something. "Belinda has a new man in her life. I know the signs. She starts dressing up and, I don't know, acting different. The man can't be Nick. That photo doesn't look recent of her and Nick. Why would she be acting as if there was someone new if it was Nick all these months?"

"Maybe he's been hiding out and has only now returned to the canyon."

That thought turned her stomach. "If he's come back…"

"Then whoever has been gaslighting you must be planning on stepping up their plan," Jackson said.

She turned to look at him as a shiver raced through her. "The psychic. Maybe this is their grand finale, so to speak, and they have something big planned tonight to finally send me to the loony bin."

"Maybe you shouldn't go—"

"No. Whatever they have planned, it won't work. They've done their best to drive me crazy. I know now what they're up to. I'll be fine."

"I sure hope so," Jackson said.

"What is the lowdown on the Taylor family?" Jackson asked Hud after dinner that evening at the ranch. They'd had beef steaks cooked on a pitchfork in the fire and eaten on the wide porch at the front of the house. The night had been beautiful, but Jackson was too antsy to appreciate it. He was worried about Allie.

She'd dropped Natalie by before she and Belinda had left. He hadn't had a chance to speak with her without raising suspicion. All he could do was try his best to find out who was behind the things that had been happening to her.

"Old canyon family," Hud said. "Questionable how they made their money. It was rumored that the patriarch killed someone and stole his gold." Hud shrugged. "Mildred? She married into it just months before Bud Taylor died in a car accident. She's kept the name even though she's been through several more husbands. I believe she is on number four now. Didn't take his name, though. He's fifteen, twenty years older and spends most of his time with his grown children back in Chicago."

"And the daughter?"

"Sarah?" Hud frowned. "Never been married that I know of. Lives in the guesthouse behind her mother's. No visible means of support."

"The brothers had a construction company together?"

"They did. Nick was the driving force. With him gone, I don't think Drew is working all that much."

"Just between you and me, Allie was planning to leave Nick Taylor before he went up in the mountain and disappeared," Jackson said, taking the marshal into his confidence.

Hud looked over at him. "What are you getting at?"

"Is there any chance Nick Taylor is alive?"

Hud frowned. "You must have some reason to believe he is."

"Someone has been gaslighting Allie."

"For what purpose?"

"I think someone, probably in the Taylor family, wants to take Natalie away from her."

"YOU SEEM BETTER," Belinda noted on the drive out of the canyon. She'd insisted on driving Allie to the psychic's house, saying she didn't trust Allie to drive herself if the psychic said anything that upset her.

Allie had been quiet most of the drive. "*Do* I seem better?" Did her friend seem disappointed in that?

"Maybe this isn't necessary."

That surprised her. "I thought you were the one who said I had to talk to this psychic?"

"I thought it would help."

"And now?" Allie asked.

"I don't want her to upset you when you seem to be doing so well."

"That's sweet, but I'm committed…so to speak."

Belinda nodded and kept driving. "Seriously, you seem so different and the only thing that has changed that I can tell is Jackson Cardwell showing up."

Allie laughed. "Just like you to think it has to be a man. Maybe I'm just getting control of my life."

Her friend looked skeptical. "Only a few days ago you were burning Nick's favorite shirt so it didn't turn up again."

"Didn't I tell you? The shirt *did* turn up again. I found

it hanging in the shower this morning. Now I ask you, how is that possible?"

"You're sure you burned it? Maybe you just—"

"Dreamed it?" Allie smiled. That was what they wanted her to think. She looked over at Belinda, worried her old friend was up to her neck in this, whatever it was.

Allie fought the urge to confront her and demand to know who else was behind it. But Belinda turned down a narrow road, slowing to a stop in front of a small house with a faint porch light on.

Showtime, Allie thought as she tried to swallow the lump in her throat.

CHAPTER NINE

BELINDA'S APARTMENT HOUSE was an old, five-story brick one a few blocks off Main Street in Bozeman.

Laramie waited in the car as lookout while Jackson and Hayes went inside. There was no password entry required. They simply walked in through the front door and took the elevator up to the third floor to room 3B. It was just as Allie had described it, an apartment at the back, the door recessed so even if someone had been home on the floor of four apartments, they wouldn't have seen Hayes pick the lock.

"You're fast," Jackson said, impressed.

Hayes merely smiled and handed him a pair of latex gloves. "I'm also smart. If you're right and Nick Taylor is alive and this becomes a criminal case... You get the idea. It was different up on the ranch. This, my brother, is breaking and entering."

Jackson pulled on the gloves and opened the door. As he started to draw his flashlight out of his pocket, Hayes snapped on an overhead light.

"What the—"

"Jackson," his brother said and motioned toward the window. The curtains were open, the apartment looking out onto another apartment building. While most of the curtains were drawn in those facing this way, several were open.

Hayes stepped to the window and closed the curtains.

"Nothing more suspicious than two dudes sneaking around in a woman's apartment with flashlights."

He had a point. "Let's make this quick."

"I'm with you," Hayes said and suggested the best place to start.

"If I didn't know better, I'd think you'd done this before," Jackson joked.

Hayes didn't answer.

In the bedroom in the bottom drawer of the bureau under a bunch of sweaters, Jackson found more photos of Belinda and Nick, but left them where he'd found them.

"So you think I'm right and Nick is alive," Jackson said.

Hayes shrugged.

Jackson finished the search of the bedroom, following his brother's instructions to try to leave everything as he had found it.

"Find anything?" he asked Hayes when he'd finished.

"She recently came into thirty-eight thousand dollars," Hayes said, thumbing through a stack of bank statements he'd taken from a drawer.

"Maybe it's a trust fund or an inheritance."

"Maybe. Or blackmail money or money Nick had hidden from Allie," Hayes said as he put everything back. "Laramie would probably be able to find out what it was if we had more time. Did you put the photos back?"

"All except one. I want to show it to Allie. It looks more recent to me."

Hayes looked as if he thought that was a bad idea. "You're messing with evidence," he reminded him.

"I'll take that chance," Jackson said.

His brother shook his head as he turned out the light and moved to the window to open the curtains like he'd found them.

"Does anyone else know how involved you are with the

wedding planner?" Silence. "I didn't think so. Better not let cousin Dana find out or there will be hell to pay. She is very protective of people she cares about. She cares about that woman and her child. If you—"

"I'm not going to hurt her." He couldn't see his brother's expression in the dark. He didn't have to.

ALLIE BRACED HERSELF. She hadn't shared her fears about the visit with the psychic with Jackson before she'd left. She hadn't had to. She'd seen the expression on his face as he watched her leave. He was terrified for her.

For months someone had been trying to push her over the edge of sanity. She had a bad feeling that the psychic was part of the master plan, a shocker that was aimed at driving her insane. By now, they probably thought she was hanging on by a thread. While she was stronger, thanks to Jackson and his determination that she was perfectly sane and those around her were the problem, there was a part of her that wasn't so sure about that.

Just this morning, she'd stepped into the bathroom, opened the shower curtain and let out a cry of shock and disbelief. Nick's favorite shirt was hanging there, the same shirt she'd burned in the fireplace a few nights ago. Or at least one exactly like it. Worse, she smelled his aftershave and when she opened the medicine cabinet, there it was in the spot where he always kept it—right next to his razor, both of which she had thrown out months ago.

Had he hoped she would cut her wrists? Because it had crossed her mind. If it hadn't been for Natalie…and now Jackson…

"Remember, you're that strong woman you were before you met Nick Taylor," Jackson had said earlier.

She'd smiled because she could only vaguely remember that woman. But she wanted desperately to reacquaint herself with her. Now all she could do was be strong for her daughter. She couldn't let these people get their hands on Natalie.

Belinda parked in front of a small house and looked over at her. "Ready?"

Allie could hear reluctance in her friend's voice. If Jackson was right and Nick was behind this, then Allie suspected he was forcing Belinda to go through with the plan no matter what.

But that's what she had to find out. If Nick was alive. She opened her car door and climbed out. The night air was cool and scented with fresh-cut hay from a nearby field. It struck her how remote this house was. The closest other residence had been up the road a good half mile.

If a person was to scream, no one would hear, Allie thought, then warned herself not to bother screaming. Belinda and the psychic were probably hoping for just such a reaction.

"I was surprised when you agreed to do this," Belinda said now, studying her as she joined Allie on the path to the house.

"I told you. I would do anything to make whatever is happening to me stop." Allie took a deep breath and let it out. "Let's get this over with."

They walked up the short sidewalk and Belinda knocked. Allie noticed that there weren't any other vehicles around except for an old station wagon parked in the open, equally old garage. If Nick was here he'd either been dropped off or he'd parked in the trees at the back of the property.

The door was opened by a small, unintimidating woman wearing a tie-dyed T-shirt and worn jeans. Her feet were bare. Allie had been expecting a woman in a bright caftan wearing some sort of headdress. She was a little disappointed.

"Please come in," the woman said in what sounded like a European accent. "I am Katrina," she said with a slight nod. "It is so nice to meet you, Allie. Please follow me. Your friend can stay here."

Belinda moved to a couch in what Allie assumed was the sparsely furnished living area.

Allie followed the woman down a dim hallway and through a door into a small room dominated by a table and two chairs. The table was bare.

Katrina closed the door, making the room feel even smaller. She took a seat behind the desk and motioned Allie into the chair on the opposite side.

This felt silly and it was all Allie could do not to laugh. She and a friend in the fifth grade had stopped at the fortune teller's booth at the fair one time—her friend Willow's idea, not hers.

"I want to know if I am going to marry Curt," her friend had said.

Allie could have told her that there was a good chance she wasn't going to marry some boy in her fifth grade class.

The fortune teller had told them they would have long, happy lives and marry their true loves. Five dollars each later they were standing outside the woman's booth. Willow had been so excited, believing what the fortune teller had said was that she would marry Curt. She'd clearly read what she wanted into the woman's words.

Willow didn't marry Curt but maybe she had found her true love since she'd moved away in sixth grade when her father was transferred. Allie hadn't had a happy life nor had she apparently married her true love and now here she was again sitting across from some woman who she feared really might know her future because she was about to control it.

"I understand you want me to try to reach your husband who has passed over," Katrina said. "I have to warn you that I am not always able to reach the other side, but I will try since your friend seems to think if I can reach…"

"Nick," Allie supplied.

"Yes, that it will give you some peace." The woman hesitated. "I hope that will be the case. It isn't always, I must warn you. Do you want to continue?"

Allie swallowed and nodded.

"Give me your hands. I need you to think of your husband." Katrina dimmed the lights and reached across the table to take Allie's hands in hers. "It helps if you will close your eyes and try to envision your husband."

That was about the last thing Allie wanted to do, but as Katrina closed hers, Allie did the same. She couldn't help but think of Nick and wonder if he was watching her at this very moment.

"WHILE WE'RE BREAKING the law, there is one other place I'd like to have a look before we head back," Jackson said to his brothers.

Hayes looked disapproving. "What part of breaking and entering don't you understand?"

"You can wait in the car."

Gallatin Canyon Specialty Construction was located on the outskirts of town next to a gravel pit. The industrial area was dark this time of the night as Jackson pulled in with his lights out and parked.

"Allie said the company hasn't been doing very well without Nick and wasn't doing that well even before Nick allegedly died," Jackson said. "I just want to take a look at the books."

"Good thing you brought me along," Laramie said. "You did mean, you want me to take a look, right?"

Jackson laughed. "Yeah, if you don't mind."

Hayes sighed and they all got out and walked toward the trailer that served as the office. Hayes unlocked the door then said, "I'll stand guard. Make it quick," before disappearing into the darkness.

"You do realize you might be jeopardizing everything by doing this," Laramie said. "Is this woman worth it?"

Jackson didn't answer as he pulled on the latex gloves Hayes had shoved at him in the car and handed his brother a pair before turning on a light and pointing at the file cabinets.

It wasn't until they were all three back in the car and headed south toward Cardwell Ranch that Jackson asked his brother what he'd found, if anything.

After Laramie tried to explain it in fiduciary terms, Hayes snapped, "The bottom line, please."

Laramie sighed. "It is clear why you all leave the business part of Texas Boys Barbecue up to me. All right, here it is. Drew Taylor is broke and has been siphoning off the money from the business before the sale."

"Sale?" Jackson said.

"While not of general knowledge, Drew has been trying to sell the business through a company in other states."

"That's suspicious," Hayes said.

"Is his mother involved in the construction business?" Jackson asked.

Laramie chuckled. "Excellent question. I believe she might have been a silent partner, which I take to mean she provided some of the money. Until recently, Drew was writing her a check each month."

"Think she knows what her son is up to?" Hayes asked.

"Doubtful. According to Allie, Mother Taylor rules the roost. Everyone is afraid of her."

"Sounds like our boy Drew is planning to escape in the dark of night," Hayes commented and Jackson agreed.

"As for the rest of the people you asked me to look at the finances of, Mildred Taylor is fine as long as her old, absentee husband sends her a check each month. She and her daughter live off the old man. Nick wasn't much of a breadwinner. Montana winters slow down construction, apparently. But he did okay. After his death, there wasn't much in his personal account."

"So the thirty-eight thousand Belinda just received wasn't from Nick, then," Hayes said.

Laramie continued, "Nick did, however, leave a hundred-thousand-dollar insurance policy, which is supposed to pay out any day once Nick has finally been ruled legally deceased."

"A hundred thousand?" Jackson exclaimed. "That doesn't seem like enough money to put Allie into the nuthouse for."

Laramie and Hayes agreed. "There could be other insurance policies I'm not aware of."

"What about Megan Knight?" Jackson asked.

"Just finished college, has thousands of dollars in student loans," Laramie said. "Majored in psychology so unless she goes to grad school…"

"What do you all make of this?" Jackson asked.

"Well," his brother Laramie said. "I've always said follow the money. That will usually take you to the source of the problem."

"So we have Drew siphoning money from the business and Belinda coming into some money and Megan needing money to pay off her student loans," Jackson said. "So which of them has motive to want Allie in the nuthouse?"

"Your guess is as good as mine," Hayes said. "That

photo you took from Belinda's apartment of her and Nick? The lovebirds didn't look like they were getting along."

"Wait a minute," Laramie said from the backseat. "Are you thinking with Nick gone, Drew and Belinda hooked up?"

"Good question," Jackson said.

"I've heard of stranger things happening," Hayes said.

"Or maybe it's blackmail money," Jackson said. "Maybe Belinda has something on Drew and he's the source of the thirty-eight thousand."

"Or Drew is simply taking money from the business and giving it to Belinda to give to Nick," Hayes threw in.

"Which would mean that Drew knows Nick is alive," Jackson said.

"Or at least he has been led to believe his brother is alive according to Belinda," Hayes said.

"You two are making my head spin," Laramie cried and both brothers laughed. "No wonder I prefer facts and figures. They are so much less confusing."

"He's right," Hayes said. "It could be simple. Nick's dead, Belinda got her money from another source entirely and Drew is blowing his on beer."

As they reached Cardwell Ranch, Jackson glanced at the time. "Let's hope Allie gets some answers tonight," he said, unable to keep the worry out of his voice. "Who knows what horrors they have planned for her."

"ALLIE."

Nick's voice made Allie jump, but Katrina held tight to her hands. Goose bumps skittered over her skin as Nick spoke again.

"Allie?" His voice seemed to be coming from far away.

"We're here, Nick," Katrina said after she'd spent a good

five minutes with her eyes closed, calling up Nick's spirit. "Is there something you want to say to Allie?"

She heard him groan. The sound sent her heart pounding even harder. Somehow it was more chilling than his saying her name.

"Please, Nick, do you have a message for Allie?"

Another groan, this one sounding farther away. Katrina seemed anxious as if she feared she was going to lose Nick before he said whatever it was he wanted to say.

Allie doubted that was going to happen, but maybe the woman would try to drag this out, get more money from her by making her come back again.

She tried to pull away, but Katrina tightened her hold, pulling her forward so her elbows rested on the table.

"Nick, please, give your wife the peace she desperately needs."

Another groan. "Allie, *why?*" The last word was so ghostly that Allie felt her skin crawl. At that moment, she believed it was Nick calling to her from the grave.

"What are you asking?" Katrina called out to him.

Silence. It was so heavy that it pressed against Allie's chest until she thought she couldn't breathe.

Then a groan as forlorn as any she'd ever heard filled the small room. She shivered. "Allie," Nick said in a voice that broke. "Why did you kill me?"

CHAPTER TEN

ALLIE JERKED HER hands free and stumbled to her feet. She didn't realize she'd made a sound until she realized she was whimpering.

As the lights came up, she saw that Katrina was staring at her in shock as if whoever was behind this hadn't taken her into their confidence. Either that, or she was a good actress.

Allie rushed out of the room and down the hallway. Belinda wasn't in the living room where she'd been told to wait. Opening the door, Allie ran outside, stopping only when she reached Belinda's car.

None of that was real. But it had been Nick's voice; there was no doubt about that. He was either alive...or they'd somehow gotten a recording of Nick's voice. *That wasn't Nick speaking from his grave.* Intellectually, she knew that. But just hearing Nick's voice and those horrible groans...

Belinda came bursting out of the house. Allie turned to see Katrina standing at the doorway looking stunned. Or was that, too, an act?

"Allie?" Belinda ran to her looking scared. "What happened in there?"

She ignored the question. "Where were you?"

Belinda seemed taken aback by her tone, if not her question. "I had to go to the bathroom. I was just down the hall. Are you all right?"

"I want to go." Katrina was still standing in the doorway. Allie reached for the door handle but the car was locked. "Belinda, I want to *go*."

"Okay, just a sec." She groped in her purse for her keys.

"Can't find them?" Allie taunted with a sneer. "Maybe you left them in the bathroom sink."

Belinda glanced up in surprise, frowning as if confused. "No, I have them. Honey, are you sure you're all right?"

Allie laughed. "How can you seriously ask that?"

Belinda stared at her for a moment before she opened the car doors and went around and slid behind the wheel.

They rode in silence for a few minutes before Belinda said, "I'm sorry. Clearly, you're upset. I thought—"

"What did you think?" Allie demanded.

Belinda shot her a glance before returning to her driving. "I seriously thought this might help."

"Really? Was it your idea or Nick's?"

"Nick's?" She shot her another quick look.

"I *know,* Belinda." Silence. "I know about you and Nick." Belinda started to deny it, but Allie cut her off. "You two had me going for a while, I'll give you that. I really did think I was losing my mind. But not anymore. How long have you and Nick been having an affair?"

"Allie—"

"I don't have to ask whose plan this was. It has Nick written all over it."

"Honey, I honestly don't know what you're talking about."

"No?" Allie reached into her pocket and pulled out the photo of Belinda and Nick standing next to the trailhead sign at Grouse Creek. "As you've often said, a picture is worth a thousand words."

Belinda groaned, not unlike Nick had back at the alleged psychic's. "It isn't what you think."

Allie laughed again as she put the photo back in her pocket. "It never is."

"I'm sorry." She sounded as if she were crying, but Allie could feel no compassion for her.

"What was the point of all that back there?" Allie demanded as they left the Gallatin Valley behind and entered the dark, narrow canyon.

"I swear I don't know what you're talking about. What happened in there that has you so angry and upset?"

"Don't play dumb, Belinda. It doesn't become you. But tell me, what's next?" Allie demanded. "You failed to make me crazy enough that you could take Natalie. Is it the insurance money? Is that what you're planning to use to open your own studio? But in order to get it, you're going to have to kill me. Is that the next part of your plot, Belinda?"

The woman gasped and shot her a wide-eyed look. "You sure you aren't crazy, because you are certainly talking that way. That photo of me and Nick? That was before he met and married you. I broke up with him. Why do you think he didn't like me? Why do you think he put up with me? Because I threatened to tell you about the two of us." She took a breath and let it out. "As for me trying to make you think you were crazy..." Belinda waved a hand through the air. "That's ridiculous. I'm the one who has been trying to help you. I should have told you about me and Nick, but it was water under the bridge. And Nick's insurance money? I don't need it. Remember I told you about my eccentric aunt Ethel? Well, it seems she'd been socking money away in her underwear drawer for years. Thirty-eight thousand of it was left to me, tax free. That's what I plan to use to start my own photo studio. Allie, no matter what you think, I'm your *friend*."

She had thought so, but now she didn't know what to

believe. "How did you come up with the idea of me going to see Katrina?" she challenged.

Belinda drove in silence, the canyon highway a dark ribbon along the edge of the river. "I told you. I'd seen Katrina a few times. But the idea for you to go see her so you could try to reach Nick and get closure? That was your sister *Megan*'s idea."

JACKSON FOUND HIMSELF walking the floor of his cabin until he couldn't take it anymore. Finally, he heard the sound of a vehicle, saw the headlights coming up the road and hurried down to the barn where Allie had left her van.

He waited in the shadows as both women got out of Belinda's car, neither speaking as they parted ways.

"Are you all right?" Jackson asked Allie as he stepped from the shadows. She jumped, surprised, and he mentally kicked himself for scaring her. "I'm sorry. I've been pacing the floor. I was so worried about you."

Her features softened. "I'm okay." She looked drained.

"If you don't want to talk about it tonight…"

Allie gave him a wane smile. "Natalie is staying with your family and I'm not going to be able to sleep, anyway."

"Do you mind coming up to my cabin?"

She shook her head and let him lead her up the mountainside through the pines. It was only a little after ten, but most everyone had turned in for the night so there was little light or sound on the ranch. Under the thick pine boughs, it was cool and dark and smelled of summer.

Jackson realized he was going to miss that smell when he returned to Texas. He didn't want to think about what else he might miss.

Once inside the cabin, they took a seat on the couch, turning to face each other. It was warm in the cabin away from the chill of the Montana summer night. Without prompting, Allie began to relate what had happened slowly as if she was exhausted. He didn't doubt she was.

He hated putting her through this. She told him about the ride to the psychic's and Belinda's apparent hesitancy to let her go through with it. Then she told him about Katrina and the small remote house.

"It all felt silly and like a waste of time, until I heard Nick's voice."

He looked at her and felt his heart drop. Hearing her husband's voice had clearly upset her. It surprised him that whoever was behind this had gone that far.

"You're sure it was Nick's voice."

She nodded. "It sounded as if it was far away and yet close."

"Could it have been a recording?"

"Possibly. His words were halting as if hard for him to speak and he...groaned." She shuddered. "It was an awful sound, unearthly."

"I'm so sorry. After you left, I regretted telling you to go." He sighed. "I was afraid it would just upset you and accomplish nothing."

"It gets worse. Nick...accused me of...killing him."

"*What?* That's ridiculous. I thought a grizzly killed him."

She shrugged. "The psychic believed it. You should have seen her face."

"Allie, the woman was in on it. This was just another ploy. You knew that going in."

"But I didn't know I would hear his voice. I didn't know he would ask me why I'd killed him. I didn't..." The tears came in a rush, dissolving the rest of whatever she was going to say.

Jackson pulled her to him. She buried her face into his

chest. "None of this is real, Allie. Are you listening to me? None of it. They just want you to believe it is."

After a few moments, the sobs stopped. He handed her a tissue from the box by the couch and she got up and moved to the window. His cabin view was the rock cliff across the valley and a ribbon of Gallatin River below it.

As he got up, he moved to stand behind her. He could see starlight on that stretch of visible river. It shone like silver.

"If Nick is alive and I believe he is, then he has tried to do everything he can to make you think you're losing your mind. It hasn't worked. This isn't going to work, either. You're stronger than that."

"Am I?" she asked with a laugh. "I am when I'm with you, but…"

He turned her to face him. "You just needed someone to believe in you. I believe in you, Allie."

She looked up at him, her green eyes full of hope and trust and—

His gaze went to her mouth. Lowering his head, he kissed her.

A LOW MOAN escaped her lips. As he drew her closer, Allie closed her eyes, relishing in the feel of her body against his. It had been so long since a man had kissed her let alone held her. She couldn't remember the last time she'd made love. Nick had seemed to lose interest in her toward the end, which had been more than fine with her.

She banished all thoughts of Nick as she lost herself in Jackson's kiss. Her arms looped around his neck. She could feel her heart pounding next to his. Her breasts felt heavy, her nipples hard and aching as he deepened the kiss. A bolt of desire like none she'd ever known shot through her veins as he broke off the kiss to plant a trail of kisses down the column of her neck to the top of her breasts.

At her cry of arousal, Jackson pulled back to look into her eyes. "I've told myself all the reasons we shouldn't do this, but I want to make love to you."

"Yes," she said breathlessly, throwing caution to the wind. She wanted him, wanted to feel his bare skin against her own, to taste his mouth on hers again, to look up at him as he lowered himself onto her. She ached for his gentle touch, needed desperately to know the tenderness of lovemaking she'd never experienced with Nick but sensed in Jackson.

He swept her up in his arms and carried her to the bedroom, kicking the door closed before he carefully lowered her to the bed. She looked into his dark eyes as he lay down next to her. He touched her face with his fingertips, then slipped his hand around to the nape of her neck and drew her to him.

His kiss was slow and sensual. She could feel him fighting his own need as if determined to take it slow as he undid one button of her blouse, then another. She wanted to scream, unable to stand the barrier of their clothing between them. Grabbing his shirt, she pulled each side apart. The snaps sung as the Western shirt fell open exposing his tanned skin and the hard muscles under it.

She pressed her hands to his warm flesh as he undid the last button on her blouse. She heard his intake of breath an instant before she felt his fingertips skim across the tops of her breasts. Pushing her onto her back, he dropped his mouth to the hard points of her nipples, sucking gently through the thin, sheer fabric of her bra.

She arched against his mouth, felt him suck harder as his hand moved to the buttons of her jeans. With agonizing deliberate movements, he slowly undid the buttons of her jeans and slipped his hand beneath her panties. She cried out and fumbled at the zipper of his jeans.

"Please," she begged. "I need you."

"Not yet." His voice broke with the sound of his own need. "Not yet."

His hand dipped deeper into her panties. She arched against it, feeling the wet slickness of his fingers. He'd barely touched her when she felt the release.

"Oh, Allie," he said as if he, too, hadn't made love for a very long time. He shifted to the side to pull off her jeans and panties. She heard him shed the rest of his own clothing and then he was back, his body melding with hers in a rhythm as old as life itself.

THEY MADE LOVE twice more before the dawn. Jackson dozed off at some point, but woke to find Allie sleeping in his arms.

She looked more peaceful than she had since he'd met her. Like him, he suspected she hadn't made love with anyone for a very long time—much longer than her husband had allegedly been dead.

He cursed Nick Taylor. How could the fool not want this woman? How could the man mistreat someone so wonderful, not to mention ignore a child like Natalie? When he found the bastard...

When is it that you plan to find him?

The thought stopped him cold. There were only two more days until the wedding. He and Ford had tickets to fly out the following day.

He couldn't leave Allie now when she needed him the most. But how could he stay? He had Ford to think about. His son would be starting kindergarten next month. Jackson wasn't ready. He'd received a list from the school of the supplies his son would need, but he hadn't seen any reason to get them yet, thinking there was plenty of time. Same with the boy's new clothes.

He thought of his small ranch in Texas. Most of the land was leased, but he still had a house down there in the summer heat. He couldn't stay away indefinitely. What if he couldn't find Nick Taylor before Ford's school started?

His thoughts whirling, he looked down at Allie curled up next him and felt a pull so strong that it made him ache. What was he going to do?

Whatever it was, he couldn't think straight lying next to this beautiful, naked woman. As he tried to pull free, she rolled away some, but didn't wake.

Slipping out of bed, he quickly dressed and stepped outside. The fresh Montana morning air helped a little. Earlier he'd heard voices down by the main house. He hoped to catch his brothers as he headed down the mountain. He needed desperately to talk to one of them, even though he had had a bad feeling what they were going to say to him. He'd been saying the same thing to himself since waking up next to Allie this morning.

ALLIE WOKE TO an empty bed. For a moment, she didn't know where she was. As last night came back to her with Jackson, she hugged herself. The lovemaking had been… amazing. This was what she'd been missing out on with Nick. Jackson had been so tender and yet so…passionate.

She lay back listening, thinking he must be in the bathroom or maybe the small kitchen. After a few minutes, she sat up. The cabin was too quiet. Surely Jackson hadn't left.

Slipping her feet over the side of the bed, she tiptoed out of the bedroom. The bathroom was empty. So was the living room and kitchen. Moving to the front window, she glanced out on the porch. No Jackson.

For a moment, she stood staring out at the view, trying

to understand what this meant. Had he finally come to his senses? That was definitely one explanation.

Had he realized they had no future? That was another.

Hurrying into the bathroom, she showered, and, forced to put on the clothes she'd worn the night before, dressed. Fortunately, she'd been wearing jeans, a tank top and a blouse. She tucked the blouse into her large shoulder bag, pulled her wet hair up into a ponytail and looked at herself in the mirror.

Her cheeks were flushed from the lovemaking and the hot shower. Her skin still tingled at even the thought of Jackson's touch. She swallowed. Hadn't she warned herself last night of all the reasons they shouldn't make love?

At a knock on the cabin door, she jumped. Her heart leaped to her throat as she saw a dark, large shadow move on the porch beyond the curtains. Jackson wouldn't knock. Maybe it was one of his brothers.

She held her breath, hoping he would go away. She didn't want to be caught here, even though she knew his brothers wouldn't tell anyone.

Another knock.

"Jackson?" Drew Taylor's voice made her cringe. She put her hand over her mouth to keep from crying out in surprise. "I need to check something in your cabin." She heard him try the door and felt her heart drop. What if Jackson had left the door open?

She was already backing up, frantically trying to decide where she could hide, when she heard Drew try the knob. Locked.

He swore, thumped around on the porch for a moment then retreated down the steps.

Allie finally had to let out the breath she'd been holding. If Drew had caught her here... What would he have done? Tell Nick. But what would a man who had faked his death do to stop his plan from working? She thought of Jackson and felt her heart drop. She'd put Jackson's life in danger, as well.

She waited until she was sure Drew had gone before she cautiously moved to the door, opened it and peered out. She could see nothing but pines as she slipped out and hurried across the mountainside, planning to slip into the barn as if she'd come to work early.

With luck, no one would be the wiser.

Allie didn't see Drew. But he saw her.

CHAPTER ELEVEN

DANA WAS SITTING on the porch as Jackson approached the house. She motioned for him to join her.

"Where is everyone?" he asked, taking the rocker next to her.

"Early morning ride. Hud took everyone including the kids. Quiet, isn't it?" She glanced over at him. "How are you this morning?"

"Fine." He would have said great, but he had a bad feeling where Dana was headed with the conversation.

"I'm worried about Allie," she said, looking past him to the mountainside.

He glanced back toward the cabins in time to see Allie hurrying toward the barn from the direction of his cabin.

"Is she all right?"

In truth, he didn't know how she was. He regretted leaving before she'd awakened, but he'd needed to get out of there. "I—"

"She's been through so much. I would hate to see her get hurt. Wouldn't you?"

He felt as if she'd slapped him. He closed his eyes for a moment before he turned to look at her. "I told myself not to get involved, but…"

"So now you are involved?" Dana frowned. "She's in trouble, isn't she?"

Jackson nodded. "I have to help her." Even if it meant staying in Montana longer, he couldn't abandon her. Isn't that what had scared the hell out of him when he'd awakened this morning? He was in deep, how deep, he didn't want to admit. "She's going through some things right now but she's working so hard on the wedding, it will be fine."

Dana studied him openly. "You care about her."

"I'm not going to hurt her."

"I hope not." She gave him a pat on the shoulder as she rose and went inside the house.

Jackson sat looking after his cousin, mentally kicking himself. *"What the hell are you doing?"*

"I was going to ask you the same thing." Laramie came walking up.

As he climbed the porch, Jackson said, "I thought you went riding with the others."

"I've been working," his brother said as he took a seat next to him. He shook his head. "I hope you know what you're doing, Jackson." He sighed and pulled out a sheet of paper. "Allie's mother spent the last seven years of her life in a mental institution. Paranoid schizophrenia."

As ALLIE SLIPPED into the barn, she was surprised to see Belinda setting up her gear for a shoot. She'd half expected Belinda to be gone after their argument last night. In fact, Allie had almost called several photographers she knew to see if they could possibly fill in at the last minute.

"So you're still here," she said as she approached Belinda.

"Where did you think I would be?"

"I wasn't sure. I thought you might have quit."

Belinda shook her head. "You really do have so little faith in me. I'm amazed. I'm the one who has stuck by you all these years. I'm sorry about…everything. But I'm here to do a job I love. Surely you understand that."

Allie did and said as much. "If I've underestimated you—"

Her friend laughed. "Or overestimated me given that you think I'm capable of some diabolical plot to destroy you. And what? Steal your cabin on the river? Steal Nick's insurance money?" Her eyes widened. "Or was it steal Natalie?" Belinda looked aghast. "Oh, Allie, no wonder you're so upset. I get it now."

She felt tears rush her eyes as Belinda pulled her into a stiff, awkward hug.

"No matter what you believe, I'm still your friend," Belinda said as she broke the embrace and left the barn, passing Megan who looked bewildered as she came in.

Allie waited until she and Megan were alone before she spoke to her stepsister about what Belinda had told her. She didn't want to believe Megan had anything to do with the psychic or what had happened last night. Either Belinda was lying or there had to be another explanation.

"I need to ask you something."

"You sound so serious," Megan said. "What is it?"

"Was it your idea for me to see the psychic?"

Megan frowned. "I guess I was the one who suggested it. When Belinda told me about some of the things you'd been going through, I thought— Allie, why are you so upset?"

Allie had turned away, unable to look at her sister. Now she turned back, just as unable to hide her disappointment. "Why would you do that?"

"I just told you. I thought it would help."

"Trying to reach Nick on...the other side?" she demanded. "You can't be serious."

"A girl I knew at college lost her mother before the two of them could work some things out. She went to a psychic and was able to put some of the issues to rest. I thought…" Her gaze locked with her sister's. "I wanted to help you. I couldn't bear the things Belinda was telling me. It sounded as if you'd been going through hell. If I was wrong, I'm sorry."

Allie studied her for a moment. "You would never betray me, would you, Megan?"

"What a strange question to ask me."

"This past year since you came into my life and Natalie's… It's meant so much to both of us. Tell me you wouldn't betray that trust."

Megan frowned. "Does this have something to do with Jackson Cardwell? Is he the one putting these ideas in your head?"

"He has a theory about the so-called incidents I've been having," Allie confided. "He thinks someone is trying to make me think I'm crazy in order to take Natalie from me."

"That sounds…crazy in itself. Allie, I hate to say this, but you are starting to sound like your "

"Don't say it," Allie cried. Wasn't that her real underlying fear, the one that had haunted her her whole life? That she was becoming sick like her mother? She rubbed a hand over the back of her neck. What was she sure of right now? She'd thought Jackson, but after this morning… "I know it sounds crazy, but if it's true, I have to find out who is behind it."

"And Jackson is *helping* you?" Megan said and frowned. "Or is he complicating things even more? You aren't… falling for him, are you?"

JACKSON WASN'T SURE what he was going to say to Allie. He felt like a heel for leaving her alone this morning. She must be furious with him. No, he thought, not Allie. She would be hurt, and that made him feel worse than if she was angry.

He headed for the barn to apologize to her. Once inside, though, he didn't see Allie.

"She said she had to run an errand," Megan told him with a shrug.

Glancing outside, he saw her van still parked where it had been last night. "Did she go on foot?"

"Her brother-in-law offered her a ride."

"Drew?" Jackson felt his heart race at the thought of Allie alone with that man. "Do you know where they went?"

Megan shook her head and kept working.

"You don't like me," he said, stepping farther into the barn. "Why is that?"

"I don't think you're good for my sister."

"Based on what?" he had to ask. "We have barely met."

"She told me about this crazy idea you have that someone is causing these incidents she's been having."

"You disagree?"

Megan gave him an impatient look. "I know the Taylors. The last thing they want is a five-year-old to raise."

"So you think what's been happening to Allie is all in her head?"

She put down what she'd been working on and gave him her full attention for the first time. "You just met her. You don't know anything about her. I love my stepsister, but I don't think she has been completely honest with you. Did you know that her mother spent her last years in a mental hospital? Or that she killed herself?"

"You aren't trying to tell me it runs in the family."

Megan raised a brow. "Allie's been through a lot. She has some issues she hasn't gotten past, including the fact that she wanted her husband gone. So she already told you about that, huh?" He nodded. "Did she also tell you that she bought a gun just before Nick went up into the

mountains? That's right. I wonder what happened to it."
She shrugged. "Like I said, I love Allie and Nat, but I also
know that Allie hated her husband and would have done
anything to escape him."

ALLIE HAD BEEN on her way to her van when Drew had suddenly appeared next to her.

"Where you off to?" he'd asked.

"I just have to pick up some ribbon at the store," she'd
said, trying to act normal. What a joke. She hadn't felt
normal in so long, she'd forgotten what it felt like. Worse,
she feared that Drew would find out about last night. The
Taylors wouldn't hesitate to use it against her, claiming it
proved what a terrible mother she was.

Allie felt guilty enough. Her husband had been dead
only months and here she was making love with another
man. Did it matter that she hadn't loved Nick for years?
She had a child to think about and Jackson Cardwell would
be leaving in two days' time. Then what?

It would be just her and Nat and the Taylors.

"I'll give you a ride," Drew said. She started to argue
but he stopped her. "It would be stupid to take your van
when I'm going that way, anyway. You pick up your ribbon. I'll pick up the chalk I need next door at the hardware
store. We'll be back here before you know it."

All her instincts warned her not to get into the pickup
with him, but she couldn't think of a reason not to accept
the ride without acting paranoid. Did she really think he
would take her somewhere other than the store and what?
Attack her?

She climbed into the passenger side of the pickup and
remembered something Nick had said not long before he'd
left to go hunting that day.

"You're so damned trusting, Allie. I worry about you.

Don't you get tired of being so nice?" He'd laughed and pretended he was joking as he pulled her close and kissed the top of her head. "Don't change. It's refreshing."

It also had made it easier for him to control her.

"You want to know something crazy?" Drew said as he started the engine and drove down the road toward Big Sky. "When I got here this morning, your van was where you'd left it last night. There was dew on the window. I checked the motor. It hadn't been moved and even more interesting, you were nowhere to be found."

She didn't look at him as he roared down the road. Ahead she could see the bridge that spanned the Gallatin River. Why hadn't she listened to her instincts and not gotten into the vehicle with Drew?

"It was like a mystery. I love mysteries. Did I ever tell you that?"

A recent rainstorm had washed out some of the road just before the bridge, leaving deep ruts that were to be filled this afternoon. Couldn't have the wedding guests being jarred by the ruts.

"I saw you come out of Jackson Cardwell's cabin this morning." Drew swore as he braked for the ruts. "You slut." He started to backhand her, but had to brake harder as he hit the first rut so his hand went back to the wheel before it reached its mark. "How could you screw—"

Allie unsnapped her seat belt and grabbed the door handle.

As the door swung open, Drew hit the brakes even harder, slamming her into the door as she jumped. She hit the soft earth at the side of the road, lost her footing and fell into the ditch.

Drew stopped the truck. She heard his door open and the shocks groan as he climbed out. By then she was on her feet and headed into the pines next to the road, running, even though her right ankle ached.

"Allie!" Drew yelled from the roadbed. "You could have killed yourself. You're crazy, you know that?"

She kept running through the pines. Her brother-in-law was right. She had been stupid. Stupid to get into the truck with him when all her instincts had been telling her not to, and crazy to jump out.

Behind her, she heard the truck engine rev, then the pickup rumble over the bridge. She slowed to catch her breath then limped the rest of the way back to the barn, telling herself she was through being naive and trusting.

JACKSON DIDN'T SEE ALLIE until that evening at the wedding rehearsal so he had no chance to get her alone. "We need to talk," he whispered in those few seconds he managed to get her somewhat alone.

She met his gaze. "Look, I think I already know what you're going to say."

"I doubt that." She wore a multicolored skirt and top that accentuated her lush body. "You look beautiful. That top brings out the green in your eyes."

"Thank you." Something glinted in those eyes for a moment. "Jackson—"

"I know. This isn't the place. But can we please talk later? It's important."

She nodded, though reluctantly.

He mentally kicked himself for running out on her this morning as he stood there, wanting to say more, but not able to find the right words.

Allie excused herself. He watched her head for the preacher as the rehearsal was about to begin. Was she limping?

All day he'd stewed over what Megan had told him. She

was wrong about Allie, but he could understand why she felt the way she did. Maybe she really did love her sister. Or maybe not.

Belinda was busy behind her camera, shooting as they all went to their places. As one of the best men, Jackson was in a position to watch the others. He hadn't seen much of Sarah Taylor. But Sarah, her mother and brother would be at the rehearsal dinner tonight. He watched Sarah enter the barn and start up the aisle toward the steps to where the preacher was standing along with the best men and the groom.

An overweight woman with dull, brown hair pulled severely back from her face, Sarah seemed somewhere else, oblivious to what was happening. Either that or bored. Four more bridesmaids entered and took their places.

Harlan and Angus broke into "Here Comes the Bride" on their guitars and Lily came out of a small-framed building next to the meadow with her father and mother. Jackson hadn't met either of them yet but he wanted to laugh when he saw them looking as if in horror. Lily was smiling from ear to ear. So was her brother Ace from the sidelines. But clearly her parents hadn't expected this kind of wedding for their only daughter.

Jackson looked over at Allie. She really was beautiful. She glanced to the parking lot and quickly looked away as if she'd seen something that frightened her.

He followed her gaze. Drew Taylor stood lounging against his pickup, a malicious smirk on his face as if he was up to something.

THE REHEARSAL WENT OFF without a hitch. Allie tried to breathe a sigh of relief. Dana had booked an Italian restaurant in Bozeman for the night of the rehearsal dinner.

"I know it's not the way things are normally done," she'd said with a laugh. But Lily and I discussed it."

Dana had insisted anyone involved in the wedding had to be there so that meant Allie and Natalie as well as Megan and Belinda.

They'd just gotten to the restaurant when Allie heard a strident voice behind her say, "There you are."

She bristled but didn't turn, putting off facing her mother-in-law as long as possible.

"Sarah thinks you're avoiding us," Mildred said. "But why would you do that?"

Allie turned, planting a smile on her face. "I wouldn't."

"Hmmm," her mother-in-law said. She gave Allie the once-over. "You look different."

Allie remembered that she was wearing one of two outfits that she hadn't taken back to the store. This one was a multicolored top and skirt that Jackson had said brought out the green in her eyes. She loved it and while it was more expensive than she could really afford, she'd needed something to wear tonight.

"Where did you get that outfit?" Mildred asked, eyeing her with suspicion.

"I found it in my closet," Allie said honestly.

"Really?"

Allie felt a hand take hers and looked up to see Jackson.

"I saved you a spot down here," he said and led her to the other end of the table, away from the Taylors.

Dana had insisted that there be no prearranged seating. "Let everyone sit where they want. I like people to be comfortable." Lily had seemed relieved that she could sit by Tag, away from her parents.

Allie was grateful to Jackson for saving her. Dinner was served and the conversation around the table was light with lots of laughter and joking. She was glad Jackson didn't try to talk to her about last night.

It had been a mistake in so many ways. But tomorrow after the wedding, they would say goodbye and he and Ford would fly out the next day. She told herself that once the wedding was over, everything would be all right.

A part of her knew she was only kidding herself. There hadn't been any more incidents, no misplaced keys, no Nick sightings, no "black cat" scares and that almost worried her. What had changed? Or was Nick and whomever he had helping him just waiting to ambush her?

She had a feeling that the séance with the psychic hadn't produced the results they'd wanted. Now she, too, was waiting. Waiting for the other shoe to drop.

Just let it drop after the wedding, she prayed. Jackson and Ford would be back in Texas. Whatever was planned for her, she felt she could handle it once this job was over. The one thing Jackson had done was made her feel stronger, more sure of herself. He'd also reminded her that she was a woman with needs that had long gone unmet until last night.

"Stop telling stories on me," Tag pleaded at the dinner table across from her. "Lily is going to change her mind about marrying me."

"Not a chance, cowboy," Lily said next to him before she'd kissed him to hoots and hollers.

Even Sarah seemed to be enjoying herself with the other bridesmaids since they had all worked together at Lily's brother's bar.

Allie avoided looking down the table to see how the Taylors were doing. She was so thankful to be sitting as far away from them as possible, especially Drew. To think that she'd trusted him and thought he'd really had her and Nat's best interest at heart. She'd felt his eyes on her all night. The few times she'd met his gaze, he'd scowled at her.

She glanced over at the children's table to see her daughter also enjoying herself. Dana's sister Stacy had the children at a separate table. Allie saw that her daughter was being on her best behavior. So ladylike, she was even using the manners Allie had taught her. She felt a swell of pride and told herself that she and Natalie were going to be all right no matter what happened after the wedding.

To her surprise, her eyes welled with tears and she quickly excused herself to go to the ladies' room. The bathroom was past an empty section of the restaurant, then down a long hallway. She was glad that no one had followed her. She needed a few minutes alone.

Inside the bathroom, she pulled herself together. Last night with Jackson had meant more to her than she'd admitted. It had hurt this morning when he hadn't been there, but she could understand why he'd panicked. Neither of them took that kind of intimacy lightly.

Feeling better, she left the bathroom. As she reached the empty section of the restaurant, Drew stepped in front of her, startling her. She could smell the alcohol on him. The way he was standing... She recognized that stance after five years of being married to his brother.

Drew was looking for a fight. How had she thought the brothers were different? Because she hadn't seen this side of Drew. Until now.

"You *jumped* out of my truck. What the hell was that? Do I scare you, Allie?" he asked, slurring his words and blocking her way.

"Please, Drew, don't make a scene."

He laughed. "Oh, you don't want Dana to know that you slept with her cousin?"

"Drew—"

"Don't bother to lie to me," he said as he stepped toward her, shoving her back. "I *saw* you." His voice broke. "How can you do this to my brother?"

"Nick's...gone."

"And forgotten. Is that it?" He forced her back against the wall, caging her with one hand on each side of her.

"Please, Drew—"

"If Nick really was out of the picture..." He belched. "You have to know I've always wanted you," he said drunkenly. Before she could stop him, he bent down and tried to kiss her.

She turned her head to the side. He kissed her hair, then angrily grabbed her jaw in one hand. His fingers squeezed painfully as he turned her to face him.

"What? Am I not good enough for you?"

"Drew—"

Suddenly he was jerked away. Allie blinked as Jackson hauled back and swung. His fist connected with Drew's jaw and he went down hard, crashing into a table.

"Are you all right?" Jackson asked, stepping to her.

She nodded and glanced at her brother-in-law. He was trying to get up, but he seemed to take one look at Jackson and decided to stay down.

"You'll pay for that!" he threatened as she and Jackson headed back toward their table. Allie knew he wasn't talking to Jackson. She would pay.

"If he bothers you again—" Jackson said as if reading her mind.

"Don't worry about me."

"How can I not?" he demanded. "That was about me, wasn't it?"

"Drew was just looking for a reason."

"And I provided it."

"He saw me leaving your cabin this morning," she said.

"I don't think he's told anyone, but he will. I just wanted to warn you. I'm afraid what Nick might do to you."

"Allie, I don't give a damn about any of that. What I'm sorry about was leaving you this morning," he said, bringing her up short as he stopped and turned her to face him. "There is so much I want to say to you—"

"Oh, there you are," Mildred Taylor said as she approached. "I was just looking for Drew. I thought you might have seen him. Allie, you look terrible. I knew this job was going to be too much for you."

Natalie and Ford came running toward them. Mildred began to say something about giving Allie and Nat a ride home, but then Drew appeared, rubbing his jaw.

"Drew, whatever happened to you?" Mildred cried.

"I still need to talk to you," Jackson whispered to Allie, who was bending down to catch her daughter up into her arms.

"After the wedding," she said as she lifted Natalie, hugging her tightly. "Tonight I just need to take my daughter home."

Jackson wanted to stop her. But she was right. The wedding was the important thing right now. After that…

CHAPTER TWELVE

WEDDING DAY. Allie woke at the crack of dawn. She couldn't help being nervous and excited. The wedding was to be held in a beautiful meadow near the house. Those attending had been told to wear Western attire as the seating at the wedding would be hay bales.

Drew had constructed an arch for the bride and groom to stand under with the preacher. Allie had walked through everything with the bride and groom, the caterer and the musicians. The barn was ready for the reception that would follow. But she still wanted to get to the ranch early to make sure she hadn't forgotten anything.

The last few days had felt like a roller-coaster ride. Today, she needed calm. Jackson hadn't tried to contact her after she and Natalie left the restaurant with Dana and family last night and she was glad. She needed time with her daughter.

Natalie hadn't slept in her own bed for several nights now. Allie made sure her daughter's window was locked as she put her to bed. She checked the other windows and the door. Then, realizing that any of the Taylors could have a key to her cabin, she pushed a straight-back chair under the doorknob.

She and Natalie hadn't been disturbed all night. At least not by intruders. In bed last night, Allie couldn't help but think about Jackson. And Nick.

"Please, just let me get through this wedding," she'd prayed and had finally fallen asleep.

Now as she drove into the ranch, she saw that Dana and the kids were waiting for Natalie.

"We have a fun morning planned," Dana said with a wink. "You don't have to worry about anything today."

Allie wished that was true. She looked down at the meadow to see that Megan was up early. She was sitting on a hay bale looking as if she were staring at the arch. Imagining her own wedding? Allie wondered as she approached.

"Good morning," she said and joined her sister on the bale.

"It's perfect. Drew really did do a good job," Megan said.

The arch had been made out of natural wood that blended in beautifully with its surroundings. Allie had asked Lily if she wanted it decorated with flowers.

"There will be enough wildflowers in the meadow and I will be carrying a bouquet. I think that is more than enough."

She had agreed and was happy that Lily preferred the more minimalist look.

"Have you been up to the barn?" Allie asked.

"Not yet." Megan finally looked over at her. "How are you?"

"Fine."

Her sister eyed her. "You can lean on me. I'm here for you and Natalie."

Allie hugged her, closing her eyes and praying it was true. She couldn't bear the thought of Megan betraying not only her but Natalie, as well.

Together they walked up to the barn. Allie turned on the lights and gasped.

JACKSON HAD TOSSED and turned all night—after he'd finally dropped off to sleep. He felt as if he'd let Allie down. Or maybe worse, gotten involved with her in the first place, knowing he would be leaving soon.

She wasn't out of the woods yet. She had to know that whoever was messing with her mind wasn't through. He still believed it had to be Nick. He had the most to gain. It scared Jackson to think that whoever was behind this might try to use Tag's wedding to put the last nail in Allie's coffin, so to speak.

His fear, since realizing what was going on, was that if they couldn't drive her crazy, they might actually try to kill her.

He was just getting dressed when he heard the knock at his cabin door. His mood instantly lifted as he thought it might be Allie. She'd said she would talk to him *after* the wedding. Maybe she had changed her mind. He sure hoped so.

Jackson couldn't hide his disappointment when he opened the door and saw his brothers standing there.

"I found something that I think might interest you," Laramie said and he stepped back to let them enter.

"Shouldn't you be getting ready for your wedding?" he asked Tag, who laughed and said, "I have been getting ready for months now. I just want this damned wedding over."

They took a seat while he remained standing. From the expressions on their faces, they hadn't brought good news.

"Nick and his brother, Drew, took out life insurance policies on each other through their construction business," Laramie said.

"That isn't unusual, right?" he asked.

"They purchased million-dollar policies and made each

other the beneficiary, but Nick purchased another half million and made Allie the beneficiary."

Jackson let out a low whistle. "All Allie knew about was the hundred-thousand-dollar policy." He saw Hayes lift a brow. "She didn't kill her husband."

"Whether she knew or not about the policies, I believe it supports your theory that Nick is alive and trying to get that money," Laramie said.

"It hasn't paid out yet, right?"

"She should be getting the checks next week."

Jackson raked a hand through his hair. Allie was bound to have been notified. Maybe it had slipped her mind. "You're sure she is the beneficiary?"

Laramie nodded.

"Who gets the money if Allie is declared incompetent?"

"Her daughter, Natalie."

Jackson groaned. "Then this is why Nick is trying to have Allie committed. He, and whoever he is working with, would get the money and Natalie."

"Only if Nick is alive and *stays* dead," Hayes pointed out.

"If Nick stays dead the money would be used at the discretion of Natalie's *guardian*."

Jackson looked at his brother, an ache starting at heart level. "Who is her guardian?"

"Megan Knight. The policy was changed eight months ago—just before Nick Taylor went up into the mountains hunting and a guardian was added."

ALLIE COULDN'T EVEN SCREAM. Her voice had caught in her throat at the sight in the barn. Last night when she'd left, the barn had been ready for the reception except for putting out the fresh vases of flowers at each setting. The tables had been covered with the checked tablecloths and all the overhead lanterns had been in place along with the decorations on the walls and in the rafters.

"Oh, my word," Megan said next to her.

Allie still couldn't speak. Someone had ripped the tablecloths from the tables and piled them in the middle of the dance floor. The old boots that served as centerpieces that would hold the fresh flowers were arranged on the floor in a circle as if the invisible people in them were dancing.

Megan was the first one to move. She rushed to the tablecloths and, bending down, picked up the top one. "They've all been shredded." She turned to look at Allie, concern in her gaze.

"You can't think I did this."

Her sister looked at the tablecloth in her hand before returning her gaze to Allie. "This looks like a cry for help."

Allie shook her head. "It's someone who hates me."

"Hates you? Oh, Allie."

"What's happened?"

She swung around to see Jackson standing in the doorway. Tears filled her eyes. She wanted to run out the barn door and keep running, but he stepped to her and took one of her hands.

"I was afraid they weren't done with you," he said. "How bad is it?" he asked Megan.

"The tablecloths are ruined. Fortunately, whoever did this didn't do anything to the lanterns or the other decorations in the rafters. Probably couldn't reach them since the ladders have all been packed away." This last was directed at Allie, her meaning clear.

"Tag already ordered tablecloths for the restaurant," Jackson said, pulling out his cell phone. "I'll see if they've come in. We can have this fixed quickly if they have." He spoke into the phone for a moment. When he disconnected, he smiled at Allie and said, "Tag will bring up the red-checked cloths right away. With their help, we'll have it fixed before anyone else hears about it."

Allie went weak with relief as he quickly got rid of the ruined tablecloths and Tag showed up with new ones from the restaurant. With the Cardwell brothers' help, the problem was solved within minutes.

"I want at least two people here watching this barn until the wedding is over," Jackson said.

"I'll talk to Dana and see if there are a couple of ranch hands who can help," Laramie said.

"That really isn't necessary," Megan said. "I will stay here to make sure nothing else happens."

Jackson shook his head. "I'm not taking any chances. I'll feel better if you aren't left alone here. Whoever is doing this... Well, I think it might get dangerous before it's over."

"Why don't you just admit that you think I'm involved in this," Megan said and looked sadly at her sister. "Apparently, you aren't the only one who's paranoid." She sighed. "Whatever you need me to do. I don't want anything to spoil this wedding."

JACKSON HAD PLANNED to talk to Allie about the insurance policies, but he realized it could wait until after the wedding. Allie's spirit seemed buoyed once the barn was ready again and a ranch hand stayed behind with Megan to make sure nothing else went wrong.

He was having a hard time making sense of the insurance policy news. Why would Nick Taylor change the guardian from his brother to Allie's stepsister, Megan? The obvious answer would be if the two were in cahoots.

That would break Allie's heart, but a part of her had to know that her sister thought all of this was in her head.

Megan had given him the impression that she was ready to step in as more than Natalie's guardian.

Jackson reminded himself that it was his brother's wedding day. As much as he didn't like weddings and hadn't attended one since his marriage had ended, he tried to concentrate on being there for Tag. He couldn't help being in awe as Allie went into wedding-planner mode. He admired the way she handled herself, even with all the stress she was under in her personal life. The day took on a feeling of celebration; after all it was the Fourth of July.

At the house, Allie made sure they were all ready, the men dressed in Western attire and boots, before she went to help the bride. Jackson had seen his father and uncle with their guitars heading for the meadow. They would be playing the "Wedding March" as well as accompanying several singers who would be performing. He just hoped everything went smoothly for Tag and Lily's sake, as well as Allie's.

"Look who's here," Laramie said, sounding too cheerful.

Jackson turned to see his mother on the arm of a nice-looking gray-haired Texas oilman. Franklin Wellington IV had oil written all over him. Jackson tried not to hold it against the man as he and his brothers took turns hugging their mother and wishing her well before shaking hands with Franklin.

His mother *did* look deliriously happy, Jackson had to admit, and Franklin was downright friendly and nice.

"Time to go," Allie said, sticking her head into the room where he and his brothers had been waiting.

Jackson introduced her to his mother and Franklin. He saw his mother lift a brow in the direction of Laramie and groaned inwardly. She would trust Laramie to tell her why she was being introduced to the wedding planner.

Allie didn't notice the interplay as she smiled at Tag. "Your bride looks absolutely beautiful and you don't look so bad yourself."

She was quite pretty, as well, in her navy dress with the white piping. She'd pulled her hair up. Silver earrings dangled at her lobes. She looked professional and yet as sexy as any woman he'd ever known. He felt a sense of pride in her, admiring her strength as well as her beauty. She'd been through so much.

Hell, he thought as he took his place, I *am* falling for her. That realization shook him to the soles of his boots.

In the meadow, his father and uncle began to play the "Wedding March" at Allie's nod. Compared to most, the wedding was small since Tag and Lily knew few people in Big Sky. But old canyon friends had come who had known the Cardwells, Savages and Justices for years.

As Lily appeared, Jackson agreed with Allie. She looked beautiful. He heard his brother's intake of breath and felt his heart soar at the look on Tag's face when he saw his bride-to-be. For a man who had sworn off weddings, Jackson had to admit, he was touched by this one.

The ceremony was wonderfully short, the music perfect and when Tag kissed the bride, Jackson felt his gaze searching for Allie. She was standing by a tree at the edge of the meadow. She was smiling, her expression one of happy contentment. She'd gotten them married.

Now if they could just get through the reception without any more trouble, he thought.

AT THE RECEPTION, Jackson watched the Taylor family sitting at a table away from the others. Mildred had a smile plastered on her face, but behind it he could see that she was sizing up everyone in the room. Her insecurities were showing as she leaned over and said something to her daughter.

Whatever her mother said to her, Sarah merely nodded. She didn't seem to have any interest in the guests, unlike her mother. Instead, she was watching Allie. What was it that Jackson caught in her gaze? Jealousy? Everyone at the wedding had been complimenting Allie on the job she'd done. Sarah couldn't have missed that.

Nor, according to Hud, had Sarah ever been married. She had to be in her late thirties. Was she thinking that it might never happen for her? Or was she content with living next to her mother and basically becoming her mother's caregiver?

Sarah reached for one of the boot-shaped cookies with Tag and Lily's wedding date on them. Her mother slapped her hand, making Sarah scowl at her before she took two cookies.

He wondered what grudges bubbled just below the surface in any family situation, let alone a wedding. Weddings, he thought, probably brought out the best and worst of people, depending how happy or unhappy you were in your own life.

As happy as he was for Tag, it still reminded him of his own sorry marriage. What did this wedding do to the Taylor clan? he wondered as he studied them. It certainly didn't seem to be bringing out any joy, that was for sure.

But his side of the family were having a wonderful time. He watched his brother Tag dancing with his bride. Their mother was dancing with her new husband, both women looking radiant. It really was a joyous day. Dana and Hud had all the kids out on the floor dancing.

Jackson thought the only thing that could make this day better would be if he could get the wedding planner to dance with him.

ALLIE TRIED TO breathe a little easier. The wedding had gone off without a hitch. Lily had been exquisite and Tag as handsome as any Cardwell, which was saying a lot. Allie had teared up like a lot of the guests when the two had exchanged their vows. She'd always loved weddings. This one would remain her favorite for years to come.

When the bride and groom kissed, she'd seen Jackson looking for her. Their eyes had locked for a long moment. She'd pulled away first, a lump in her throat, an ache in her heart. The wedding was over. There was nothing keeping Jackson and Ford in Montana.

Whoever had been trying to gaslight her, as Jackson had called it, hadn't succeeded. Maybe now they would give up trying. She certainly hoped so. If Nick was alive, then she should find out soon. The insurance check for the hundred thousand would be deposited into her account next week. She'd already made plans for most of it to go into an interest-bearing account for Natalie's college.

Allie wondered what would happen then. If Nick was alive, would he just show up at her door? Or would the media be involved with reporters and photographers snapping photos of him outside the cabin as he returned from his ordeal?

All she knew was that the only way Nick could get his hands on the insurance money would be if he killed her. That thought unnerved her as she surveyed the reception. Belinda was busy shooting each event along with some candid shots of guests. Allie had to hand it to her, she appeared to be doing a great job.

Everything looked beautiful. Megan had taken care of the flowers in the boot vases, put the attendees' gifts on the tables and made sure the bar was open and serving. Appetizers were out. Allie checked to make sure the caterer was ready then looked around for her daughter. Nat

was with the other kids and Dana. Allie had bought her
a special dress for the wedding. Natalie looked beautiful
and she knew it because she seemed to glow.

Her tomboy daughter loved getting dressed up. She
smiled at the thought. She was thinking that they should
dress up more when Mildred Taylor let out a scream at a
table near the dance floor and stumbled to her feet.

Allie saw that she was clutching her cell phone, her
other hand over her mouth.

"What is it?" Dana demanded, moving quickly to the
Taylors' table.

"It's *my Nicky,*" Mildred cried, her gaze going to Allie,
who froze thinking it was already happening. She was so
sure she knew what her mother-in-law was about to say,
that she thought she'd misunderstood.

"His body has been found," Mildred managed to say between sobs. She cried harder. "They say he was *murdered.*"

CHAPTER THIRTEEN

PANDEMONIUM BROKE OUT with Mildred Taylor shrieking uncontrollably and everyone trying to calm her down.

Jackson looked over at Allie. All the color had bled from her face. He moved quickly to her. "Let's get you out of here," he said, taking her hand. "You look like you could use some fresh air."

"I'll see to Natalie," Dana said nearby as she motioned for Jackson and Allie to go.

Allie looked as if she were in shock. "It just won't end," she said in a breathless rush as he ushered her outside. "It just won't end."

"I'm so sorry," Jackson said, his mind reeling, as well.

"I was so sure he was *alive*." She met his gaze. "I thought..."

"We both thought he was alive. I'm as floored as you are." He realized that wasn't possible. Nick Taylor had been her husband, even if he had been a bad one, she would still be shocked and upset by this news. He was the father of her child.

"Nick was *murdered*? How is that possible? They found his backpack and his gun and the grizzly tracks."

"We need to wait until we have all the details," he said as his brothers Hayes and Laramie joined them.

"We're headed down to the police station now," Hayes said. "I'll let you know as soon as I have any information."

"Thank you." Jackson swallowed the lump in his throat.

His brothers had been so great through his divorce and custody battle, and now this. He couldn't have been more grateful for them.

"The police will be looking for me," Allie said, her eyes widening.

He saw the fear in her eyes and at first had misunderstood it then he remembered what had happened at the psychic's. "No one believes you killed your husband."

"*Someone* already does."

"That's crazy. How could whoever was behind the séance know that Nick was even murdered unless they did the killing?"

She shook her head. "Mildred has blamed me for his death all along. Belinda thought I drove him to kill himself. Don't you see? They didn't have to know it was true. They just wanted me to feel responsible. Now that it *is* true… Even dead, he's going to ruin my life."

The last of the sun's rays slipped behind the mountains to the west, pitching the canyon in cool twilight. Inside the barn, the reception was continuing thanks to Megan and Dana, who had taken over.

"I need to go back in."

"No." Jackson stopped her with a hand on her arm. "You did a great job. No one expects you to do any more. You don't have to worry about any of that."

She met his gaze. "I don't understand what's going on."

"My brothers will find out. Allie, I'm sorry I left you the other morning. I…panicked. But I'm not leaving you now."

Allie shook her head and took a step back from him. "This isn't your problem. You should never have gotten involved because it's only going to get worse."

He remembered what Laramie had told him about the insurance policy and realized she was right. The money would definitely interest the police. He looked toward the barn. Some guests had come out into the evening air to admire the sunset.

"Please, come up to my cabin with me so we have some privacy. There's something important I need to tell you." He saw her expression and realized that she'd misunderstood.

She looked toward the barn, then up the mountain in the direction of his cabin.

"I just need to talk to you," he assured her.

"That wasn't what I…" She met his gaze. "Jackson, I've caused you enough grief as it is. If the Taylors come looking for me—"

"Let me worry about your in-laws. As for Drew, he won't be bothering you as long as I'm around."

She smiled at that. They both knew that once he left she would again be at the mercy of not just Drew but also the rest of the Taylor family.

He wanted to tell her he wouldn't leave her. But he couldn't make that promise, could he?

She was on her own and she knew it.

"Come on," he said and reached for her hand.

DARKNESS CAME ON quickly in the narrow canyon because of the steep mountains on each side. Allie could hear the fireworks vendors getting ready for the wedding grand finale and glanced at her watch. They were right on time. Maybe she wasn't as necessary as she'd thought since everything seemed to be going on schedule without her.

Overhead the pines swayed in the summer night's breeze. Jackson was so close she could smell his woodsy aftershave and remember his mouth on hers. The perfect summer night. Wasn't that what she'd been thinking earlier before her mother-in-law had started screaming?

Nick was dead. Murdered.

For days now she'd believed he was alive and behind all the weird things that had been happening to her. Now how did she explain it?

Jackson stopped on the porch. "We can talk privately here, if you would be more comfortable not going inside." He must have seen the answer in her expression because he let go of her hand and moved to the edge of the porch.

Inside the cabin she would remember the two of them making love in his big, log-framed bed. Her skin ached at the memory of his touch.

"Allie, I hate to bring this up now, but the police will ask you…" He leaned against the porch railing, Allie just feet away. "Were you aware that your husband and brother-in-law took out life insurance policies on each other when they started their construction business?"

"No, but what does that have to do with me?"

"They purchased million-dollar policies and made the other brother the beneficiary, but Nick purchased another half million and made you beneficiary. He never mentioned it to you?"

She shook her head, shocked by the news and even more shocked by how it would look. "You think a million and a half dollars in insurance money gives me a motive for killing him."

"I don't, but I think the police might, given that just before your husband went up into the mountains on his hunting trip, he changed the beneficiary of his million-dollar insurance policy from Drew to you."

Allie didn't think anything else could surprise her. "Why would he do that?" Her eyes filled with tears as a reason came to her. She moved to the opposite railing and looked out across the darkening canyon. "Maybe he did go up there to kill himself," she said, her back to Jackson.

"Hayes will find out why they think he was murdered. In the meantime—"

All the ramifications of this news hit her like a battering ram. "What happens if I'm dead?" She had been looking out into the darkness, but now swung her gaze on him. "Who inherits the money?"

"Natalie. The money would be used for her care until she was twenty-one, at which time her guardian—"

"Her *guardian?*"

"Nick named a guardian in case of your…death or incarceration."

Allie's voice broke. *"Who?"*

"Originally Drew was listed as guardian on the policies, but Nick changed that, too, right before he headed for the mountains." He met her gaze. "Megan, as your next closest kin, even though she isn't a blood relative."

She staggered under the weight of it. She couldn't deal with this now. She had the wedding. "The fireworks show is about to start," she said. "I have to finish—"

"I'm sure Dana will see that the rest of the wedding goes off like it is supposed to," Jackson said, blocking her escape. "No one expects you to continue, given what's happened."

"I took the job. I want to finish it," Allie said, hugging herself against the evening chill. "I thought you would understand that."

"I do. But—" His cell phone rang. "It's Hayes." He took the call.

She had no choice but to wait. She had to know what he'd found out at the police station. As she waited, she watched the lights of Big Sky glitter in the growing darkness that fell over the canyon. A breeze seemed to grow in the shadowed pines. The boughs began to move as if with the music still playing down in the barn.

After a moment, Jackson thanked his brother and disconnected. She remained looking off into the distance, her back to him, as he said, "Nick Taylor's remains were found in a shallow grave. There was a .45 bullet lodged in his skull. The trajectory of the bullet based on where it entered and exited, along with the fact that it appears someone tried to hide the body... It's being investigated as a homicide."

She felt a jolt when he mentioned that the bullet was a .45 caliber and knew Jackson would have seen it. Still, she didn't turn.

"Megan told me you bought a gun and that it disappeared from the cabin," he said. She could feel his gaze on her, burning into her back. He thought he knew her. She could imagine what was going through his mind. He would desperately want to believe she had nothing to do with her husband's murder. "Was the gun you purchased a—"

"Forty-five?" She nodded as she turned to look at him. "Everyone will believe I killed him. You're not even sure anymore, are you?"

"Allie—" He took a step toward her, but she held up her hand to ward him off. It had grown dark enough that she couldn't make out his expression unless he came closer, which was a godsend. She couldn't bear to see the disappointment in his face.

Below them on the mountain everyone was coming out of the barn to gather in the meadow for the fireworks. She suddenly ached to see her daughter. Natalie had been all that had kept her sane for so long. Right now, she desperately needed to hold her.

What would happen to Natalie now? She was trembling with fear at the thought that came to her and would no doubt have already come to the police—and eventually Jackson. She didn't want to be around when that happened.

"With my husband dead, that is three insurance policies for more than a million and a half," she said. "Mother Taylor is convinced I've made up all the stories about someone gaslighting me, as you call it. She thinks I have some plot to make myself rich at her poor Nicky's expense. I'm sure she's shared all of that with the police by now. Maybe I did do it."

He stepped to her and took her shoulders in his hands. "Don't. You didn't kill your husband and you *know* damned well that I believe you."

"Your ex-wife, she was a liar and con woman, right? Isn't that why you were so afraid to get involved with me? What makes you so sure I'm not just like her?"

"You can't push me away." He lifted her chin with his fingers so she couldn't avoid his gaze. Their faces were only a few inches apart. "You aren't like her."

"What if I'm crazy?" Her voice broke. "Crazy like a fox?" The first of the fireworks exploded, showering down a glittering red, white and blue light on the meadow below them. The boom echoed in her chest as another exploded to the oos and ahs of the wedding party. She felt scalding tears burn her throat. "What if Mother Taylor is right and all of this is some subconscious plot I have to not only free myself of Nick, but walk away with a million and a half dollars, as well?"

JACKSON COULDN'T BEAR to see Allie like this. He pulled her to him and, dropping his mouth to hers, kissed her. She leaned into him, letting him draw her even closer as the kiss deepened. Fireworks lit the night, booming in a blaze of glittering light before going dark again.

Desire ignited his blood. He wanted Allie like he'd never wanted anyone or anything before. She melted into him, warm and lush in his arms, a moan escaping her lips.

Then suddenly he felt her stiffen. She broke away. "I can't keep doing this," she cried and, tearing herself from his arms, took off down the steps and through the trees toward the barn.

He started after her, but a voice from the darkness stopped him.

"Let her go."

He turned to find his brother Laramie standing in the nearby trees. More fireworks exploded below them. "What are you doing, little brother?"

"I'm in love with her." The words were out, more honest than he'd been with even himself—let alone Allie.

"Is that right?" Laramie moved to him in a burst of booming light from the meadow below. "So what are you going to do about it?"

Jackson shook his head. "I…I haven't gotten that far yet."

"Oh, I think you've gotten quite far already." Laramie sighed. "I don't want to see you jump into anything. Not again."

"She is nothing like Juliet."

His brother raised a brow. "I knew one day you would fall in love again. It was bound to happen, but Jackson, this is too fast. This woman has too many problems. Hayes and I just came from the police station. They are going to be questioning her about her husband's murder. It doesn't look good."

"She had nothing to do with his death."

"She owns a .45 pistol, the one they suspect is the murder weapon."

Jackson sighed and looked toward the meadow below. It was cast in darkness. Had the fireworks show already ended? "She did but whoever is trying to have her committed, took it to set her up. You know as well as I do that someone has been gaslighting her."

Laramie shook his head. "We only know what Allie has been telling you."

His first instinct was to get angry with his brother, but he understood what Laramie was saying. There was no proof. Instead, the evidence against her was stacking up.

"I believe her and I'm going to help her," he said as he stepped past his brother.

"I just hope you aren't making a mistake," Laramie said behind him as Jackson started down the mountainside.

He'd only taken a few steps when he saw people running all over and heard Allie screaming Natalie's name. He took off running toward her.

"What's wrong?" he demanded when he reached her.

"Nat's gone!" Allie cried.

CHAPTER FOURTEEN

"SHE *CAN'T* BE GONE," Jackson said. "She was with Dana, right?"

"Dana said the kids were all together, but after one of the fireworks went off, she looked over and Nat wasn't with them. She asked Hank and he said she spilled her lemonade on her dress and went to the bathroom to try to wash it off. Dana ran up to the house and the barn, but she wasn't there." Allie began to cry. "She found this, though." She held up the tie that had been on Nat's dress. "Natalie might have gone looking for me. Or someone took her—"

"Allie," he said, taking her shoulders in his hands. "Even if she left the meadow to go to the house, she couldn't have gotten far. We'll find her."

The search of the ranch area began quickly with everyone from the wedding party out looking for the child.

"I turned my back for just a moment," Dana said, sounding as distraught as Allie when Jackson caught up with her.

"It's not your fault. If anyone is to blame, it's me. I've been trying to help Allie and have only made things worse. I need to know something," he said as he watched the searchers coming off the mountain from the cabins. No Natalie. "Did you see anyone go toward the house about the time you realized she was gone?"

She shook her head. "You mean Drew or his mother? They both left earlier to go talk to the police."

"What about his sister, Sarah? Have you seen her?"

Dana frowned. "She didn't leave with them, now that I think about it, and I haven't seen her since Nat went missing."

Jackson spotted Belinda trying to comfort Allie down by the main house. "How about Megan?"

She shook her head. "I haven't seen either of them." Dana looked worried. "You don't think—"

He did think. He ran down the slope toward the house and Allie. "Did either of you see Sarah or Megan?"

They looked at him in surprise.

"They left together not long after the fireworks started," Belinda said. "Sarah said she had a headache and asked Megan to give her a ride."

Jackson looked at Allie. "You know where Sarah lives, right?"

"You think they took Nat?" Allie looked even more frightened.

"Belinda, stay here and keep us informed if the searchers find Nat. Come on. Let's see if they have Natalie or might have seen her since they left about the time she went missing."

EACH BREATH WAS a labor as Allie stared out the windshield into the darkness ahead. She fought not to break down but it took all of her strength. She'd never been so frightened or felt so helpless. All she could do was pray that Natalie was safe.

"If they took her, then I'm sure they wouldn't hurt her," she said, needing desperately to believe that. "Sarah might have thought it was getting too late for Natalie to be out. Or maybe Nat's dress was so wet—"

"We're going to find her." Jackson sounded convinced of that.

She glanced over at him. His strong hands gripped the

wheel as he drove too fast. He was as scared as she was, she realized. Like her, he must be blaming himself. If the two of them hadn't left the wedding…

"Tell me where to turn. I don't know where they live."

"Take a left at the Big Sky resort turnoff. Mother Taylor… Mildred lives up the mountain."

"They don't have that much of a head start," he said, sounding as if he was trying to reassure himself as much as her.

"This is all my fault." She didn't realize she'd said the words aloud until he spoke.

"No, if anyone is to blame it's me," he said as he reached over and squeezed her hand. "You have been going through so much and all I did was complicate things for you."

She let out a nervous laugh. "Are you kidding? I would have been in a straitjacket by now if it wasn't for you. I still might end up there, but at least I had this time when there was someone who believed me."

"I *still* believe you. You're not crazy. Nor did you have anything to do with your husband's death. You're being set up and, if it is the last thing I do, I'm going to prove it."

Allie couldn't help but smile over at him. "Thank you but I can't ask you to keep—"

"You're not asking. There's something else I need to say." He glanced over at her before making the turn at Big Sky then turned back to his driving. "I hadn't been with another woman since my ex. I didn't *want* anyone. The mere thought of getting involved again… Then I met you," he said shooting her a quick look as they raced up the mountain toward Big Sky Resort.

"Turn at the next left when we reach the top of the mountain," she said, not sure she wanted to hear what he had to say.

"I hadn't felt anything like that in so long and then we made love and…"

She really didn't need him to let her down easy. Not right now. All she wanted to think about was Natalie. If he was just doing this to keep her from worrying… "You don't have to explain."

"I do. I panicked because making love with you was so amazing and meant so much and…" He shook his head. "I…I just needed time to digest it all. And, truthfully, I was scared. Ford's mom did a number on me. Admittedly, we were both young, too young to get married, let alone have a child together. I had this crazy idea that we wanted the same things. Turned out she wanted money, a big house, a good time. When she got pregnant with Ford…" He slowed to make the turn.

"It's up this road about a mile. Turn left when you see the sign for Elk Ridge."

He nodded. "Juliet didn't want the baby. I talked her into having Ford. She hated me for it, said it was going to ruin her figure." He shook his head at the memory. "I thought that after he was born, her mothering instincts would kick in. My mistake. She resented him even more than she did me. She basically handed him to me and went out with her friends."

"I can't imagine."

He glanced over at her. "No, *you* can't." He sighed. "After that, she started staying out all night, wouldn't come home for days. Fortunately, the barbecue businesses took off like crazy so I could stay home with Ford. I asked for a divorce only to find out that my wife liked being a Cardwell and didn't want to give up what she had, which was basically no responsibilities, but lots of money and freedom to do whatever she wanted."

"Keep going up this road," she told him. Then after a moment, said, "She didn't want a divorce."

"No. She said that if I pushed it, she would take Ford."

"How horrible," Allie cried. Hadn't that been her fear with Nick? Hadn't she worried that he would be a bastard and try to hurt them both when she told him she was leaving him?

"After the battle I fought to keep my son, I was...broken."

"I understand. The last thing you wanted was to get involved with a woman who only reminded you of what you'd been through."

He glanced over at her. "That was part of it." He didn't say more as he reached the turnoff for Mildred Taylor's house and the guesthouse where her daughter, Sarah, lived. He turned down it and Mildred's house came into view.

JACKSON HAD ALMOST told Allie how he felt about her. That he loved her. But as he'd turned and seen Mildred Taylor's big house, he'd realized the timing was all wrong. First they had to find Natalie.

He prayed she would be here, safe. But if so, did the Taylors seriously think they could get away with this? Had they told someone they were taking Natalie and the person just forgot or couldn't find Allie and left? Was there a logical explanation for this?

He hoped it was just a misunderstanding. But in his heart, he didn't believe for a minute that Allie had imagined the things that had been happening to her. Someone was behind this and they weren't finished with Allie yet. What scared him was that one of them could have murdered Nick.

His heart began to pound harder as he pulled in front of the large stone-and-log house set back against the mountainside. There were two vehicles parked in front and the lights were on inside the massive house. He parked and opened his door, anxious to put Nat in her mother's arms. Allie was out her door the moment he stopped.

"Who all lives here?" Jackson asked as he caught up to her.

"Just Mildred in the main house. Sarah stays in the guesthouse behind it. Drew lives down in Gateway but he stays with his mother a lot up here. That's his pickup parked next to Mildred's SUV so he must be here."

As Jackson passed Mildred's SUV, he touched the hood. Still warm. They at least hadn't been here long.

"What does Sarah drive?" he asked, glancing toward the dark guesthouse.

"A pearl-white SUV. I don't see it."

At Allie's knock, he heard movement inside the house. If they were trying to hide Natalie, it wouldn't do them any good. He looked back down the mountainside telling himself that if Natalie was in this house, he'd find her.

Drew opened the door and looked surprised to see them standing there.

"Where is Natalie?" Allie cried as she pushed past him.

"Natalie?" Drew barely got the word out before Jackson pushed past him, as well. The two of them stormed into the main part of the house.

Mildred was seated on one of the large leather couches facing the window in the living room, a glass of wine in her hand. She looked up in surprise.

"Where is she?" Allie demanded. "I know you have my daughter."

"Natalie?" Mildred asked, frowning. "You can't *find* her?"

"They seem to think we have her," Drew said, closing

the front door and joining them. "We've been at the police station. Why would you think we had Natalie?"

"Allie, stay here. I'll search the house," Jackson said.

"You most certainly will not," Mildred cried. "I'll call the cops."

"Call the cops, but I suspect the marshal is already on his way here," he told her and wasn't surprised when Drew stepped in front of him as if to block his way.

"You really want to do this now? Your niece is missing. If you don't have her, then we need to be out looking for her, not seeing who is tougher between you and me."

"We don't have her," Drew said, "and you're not—"

Jackson hit him and didn't wait around to see if he got up.

He stormed through the house, calling Nat's name. There were a lot of rooms, a lot of closets, a lot of places to look. But it didn't take him long to realize she wasn't here. Whatever they might have done with her, she wasn't in this house.

"I'm going to have you arrested for trespassing and barging into our house and attacking my son," Mildred threatened but hadn't made the call when he returned. Drew had a package of frozen peas he was holding to his eye as he came out of the kitchen.

"Mildred swears she hasn't seen Sarah," Allie told him.

"Well, Natalie isn't here. I think we should still check the guesthouse."

"You planning to break in?" Drew asked. "Or would you like me to get the key?"

Mildred pushed to her feet. "Drew, you are most certainly not going to—"

"Shut up, Mother," he snapped. "Aren't you listening? Natalie is missing. If I can help find her, I will. What I'd like to know is why you aren't upset about it. If you know where Nat is, Mother, you'd better tell me right now."

Jackson felt his cell phone vibrate, checked it and said, "I just got a text that the marshal is on his way. Mrs. Taylor, you could be looking at felony kidnapping," he warned.

ALLIE STARED AT HER mother-in-law, seeing a pathetic, lonely woman who now looked trapped.

"She's not in the guesthouse," Mildred said. "She's *fine*. She's with Sarah and Megan."

"Where?" Allie demanded, her heart breaking at the thought of Megan being involved in this. "Why would they take her?"

Mildred met her gaze. "Because you're an unfit mother. Megan told me all about your mother and her family. Crazy, all of them. And you? You see things and do things that prove you can't raise my Nicky's baby girl. She needs *family*. Natalie needs her *grandmother*," she said before bursting into tears.

"Call them and tell them to bring Natalie back," Jackson ordered.

"He's right, Mother. Natalie belongs with her mother."

"How can you say that?" Mildred cried, turning on her son. "I told you about all the crazy things she's been doing. Did you know she cut up all those lovely dresses my Nicky had bought her? She never liked them and with him gone—" Mildred stopped as if she felt Allie staring at her in shock. "She's *crazy*. Just look at her!"

"The dresses. I never told anyone other than Jackson about finding them cut up on my bed," Allie said, surprised by how normal her voice sounded. Even more surprised by the relief she felt. "It was the night Drew took Natalie and me to dinner. *You?* You bought the clothes in the closet that I found. No wonder you asked me about what I was wearing at the rehearsal dinner. You knew where I kept my checkbook in the desk drawer. Nick would have told you about the kind of clothes I liked. Forging my signature on a check wouldn't have been hard, not for a woman who has been forging her husband's signature on checks for years."

Mildred gasped. "Where would you get an idea like that?"

"*Your Nicky* told me. You've been stealing from the elderly man you married to keep up the lifestyle you believe you deserve. But you don't deserve my daughter."

"Is that true, Mother?" Drew asked with a groan.

"Never mind that cheap bastard. Men never stay so yes, I took advantage while it lasted and now he's divorcing me. Happy?" Mildred thrust her finger at Allie. "But you, you killed my Nicky!"

"How can you say that?" Allie demanded. "You can't really believe I followed him up into the mountains."

"You *paid* someone to kill him. I know you did," the older woman argued. "When I came over that weekend, you were packing up some of Nicky's belongings. You knew he was dead before we even heard."

"That was just some things he left out before he went hunting."

"She's lying," Mildred cried as she looked from Jackson to Drew. "She knew Nicky wasn't coming back. She was packing. I saw that she'd cleaned out the closet before she closed the bedroom door."

"I was packing my own things and Natalie's," Allie said. "I was planning to leave Nick. Ask Belinda. She'll tell you. I wanted a divorce."

Mildred looked shocked. "Why would you want to leave my Nicky? You must have found another man."

"No," Allie said, shaking her head. "I know how much

you loved him but I didn't see the same man you did. Nick wasn't any happier than I was in the marriage."

"Oh, I have to sit down," Mildred cried. "Can't you see? She had every reason to want Nicky dead. She's admitted it."

"Make the call to your daughter, Mrs. Taylor," Jackson said, handing her his phone.

At the sound of a siren headed toward the house, Mildred took his phone.

"You'll get your daughter back, but only temporarily," her mother-in-law spat after making the call. "Once you go to prison for my Nicky's murder, you will get what you deserve and I will get my Nicky's baby."

"And all Nick's insurance money," Jackson said. "Isn't that what this is really about?"

Mildred didn't answer as Marshal Hud Savage pulled up out front.

CHAPTER FIFTEEN

EMOTIONALLY EXHAUSTED, all Allie could think about was holding her daughter. They'd all waited, the marshal included, until Megan and Sarah brought Natalie to the Taylor house.

Allie swept her daughter up into her arms, hugging her so tightly that Natalie cried, "Mama, you're squishing me!"

Hud took Mildred, Drew, Megan and Sarah down to the marshal's office to question them.

"Why don't you come stay at the ranch," Jackson suggested, but all Allie wanted to do was take her daughter home. "Okay, I'll drop you off there. I can give you a ride to the ranch in the morning to pick up your van."

She looked into his dark eyes and touched his arm. "Thank you."

They didn't talk on the drive to her cabin. Natalie fell asleep after complaining that she'd missed most of the fireworks. Apparently, Sarah and Megan had told her they were taking her to see her mama and that it was important.

As they drove, pockets of fireworks were going off around them. Allie had forgotten it was the Fourth of July. Even the wedding seemed like it had been a long time ago.

"If you need anything..." Jackson said after he'd insisted on carrying Natalie into her bed. He moved to the cabin door. "I'm here for you, Allie."

She could only nod, her emotions long spent.

"I'll see you tomorrow."

Allie doubted that. Jackson and Ford would be flying out. She told herself that she and Natalie were safe as she locked the front door, leaned against it and listened to Jackson drive away.

But in her heart she knew they wouldn't be safe until Nick's killer was caught.

"I RUINED TAG and Lily's wedding," Jackson said with a groan the next morning at breakfast.

"You did not," Dana said, patting his hand as she finished serving a huge ranch breakfast of elk steaks, biscuits and gravy, fried potatoes and eggs. She had invited them all down, saying that she knew it had been a rough night. Hud had left for his office first thing this morning.

The wedding couple had stayed at Big Sky Resort last night and flown out this morning to an undisclosed location for their two-week-long honeymoon.

"They loved everything about the wedding," Dana said. "They were just worried about Allie after Mildred's announcement and then concerned for Natalie. I'm just so thankful that she was found and is fine. I can't imagine what Sarah and Megan were thinking."

Jackson had filled everyone in on what had happened at the Taylors' and how apparently Mildred, Sarah and Megan had been gaslighting Allie.

"Oh, Allie must be heartbroken to find out her stepsister was in on it," Dana said.

"I'm sure Hud will sort it out," Jackson said as he watched his son eating breakfast with the Savage clan at the kid table. Ford, he noticed, had come out of his shell. Jackson couldn't believe the change in the boy from when they had arrived at the ranch. Montana had been good for his son.

"Natalie is safe and so is Allie, at least for the moment,"

he said. "The problem is Nick's murder," he said, dropping his voice, even though he doubted the kids could hear, given the amount of noise they were making at their table.

"They still don't know who killed him?" Dana asked.

Jackson shook his head. "Mildred is convinced Allie paid someone to do it. The police want to talk to her."

"You sound worried," Dana noted. "And your brothers haven't said a word," she said, looking from Hayes to Laramie and finally Jackson. "Why is that?"

"They've been helping me do some investigating," he admitted.

Dana rolled her eyes. "I should have known that was what was going on." She glanced at Hayes and Laramie. "You found something that makes her look guilty?"

"Someone is setting her up," Jackson said.

"The same people who tried to drive her crazy?" she asked.

"Maybe not. There could be more going on here than even we know." Jackson couldn't help sounding worried as he got to his feet. "Hayes and I are going to take her van to her. She called this morning. A homicide detective from Bozeman wants to see her."

ALLIE HAD AWAKENED in Natalie's bed to the sound of the phone. She'd expected it to be Jackson. That sent her heart lifting like helium. But as she reminded herself he was leaving today, her moment of euphoria evaporated.

Reaching for the receiver, she had a bad feeling it wasn't going to be good news. "We would like to ask you a few questions," the homicide detective told her. "When would be a good time?"

After she'd hung up, she'd called Jackson and told him the news.

"You knew this was coming. It's nothing to worry

about," he'd told her, but she'd heard concern in his voice. "Do you want me to go with you?"

"No. This is something I have to do alone. Anyway, aren't you flying out today?"

Silence, then, "I canceled our flight."

"You shouldn't have done that," she said after a moment.

"Allie, I can't leave yet. I saw that the key is in the van. Hayes and I will bring it over."

"There is no hurry. I don't see the homicide detective until later."

Their conversation had felt awkward and ended just as badly. Allie told herself she couldn't keep leaning on Jackson. She knew now what Mildred and her daughter and Megan had done to her. She could understand Sarah going along with whatever her mother said, but Megan?

She'd felt like family. But then so had Drew.

Allie made Natalie her favorite pancakes when she woke up, then they went for a walk down by the river. Nat did love to throw rocks into the water. Allie watched the ripples they made, thinking about Jackson and the ripples he'd made in her life.

After a while, they walked back to the cabin. Dana had called saying she would love to take Natalie while Allie went to talk to the detective.

"If you trust me with her. I wouldn't blame you if you didn't. Just let me know."

Allie called Dana right back. "I would always trust you with Natalie and she would love to see the kids, not to mention Sugar, the horse."

Dana laughed and Allie could hear tears in her voice. "I was afraid you would never forgive me."

"There is nothing to forgive. Megan and Sarah took advantage of the fireworks show and the wedding."

"What were they thinking? Did they really believe they could get away with keeping her?"

"I suppose they thought I would come unglued, which I did, proving that I was unbalanced. If it hadn't been for Jackson..." She really hadn't meant to go there.

"Is Natalie all right?"

"She didn't even realize anything was amiss. Apparently, they told her they were taking her to me, but when they reached Megan's motel room, they told her I was going to meet them there. Nat ended up falling asleep. So she had no idea what was going on."

"Thank goodness."

"I'll drop Nat off on my way, if that's okay."

"That's wonderful. We can't wait to see her. Tell her to wear her boots. We'll go for a ride."

"You need to take the hint," Hayes said as he and Jackson drove away from Allie's cabin. They'd dropped off the van, Allie had thanked them and that was that, so Jackson knew what his brother was getting at. "Allie is handling all of this fine. I'm not sure there is anything you can do from here on out."

"You think she had him killed?" Jackson demanded.

Hayes shrugged. "I don't know her as well as you think you do. I don't think she paid anyone to do it. But if she gave Drew any kind of opening with her, I think he would have killed his brother for her—and the insurance money."

"She wasn't in cahoots with Drew. And stop doing that," he snapped as his brother shrugged again. "Do you realize how cynical you've become? Worse, does McKenzie?"

Hayes smiled. "Speaking of McKenzie... I'm opening a private investigator business here."

"You think that's a newsflash?" Jackson laughed.

"We've all seen that coming for a mile. So when is the wedding?"

"I'm thinking we might elope. I'm not sure the family can live through another Cardwell Ranch wedding."

"Which reminds me, still no word from Austin?"

"You know our brother when he's on a case. But I am a little worried about him. I really thought he'd make Tag's wedding."

"Yeah, me too. Maybe I'll give a call down there. Knowing him, he probably didn't list any of us as emergency contacts."

ALLIE TRIED TO get comfortable in the chair the homicide detectives offered her. The room was like any office, no bare lightbulb shining into her eyes, no cops threatening her. But she still shifted in her chair.

On the drive here, she'd tried to concentrate on who might have killed Nick. Belinda had been up that trail with Nick when the two of them had been dating. Drew usually went hunting with his brother. Had Drew gone this time, as well, gotten in an argument with Nick and killed him?

She shuddered at the path her thoughts had taken. Did she really think someone in Nick's own family had killed him?

Better that than to think that her stepsister, Megan, had. Allie felt sick at the thought. Her sister had called this morning but Allie hadn't picked up.

"I need to explain," Megan had said on voice mail. "I did what I did for Natalie's sake. I love you and my niece. I really believed I was protecting you both. I had no idea Mildred and Sarah were doing those things to you, making you behave the way they told me you were. Please call me so we can talk about this."

The larger of the two homicide detectives cleared his

voice. His name tag read Benson. "We need to know where you were the weekend your husband went up into the mountains."

"I was home that whole weekend."

"Did you talk to anyone? Anyone stop by?"

Allie tried to remember. Her mind was spinning. They thought she'd had something to do with Nick's death? Of course they did, given the insurance policies and her mother-in-law's rantings and ravings.

Just yesterday, she'd been sure that Nick was alive. Jackson had been convinced, as well. She'd been even more convinced when she'd heard his voice at the séance. Nick's voice accusing her of killing him. She shivered at the memory.

"Mrs. Taylor?" the smaller of the two, whose name tag read Evans, asked.

She blinked. No one called her Mrs. Taylor. Mrs. Taylor was Nick's mother. "Please, call me Allie. I just need a moment to think." Had anyone stopped by that weekend?

Fighting all her conflicting thoughts, she tried to remember. Nick had left early, having packed the night before. He'd seemed excited about the prospect of going alone on this hunt. Why hadn't she noticed that something was wrong right there? It was the first red flag.

Had anyone stopped by? No. She frowned. She'd tried to call Belinda but hadn't been able to reach her, she recalled now. She'd wanted to tell her what Nick had said about making some changes when he returned from his hunting trip. She'd had misgivings about the trip even then and she'd needed to talk to someone. Had she worried that he might be thinking of killing himself?

"I don't remember anyone stopping by," she said, trying to keep her thoughts on the question. She ticked off everyone on her fingers. "I couldn't reach my friend Belinda."

Had she tried Megan? "Or my stepsister, Megan. And my in-laws. I think that was the weekend that Mildred and Sarah went on a shopping trip to Billings. Drew... I don't know where he was. I didn't talk to him."

She looked up to see that both detectives were studying her. They were making her even more nervous.

"I was alone with my daughter that whole weekend." She had no alibi. But they didn't really think she'd followed Nick up in the mountains and killed him, did they?

"Was it unusual for your husband to go hunting alone?"

"Very. I didn't think he had. I thought he was having an affair. I was surprised when I learned that he really had gone into the mountains."

The detectives shared a look before the lead one asked, "Did you have any reason to believe your husband was having an affair?"

"No. I guess it was wishful thinking. It would have made it easier for me."

The two shared another look. "Easier?"

She met the smaller detective's gaze. "I was going to leave Nick." Why not admit it? They probably already knew this after talking to her in-laws and Belinda and Megan. "But I didn't want him dead. You asked what I was doing that weekend? I didn't leave the house. I had my five-year-old daughter to take care of that weekend and I was busy packing."

"When were you planning to tell him?" Benson asked.

"As soon as he returned."

Evans picked up a sheet of paper from the desk. "Mrs. Tay— Excuse me, Allie, you own a .45 pistol?"

CHAPTER SIXTEEN

THE GUN. WHAT HAD SHE been thinking when she'd bought it? Had she really thought that pulling it on Nick would be a good idea? She'd wanted something to protect herself for when she told him she was leaving.

Now she saw how ridiculous that was. Nick would have taken it away from her, knowing she couldn't shoot him and then he would have been so furious....

"Yes, I bought the gun for protection."

Benson raised a brow. "Protection? Against whom?"

"I was planning to leave my husband. My daughter and I would be alone—"

"But you hadn't left him yet," Evans pointed out. "So why buy a .45 pistol only days before your husband was to go on his hunting trip?"

"I...I...was afraid of how Nick was going to take it when he returned and I told him I was leaving him. Sometimes he scares me."

The two detectives exchanged another look.

"But it was impulsive and silly because Nick would have known I couldn't use it on him. He would have taken it away from me and..." She swallowed.

"You were afraid of your husband," Benson said.

"Sometimes."

"Where is the gun now?" Evans asked.

"I don't know. When I heard that Nick had been killed with a .45, I looked for it, but it was gone." Allie could see the disbelief written all over their faces. Hadn't she known when she looked that it would be gone?

"I think someone is trying to set me up for his murder," she blurted out and instantly regretted it when she saw their expressions. Apparently, they'd heard this type of defense before.

"You're saying someone took the gun to frame you?" Benson asked. "Who knew you'd bought it?"

Allie met his gaze. "I didn't tell anyone, if that is what you're asking."

"Who had access to your house?" Evans asked.

"It's an old cabin. I don't know how many people might have a key. Nick was always going to change the locks..."

"Your in-laws? Did they have keys?" Benson asked.

"Yes."

"Friends?"

"Belinda and my stepsister, Megan, know where there's a key to get in."

"Where did you keep the gun that someone could have found it? You have a five-year-old. I assume you didn't just leave the gun lying around," Benson asked.

"Of course not. I put it on the top shelf of the closet. It wasn't loaded."

"But there were cartridges for it with the gun?"

She nodded.

"When was the last time you saw it?" Evans asked.

"The day I bought it. I put it on the shelf behind some shoe boxes... I'd forgotten all about it with Nick's... death...and all."

"So you were just going to leave him," Evans said. "This man who you said scared you sometimes, you were going to allow him to have joint custody of your child?"

"It hadn't gotten that far. I guess it would have been up to the court—"

"Oh, so you'd already seen a lawyer about a divorce?" Benson asked.

"Not yet. I couldn't afford to see one until I got a job and Nick wouldn't allow me to work."

The detectives exchanged looks.

"Was your husband abusive?" Benson asked not unkindly.

Allie hesitated. "He was…controlling."

"And he scared you," Evans said.

"Yes, sometimes. What is it you want me to say? He wasn't a good husband or father to our daughter. And yes, sometimes he scared me."

"Mrs. Taylor, did you kill your husband?" Evans asked.

"No. I told you. I could never—"

"Did you get your brother-in-law, Drew, or someone else close to you to do the killing for you?" Benson asked.

"*No!* I didn't want to be married to Nick anymore but I didn't want him dead."

Evans leaned forward. "But look how it turned out. Nick is no longer around to scare you, even sometimes. Your daughter is safe from him. And you are a wealthy woman thanks to his insurance money. Better than a divorce and a lengthy battle over your daughter, wouldn't you say?"

Allie felt as if the detectives had beaten her as she stumbled out of the police station. For a moment she forgot where she'd parked the van. Panic sent her blood pressure soaring before she spotted it. There it was, right where she'd left it. And there was…

"Jackson?"

He pushed off the van and moved quickly to her. "I had to see you before I left."

She frowned, still feeling off balance. "I thought you weren't flying out yet?"

"It's my brother Austin. He's a sheriff's deputy in Texas.

He's been shot. He's critical. I have to fly out now. Franklin and Mom already left. Hayes, Laramie and I are taking the corporate jet as soon as I get to the airport."

"I'm so sorry, Jackson. Does Tag know?"

"We weren't able to reach him. He and Lily wanted their honeymoon to be a secret... Ford is staying with Dana until I get back. But I couldn't leave without seeing you. Are you all right?"

She started to say she was fine, but she couldn't get the lie past her lips. Her eyes filled with tears. "They think I killed Nick. Everyone does."

"Not me," he said and pulled her into his arms. "When I get back, we'll sort this out. I'm sorry I have to go."

She pulled back, brushed at her tears. "I'll say a prayer for your brother." As he ran to his rented SUV, she turned in time to see Detective Evans watching her from the front of the building. He looked like a man who'd just received a gift he hadn't expected. Jackson Cardwell. Another motive as to why she'd want her husband gone for good.

THE JET OWNED by the corporation was waiting on the tarmac when Jackson arrived at the airport. He ran to climb aboard and Laramie alerted the captain that they were ready.

"Have you heard any more from Mom or the hospital?" Jackson asked as he buckled up.

"I just got off the phone with Mom," Hayes said. "Austin's still in surgery." His tone was sufficient for Jackson to know it didn't look good.

"Do we know what happened?" he asked as the plane began to taxi out to the runway.

"You know how hard it is to get anything out of the sheriff's department down there," Hayes said. "But I got the impression he was on one of the dangerous cases he seems to like so well." He raked a hand through his hair. "There was a woman involved. He'd apparently gone into a drug cartel to get her out."

"That sounds just like Austin," Jackson said with a sigh as the jet engine roared and the plane began to race down the runway. "Did he get her out?"

"Don't know. Doubtful, though, since some illegal immigrants found him after he'd been shot and got him to a gas station near the border."

Hayes shook his head. "Some of the same illegal immigrants his department is trying to catch and send back over the border. What a mess down there. I'm glad I'm done with it."

His brothers looked at him in surprise as the plane lifted off the ground.

"McKenzie and I signed the papers on a ranch in the canyon not far from Cardwell Ranch. When I get back, we're eloping. She's already looking for some office space for me at Big Sky to open a private investigation office up here."

"Congratulations," Laramie said.

"Have you told Mom?" Jackson asked. "I'm wondering how she is going to feel losing another son to Montana?" The plane fell silent as he realized she might be losing another son at this very moment, one that not even Montana got a chance to claim.

Speaking of Montana, he thought as he looked out the window at the mountains below them. He'd hated leaving Allie, especially as upset as she'd been. He promised himself he would return to the canyon just as soon as he knew his brother was going to be all right.

He said a prayer for Austin and one for Allie, as well.

DANA HAD CALLED to say she was taking the kids on a horseback ride and that Allie could pick Natalie up later, if that was all right. Ford apparently was very upset and worried about his uncle Austin, so Dana was trying to take their minds off everything for a while.

Not wanting to go back to an empty cabin, Allie had busied herself with errands she'd put off since the wedding preparation. It was late afternoon by the time she got home. She'd called the ranch only to find out that Dana and the kids had gone to get ice cream and would be back soon.

Allie was carrying in groceries and her other purchases when she heard the vehicle pull up. She'd hoped to get everything put away before she went to pick up Natalie. She carried the bags into the cabin, dumping them on the kitchen counter, before she glanced out the window to see her mother- and sister-in-law pull up. She groaned as the two got out and came to the door.

For just an instant, she thought about not answering their knock, but they must have seen her carrying in her groceries. Mildred wasn't one to take the hint and go away.

"I just got back from the police station," she said as she opened the door. "I'm really not in the mood for visitors." She couldn't believe either of them would have the gall to show their faces around here after what they'd done. Well, they weren't coming in. Whatever they had to say, they could say it on the front step.

Allie had already talked to Hud this morning. He'd questioned all of them last night, but had had to let them all go. Maybe they had come by to apologize, but Allie doubted it.

"I just got a call from the police," Mildred said indignantly. "Why would you tell them that Sarah and I went to Billings the weekend my Nicky was killed?"

"I thought you had." She knew she shouldn't have been surprised. No apology for what they had tried to do to her.

"We'd planned to go, but Sarah was sick that whole

weekend." She sniffed. "I was alone when I got the call about my Nicky." She glared at her daughter for a moment. "Sarah had taken my car down to the drugstore to get more medicine since her car was in the shop. I couldn't even leave the house to go to Drew." Mildred sighed.

"I'm sorry you were alone, Mother. I came right back. I couldn't have been gone more than five minutes after you got the call," Sarah said.

"That was the longest five minutes of my life," Mildred said with another sniff.

"I guess I had forgotten the two of you hadn't gone to Billings, but I'm sure you straightened it out with the police," Allie said. "And Sarah couldn't have known that would be the time you would get the call about Nick," Allie pointed out.

Sarah gave her a grateful smile, then added, "I hate to ask, but do you happen to have a cola in your fridge?"

"Oh, for crying out loud, Sarah, how many times have I told you that stuff is horrible for you?" her mother demanded.

"Help yourself," Allie said, moving to the side of the doorway to let her pass. She saw that the sun had disappeared behind Lone Mountain, casting the canyon in a cool darkness. Where had this day gone? "I hate to run you off, but I have to go pick up Natalie."

"Once this foolishness is over, I hope you'll forgive me and let me spend some time with my granddaughter," Mildred said.

As Sarah came out with a can of cola, Allie moved aside again to let her pass, hoping they would now leave.

Mildred looked in the yard at Nick's pickup, where it had been parked since someone from the forest service had found it at the trailhead and had it dropped off. "Why are you driving that awful van of yours? You should either drive Nicky's pickup or sell it. Terrible waste to just let it sit."

Allie planned to sell the pickup but she'd been waiting, hoping in time Mildred wouldn't get so upset about it.

"I'd like to buy it," Sarah said, making them both turn to look at her in surprise.

"What in the world do you need with Nicky's pickup?" Mildred demanded. "I'm not giving you the money for it and I couldn't bear looking at it every day."

"It was just a thought," Sarah said as she started toward her SUV. The young woman took so much grief from her mother.

Her gaze went to Nick's pickup. The keys were probably still in it, she realized. As Sarah climbed behind the wheel and waited for her mother to get into the passenger side of the SUV, Allie walked out to the pickup, opened the door and reached inside to pull the keys.

The pickup smelled like Nick's aftershave and made her a little sick to her stomach. She pocketed the keys as she hurriedly closed the door. The truck was Nick's baby. He loved it more than he did either her or Natalie. That's why she was surprised as she started to step away to see that the right rear panel near the back was dented. She moved to the dent and ran her fingers over it. That would have to be fixed before she could sell it since the rest of the truck was in mint condition.

Just something else to take care of, she thought as she dusted what looked like chalky white flakes off her fingers. She looked up and saw that her in-laws hadn't left. Mildred was going on about something. Sarah was bent toward the passenger seat apparently helping her mother buckle up. Mildred was probably giving her hell, Allie thought.

When Sarah straightened, she looked up from behind the wheel and seemed surprised to see Allie standing by

Nick's truck. Her surprise gave way to sadness as she looked past Allie to her brother's pickup.

Was it possible Sarah really did want Nick's pickup for sentimental reasons? Maybe she should have it. Allie had never thought Sarah and her brother were that close. Well, at least Nick hadn't been that crazy about his sister. He'd been even more disparaging than his mother toward Sarah.

Allie met her sister-in-law's dark gaze for a moment, feeling again sorry for her. Maybe she would just give her the pickup. She waved as Sarah began to pull away, relieved they were finally leaving.

Her cell phone rang. She hoped it was Jackson with news of his brother. She said a silent prayer for Austin before she saw that it was Dana.

"Is everything all right?" Allie asked, instantly afraid.

"Ford is still upset about his uncle. Natalie told him that you were picking her up soon…"

Allie knew what was coming. She couldn't bear the thought. She wanted Natalie home with her. The way things were going, she feared she might soon be under arrest for Nick's murder. She didn't know how much time she and Nat had together.

"Natalie wishes to speak with you," Dana said before Allie could say no.

"Mama?" Just the sound of her daughter's voice made her smile. "Please say I can stay. Ford is very sad about his uncle. Please let me stay."

"Maybe Ford could come stay with you—"

"We're all going to sleep in the living room in front of the fire. Mrs. Savage said we could. She is going to make popcorn. It is Mary and Hank's favorite."

Allie closed her eyes, picturing how perfect it would be in front of Dana's fireplace in that big living room with the smell of popcorn and the sound of children's laughter. She wanted to sleep right in the middle of all of them.

"Of course you need to stay for your new friend," she heard herself say as tears burned her eyes. "Tell Mrs. Savage that I will pick you up first thing in the morning. I love you."

"I love you, too, Mama." And Natalie was gone, the phone passed to Dana who said, "I'm sorry. This was the kids' idea."

"It's fine."

"What about you? How did it go with the police?"

"As expected. They think I killed Nick. Or at least got someone to do it for me."

"That's ridiculous. Allie, listen, you shouldn't be alone. Why don't you come stay here tonight? I think you need your daughter. Do you like butter on your popcorn? Come whenever you want. Or take a little time for yourself. If you're like me, when was the last time you got a nice leisurely bath without being interrupted? Whatever you need, but bring your pjs. We're having a pajama party. Right now the kids all want to go help feed the animals. See you later."

AS THE JET touched down just outside of Houston, Hayes got the call from their mother. Jackson watched his expression, waiting for the news. Relief flooded his brother's face. He gave thumbs up and disconnected.

"Mom says Austin is out of surgery. The doctor says he should make it."

Jackson let out the breath he'd been holding. As the plane taxied toward the private plan terminal, he put in a call to Allie. It went straight to voice mail.

He left a message, telling her the good news, then asking her to call when she got the message. "I'm worried about you." As he disconnected, he realized he'd been worried the entire flight about both his brother and Allie.

"I can't reach Allie."

His brothers looked at him in concern as the plane neared the small brightly lit terminal. It was already dark here, but it would still be light in Montana.

"Call Dana," Hayes said. "She's probably over there."

He called. "No answer."

"They probably went for a horseback ride," Laramie said. "Wasn't that what Ford told you they were going to do the last time you talked to him?"

Jackson nodded, telling himself his brother was probably right. He glanced at Hayes. He understood what Laramie couldn't really grasp. Laramie was a businessman. Hayes was a former sheriff's deputy, a private investigation. He understood Jackson's concern. There was a killer still loose in Montana.

The plane came to a stop. Jackson tried Allie again. The call again went straight to voice mail. He got Mildred Taylor's number and called her.

"Have you seen Allie?" he asked. He couldn't explain his fear, just a feeling in the pit of his stomach that was growing with each passing minute.

"Earlier. She wouldn't even let me in her house." She sniffed. "She was on her way to Cardwell Ranch to pick up Natalie the last I saw of her. Driving that old van. Why she doesn't drive Nickie's pickup I will never—"

He disconnected and tried Dana. Still no answer. He tried Allie again. Then he called the marshal's office in Big Sky.

"Marshal Savage is unavailable," the dispatcher told him.

"Is there anyone there who can do a welfare check?"

"Not at the moment. Do you want me to have the marshal call you when he comes in?"

Jackson started to give the dispatcher his number but Hayes stopped him.

"Take the plane," Hayes said. "Mother said it would be hours before we could even see Austin. I'll keep you informed of his progress."

"Are you kidding?" Laramie demanded. "What is it with you and this woman? Have you forgotten that she's the number one suspect in her husband's murder?"

"She didn't kill him," Jackson and Hayes said in unison.

"Let us know as soon as you hear something," Hayes said.

Jackson hugged his brother, relieved that he understood. He moved to cockpit and asked the pilot how long before they could get the plane back in the air. As Hayes and Laramie disembarked, he sat down again and buckled his seatbelt, trying to remain calm.

He had no reason to believe anything had happened. And yet...that bad feeling he'd gotten when her phone had gone to voice mail had only increased with each passing second. His every instinct told him that Allie was in real trouble.

CHAPTER SEVENTEEN

ALLIE HAD TAKEN a hot bath, but had kept it short. She was too anxious to see her daughter. She changed her clothes, relieved she was going to Dana's. She really didn't want to be alone tonight. She'd heard Natalie's happy chatter in the background and couldn't wait to reach the ranch.

In fact, she had started out the door when she realized she didn't have her purse or her van keys. Leaving the door open, she turned back remembering that she'd left them on the small table between the living room and kitchen when she brought in her groceries earlier.

She was sure she'd left her purse on the table, but it wasn't there. As she started to search for it, she began to have that awful feeling again. Her mind reeled. Mildred wasn't still fooling with her, was she? No Mildred hadn't come into the cabin. But Sarah had. Why would Sarah hide her purse? It made no sense.

Racking her brain, she moved through the small cabin. The purse wasn't anywhere. On her way back through, she realized she must have left it in the van. She was so used to leaving her purse on that small table, she'd thought she remembered doing it again.

She started toward the open door when a dark figure suddenly filled the doorway. The scream that rose in her throat came out a sharp cry before she could stop it.

"Drew, you scared me. I didn't hear you drive up."

"My truck's down the river a ways. I was fishing...."

The lie was so obvious that he didn't bother finishing it. He wasn't dressed for fishing nor was he carrying a rod.

"The truth is, I wanted to talk to you and after everything that's happened, I thought you'd chase me off before I could have my say."

"Drew, this isn't a good time. I was just leaving."

He laughed. "That's exactly why I didn't drive up in your yard. I figured you'd say something just like that."

"Well, in this case, it's true. Natalie is waiting for me. I'm staying at Cardwell Ranch tonight. Dana is going to be wondering where I am if I don't—"

"This won't take long." He took a breath. "I'm so sorry for everything."

Allie felt her blood heat to boiling. No one in this family ever listened to her. How dare he insist she hear him out when she just told him she was leaving? "You and your mother tried to drive me insane."

"I didn't know anything about that, I swear," Drew cried. "Mother told me that you had already forgotten about Nick. It was breaking her heart. She said you needed to be reminded and if you saw someone who looked like Nick…"

"You expect me to believe that?"

He shrugged. "It's true. I did it just to shut her up. You know how Mother is."

She did. She also knew arguing about this now was a waste of time and breath. She glanced at the clock on the mantel. "I really need to go."

"Just give me another minute, please. Also I wanted to apologize for the other night. I had too much to drink." He shook his head. "I don't know what I was thinking. But you have to know, I've always liked you." He looked at her shyly. "I would have done anything for you and now the cops think I killed Nick for you."

Her pulse jumped, her heart a thunder in her chest. "That's ridiculous."

"That's what I told them. I could never hurt my brother. I loved Nick. But I have to tell you, I was jealous of him when he married you."

"Drew, I really don't have time to get into this right—"

"Don't get me wrong," he said as if she hadn't spoken. "If I thought there was chance with you..."

A ripple of panic ran up her spine. "There isn't, Drew."

"Right. Jackson Cardwell."

"That isn't the reason."

"Right," he said sarcastically. His jaw tightened, his expression going dark. She'd been married to his brother long enough to know the signs. Nick could go from charming to furious and frightening in seconds. Apparently so could his brother.

"Drew—"

"What if I did kill him for you, Allie?" He stepped toward her. "What if I knew where he would be up that trail? What if I wanted to save you from him? You think I don't know how he was with you?" He let out a laugh. "Jackson Cardwell isn't the only knight in shining armor who wants to come to your rescue."

She didn't want to hear his confession and feared that was exactly what she was hearing. "Drew, I would never want you to hurt your brother for any reason, especially for me."

"Oh yea? But what if I did, Allie? Wouldn't you owe me something?"

He took another a step toward her.

She tried to hold her ground but Drew was much stronger, much larger, much scarier. With Nick, she'd learned that standing up to him only made things worse. But she was determined that this man wasn't going to touch her. She'd backed down too many times with Nick.

"This isn't happening, Drew." She stepped to the side and picked up the poker from the fireplace. "It's time for you to go."

She could almost read his mind. He was pretty sure he could get the poker away from her before she did much bodily harm to him. She lifted it, ready to swing, when she heard a vehicle come into the yard.

Drew heard it to. "Jackson Cardwell to the rescue again?"

But it couldn't be Jackson. He was in Texas by now.

Allie was relieved to see his sister Sarah stick her head in the door. "I hope I'm not interrupting anything," she said into the tense silence.

"Not at all," Allie assured her sister-in-law. Her voice sounded more normal than she'd thought it would. Had Drew just confessed to killing Nick? "Drew was just leaving."

"We're not through talking about this," he said as he started for the door.

"Oh, I think we already covered the subject. Goodbye Drew."

"Is everything all right?" Sarah asked as Allie returned the poker to its spot next to the fireplace. She stepped in and closed the door behind her.

"Fine. You didn't happen to see my purse when you were here earlier, did you? Dana is expecting me and I can't seem to find it."

"No. You still haven't picked up Natalie?"

"No, Dana invited me for a sleepover with the kids. I was just heading there when Drew arrived."

"I didn't see his truck," Sarah said glancing toward the window.

"He said he parked it down river where he was fishing." She glanced around the living room one more time. "I need to find my purse and get going."

"Your purse? Oh, that explains why you didn't answer your cell phone. I tried to call you," Sarah said. "Do you want me to help you look?"

"No, maybe I'll just take Nick's truck." The idea repulsed her, but she was anxious to get to the ranch. "I'm sure my purse will turn up. Oh, that's right, I was going out to check the van and see if I left it there when Drew showed up."

"So you're off to a kids sleepover?"

Allie knew she should be more upset with Sarah for taking Natalie last night, but Sarah had always done her mother's bidding. Allie couldn't help but feel sorry for the woman.

"Nat wanted to spend the night over there for Ford. He's upset about his uncle Austin who was shot down in Texas. His brothers should be at the hospital by now. No wonder I haven't heard anything with my cell phone missing."

"Natalie and Ford sure hit it off, didn't they? It's too bad Nat doesn't have a sibling. I always thought you and Nick would have another child."

Allie found Nick's truck keys in her jacket pocket and held them up. "If you still want Nick's truck, you can have it. I was planning to sell it. But the back side panel is dented." She frowned. "It's odd that Nick didn't mention it. You know how he was about truck…"

Her thoughts tumbled over each other in a matter of an instant as her gaze went to her fingers and she remembered the white flakes she'd brushed off the dent. It hadn't registered at the time. The dent. The white paint from the vehicle that had hit it. Pearl white on Nick's black pickup.

Nick would have been out of his mind if someone had

hit his pickup. So it couldn't have happened before his hunting trip, which meant it happened where? At the trailhead?

ANOTHER VEHICLE MUST have hit the pickup. Allie's thoughts fell into a straight, heart-stopping line. A pearl-white vehicle like the one Sarah was having repaired the day the call came about Nick's death.

Allie felt the hair rise on the back of her neck as she looked up and saw Sarah's expression.

"I knew you would figure it out the minute I saw you standing next to the dent in Nick's pickup. Nick was so particular about his truck. One little scratch and he would have been losing his mind. Isn't that what you were realizing?"

"Oh Sarah," she said, her heart breaking.

"That's all you have to say to the woman who killed your husband?" she asked as she pulled Allie's .45 out of her pocket and pointed the barrel at Allie's heart.

JACKSON HAD LEFT his rental car at the Bozeman airport. The moment the jet landed he ran to it and headed up the canyon. He tried Allie again. Still no answer. He left a message just in case there was a good reason she wasn't taking calls.

The only reason he could come up with was that she was at Dana's with the kids and didn't want to be disturbed. But she would have taken his calls. She would have wanted to know how Austin was doing.

He tried Dana and was relieved when at least she answered. "I'm looking for Allie. Have you seen her?"

"Not yet. I talked to her earlier. I told her to take a nice hot, long bath and relax, then come over for a sleepover." He could hear Dana let out a surprised sound. "I didn't realize it was so late. She should have been here by now."

"Her calls are going straight to voice mail."

"I'm sure she's just running late…" Dana sounded worried. "How is Austin?"

"He's out of surgery. The doctor said he should make it. I left Hayes and Laramie in Houston."

"Where are you now?"

"On my way to Allie's cabin. If you hear from her, will you please call me?"

He disconnected and drove as fast as he could through the winding narrow canyon. Something was wrong. Dana felt it, too. He prayed that Allie was all right. But feared she wasn't.

Realizing his greatest fear, he called Drew's number. When he'd heard the part Allie's brother-in-law had played in gaslighting her, he'd wanted to punch Drew again. He didn't trust the man, sensed he was a lot like Nick had been; another reason to hate the bastard.

But Jackson also worried that Drew might have killed Nick. The problem was motive. He wouldn't benefit from his brother's death since Nick had changed his beneficiaries on his insurance policy. Or was there something else Drew wanted more than money?

It came to him in a flash. Allie. If he had her, he would also have Nick's money and Nick's life.

Drew answered on the third ring. "What?" He sounded drunk.

Jackson's pulse jumped. "Have you seen Allie?"

"Who the hell is this?"

"Jackson Cardwell." He heard Drew's sneer even on the phone.

"What do *you* want? Just call to rub it in? Well, you haven't got Allie yet so I wouldn't go counting your chickens—"

His heart was pounding like a war drum. "Is she with you?"

Drew laughed. "She's having a sleepover but not with me. Not yet."

"She isn't at the sleepover. When did you see her?"

Finally picking up on Jackson's concern, he said, "She was with my sister at the cabin."

Jackson frowned. "Your sister?"

"They both think I killed Nick. But Sarah had more of a motive than I do. She hated Nick, especially since he'd been trying to get Mother to kick her out. Sarah might look sweet, but I have a scar from when we were kids. She hit me with a tire iron. A tire iron! Can you believe that?"

Jackson saw the turnoff ahead. As he took it, his headlights flashed on the cabin down the road. There were three vehicles parked out front. Nick's black pickup. Allie's van. Sarah's pearl-white SUV.

CHAPTER EIGHTEEN

"I DON'T UNDERSTAND," Allie said. "Why would you kill your brother?"

Sarah smiled. "Sweet, lovable *Nickie?* You of all people know what he was like. You had to know the way he talked about me."

Allie couldn't deny it. "He was cruel and insensitive, but—"

"He was trying to get Mother to kick me out without a cent!" Her face reddened with anger. "I gave up my life to take care of her and Nickie is in her ear telling her I am nothing but a parasite and that if she ever wants to see me get married, she has to kick me out and force me to make it on my own. Can you believe that?"

She could. Nick was often worried about any money that would be coming to him via his mother. He was afraid Sarah would get the lion's share because his mother felt sorry for her.

"He was jealous," Allie said. "He was afraid you were becoming her favorite just because she depends on you so much."

Sarah laughed. "Her *favorite?* She can't stand the sight of me. She'd marry me off in a heartbeat if she could find someone to take me off her hands."

"That isn't true. You know she would be lost without you." With a start, Allie realized that Mildred was going to get a chance to see what life was like without Sarah once Sarah went to prison. That is, unless she got away with murdering Nick. With Allie out of the way, Sarah just might.

"I still can't believe you killed him," Allie said as she searched her mind for anything within reach of where she was standing that she could use to defend herself. Something dawned on her. "How did you get my gun?"

"Mother had sent me to your cabin to see if you still had that pink sweater she gave you for Christmas. You never wore it and it was driving her crazy. I told her pink didn't look good on you, but she got it on sale… You know how she is."

Oh yes, she knew. That ugly pink sweater. Allie had put the gun under it behind the shoe boxes.

"When I found the gun, I took it. I was thinking I would try to scare Nick. After all, we have the same genes. He should have known I could be as heartless as him. But Nick had always underestimated me. I tried to talk to him, but he went off on women, you in particular."

Allie blinked in surprise. *"Me?"*

"He said some women needed to be kept in their place and that you thought you were going to leave him and take his child. He had news for you. He laughed, saying how you'd been stealing small amounts of his money thinking he wouldn't notice but he was on to you. He'd given you a few days to think about what you were doing, but when he came back there were going to be big changes. He was going to take you in hand. He said, 'I'll kill her before I'll let her leave me.' Then he told me to get out of his way and took off up the trail."

So Nick hadn't been promising to change, she thought. He was going to change her when he got back. Allie felt sick to her stomach, imagining what Nick would have been like if he had ever returned home to find her packing to leave him.

"His parting shot was to yell back at me. 'You big fat ugly pig. Go home to your mommy because when I get back your butt is out of that guesthouse.' Then he laughed and disappeared into the trees."

"Oh, Sarah, I'm so sorry. Nick was horrible. If you tell the police all of this—and I will back you up—I'm sure they will—"

"Will what? Let me go? You can't be that naive. I'll go to prison."

Allie had a crazy thought that prison would be preferable to living with Mildred Taylor.

"No, Allie, there is another way. You are the only one who knows what I did."

"If you kill me, they'll eventually catch you and since this will be cold-blooded murder, you will never get out of prison. Don't throw your life away because of Nick."

"I'm going to make you a deal," Sarah said. "I will spare your daughter if you do what I say."

"What? You would hurt Natalie?" Allie's terror ramped up as she realized this was a woman who felt no remorse for killing her own brother. Nor would she feel any for killing her sister-in-law now. That she could even think of hurting Natalie...

"Do you know why I look like I do?" Sarah asked. "I made myself fat after my mother's first divorce when I was just a little older than Natalie." She stepped closer, making Allie take a step back. "My stepfather thought I was adorable and couldn't keep his hands off me. My other stepfathers were just as bad until I gained enough weight that, like my mother, they only had contempt for me."

Allie couldn't hold back the tears. "I'm so sorry. I had no idea."

"No one did. My mother knew, though." Her eyebrow shot up. "That surprises you?" She laughed. "You really have no idea what *Mother Taylor* is capable of doing or why she dotes on her granddaughter. This latest husband is divorcing her, but there will be another husband, one who will think your little Natalie is adorable. Think about that. You do what I say and I will make sure what happened to me doesn't happen to Nat."

Allie was too stunned almost to breathe. What was Sarah saying?

"That's right, Mother Taylor *needs* Natalie," her sister-in-law said. "Now you can either take this gun and shoot yourself or I will shoot you. But if I have to do it, I will probably get caught as you say and go to prison. Imagine what will happen to Natalie without me here to protect her. Oh, and don't even think about turning the gun on me because trust me I will take you with me and Natalie will have a new grandpa, one who will adore her."

Allie couldn't bear the choice Sarah was demanding she make. "Natalie needs me," she pleaded as she looked at the .45 her sister-in-law held out to her.

"She needs me more. Just imagine the danger Natalie would have been in if I hadn't warned you."

"Don't you think I suspected something was wrong at that house? I didn't like Natalie going there. I didn't trust your family."

"With good reason as it turns out. You have good mothering instincts. I wonder what my life would have been like if I'd had a good mother?"

Allie's heart went out to her even though the woman was determined she would die tonight. "I'm so sorry. Sarah, but we don't have to do this. I won't tell the police about the dent in the pickup."

"You're too honest. Every time you saw me, we would both know." She shook her head. "One day you would have to clear your conscience. You know what would happen to me if I went to prison. No, this is the best way. Think of your daughter."

How could she think of anything else? That's when she heard the vehicle approaching.

Sarah got a strange look on her face as she cocked her head at the sound of the motor roaring up into the yard. "This has to end now," she said.

Allie couldn't imagine who had just driven up. Dana and the kids? She couldn't take the chance that someone else would walk into this.

She grabbed for the gun.

JACKSON HIT THE door running. He told himself he was going to look like a damned fool barging in like this. But all his instincts told him something was very wrong.

As he burst through the door, he saw Allie and Sarah. Then he saw the gun they were struggling over.

The sound of the report in the tiny cabin was deafening. Jackson jumped between them going for the gun that Sarah still gripped in her hands. The silence after the gunshot was shattered as Allie began to scream.

Jackson fought to get the gun out of Sarah's hands. She was stronger than she looked. Her eyes were wide. She smiled at him as she managed to pull the trigger a second time.

The second silence after the gunshot was much louder.

"Allie, are you hit?" Jackson cried as he wrenched the gun from Sarah's hand.

She looked at him, tears in her eyes, and shook her head.

For a moment all three of them stood there, then Sarah fell to her knees, Allie dropping to the floor with her, to take the woman in her arms.

"She killed herself," Allie said to Jackson. "She could have killed me, but she turned the gun on herself." Still holding Sarah, Allie began to cry.

Jackson pulled out the phone, tapped in 911 and asked for an ambulance and the marshal, but one look at Sarah and he also asked for the coroner.

EPILOGUE

BE CAREFUL WHO YOU MARRY—including the family you marry into. That had been Jackson's mother's advice when he'd married Juliet. He hadn't listened. But Allie's in-laws made Juliet's look like a dream family.

"If you want to file charges," Marshal Hud Savage was saying. "You can get your mother-in-law for trespassing, vandalism, criminal mischief…but as far as the gaslighting…"

"I don't want to file charges," Allie said. "The real harm she's done… Well, there isn't a law against it, at least not for Mildred. And like you said, no way to prove it. How is Mildred?"

After what Allie had told him, Jackson hoped the woman was going through her own private hell. She deserved much worse.

"She's shocked, devastated, but knowing Mildred, she'll bounce back," Hud said. "How are you doing?"

"I'm okay. I'm just glad it's over."

Jackson could see the weight of all this on her. He wanted to scoop her and Natalie up and take them far away from this mess. But he knew the timing was all wrong. Allie had to deal with this before she would be free of Nick and his family.

"I did talk to the psychic Belinda took you to," Hud said. "She claims she didn't know what was planned. Mildred had given her a recording of Nick's voice that had been digitally altered with Drew helping with any extra words that were needed. She alleges she was as shocked as anyone when Nick said what he did."

"I believe her," Allie said.

"As for who shot your horse up in the mountains…" Hud rubbed a hand over his face. "I've arrested Drew for that. I can't hold him for long without evidence, but he does own a .22 caliber rifle and he did have access to the ranch."

"So that whole family gets off scot-free?" Jackson demanded.

Hud raised a brow. "I wouldn't say scot-free. I'd love to throw the book at Mildred and Drew, believe me. But neither will see jail time I'm afraid. Their justice will have to come when they meet their maker." Hud shook his head and turned to Jackson. "I heard Austin is recovering fine."

"It was touch and go for a while, but he's tough. The doctor said he will be released from the hospital in a week or so, but he is looking at weeks if not months before he can go back to work. He might actually get up to Montana to see the Texas Boys Barbecue joint before the grand opening."

"I suppose you're headed back to Texas then?" Hud asked. "Dana said Ford will be starting kindergarten his year?"

Jackson nodded. "I suppose I need to get a few things sorted out fairly soon."

ALLIE COULDN'T FACE the cabin. She had nothing but bad memories there. So she'd been so relieved when Dana had insisted she and Natalie stay in one of the cabins. All but one of them was now free since Laramie had gone back to Texas, and Hayes and McKenzie had bought a ranch down the highway with a large house that they were remodeling. Only Jackson and Ford were still in their cabin, not that

Ford spent much time there since he was having so much fun with his cousins.

The same with Natalie. Allie hardly saw her over the next few days. She'd gotten through the funerals of Sarah and a second one for Nick. Mildred had tried to make her feel guilty about Sarah's death. But when Mildred started insisting that Natalie come stay with her, Allie had finally had to explain to her mother-in-law that she wouldn't be seeing Nat and why.

Of course Mildred denied everything, insisting Sarah had been a liar and blamed everything on her poor mother.

"We're done," Allie said. "No matter what I decide to do in the future, you're not going to be a part of my life or Natalie's."

"I'll take you to court, I'll…" Mildred had burst into tears. "How can you be so cruel to me? It's because you have all my Nickie's money now. I can't hold my head up in this canyon anymore, my husband is divorcing me, Drew is selling out and leaving… Where am I supposed to go?"

"I don't care as long as I never have to see you." Allie had walked away from her and hadn't looked back.

"I don't want Nick's insurance money," she'd told Dana the day she and Natalie had moved into one of the ranch cabins.

"Use just what you need and put the rest away for Natalie. Who knows what a good education will cost by the time Nat goes to college? Then put that family behind you."

But it was her own family that Allie was struggling to put behind her, she thought as she saw Megan drive up in the ranch yard. Megan had been calling her almost every day. She hadn't wanted to talk to her. She didn't want to now, but she knew she had to deal with it, no matter how painful it was.

Stepping out on the porch, she watched her half sister

get out of the car. Natalie, who'd been playing with the kids, saw her aunt and ran to her. Allie watched Megan hug Natalie to her and felt a lump form in her throat.

"We can talk out here," she told Megan as Natalie went to join her friends.

Allie took a seat on the porch swing. Megan remained standing. Allie saw that she'd been crying.

"I used to ask about you when I was little," Megan said. "I'd seen photographs of you and you were so pretty." She let out a chuckle. "I was so jealous of your green eyes and your dimples. I remember asking Dad why I got brown eyes and no holes in my cheeks."

Allie said nothing, just letting her talk, but her heart ached as she listened.

"I always wanted to be you," Megan said. "Dad wouldn't talk about your mother, so that made me all the more curious about what had happened to her. When I found out… I was half afraid when I met you, but then you were so sweet. And Natalie—" she waved a hand through the air, her face splitting into a huge smile "—I fell in love with her the moment I saw her. But I guess I was looking for cracks in your sanity even before Nick was killed and Mildred began telling me things. I'm sorry. Can you ever forgive me?"

Allie had thought that what she couldn't do was ever trust Megan again, especially with Natalie. But as she looked at her stepsister, she knew she had to for Natalie's sake. She rose from the chair and stepped to her sister to pull her into her arms.

They both began to cry, hugging each other tightly. There was something to this family thing, Allie thought. They might not be related by blood, but Allie couldn't cut Megan out of their lives, no matter where the future led them.

ALLIE WATCHED HER SISTER with Natalie and the kids. Megan, at twenty-three, was still a kid herself, she thought as she watched her playing tag with them. She knew she'd made the right decision and felt good about it.

She felt freer than she had in years. She'd also made up with Belinda. They would never be as close, not after her friend had kept her relationship with Nick from her. But they would remain friends and Allie was glad of it.

Belinda said she wanted her to meet the man in her life. Maybe Allie would, since it seemed that this time the relationship was serious.

Drew had tried to talk to her at the funeral, but she'd told him what she'd told his mother. She never wanted to see either of them again and with both of them leaving the canyon, she probably never would.

Beyond that, she didn't know. She would sell the cabin, Nick's pickup, everything she owned and start over. She just didn't know where yet, she thought as she saw Jackson coming up the mountainside.

He took off his Stetson as he approached the steps to her cabin and looked up at her. "Allie," he said. "I was hoping we could talk."

She motioned him up onto the porch. He looked so bashful. She smiled at the sight of his handsome face. The cowboy had saved her more times than she could count. He'd coming riding in on his white horse like something out of a fairytale and stolen her heart like an old-time outlaw.

"What did you want to talk about?" she asked. He seemed as tongue tied as Ford had been when he'd met Natalie.

"I…I…" He swallowed. "I love you."

Her eyes filled with tears. Those were the three little words she had ached to hear. Her heart pounded as she stepped to him. "I love you, Jackson."

He let out a whoop and picking her up, spun her around. As he set her down, he was still laughing. "Run away with me?"

"Anywhere."

"Texas?"

"If that's where you want to go."

"Well, here is the problem. You know my father, Harlan? I think he might just make a better grandfather than he ever did a father. I want Ford to have that."

She smiled. "Montana?"

"This is where I was born. I guess it is calling back my whole family. Did I tell you that my mother's new husband, Franklin, owns some land in the state? They're going to be spending half the year here. Hayes and McKenzie bought a place up the road and Tag and Lily will be living close by, as well. Dana said we can stay on the ranch until we find a place. The only thing we have to do is make sure our kids are in school next month."

"Montana it is then."

"Wait a minute." He looked shy again as he dropped to one knee. She noticed he had on new jeans and a nice Western dress shirt. Reaching into his pocket, he pulled out a ring box. "You're going to think I'm nuts. I bought this the day Tag and I went to pick up his rings for the wedding. I saw it and I thought, 'It's the same color as Allie's eyes.' Damned if I knew what I was going to do with it. Until now." He took a breath and let it out. "Would you marry me, Allie?"

She stared down at the beautiful emerald-green engagement ring set between two sparkling diamonds and felt her eyes widen. "It's the most beautiful thing I have ever seen."

He laughed. "No, honey, that would be you," he said as he put the ring on her finger, then drew her close and kissed her. "I can't wait to tell the kids. I have a feeling

Ford and Natalie are going to like living in Montana on their very own ranch, with their very own horses and lots of family around them."

Allie felt like pinching herself. She'd been through so much, but in the end she'd gotten something she'd never dreamed of, a loving man she could depend on and love with all her heart. For so long, she'd been afraid to hope that dreams could come true.

She smiled as Jackson took her hand and they went to tell the kids the news.

* * * * *

THE COWGIRL
IN QUESTION

I dedicate this book to my editor, Denise O'Sullivan.
Thank you for your faith, support and encouragement
over the years. It's a privilege to work with you.

PROLOGUE

Maybe if Forrest Danvers hadn't been half-drunk or spitting mad, he might have seen it coming.

But then he wasn't expecting any real trouble as he drove up Wild Horse Gulch in the late-night darkness.

The road cut through sheer rock cliffs, then opened to towering ponderosa pines before topping out on a sagebrush-studded bench that overlooked the Tongue River.

Forrest was a little uneasy, given his reason for being there in the first place. Nor did it help that the night was blacker than the inside of a boot and a storm was coming.

But he was feeling too good to go home yet. For the first time in his twenty-one years of miserable life, he felt he could be somebody. Somebody people respected. Not just another one of those no-count Danvers like his brother Cecil.

He parked his pickup on the bench above the river and rolled down his window, feeling closed in, anxious to hear the sound of the other vehicle coming up the narrow mountain road. She was late. As usual. *Women.*

The air had an edge to it, a kind of jittery current that set his nerves on end. He blamed the approaching thunderstorm and the lightning that flickered behind dark bruised clouds at the edge of the horizon.

It promised to be one hell of a storm. In this part of Montana, thunderstorms often swept across the vast open landscape, bringing wind that tore branches from the cottonwoods and rain as large and hard as stones that ran in torrents down the dry creek beds like rivers.

Beyond the closer smell of sagebrush and dust, he picked up the welcome scent of the coming rainstorm. It had been far too hot and dry this summer. The ground needed a good soaking and he needed to cool down in more ways than one.

It had been one hell of a night at the Mello Dee Lounge and Supper Club. At the memory, he flexed his right hand. It hurt like hell, the knuckles skinned and bloody. He smiled at the memory of his fist connecting with Rourke McCall's face.

Forrest could feel his left eye swelling shut. At least the cut over his right had stopped bleeding. That was something. And, he thought taking a shaky breath, his ribs hurt where he'd taken a punch, but Forrest had got in a few good licks himself.

Rourke McCall had just been itching for a fight. Forrest saw that now. Saw that he'd been a fool to oblige the crazy bastard. But what else could he have done? Just let Rourke cut in on the dance floor when Forrest was enjoying himself with Blaze Logan?

That was the problem with Rourke. He thought he owned Blaze, had ever since junior high. What a fool. Anyone with a pocketful of money could have Blaze—at least until the cash ran out.

Forrest rolled a cigarette, lit it and glanced at his watch before tossing the match to the floorboard. In that instant between light and darkness, he looked out and thought he saw someone silhouetted against the storm.

He stared into the darkness, unnerved until lightning lit the horizon and he could see that there was nothing out there but clumps of silver sage and sun-golden grasses bent to the breeze.

Just the booze playing tricks on him. He crushed out the last of his cigarette, wishing now he'd just gone home. Leaning back, he pulled his cowboy hat down over his face and closed his eyes. He was tired and sore and already feeling a little hungover. This had been a bad idea, but if she'd ever get here...

The night air felt good coming in through his open window. He half listened for the sound of the vehicle coming up the creek road, half dozed.

He'd dropped off into a deep, alcohol-drenched sleep when he was startled awake. At first all he heard was the whine of a vehicle engine coming up the road and the low rumble of thunder. Lightning flickered across the horizon, then died, leaving the night even darker.

But as he listened, he realized that wasn't what had awakened him.

He sat up a little, trying to place the sound. Then he heard it again. The soft scrape of boot leather brushing against sagebrush.

He sat up straight, pushed back his hat and, rubbing his hand over his face to wake up, stared out his open side window into the blackness.

The air seemed to change around him an instant before he saw the barrel of the pistol. Just a glint of blued steel appearing out of the night right next to him and the open window.

He stared at the gun, more than a little startled to realize that he really *wasn't* alone, probably hadn't been for most of the time he'd been sitting there.

He frowned, uncomprehending. In the distance, the sound of the vehicle coming up the road grew closer and closer.

For just a split second, the gun, the gloved hand holding it and the face of the person were illuminated in a flash of lightning. Just long enough for Forrest Danvers to face his killer.

"No!" The deafening boom of the gunshot drowned out his cry. He felt the burning heat as the lead entered his chest. The second shot exploded from the barrel of the gun. He barely noticed it. In the flare of the gunshot, he studied the killer's face, wanting to hang on to every familiar feature until they met again in hell.

CHAPTER ONE

Eleven years later

A STORM BLEW in the day Rourke McCall got out of prison.

At the Longhorn Café, Cassidy Miller brushed back an errant strand of hair from her face and tried to pretend it was just another day as she picked up the coffeepot and headed for the table in the corner now full of ranch hands from the VanHorn spread.

On the way, she made the mistake of looking out the window. The sky outside had turned dark and ominous, dust devils swirled in the street, the first drops of rain pelted the front window and streaked the glass.

Past the rain and dust, someone else was also staring out at the storm—and her. Blaze Logan stood at the window of the Antelope Development Corporation. Their eyes met across Main Street and Cassidy felt a chill rattle through her.

"I'll take a little more of that coffee, Cass," called Dub Morgan, the VanHorn Ranch foreman, from the table she'd been heading toward.

Cassidy dragged her gaze away from the window and Blaze, not realizing that she'd stopped walking, and took the pot of coffee over to the tableful of cowboys. But as she filled their coffee cups and joked and smiled, her mind was miles away in Deer Lodge, Montana, where Rourke

McCall, the wildest of the McCall boys, would be walking out the gate of the Montana State Prison this morning.

None of her patrons had mentioned it, but everyone in town knew. That was one reason the café was packed this morning and she'd had to call in an extra waitress.

Everyone was wondering if Rourke would come back to town and make good on the threat he'd made against her eleven years ago.

As he was being dragged out of the courtroom in handcuffs, he had called back to Cassidy, "I know you framed me. I'm going to get out and, when I do, I'll be back for you."

The judge had given him twenty-five years but Rourke was walking out a free man after only eleven. For most of those years, Rourke had worked the prison's cattle ranch. Ironic since he'd hated working the family ranch and done everything possible to avoid it in all the years Cassidy had known him.

Good behavior, the warden had told the parole board. "Rourke McCall is a changed man. A reformed man. He is no longer a threat to society."

No, he was only a threat to Cassidy Miller—no matter what he told the parole board or the warden.

"You okay, honey?" Ellie whispered, slowing as she passed Cassidy with an armload of plates headed for the VanHorn Ranch table.

Cassie nodded and glanced outside again, trying to imagine what it would be like seeing Rourke after all these years. Maybe he really was a changed man. Maybe he was reformed. Maybe he'd forgotten his threat against her.

But even as she thought it, she knew better. Rourke McCall might have fooled the prison officials but he couldn't fool her.

The bell dinged indicating that an order was up. She

moved toward the kitchen, determined to keep up a good front. She didn't want anyone to know she'd been dreading this day for eleven years. Or the real reason why.

ACROSS THE STREET, Blaze Logan stood at the window watching the crowd at the Longhorn Café and smiling to herself. How appropriate that one hell of a thunderstorm would hit town just before Rourke McCall did.

She could sense the change in the air, smell the rain and expectation, hear the hush that had fallen over Antelope Flats, Montana. She loved nothing better than a good knock-down, drag-out fight. She'd had that and more the night Forrest Danvers was murdered and she was ready for the hell Rourke was going to cause when he got back.

As she caught another glimpse of Cassidy Miller through the café window across the street, her smile broadened. Cassidy. The good girl and a thorn in Blaze's side since they were kids. Her cousin Cassidy had always been the perfect one. She now owned her own business, was president of the chamber of commerce, helped with every damned fund-raiser in town. No one ever had a bad word to say about her.

"Why can't you be more like Cassidy?" her father had said from as far back as Blaze could remember.

She and Cassidy competed against each other in regional rodeos and Cassidy always won, and Blaze always threw a fit when she lost.

"You could learn something about being a good sport from your cousin," her father would say.

But Blaze knew she should have won, had to win, was expected to win because her great-grandmother had been a trick rider with a Wild West show. Her cousin Cassidy's great-grandmother was nobody.

"Even when Cassidy loses, she's gracious," her father would say.

Yeah, well that was because Cassidy seldom lost at anything.

Except when it came to Rourke McCall. Blaze had felt not even a twinge of guilt when Cassidy had confessed back in junior high that her dream was to someday marry Rourke McCall.

Blaze had never paid much attention to Rourke before that. He was tall, sandy-blond with blue eyes and a temper. At the time, he'd been a teenager, moody and full of himself. She could tell by looking at him even back then that he would never amount to anything.

But Blaze was already developing and boys were noticing. Cassidy, on the other hand, was two years younger, and a tomboy.

Getting Rourke to notice her had been a piece of cake for Blaze, who hadn't really liked him but wanted to win just once. As it turned out, she'd not only beaten Cassidy, she'd ruined any chance her cousin ever had of ending up with Rourke McCall.

Blaze stared across the street, catching glimpses of Cassidy as she worked. Blaze still resented her. Probably because Blaze's father still threw Cassidy up to her.

The worst fight she'd ever had with her father was over Cassidy.

"My whole life you've compared me to Cassidy," she'd cried. "I'm sick of it. I'm nothing like her and I'm glad."

Her father had nodded ruefully. "No, you're right, you're nothing like your cousin. She's doing something with her life. She doesn't just live off her parents."

"Her daddy ran off and her mother is poor," Blaze had retorted. "We're not."

"*I'm* not," John Logan had snapped. "You, my daughter, are going to get a job and start growing up."

"What are you saying?"

"I'm cutting you off. No more money. You're on your own."

Blaze hadn't been able to believe her ears. She'd always been her father's favorite between her and her stepbrother, Gavin Shaw. How could her father turn against her like this? "You're doing this because of Cassidy."

He just shook his head. "You've always put your cousin Cassidy down, but it wouldn't hurt you to be a little more like her."

Well, Blaze thought wryly, she was damned glad she wasn't Cassidy now. She wouldn't want to be in that woman's shoes for anything. Not today. Not with Rourke getting out of prison and coming back to even the score.

No way was Rourke going to let Cassidy Miller get away with what she'd done to him. Blaze was almost rubbing her hands together in her excitement. Antelope Flats had been too dull for too long, but Rourke McCall was about to change all of that.

Unless *he* was the one who'd changed. Unless all that good behavior that got him released early *wasn't* an act. The thought ruined her day. What if he didn't come back? What if he really had put the past to rest?

No, not the Rourke McCall she'd known, she assured herself. He'd just sold all of that bull to the warden so he could get out early. Good behavior and Rourke McCall... The two had never gone together, she thought smiling again.

Poor Cassidy Miller. Blaze couldn't wait. Finally her cousin was going to get her comeuppance. It couldn't happen to a nicer person.

ROURKE MCCALL WALKED out of Montana State Prison, stopped and, looking up at the wide blue sky, took a deep breath of freedom.

Eleven years. Eleven years of his life.

He heard his little brother get out of the pickup and come toward him. Lowering his gaze from the sky, he took Brandon's outstretched hand and shook it firmly, smiling at the youngest of his brothers. Of his family, only Brandon and their little sister Dusty had kept in touch with him on a regular basis, and Dusty only on the Q.T. since their father had forbidden it.

"You have any plans?" Brandon asked as he led the way to one of the ranch pickups.

Rourke stopped to study the graphic painted on the pickup door. The words Sundown Ranch were printed over the top of the longhorn in a stylized print. New. He liked the old, more simple script that had been on the trucks since his grandfather's time much better, but he was sure that a lot of things had changed in the eleven years he'd been gone.

"I mean, if you don't have any plans, I have a few things going I could let you in on," Brandon said as he opened the driver's door and climbed behind the wheel.

Rourke got in the passenger side. Yeah, a lot of things had changed. He tried to remember if he'd ever ridden with Brandon, who was only nineteen when Rourke had gone to prison. Rourke had only been twenty-two himself. "What kind of things?"

Brandon smiled. "Moneymaking."

Rourke shook his head and leaned back against the seat, adjusting his cowboy hat. "Thanks, but I have plans."

He could feel Brandon's eyes on him. Unlike the warden, Brandon wouldn't even attempt to give him a pep talk about letting go of the past, starting over, looking at this as a new beginning, forgetting he'd been framed for murder and had just spent eleven years of his life in prison because of it.

He closed his eyes and let the sound of the tires on the pavement lull him. He was free. Finally. Free to do what he'd promised himself he would do all those nights in prison.

He didn't wake up until the pickup left the highway and bumped onto the dirt road. He didn't need to open his eyes to know exactly where they were. He'd been down this road enough times to remember every hill and turn and bump. How many times at night in his prison cell had he lain awake thinking about the day he would drive down this road again?

He opened his eyes and rolled down his window, realizing he'd forgotten the exact smell of the sage, the sun-baked earth and summer-dried grasses, the scent of the cool pines and the creek.

He'd forgotten too how much he loved this land. The red rock bluffs, the silken green of the ponderosa trees etched against the summer blue of the sky or the deep gold of the grass, tops heavy, bobbing in the breeze.

McCall Country. Miles and miles dotted with cattle that had been driven up here from Texas by his great-great-grandfather when this country was foreign and dangerous and full of promise.

His memory hadn't done it justice. White puffs of clouds scudded across a canvas of endless deep blue as the pickup raced along the muddy dirt road, still wet from an earlier rain. Chokecherries, dark as blood, bent the limbs of the bushes along the creek as the summer golden grasses undulated in waves over the rolling hills. And above a narrow draw, turkey buzzards circled, black wings flapping slowly over something dead below.

Rourke fought that old feeling of awe and ownership. He stared out, feeling the generations of men before him who had fought for this land, feeling its pull, its allure and the price of that enticement. No matter how he felt about his old man or how Asa McCall felt about him, Rourke was a McCall and always would be.

The pickup dropped over a rise and he saw it. The Sundown Ranch house. It seemed a mirage shimmering in the afternoon sunlight.

Rourke caught his breath, surprised by the ache in his chest, the knot in his throat. When he'd left here in handcuffs, he hadn't looked back. Afraid he would never see it again if he did.

"We had a hell of thunderstorm here this morning," Brandon said.

Rourke could feel nervous waves of energy coming off his brother as they neared the ranch. No doubt Brandon was worried about the reception the two of them would get. Rourke doubted Brandon had told their father that he was picking up the first McCall to ever go to prison.

Brandon slowed the truck, pulled up in the yard and parked. Rourke sat for a moment after the engine died just looking at the ranch house, reliving memories, the good mixed with the bad, all treasured now.

The house seemed larger than even he remembered it: the logs more golden, the tan rock fireplace chimney towering above the roofline more majestic, the porch stretching across the entire front of the building, endless.

"I've got some business in town, but I'll catch you later," Brandon said, obviously anxious to get going. "Your pickup's over there. Still runs good. I took care of it for you. Left the keys in the ignition."

"Thanks," Rourke said, looking over at his little brother, and extended his hand. "I appreciate everything you've done and thanks for coming up to get me."

"No problem," Brandon said, shaking his hand, then looking at his watch, fiddling with the band.

Rourke studied his little brother. "You're not in any kind of trouble, are you?"

"No," Brandon said too quickly. "I'm fine."

"These investments you were talking about, they're legal, right?" Rourke asked, seeing something in his brother that worried him.

Brandon fiddled with the gearshift, seeming to avoid his gaze. "Hey, it isn't like that, okay?"

It was something, Rourke thought. Something that equaled trouble, sure as hell. "If you need help for any reason—"

"Stop acting like a big brother," Brandon said, then softened his words. "I'm okay. I can take care of myself."

Rourke climbed out of the truck and Brandon took off in a cloud of dust. He watched him leave, wondering how deep Brandon was in. And to whom.

As the sound of the ranch pickup engine died off in the distance, Rourke heard the front door of the house open, heard the solid thump of boot soles on the pine floorboards and knew before he turned that it would be his father.

Asa McCall had always been a big man, tall and broad and muscular. He'd also always been a hard man, mule stubborn, the undisputed head of the McCall clan, his word the last one.

The years hadn't changed him much that Rourke could see. He was still large, rawboned, still looked strong even at sixty-eight. The hair at his temples was no longer blond but gray, the lines around his eyes a little deeper, the sun-weathered face still granite hard and unforgiving.

They stared at each other as Rourke slung his duffel over one shoulder.

"So they let you out," Asa McCall said, his deep voice carrying across the wide porch.

Rourke said nothing. There was nothing to say. He'd

told the old man he was innocent eleven years ago and hadn't been believed. Not Rourke McCall, the wildest Mc-Call.

"Don't worry, I'm not staying," Rourke said. "I just came by to pick up my things."

Asa McCall nodded. Neither moved for a few moments, then Rourke mounted the steps and walked past his father and into the ranch house without a word or a look, torn between anger and regret.

As he stepped through the front door, he saw that nothing had changed from the Native American rugs on the hardwood floors to the Western furnishings and huge rock fireplace.

He turned at a sound and was struck by the sight of a pretty young woman coming out of the kitchen. She stopped, her eyes widening. A huge smile lit her face as she came running at him, throwing herself into his arms.

"Rourke," she cried. "Oh, I'm so glad you're back."

He stepped away to hold her at arm's length to study his little sister. "Dusty? I can't believe it."

She'd been six when he'd left, a kid. Now she was a woman, although it was pretty well hidden. She wore boys' jeans, a shapeless Western shirt and boots. Her long blond hair was woven in a single braid down her back and a straw cowboy hat hung from a string around her neck. She wore no makeup.

"Dusty?"

Neither had heard the front door open. They both turned to find their father filling the doorway.

"We got fencing to see to," Asa said, and turned, letting the door slam behind him.

Rourke listened to his father's boots pound across the porch. "You best get going. We can visit later. I'll let you know where I'm staying in town."

"You're not staying here?" Dusty cried.

Rourke gave her a look.

"Daddy is so impossible," she said, sounding like the teenager she was. "I swear he gets more stubborn every day."

Rourke could believe that. "Where's everyone else?"

"Cash lives in town. You know he's still the sheriff?"

Rourke nodded.

"J.T. is running the ranch now, but Daddy and I help. Brandon is hardly ever around. J.T. is probably still out riding fence this morning. Did Brandon leave?"

"He said he had business in town," Rourke told his sister.

She nodded and frowned. "I hate to think what kind of business. Daddy says he's headed for trouble and I'm afraid he might be right."

Headed for trouble. That's what Asa used to say about him, Rourke thought.

"I'm so glad you're finally home," Dusty said, and stood on tiptoe to give him a kiss on the cheek before closing the front door behind her.

He watched Dusty join their father out in the yard, watched her walk past the old man. Rourke had to smile, recognizing the familiar anger and stubbornness in the set of her shoulders, the tilt of her head. The old man shook his own head as she sashayed past him, giving him the silent treatment just as she'd done to them all when she was mad as a child.

When Asa finally followed after her, he looked older, almost sad, as if another defiant kid would be the death of him.

Rourke's smile faded as he watched his father follow Dusty to one of the ranch pickups. He stayed there at the window until they'd driven away, then he turned and climbed the wide staircase at the center of the room. At the top, the second floor branched out in two wings. Rourke walked down the wood-floored hallway to his old room at the end of the west corridor. He tried the door, wondering if his stuff had been moved out, the room used for something else.

But as the door swung in, he saw that his room was exactly the same as it had been when he'd left eleven years before. He expected the room to smell musty, at least be covered in dust. But neither was the case. Asa must have had the housekeeper clean it each week. What the hell?

He dropped his duffel on the log-framed bed and looked around, spotting the small straw cowboy hat he'd worn the day he'd won his first rodeo event at the age of seven. His first real chaps, a birthday present for his first cattle drive at the age of nine. His first baseball glove. All gifts from his father, placed on the high shelf Asa had built to store memories.

"In the end, that's what life comes down to," his father had told him the day he'd built the shelf. "Memories. Good and bad, they're all you will ever really own, they're all that are uniquely yours and ultimately all you can take with you."

"You think Mom took memories of us to heaven with her?" Rourke had asked, looking up at his father.

Asa's weathered face had crinkled into a smile, tears in his blue eyes. "She could never forget her kids," he said without hesitation. "Never."

"Or you, Dad. I'll bet she remembers you." It was the one time he'd ever seen his father cry, and only for those few moments before Asa could get turned and hightail it out to the barn.

Rourke walked through the bedroom, past the sitting room, to open the patio doors that led to the small bal-

cony off the back. Stepping out, he gulped the afternoon
air, the familiarity of it only making the lump in his throat
harder to swallow.

As he looked out across the ranch, he spotted his brother
J.T. riding in. Rourke watched him until J.T. disappeared
behind one of the red-roofed barns, then he turned and
went back inside.

Too many memories. Too many regrets.

He looked up again at the high shelf and all his trophies
from first grade through high school for every damned
thing from best stick drawing to debate, basketball to bull
riding, baseball to target practice. And not a lick of dust
on any of them.

He shook his head, not understanding himself any better than he did his father. He'd been wild from the time
he could walk, bucking authority, getting in trouble, but
somehow he'd managed to excel in spite of it. He got good
grades without trying. Athletics came easy, as well. In fact,
he thought, studying the trophies on the shelf, maybe that
was the problem. Everything had always come too easily.

He glanced around the room suddenly wondering why
he'd come back here. Not to get his things. He hadn't left
anything here he needed. His grandfather had left all of
them money, money Rourke had never touched. He could
buy anything he needed for this new life the warden had
tried to sell him on. He didn't even need his old pickup.
Hell, it was fifteen years old.

But he couldn't leave without taking something. He
went to the chest of drawers, opened several and took out
jeans, underwear, socks, a couple of once-favorite T-shirts
he knew he would never wear again and stuffed them into
the duffel bag, zipping it closed.

Then he picked up the duffel bag and started to leave
the room. His throat tightened again as he turned and spot-

ted the faded photograph stuck in the edge of the mirror over the bureau.

It was a snapshot of Blaze and Cassidy.

He dropped the duffel bag on the bed and walked to the mirror. Blaze with her mass of long, curly fire-engine-red hair and lush body standing next to her cousin at the rodeo grounds. Blaze nineteen and full of herself, he thought with a smile.

His gaze shifted to Cassidy and the smile evaporated. Cassidy looked plain next to Blaze, with her brown hair and big brown eyes peering out of the shadow of her cowboy hat. Blaze was smiling at the camera, her hat pushed back. She was smiling at him behind the camera, flirting, being Blaze.

But Cassidy was leaning back against the fence, head angled down, peering out at the camera and him from under the brim of the hat, not smiling. Not even close. Her brown eyes were narrowed in an expression he hadn't even noticed. Probably because he'd only had eyes for Blaze.

Now, though, he recognized the expression. Anger. Cassidy Miller had been furious with him.

He swore and plucked the picture from the edge of the mirror, remembering when he'd taken it. Only a week before Forrest Danvers's murder.

Stuffing the photo into the duffel along with the clothes, he zipped it closed again and walked out of the room as he'd done eleven years ago, slamming the door behind him. He'd waited eleven years for this day. He couldn't wait to see Cassidy.

CHAPTER TWO

CECIL DANVERS WOKE that afternoon with the worst hangover of his life. He rolled off the soiled cot he called a bed and stumbled to the rusted refrigerator for his first beer of the day.

He'd downed most of the can when he remembered what day it was. He stood in front of the fridge, listening to it running, waiting for the sweet feel of justified anger.

For the past eleven years, he'd plotted and planned for this day, but now that it was here, he had trouble working up the murderous rage he'd spent years nurturing.

Rourke McCall was to blame for every bad thing that had happened to him since the night his brother Forrest was murdered.

A lot of people in the county didn't understand; they just thought Cecil was lazy, that he'd lived off Forrest's death all these years. They just didn't understand what it had been like to lose his only little brother, especially one who'd always taken care of him.

Cecil finished his beer, burped loudly and smashed the can in his fist before hurling it toward the trash can.

No matter what anyone said, he knew his life would have been better if Forrest had lived. He certainly wouldn't be living in this rathole on the tiny patch of land his mother had left him, living in the old homestead cabin that was falling down around his ears.

Nope. Forrest would have seen that he was taken care of.

After all, Forrest was the smart one, the strong one. Hadn't their old man always said so?

"Forrest is going to make something of his life," the old man would say. "And if you're lucky, Cecil, he'll take care of your sorry ass, as well."

Now he had no one, Cecil thought as he opened the fridge and downed another beer, his eyes narrowing, stomach churning. His father had died right after Forrest's murder. A farming accident. Happened all the time. Cecil's mother hadn't been far behind him. She was always moping around, crying over Forrest as if Forrest had been her only son.

Cecil shoved the memories away and concentrated on Rourke McCall. Yep, if it hadn't been for Rourke, Cecil wouldn't be forced to work when he ran out of money, mucking out other people's horse barns or swabbing the local bars after hours.

He downed the rest of the beer, crushing the can in his fist and throwing it in the general direction of the trash can. Everyone in town was going to say that Rourke McCall had paid his debt to society for killing Forrest.

They'd tell Cecil to forget it, just as they had for the past eleven years. But people had always underestimated him, he thought grimly. He was the last of his family. It was up to him now. Rourke McCall had ruined his life and Cecil wasn't about to let him get away with it.

ROURKE HAD JUST put his duffel on the seat of his pickup and was about to climb in when he saw his brother J.T. lead a large bay mare into the barn.

"Might as well get it over with," he said under his breath, and walked toward the barn.

J.T. looked up as Rourke entered the cool darkness of the horse barn. The smell of horseflesh and leather, hay and manure filled his senses, sending him back to those cold mornings when he was barely old enough to walk. He and his father would come out here.

Asa would saddle up a horse, then lift Rourke in one strong arm and swing up into the saddle. Together they would ride fence until long after the dew on the grasses dried, the sun rising high and warm over the ranch and the sound of the breakfast bell pealing in the air.

Rourke breathed in the memory as he watched his brother unsaddle the bay, more recent memories of the prison barn trying to crowd in.

"Rourke," J.T. said, looking up as he swung the saddle off. "Welcome home. So you're back."

He'd heard more heartwarming welcomes. "Thanks."

His brother studied him. "You staying?"

He shook his head.

J.T. made a face and started to walk past him.

"The old man doesn't want me here. Remember? He disinherited me. I'm not his son anymore."

J.T. sighed, stopped and turned. "He was upset. He didn't even do the paperwork. You aren't disinherited. You never were."

Rourke tried to hide his surprise.

"You know how he is," J.T. continued. "Says things when he's mad that he doesn't mean."

"Yeah, well, I just saw him and I didn't get the impression he'd changed his mind."

"He also can't say he's sorry any better than you can," J.T. said.

Rourke had been compared to his father all his life. He hated to think he might really be like Asa McCall. As if he didn't have enough problems.

"I assume you heard he had a heart attack," J.T. said. "He can't work the ranch like he used to. I'm doing the best I can with Buck's help, hiring hands for branding, calving and moving cattle to and from summer range. But Dad's going to kill himself if his sons don't start helping him."

Buck Brannigan was a fixture of the ranch. Once the ranch foreman, he was getting up in age and probably didn't do any more than give orders.

Rourke looked out the barn door, squinting into the sunlight. "Dad would rather die working than rocking on the porch. Anyway, he's got other sons."

J.T. swore. "I'd hoped you might settle down, move back here and help out."

Rourke shook his head. "Even if the old man would let me, I'm not ready right now."

"You're determined to stir it all back up, aren't you?"

"Someone owes me eleven years," Rourke said.

"Well, even if you do prove that you were framed, those years are gone," J.T. said. "So how many more years are you going to waste?"

"I didn't kill Forrest."

"Don't you think Cash tried to find evidence that would have freed you?" J.T. demanded. "Hell, Rourke, a team of experts from the state marshal's office were down here for weeks investigating this case, but you think that, after eleven years, you're going to come home and find the killer on your own?" J.T. shook his head in disgust, turned and walked off.

Not on his own. He was going to have help, he thought as he rubbed the mare's muzzle and thought of Cassidy Miller. He'd kissed her right here in this barn when she was thirteen.

Another memory quickly replaced it. Cassidy on the witness stand testifying at his trial.

"So THE DEFENDANT read the note that had been left on his pickup windshield and then what did he do?" the prosecutor, Reece Corwin, had asked her.

Cassidy hesitated.

"Remember you are under oath. Just tell the truth."

Rourke could see that she was nervous, close to tears. Her gaze came to his, then skittered away.

"He dropped the note, opened his pickup door, got in and drove away," she said.

"Oh, come on, Miss Miller, didn't the defendant ball up the note, throw it down, jerk open his pickup door so hard it wouldn't close properly the next day and didn't he drive out of the bar parking lot spitting gravel? Didn't he almost hit several people coming out of the bar?"

"Objection!" Rourke's lawyer, Hal Rafferty, had cried, getting to his feet. "He's telling her what to say."

"Overruled. We've heard this from other witnesses. Answer the question," the judge instructed Cassidy. "And Mr. Corwin, please move on."

"Yes," Cassidy said, voice barely audible.

"And what did you hear him say before he left?" the prosecutor asked. This part was new. This part would put the nail in Rourke's coffin.

Cassidy licked her lips, her eyes welling with tears as she looked at Rourke. "He said, 'I'll kill you, Forrest.'"

"Speak up, Miss Miller."

"He said, 'I'll kill you, Forrest.' But he didn't mean it. He was just—"

"Thank you. No more questions."

Cassidy had left out one important point his lawyer had been forced to remind her of on cross-examination.

"Who wrote the note that was left on my client's pickup windshield, Miss Miller?" Hal Rafferty had asked.

Again tears. "I did."

"And what did that note say?"

Cassidy twisted her hands in her lap, eyes down. "Blaze is meeting Forrest up Wild Horse Gulch."

"You *sent* my client to the murder scene?" Rafferty demanded.

"Objection. There was no murder scene until your client got there."

"Sustained."

"Why did you write that note, Miss Miller?" the attorney demanded.

She stared down at her hands, crying now, shaking her head.

"What did you hope to gain by doing that?" Rafferty asked.

Again a head shake.

"Answer the question, Miss Miller," the judge instructed.

"I don't know why I did it."

"Did someone instruct you to do it?" the attorney asked.

Her head came up. Rourke saw her startled expression. "No. I...just did it on impulse. I thought he should know what Blaze was...doing."

"You a friend of Rourke McCall's?"

She looked at Rourke, then the attorney, and shook her head.

"You were just trying to do him a favor?" the attorney asked. "Or were you trying to set him up for a murder?"

"No." Cassidy had burst into tears. She'd been just a girl, sixteen going on seventeen, shy and gangly. The jury hadn't believed that anyone like Cassidy Miller could have set him up.

"Who put you up to it?" the attorney demanded. "Who?"

"No one did."

But Rourke knew better. Cassidy had left the note. He would never have gone up to Wild Horse Gulch if she hadn't. He wouldn't have been framed for murder.

What he didn't know was why. Or who'd put her up to it.

But he was finally out of prison, finally back, and he was finally going to get the truth out of Cassidy Miller.

As THE AFTERNOON dragged on, Blaze Logan found herself pacing in front of the Antelope Development Corporation window, or ADC as it was known around the county.

"Sit down, Blaze," Easton Wells finally snapped. "You're making me nervous as hell."

She turned from the window to look at her boss. Easton Wells was thirty-nine, a little old for her in more ways than the nine years between them. He had dark hair and eyes, not bad-looking but nothing like Rourke McCall. Nothing at all. And that was part of Easton's charm. He had a good future, was divorced—no alimony or children, his ex-wife on another continent and not coming back—and Easton thought Blaze was the hottest thing going.

What could she say? She loved it.

But he didn't want to marry her. Not yet, anyway.

"What if Rourke doesn't come back to town?" she lamented out loud.

"I wouldn't blame him," Easton said, not looking up from the papers on his desk. ADC was small, a reception area and the larger office that she and Easton shared.

Blaze shifted her focus from across the street to her own reflection in the large front window. She turned to get a side view, liking what she saw, but she wasn't getting any younger. She was thirty. Almost thirty-one! She needed to think about marriage. And soon. And Rourke's getting out of prison had given her the answer.

"Rourke will bring a little life to this town," she said, trying to get a rise out of Easton. "I, for one, think the diversion will be good. I know I'm getting tired of the status quo."

Easton looked up and shook his head. "I know what you're trying to do and it isn't going to work."

"What?" she asked innocently. She'd been dating Easton for years now off and on. Believing a woman should always keep her options open, she'd also seen Sheriff Cash McCall a few times. She'd had to initiate the impromptu dates with Cash. Like all the McCalls, he was stubborn and dense as a post. She'd had to practically throw herself at him to even get him to notice her.

Easton wasn't dense. He just didn't want to get married again. But she intended to change that. And Rourke was going to help her. He just didn't know it yet.

"You're trying to make me jealous," Easton said.

She smiled and stepped over to his desk, placed both palms down on the solid oak surface and leaned toward him, making sure her silk blouse opened at the top so he got a tempting view of the cleavage bursting from her push-up bra.

"East, we both know there isn't a jealous bone in your body," she said in her most seductive voice.

He looked up, halting on the view in the V of her blouse appreciatively before looking up into her face.

"It would be a mistake to fool with Rourke," he said, looking way too serious. That was another problem with Easton. He took everything too seriously, like work. He often got mad at her because she was late in the mornings or took too long at lunch or didn't finish some job he'd given her or spent too much time on the phone.

"If I were you, I'd steer clear of Rourke," Easton said.

"Would you?" she asked, lifting a brow as she studied him. "Why, East, you and Rourke used to be best friends."

He nodded. "A long time ago. I'm sure Rourke has changed. I know I have."

Not for the better necessarily, Blaze thought.

"I think you're just mad at Asa. You wouldn't even be in business if he'd gotten his way." Asa had campaigned with all his power and money against coal-bed methane drilling in his part of Montana. "But you beat him."

Easton shook his head. "Asa McCall is never beaten. All I did was make an enemy of him, which is a very dangerous thing to do."

"And just think how much money you've made because of it," she purred.

"Like I said, I wouldn't mess with any of the McCalls if I were you. You don't want that kind of wrath brought down on you."

She studied him, a little surprised. Easton didn't scare easily. "You make it sound as if the McCalls have done something to you."

"I just wouldn't want any of them to have a reason to come gunning for me," Easton said.

Blaze straightened, a frown furrowing her brows. "Is there any reason Rourke would come after you?"

He looked up at her. "Don't you have work to do?"

"If anyone should fear Rourke it's my cousin Cassidy," she said, going over to the window to look out at the Longhorn Café again.

"You aren't on that kick again." He groaned. "You can't believe that Cassidy set him up for murder."

"Does it matter if she did or didn't as long as Rourke *thinks* she did?"

"It might to Rourke," Easton said behind her. "You're counting on him being that hothead who left here. But it's been eleven years, Blaze. He isn't going to come back the same man who left. He just might surprise you. Instead of going off half-cocked, he might have had time to figure out some things about the night Forrest was murdered."

"You think Rourke is going to blame *me?*" She let out

a laugh and turned to look at him. "Rourke was crazy in love with me."

"*Was* being the key word here," Easton said without looking up at her.

She glared daggers at him. "I take it back. I think you *are* jealous. Or afraid that Rourke might find out something about you. Let's not forget that you're sleeping with me now. Are you worried that Rourke won't like that?"

Easton laughed without bothering to look up. "I think Rourke probably learned his lesson with Forrest."

"What does *that* mean?" she demanded.

"It means Rourke won't be killing any more men who you've slept with. Anyway, where would he start?" Easton laughed.

She continued to glare at him, but he didn't look up. "Let's not forget that you were at the Mello Dee, too, the night Forrest was murdered."

Easton finally looked up at her, his eyes dark. "Yes, I witnessed the way you work men, Blaze. I saw how you got Forrest to dance with you to make Rourke jealous. I know how you operate."

He was making her angry, but she hated to show it, hated to let him know that he was getting to her. She also didn't like the fact that he thought he knew her. In fact, was wise to some of her methods when it came to men.

"You're afraid of Rourke," she challenged, wondering if she'd hit a nerve or if it was just simple jealousy. "Is there something you wanted to tell me about that night?"

Easton shot her a pitying look. "I had no reason to kill Forrest Danvers. Can you say the same thing?"

"I couldn't kill anyone," she cried, but right now the thought of shooting Easton did have its appeal.

"Take my advice," he said, going back to the work at

his desk. "Stay away from Rourke. It isn't going to make me jealous, but it might make you regret it."

"That almost sounds like a threat."

"I'm trying to save you from yourself, Blaze," he said with a bored sigh. "But I'm not sure anyone can do that."

Blaze turned her back on him again, wondering what she saw in the man. Little, other than what he could afford her, she told herself. And he'd always wanted her. No matter what he said, he'd been jealous of her and Rourke.

She turned her attention back to the Longhorn Café and her cousin Cassidy.

Easton was right about one thing. Blaze *had* danced with Forrest to make Rourke jealous—and to see what he would do. She hadn't expected Forrest to fight him. Nor had she expected Rourke to kill Forrest up at Wild Horse Gulch. At least that was her story and she was sticking to it.

But what if Rourke wasn't that hotheaded bad boy Mc-Call anymore? She hated to imagine. No, Rourke would come back hell-bent over the past eleven years he'd spent in prison, and he'd make a show of looking for the "real" killer, then he'd go berserk one night and end up back in prison. He wouldn't be here long enough to find out much of anything about the night Forrest was murdered.

She realized she could make sure of that—once she and Rourke took up where they'd left off. She would keep him so busy he would have little time to be digging into the past. And that way she'd know exactly what Rourke was finding out about the night Forrest was murdered. She'd make sure he didn't find out anything she didn't want him to. He wasn't messing up her future. She'd see to that.

She caught a glimpse of a pickup she remembered only too well from years ago. Her pulse jumped. Rourke McCall. That pickup brought a rush of memories as Rourke drove slowly up Main Street.

As the pickup passed her window, all she saw of him was his silhouette, cowboy hat, broad shoulders, big hands on the wheel, but there was no doubt about it. Rourke was back in town.

She waved excitedly, but unfortunately he was looking in the direction of the Longhorn Café—and Cassidy. Blaze let out an unladylike curse.

Wasn't this what she wanted? Rourke back? Rourke set on getting even with Cassidy? But just the thought of Rourke interested in Cassidy for any reason set her teeth on edge.

"What?" Easton said impatiently behind her.

She turned to smile at him. "Rourke. He's back."

Easton couldn't have looked more upset and she realized she had him right where she wanted him. Soon she'd have Rourke where she wanted him, too.

If Easton didn't ask her to marry him by the end of the week then her name wasn't Blaze Logan.

But as she looked at her future fiancé, she had a bad feeling he was hiding something from her.

HOLT VANHORN PICKED UP one of his father's prized bronzes from the den end table and hefted it in his hand. The bronze was of a cowboy in chaps and duster, a bridle in his hand as if headed out to saddle his horse, his hat low on his head, bent a little as if against a stiff, cold breeze. Holt had little appreciation for art. What interested him was the fact that the bronze was heavy enough to kill someone.

"Holt?"

He turned, surprised he hadn't heard his father come into the den. Mason VanHorn was frowning and Holt realized his father's gaze wasn't on him but on the bronze Holt had clutched in his fist.

He put down the work of art carefully, avoiding his

father's eye. For his thirty years of life he'd been afraid Mason could read his thoughts. It would definitely explain the animosity between them if that were the case.

"So what brings you out to the ranch, Junior?" Mason asked as he walked around his massive oak desk to sit down.

Holt heard the bitterness behind the question. Mason had never gotten over the fact that his only son hated ranching and if he could get his hands on the land, would subdivide it in a heartbeat and move to someplace tropical.

Holt had moved off the ranch as soon as he could, living on the too-small trust fund his grandfather had left him and what few crumbs Mason had thrown him over the years.

His father didn't offer him a chair. Or a drink. Holt could have used the drink at least.

Mason VanHorn was a big man, broad-shouldered with black hair streaked with gray, heavy gray brows over ebony eyes that could pierce through you faster and more painfully than a steel drill bit.

Holt looked nothing like his father, something that he knew Mason regretted deeply. Instead, Holt had taken after his mother, a small, frail blonde woman with diluted green eyes and a predilection for alcohol. His mother had been lucky, though. The alcohol had killed her by fifty. At only thirty, Holt didn't see an end in sight. At least not as long as his father kept the purse strings gripped in his iron fist.

"I need to go away for a while." Holt's voice broke and he saw his father's startled expression.

"Away where?" Mason asked.

Holt shook his head. The massive desk was between them. He had the stronger urge to shove it aside and go for his father's throat but, he thought wryly, with his luck, the desk wouldn't budge and he'd crash into it and break something. He was good at breaking things. Clumsy as an oaf, he'd once heard his father tell his mother after he had managed to break another bone. If he hadn't been aware of his father's disappointment in his only son, he certainly was then.

"I…" The words seemed to catch in his throat as if barbed, and he hated his father even more for making him feel like a boy again in his presence. "I just need to get out of town for a while."

"Where?"

Anywhere. As far away as he could get from Antelope Flats, Montana. "I'd like to go down to Texas. Maybe go back to school." He was grabbing at anything he could think of.

"What is this really about?" Mason VanHorn demanded.

His father always saw through him. Mason VanHorn held the purse strings, so he also had a stranglehold on Holt's life.

"Please just give me enough money to—"

"Is this about Rourke getting out of prison today?" Mason demanded.

Holt heard the disgust in his father's voice, saw the worry in his face. No, not worry, the affirmation of what his father had suspected for years.

"All I need is enough money to tide me over—"

"VanHorns don't run like cowards," his father said through clenched teeth.

"Right." Holt saw then that his father would freeze in hell before he'd help him get away from here. "Never mind. I should have known you wouldn't help me."

He turned too quickly, bumping into the end table. The table overturned. The bronze cowboy hit the tile floor with a crash and a curse from his father.

Holt didn't stop to pick up the bronze or the table. He

headed for the door, wondering how far he could go on thirty-seven dollars and fifty-two cents.

"If you run, everyone will know you have something to hide," Mason VanHorn yelled after him.

CHAPTER THREE

CASSIDY HAD NEVER run from anything in her life. But as she stood in the kitchen of the Longhorn Café smelling the freshly baked rolls that had just come out of the oven, every instinct told her to take off. Now.

Rourke was back. She could feel it. The rest of the town seemed to have given up on him. The café had cleared out as the day dragged on and he hadn't shown. Ellie was taking care of what few customers were left. Cassidy had gone into the kitchen to help Arthur, her cook, who was working on the nightly dinner special.

Trying to keep to her usual routine, Cassidy made the dinner rolls for that evening. She liked cooking and baking. Especially making bread. She could work out even the worst mood kneading dough.

But it didn't work today. Nothing worked. And she knew she had to get out of here. Out of the café. Maybe out of town. The state. The country. She couldn't face Rourke. Not today. Maybe not ever.

"I'm going to take off for a while," she told Ellie, who was sitting in an empty booth reading a magazine, waiting for Kit, the night-shift waitress to come in.

"You all right?" Ellie asked.

"Yeah."

"He's not coming back to town. Hell, if I were him I'd head for Mexico or maybe South America," Ellie said. "I've seen pictures of it down there. It's nice." Ellie was always dreaming of going somewhere else. But at almost fifty, it wasn't looking like she would ever go any farther than a couple of hours away to Billings or the thirty-mile drive into Wyoming to Sheridan.

"Everything under control?" Cassidy asked Arthur as she stuck her head in the kitchen.

The cook was fortysomething, tall, pencil thin, with a shock of dark hair beneath his chef's hat. He gave her a look filled with sympathy. It was the last thing she needed right now. "Take care of yourself, sweetie."

She smiled and nodded, taking off her apron and hanging it up before heading into the small office at the back. Retrieving her purse, she glanced around to make sure there was nothing she would need.

How could she know what she would need? She had no idea where she was going. Or if she was even going any farther than home. She was new to running and it already didn't suit her.

She turned out the office light and started down the hall toward the back door.

"Not planning to skip town, are you?" asked a strident voice behind her.

Cassidy froze.

"Not Cassidy Miller," the voice mocked.

She turned slowly, a curse on her lips as she met her cousin's blue-eyed gaze. "I'm going home for the day, not that it's any of your business."

Blaze Logan nodded, smiling as if she'd always been able to see through her.

Cassidy feared that might be true.

"No one would blame you if you turned tail and ran," Blaze said in her comforting, I'm-your-friend tone.

Cassidy had fallen for that act when she was young and stupidly confided in her cousin. She was no longer that young or naive. Normally she avoided Blaze when at all possible and Blaze hadn't gone out of her way, so their paths had crossed little in the past eleven years. Cassidy should have known that Rourke's return would change all of that.

"What would I have to run from?" Cassidy asked as she stepped toward her cousin.

Blaze laughed, a bray of a sound. "Rourke McCall."

"I have nothing to fear from Rourke." If only that were true.

Blaze eyed her. "I just saw his pickup go by."

Cassidy suppressed a shudder, hoping she hid her emotions, as well. "Go away, Blaze. This doesn't have anything to do with you. Or does it? I've always suspected you knew something about Forrest's murder, something you don't want Rourke to know."

Blaze paled under the thick layer of makeup she wore. "That's ridiculous."

"Is it?" Cassidy raised a brow. "I wonder if Rourke will think so?"

"Don't you dare try to incriminate me," Blaze snapped. "You start telling Rourke a bunch of lies—"

"Oh, I'm sure Rourke has had a lot of time to think about the past. He's probably figured out by now why you danced with Forrest that night."

"How could I know that Rourke would try to cut in, let alone that Forrest would pick a fight with him?"

"Oh, Blaze, I think you knew exactly what you were doing. Everyone had heard the rumors going around about you and Forrest. And all the time Rourke thought he was the only one you were seeing. It certainly gave Rourke a motive for murder, didn't it?"

All the color had gone out of Blaze's face. "You started

those rumors," she said on a whisper. "You would have done anything to break up Rourke and me."

Cassidy let out a laugh that was almost a sob. "It was a junior-high crush, Blaze. I much prefer his brother Cash." Cash had asked her out a few times. She'd declined.

But Cassidy knew Blaze was interested in Cash.

"Cash?" Blaze demanded in a choked cry. "You and Cash?"

"Oh, I'm sorry," Cassidy said. "Are you interested in him, too?" She hated the cattiness in her voice. "You change McCall brothers the way you change shoes. It's hard to keep track. Whatever happened to J. T. McCall? Didn't work out?" J.T., the eldest and the one in charge of the ranch, hadn't given Blaze the time of day. Cassidy had seen him cross the street to avoid Blaze. Cassidy knew that feeling only too well.

Blaze glared, nostrils flared. "Be careful, little cousin. If Rourke doesn't kill you just like he did Forrest, someone else might." With that, she spun around and stalked out of the café.

Cassidy stared after her, feeling weak and sick. Blaze always brought out the worst in her. But it was Blaze's last words that struck to her core. What would an embittered Rourke McCall do? Would he make good on his threat to see her pay for her part in sending him to prison?

She wondered now why she hadn't run the moment she heard Rourke was getting out of prison. Her stupid pride. She didn't want the town to think she was a coward. Or that she had anything to hide.

Both were a lie.

She took a breath, then went back into her office, turned on the light, put her purse away. She had work to do. As much as she wished otherwise, she wasn't cut out to be a runner.

ROURKE DROVE ALL the way through Antelope Flats, surprised at how little it had changed. There were a few new
houses on the edge of town, a half-dozen different businesses, but basically in eleven years the town had changed
little.

Antelope Flats was like so many other small Montana
towns. There were more bars than banks, more churches
than places to eat. There was no mall. If you wanted to
buy clothes, you either went to the department store on
Main that had had the same sign out front since the 1950s
or you went to the Western store where you could also buy
a rope or a hat or a pair of boots.

What was new was Antelope Development Corporation,
or ADC as Brandon had called it. Rourke hadn't noticed
the office the first time he drove past. He'd been too busy
looking across the street at the Longhorn Café.

He'd always asked Brandon about Cassidy, afraid she
might clear out of town before he got out of prison. So he
knew that Cassidy had bought the Longhorn Café and
it had been thriving under her management. She'd also
bought the old Kirkhoff place at the edge of town.

"And Blaze?" Rourke would ask his brother.

"She's working for Easton Wells. He started ADC
across the street from the Longhorn."

"What's ADC?" he'd questioned, frowning.

"Antelope Development Corporation. Mostly they deal
with landowners and coal-bed methane gas well leases."

"Our old man must love all those wells everywhere
around the property," Rourke had said. Asa McCall would
shoot anyone who even suggested doing anything to his
land but farming and ranching it.

"There's money in that gas," Brandon said. "A whole
lot of money. You can't believe the wells that have gone
in around the county."

"Blaze seeing anyone?"

Brandon would shrug. "You know Blaze."

Yeah. He knew Blaze, he thought as he pulled into a space in front of the Longhorn Café and sat for a moment trying to see inside the café through the front window. The afternoon sun made the glass like a mirror, reflecting him and his old pickup.

He'd been waiting for this day for so long he could hardly believe it had finally come. He got out, slammed the truck door and walked toward the entrance to the café. Town seemed a lot busier than it had eleven years ago.

He saw people he used to know, but he didn't acknowledge them. Most just stared. He knew he'd changed in the past eleven years. He told himself maybe they didn't recognize him. Or maybe they didn't want to. Maybe they were afraid of him.

He pushed open the door to the Longhorn. The bell tinkled and he stepped into the café, and was hit by the mouthwatering smell of freshly baked bread.

His stomach growled and he realized he hadn't eaten since breakfast. He took a stool at the counter. The café was empty this late in the afternoon except for one couple he didn't recognize at a booth. He could hear voices in back, the clang of pots and pans, the creak of an oven door opening and closing.

He picked up a menu, telling himself that Cassidy probably wasn't even here. The menu covers were the same plastic with a local color photograph of red bluffs, tall blue-green sage and a longhorn steer in the foreground. It had been a shot of the McCall Ranch. He liked that she hadn't changed it. And wondered why she hadn't, given how at least one McCall felt about her.

The McCall Ranch was the only one around that raised longhorns. There was no money in anything but beef cattle, but his father kept some longhorns, raising them as his great-grandfather had. A reminder of what had started the ranch, a link to the past that Asa hadn't been able to let go of.

Out of the corner of his eye, he saw Cassidy come out of the back of the café. She didn't recognize him at first. Not until he looked up from the menu and his eyes met hers.

CASSIDY STOPPED DEAD in her tracks. Although all day she'd been expecting to see him walk into the café, she was shocked to see Rourke sitting at the counter, shocked that after all these years, he really was free and home.

Her heart thudded in her chest so loudly she swore he had to have heard it. Except he wouldn't know why. He'd think it was out of fear.

Her biggest shock was how much Rourke had changed. He'd been more of a boy than a man when he'd left, tall and lanky, not yet filled out at twenty-two.

Now there was no doubt that he'd become a man, from his strong jawline to his broad, muscular shoulders. But there was a coldness to him that showed in the pale blue of his eyes, a hardness that hadn't been there before. Bitterness and anger showed in the hard set of his jaw, in the way he carried himself, a wariness, a spring-coil tension like a wild animal that knew he had predators nearby.

Her heart dropped at the thought. Rourke believed she was one of those predators. She shuddered to think what his life had been like the past eleven years in prison. And the part she'd played in sending him there.

"Rourke," she said, and forced her feet to move toward him, careful to keep the counter between them. She put down the rack of glasses she'd been carrying, shoving her shaking hands deep into her apron pockets so he wouldn't realize how much just seeing him affected her.

She glanced past him to the street and beyond it to the large window of the ADC where Blaze was standing, watching them. Her stomach churned. Blaze was hoping for a show. What *did* Rourke have planned?

"Cassidy." There was a softness to his voice that belied the icy malice in his expression.

His voice was the only thing about this man that was the same as the boy she'd been unable to get out of her thoughts for years. She hated what just the sound of that voice did to her.

"I heard you were released," she said, needing to say something. "I'm glad you're back."

He smiled at that. "I'll bet." He looked down at his menu.

"Rourke, I—"

"I'll have the same thing I used to."

A hot roast beef sandwich, a coffee and a salad with blue-cheese dressing.

She stared at him. "I was hoping—"

"You do remember what I used to order when your mother worked here, don't you?"

Fumbling, she pulled her pen and order pad from her pocket and wrote down his order, writing fast so he wouldn't see how her hands shook.

He smiled a smile that had no chance of reaching his eyes.

There was so much she wanted to say to him, but she could see he wasn't going to let her.

Back when she and Rourke were teens, Cassidy's mom would have taken Rourke's order. Cassidy would have been bussing tables, lurking in the kitchen so Rourke wouldn't see her, feeling ashamed to be caught sweaty, in her white uniform, her apron soiled from clearing dirty tables.

He was looking at her as if he knew her deepest, darkest secrets, knew that she hid in the kitchen when he came in, and listened to him talking and joking with her mother.

"Anything else?" she asked, looking down at the scribbled order on her pad, then up at him.

"No." His expression was colder than the grave.

She stared at him, confused. She'd expected him to lay into her the moment he saw her. She wished he had. His silence was more frightening. Tension arced between them like a tightwire. She felt as if she were balancing on it, unsteady, ready to fall any moment.

"I'll put your order in," she managed to say.

He picked up the menu to look at it again, then without a word turned away from her to stare out the front window, toward ADC and Blaze? He was enjoying her discomfort. He wanted to make her suffer, drag this out.

She turned and walked back to put in his order, trying hard not to run. She wished Kit would come in for her shift, but Cassidy knew she wouldn't leave anyway. She couldn't escape Rourke. Not in a town the size of Antelope Flats. Not even in a state as large as Montana.

Needing desperately to keep busy and yet not wanting to hide in the kitchen, she returned to the counter with more clean glasses and utensils.

She could feel his attention on her, hard as stones, but he didn't say a word. Nor did she try to talk to him. It was clear Rourke was calling the shots.

Kit came in finally, passing Cassidy and making big eyes at her as if to say, *Did you see who's sitting at the counter?*

"You want me to wait on him?" Kit whispered on one of Cassidy's trips to the kitchen.

"No. I have it covered," she said, wondering if Rourke was straining to hear their conversation, just as she had strained to hear his so many years ago.

She returned to the counter to refill the sugar, salt and pepper containers. The one time she looked in his direction he was smirking at her as if he knew what she was up to and it didn't fool him for a minute.

She should have picked another task to do. She spilled sugar, knocked over salt and pepper shakers, fumbled and dropped things. *Come on, Rourke. Just get it over with.*

The bell dinged that his order was up. She hurried back to get it, so nervous she felt nauseous.

She wiped perspiration from her forehead with her arm. Her skin felt flushed, then dimpled with goose bumps as a chill rippled over it. She blotted her hands on a clean towel, avoiding the sympathetic looks of Ellie, Kit and Arthur.

"Don't you want me to call the sheriff?" Arthur said.

"No!" She lowered her voice. "Please. I can handle this."

Picking up Rourke's order, she hurried back out to the counter and put it down in front of him.

"Thank you," he said, his eyes boring into her.

"Can I get you anything else?" Her voice only broke a little but she could see that he heard it, relished in the fact that he had her flustered.

"No thanks. I have everything I need. At least for the moment," he added.

She was weary of this game and desperate to say the words she'd wanted to say to him for eleven years. "Rourke, I think we should—"

"I'll let you know if I need anything else," he said, cutting her off.

He didn't want to hear her tell him how sorry she was for what had happened to him. Or how badly she felt about the part she'd played in it. He wanted to be angry. To make her suffer. Didn't he know how much she'd suffered already?

No, she thought, looking into all that icy blue. He

wanted to strike out at her for his own suffering. He wanted someone to pay. And he'd decided eleven years ago, who that person would be.

She stared at this hardened, cold, embittered man with only one thing on his mind: getting even with her. The realization left her feeling empty inside.

He'd never paid her any mind at all—except for one kiss when she was thirteen and then again after Forrest's murder. He'd looked right through her before then.

She refilled his coffee cup. He thought she'd framed him for murder. That he'd been the only one to live his life under a cloud of suspicion for the past eleven years.

If he thought he could make her feel more guilty, he was wrong. She had blamed herself all these years.

Just do it, Rourke. Do whatever it is you've been planning to do to me for the past eleven years.

He must have seen the change in her. His eyes narrowed and he frowned as if suddenly confused.

There was a crash of pots and pans from the kitchen, followed by some mild cursing. Cassidy hurriedly returned to the kitchen.

Arthur looked up sheepishly. "Nerves," he whispered.

She smiled at him, knowing how he felt, and bent to help him and Kit retrieve the clutter of pans that had fallen from the shelf. Ellie had finally left, it appeared. "These all have to be washed."

"I'll do it," Kit volunteered, kneeling beside her on the floor. "Are you all right?" she whispered.

Cassidy nodded. She felt as if she'd just gotten the news that someone close to her had died. Only she and Rourke had never been close. Their only connection was his need for revenge. And her need to set things right.

She'd tried to just before Rourke was moved to the prison in Deer Lodge. She'd gone to the jail to try to talk to him but he'd been too angry to listen—let alone believe her.

Cassidy handed Arthur a pan as she rose. Hiding her tears, she made a swipe at them, then turned to go back out to the counter. Rourke *would* talk to her. And if he didn't, well, she'd talk to *him*.

But when she reached the counter, she looked around in confusion.

He was gone.

She stared in surprise at the spot where she'd left him just minutes before. His plate was empty. He'd left the price of his meal and a generous tip on the counter.

She was torn between relief and regret. Both made her weak. She leaned against the counter, fighting back her earlier tears. She felt drained, bereft.

"Go on home," Kit said as she scooped up Rourke's empty dishes and wiped down the counter. "You've had a long day."

Cassidy could only nod. It had been the longest day of her life.

She took off her apron, hung it up and went to her office to retrieve her purse again. This time, she didn't hesitate. She opened the back door, trying not to run. She desperately wanted to go home, take a hot bath, mourn for all that had been lost.

The door swung open and she stepped out.

Rourke was leaning against his old pickup, arms folded across his chest, his cowboy hat pushed back, the last of the day's sunlight on the face she'd dreamed about for eleven years. Some of those dreams had turned into nightmares.

CHAPTER FOUR

"LET'S GO FOR A RIDE," Rourke said, motioning to his pickup as he considered what he would do when she refused.

Cassidy glanced at the truck, then at him. "If you want to talk, we can go in my office."

"Any reason you wouldn't want to go for a ride with me?" he asked.

She cocked her head at him, that look in her eyes again, the same one he'd seen earlier in the café. Anger? What the hell did *she* have to be angry about? He thought of the photo in his pocket. He didn't know what to make of it any more than he did of her now. He would have to learn to read this woman better.

"I know you're trying to intimidate me," she said quietly.

He smiled at that. He'd just graduated from the school of intimidation. "That's what you think I'm trying to do?"

"Yes," she said, but to his surprise, she walked around the front of the pickup, opened the passenger-side door and climbed in.

He was momentarily taken aback. He'd expected her to put up an argument. Maybe even yell for help. Or at least threaten to tell his brother the sheriff that she was being harassed.

She'd surprised him and he had a feeling it wouldn't be the first time. That in itself worried him as he climbed behind the wheel and glanced over at her.

"You know most people in town wouldn't have agreed to a ride with a convicted killer," he said as he shifted into first, kicking up gravel from the rear tires as he took off.

She just shot him another one of those looks he couldn't read. Everything about Cassidy was a mystery to him, he realized. He'd been four years ahead of her in school. He barely remembered her. Even after high school, when she'd gone to work at the Longbranch that summer before college bussing tables, he hardly remembered seeing her.

And even after hiring several private investigators while in prison to dig up everything they could on her, he still didn't have any idea why she'd framed him. Or who was really behind it.

Cassidy Miller appeared to be just what she seemed. A twenty-eight-year-old woman who'd grown up in Antelope Flats without a father. Her mother had been a waitress. The year her mother died, Cassidy was at Montana State University in Bozeman on a scholarship, getting a degree in business.

Cassidy had come back to Antelope Flats, bought the Longhorn Café and later the Kirkhoff Place, both with low down payments.

She was up to her eyeballs in debt but had made a go of the café and had never been late on a payment on either place. She'd never been in trouble with the law. Never even been late on returning a library book from what he could tell.

On the surface, Cassidy Miller looked squeaky clean.

He wondered what he'd missed.

"Where are you taking me?" she asked as he drove out of town headed north. There was only a slight quiver in her voice. She was trying so hard to make him think he didn't frighten her. Fool woman.

"You'll see."

She wore a pale pink short-sleeved uniform top and skirt that came down to her knees.

He remembered her in jeans, boots and a Western shirt. Now that he thought of it, she had dressed like his tomboy sister, all cowgirl. He couldn't ever remember seeing Cassidy's legs before. They were shapely, lightly tanned from the summer and long for her height of about five foot six. She was short next to him at six-two.

With her small leather purse in her lap, white cross-trainers and white socks on her feet and her hair pulled up in a ponytail, she looked like the schoolgirl he'd kissed in the barn. Except, he noticed as he drove, her body had filled out. She'd turned into a woman while he'd been gone, he thought, annoyed with himself for noticing, even more annoyed with her for not being the same person he'd imagined when he'd planned what he would do to her.

He drove north five miles, turned onto the Rosebud Creek Road and didn't go far up the winding muddy path before stopping next to a monument with the word *Crook* on it.

"Come on. Let's take a little walk." He climbed out before she could argue. He could tell she wasn't wild about the idea, but she opened her door and stepped out, squinting into the sun that was about to sink behind the bluffs.

She should have been terrified. And would have been, if she'd known how furious he was with her. He was convinced there was only one reason Cassidy Miller had gotten into the pickup with a convicted murderer. Because she knew he wasn't a killer. Because she knew who was and had kept silent all these years while he was locked up in prison.

He started up a gully through the tall grass, walking toward the bottom of the red bluffs. It was cool here with the sun almost down. The air smelled of sage and pine. A bee buzzed in the riot of wildflowers, and crickets chirped deeper in the bushes.

He'd waited so long for this day he could hardly contain himself. He took deep breaths, fighting to control his temper. He wanted to grab Cassidy and shake the truth from her.

Instead, he looked at the red bluffs, at the ponderosa pines along the top and imagined Cheyenne and Sioux warriors sitting on their horses watching them.

He'd always liked to come here. His grandfather had brought him the first time and told him the story of struggle and courage, victory and defeat, the tale of man's battle against man. He'd felt the history then, just as he did now, as if it was entrenched in the soil, in the rocks.

"Why are we here?" Cassidy asked as he stopped in a draw below the red bluffs. The breeze stirred her hair, now loose around her shoulders. She had pulled out the band that had held her hair and was nervously toying with it.

"Do you know what happened here?" he asked.

She glanced behind them, down the hillside. He followed her focus to where the lush green willows, wild roses and chokecherries hid the stream. They were completely alone. The closest ranch house was a good half mile away and there had been no vehicles at the ranger station up the road when they'd passed.

"Everyone knows what happened here," she said, turning back to look at the bluffs, then at him.

He smiled at that. "I doubt few people have even heard of the Rosebud Battlefield, let alone know the story."

General Crook and his men had stopped to water their horses at the creek on June 17, 1876—just eight days before the Battle of the Little Bighorn. Fifteen hundred Cheyenne and Sioux warriors came over the hills above where he and Cassidy now stood and attacked the cavalry unit.

Of Crook's one thousand men and three hundred and seventy-five Crow and Shoshoni scouts, only eight cavalry men were killed and fifty scouts.

It wasn't much of a battle because Crook didn't pursue when the Indians retreated. But eight days later, the warring warrior chiefs used the techniques they'd learned on the Rosebud to defeat Custer at the Little Bighorn. Custer and two hundred and sixty-one cavalry and scouts were killed.

Cassidy gave him a look that he *could* read. What was the point of all this?

"Crook didn't go after the Cheyenne and Sioux that day," Rourke said. "If he had, who knows how history might have been written. Instead he just let it go not realizing he would contribute to many more deaths at the Little Bighorn."

She shook her head and met his gaze. Her eyes, he noticed, were the same color as her hair, shades of rich brown in the sunset with splashes of gold.

"You're not going to let it go," she said. She didn't sound in the least surprised as she turned her back on him to look down at his pickup parked below them on the hillside. If anything, she sounded sad.

"There are some battles that you just can't walk away from," he said. "But that isn't my point. Crook was in the wrong place at the wrong time. Historians disagree, but I think he made a mistake not finishing the battle and I—"

"I'm sorry." Her voice broke as she turned to face him. "I never meant to hurt you. I tried to explain about that night."

Rourke squeezed his eyes closed, that night too clear in his memory. Driving up the dark gulch, driven by his anger. Forrest's pickup flashed in his headlights. He'd swung his truck in front of Forrest's because he thought Forrest would try to make a run for it. And then he'd stormed over to Forrest's truck and jerked open the driver's door.

Forrest had fallen toward him and, without thinking, he'd caught him. Blood. It was all over his hands, his shirt, as he'd pushed Forrest back up in a sitting position behind the wheel. Everything registered at once. The gunshot wound to Forrest's chest, the dead, hollow look in his eyes, the empty seat beside him.

He'd stared at Forrest, trying to make sense of it, then turned and ran back toward his pickup. He'd left it running, the lights on. He had to get help. That was what he'd been thinking and yet he'd known Forrest was dead. Did he reach his pickup? Rourke couldn't be sure.

All he remembered was Cash waking him up in the wee hours of the morning. He had Forrest's blood all over him and the murder weapon was on the seat next to him with only his fingerprints on it. And Cassidy. She stood out in the darkness, hugging herself, beside Cash's patrol car.

And Cash was saying, "Cassidy called, worried after you left the Mello Dee." Cassidy, the one who'd tricked him into going up Wild Horse Gulch in the first place.

He fought to keep eleven years of anger and frustration and bitterness out of his voice and failed. "Stop lying to me. You wouldn't have gotten into my pickup today if you thought I really was a murderer. You know I didn't kill Forrest, because you framed me for his murder. I want to know why. And who was in on it with you."

She had to have heard the rage in his voice, seen it in his eyes, in his balled fists at his side. And yet she met his eyes and didn't veer away. "I don't know who killed Forrest. I just know in my heart that you didn't do it. You couldn't kill a man in cold blood, not even out of jealousy." She shook her head. "Why can't you believe me?"

"Because I didn't believe your story at the trial and I sure as hell don't believe it now."

"The prosecutor used me to help convict you. I'm sorry about that. But I told the truth and I give you my word that I'm telling you the truth now. There is nothing more I can do." She started to walk past him back down the hillside to the pickup, but he grabbed her arm and spun her around to face him.

"Not so fast, sugar." He smiled at her. "Your *word?*"

She raised her chin, her spine a rod of steel. "It's all I have."

He felt the fury, banked for so many years, bubble up inside him. "I'm not taking your word on anything, all right? You wrote the note that put me up Wild Horse Gulch, that put me at the scene of the crime."

Her chin came down a little, some of the steel melting out of her spine. "I'm not proud of what I did."

"Not *proud?*" he echoed. "It cost me eleven years of my life. You set me up. The killer couldn't have framed me without you leaving me that damned note!" He was towering over her, his fingers digging into her arm.

"Do you think that I haven't agonized over this every day for the past eleven years? I tried to save you at the trial. You know I did." Tears welled in her eyes but she didn't look away. "You're hurting me." It came out little more than a whisper.

He released her at once, swallowed and stepped back, afraid of what he might do to her. Overhead, a hawk sailed soundlessly across the fading blue sky. "Why did you write that note?"

THE PAIN IN HIS VOICE crushed her heart like a blow. She felt hot with shame just as she had at seventeen when she'd taken the stand to explain that she'd left a note on Rourke's pickup windshield telling him that Blaze was meeting Forrest up Wild Horse Gulch.

That spiteful note, written out of her schoolgirl jealousy over Rourke and Blaze, had cost Rourke eleven years of his life. She'd helped send him to prison, destroying the young man he'd been. All these years she'd hoped that when he got out of prison he might finally believe her. What a fool she'd been. Then. And now.

He stepped back, shoved his hands deep into the pockets of his jacket, as if fighting to control his anger. "Tell me something. What would *you* do if you'd just spent eleven years of your life behind bars for a crime you didn't commit?"

"I would find the real killer or die trying," she said without hesitation.

He smiled at that. "And what would you do once you found him? Or *her*," he added.

She swallowed, afraid of where he was going with this. "I would prove the person was guilty and turn the evidence over to the authorities."

His laugh held no humor. "Then I guess you and I are different."

"I hope you don't intend to take the law in your own hands," she said, her voice cracking. "It will only get you sent back to prison."

Rourke closed the distance between them in a stride, his hand coming out of his pocket to cup her jaw. He moved so fast she didn't have time to react. But she couldn't help flinching at his touch.

He smiled, obviously pleased to think that he'd frightened her. It had been fear that his touch induced and something much more primitive.

He said between gritted teeth, "If I was going to take

the law into my own hands, don't you think I would do it right now?" His thumb caressed her cheek.

She didn't move, didn't breathe.

"I was headed home that night," he said, his voice breaking with emotion. He released her but stayed so close she could smell his masculine scent, feel his heat. "Blaze had already left to go to her apartment. I only went up Wild Horse Gulch because of your note. *You* put me at the murder scene. Don't you dare tell me it was just a coincidence." He glared at her, his eyes a dark blue under the brim of his cowboy hat. "Either *you* framed me. Or you helped someone else frame me and I will get the truth out of you—one way or the other."

She swallowed, her heart breaking at the sight of his raw pain. "What do you want from me, Rourke? I've told you everything I know. I left the note. It was a childish, spiteful thing to do and I've regretted it for eleven years. At the time, I just wanted you to know the truth about Blaze. I thought I was protecting you."

"You did it for my own good," he mocked.

"No, I did it for very selfish reasons. I thought if you knew the truth…" Her eyes came up to meet his.

"What?" He grabbed her arm and shook her gently. "What were you going to say?"

"I was seventeen." Her voice broke. "I was in…love with you."

He stared at her, stepping back as if in shock.

"You really didn't know." She smiled ruefully, seeing the truth in his eyes.

"You and I never said two words to each other. How could you…" He reached into his pocket and shoved a photograph at her. "That's what you call love?"

With trembling fingers, she took the snapshot from him and looked down at the two young women in the snapshot.

"How do you explain your anger at me in that photograph?" he demanded. "That was taken just days before Forrest's murder."

"I thought you were taunting me with Blaze."

"What?"

"You were the one who insisted I stand next to Blaze for the photograph. I thought you knew how I felt about you, that you were enjoying rubbing it in my face, maybe hoping Blaze and I would fight over you," she said, and handed him back the photograph.

He stared at her, frowning. "The photo was Blaze's idea. I had no idea how you felt. You never said anything."

She smiled and nodded. "I thought maybe you liked me because— You probably don't even remember that day in the barn." Her eyes burned with humiliation.

"You framed me for murder because I chose Blaze over you, is that what this has been about?" His words hit her like a whip. "I went to prison because of some schoolgirl crush?"

She brushed at her tears, anger replacing the hurt and humiliation. "You didn't go to prison because of some schoolgirl crush. You could have thrown away the note I left on your pickup, and you would have, if you had trusted Blaze. Or if Blaze was trustworthy."

"Oh yeah? Why *did* I go to prison?"

"Because you left your gun sitting out in your bedroom where anyone could take it," she said. "Even if you hadn't gone up Wild Horse Gulch that night, the killer had your gun with only your prints on it. You had motive. You'd just beat the devil out of Forrest Danvers at the bar because he was seeing your girlfriend."

"He wasn't seeing my girlfriend."

She raised a brow. "Wasn't he?"

Rourke swore. "This isn't about Blaze."

She stared at him. "Obviously you're as blind to the truth as you were eleven years ago." She started past him, but he stopped her with a hand on her arm.

"Admit it, you wanted me sent to prison."

She shook her head in disbelief. "If I wanted you in prison, all I would have to do is call the sheriff and tell him you are threatening me."

With an angry gesture, Rourke pulled his cell phone from his pocket and held it out to her. "Go ahead. Call the sheriff. Get me thrown back into prison. Finish what you started."

She stared at him. "Don't you know I would never do that to you?"

"No. Who else hated me enough to frame me for murder besides you?"

"What makes you so sure it was even about you?" she demanded angrily.

"Because I just spent eleven years in prison," he shot back.

"You're that sure you were the target? What if you're wrong? What if it wasn't about framing you but simply about killing Forrest?"

"That's ridiculous."

"Oh? Haven't you been looking for reasons someone wanted to frame you and all you've come up with so far is me? And my motive was that I was jealous of you and Blaze and I set this whole thing up to get back at *you?* I always knew you were arrogant, but I never thought you were stupid."

He looked at her as if he could kill her.

"What if you were just an easy scapegoat?"

He shook his head. "Don't you think I know what you're doing? You're just trying to get yourself off the hook."

She could see from his expression that he didn't want to

believe that he'd lost eleven years just because he'd been a convenient patsy. That, she realized, made it worse for him, but it didn't change what she believed had happened the night Forrest was killed and if Rourke was determined to find out the truth—

"I've had a long time to think about this," she said.

"So have I."

"Just consider this. What if the killer wanted to get rid of Forrest and looked around for someone to take the fall?" She hurried on. "You were the McCall bad boy, you kept a gun on a shelf in your bedroom, you were a hothead, you didn't like Forrest and you were going to like him a lot less when you found out about him and Blaze." She waved off his denial. "You were *perfect*."

He stared at her, his expression grim, as if she'd just voiced his worst fear. Without a word, he turned and walked on up the trail as if wanting to distance himself from her words, from even the thought that they might be true. His lawyer had to have told him the same thing eleven years ago, but he hadn't wanted to believe it. Still didn't.

Cassidy watched him go, his pain so obvious it made her hurt. Could he hate her any more than he had? She hadn't thought so.

Blindly she turned and started down the hill to the pickup. A sob caught in her throat at the thought that the old Rourke McCall was gone forever, destroyed by prison and injustice and his own bitterness, and that the stranger on the hillside wouldn't stop until he destroyed them both.

Rourke didn't go after her. He couldn't. He fought back the pain and rage that threatened to overwhelm him. He'd had a death grip on one single-minded resolve. To find the real killer when he got out. It was how he had survived prison.

For eleven years, he'd been convinced Cassidy was part

of an elaborate setup to frame him for Forrest's murder. He had planned what he would do when he got out. Starting with the note that had gotten him up Wild Horse Gulch that night. Starting with breaking Cassidy Miller. Forcing the truth out of her.

He swore again. He'd had eleven years to think about nothing else. He knew he wasn't without blame. He'd been stupid and hotheaded. What he wouldn't give for another chance to do things differently.

He shook his head, trying to make sense of it. But he'd been trying to do that for eleven years. Except he hadn't known that Cassidy Miller had been in love with him. Is that what this had all been about? She'd left the note that had sent him to prison because she thought she was in love with him?

Or was she right and he had just been a pawn, his own character flaws used against him?

He faced the bluffs and imagined fifteen hundred warriors swarming over the rise. He knew how General Crook had felt.

He wished his grandfather were still alive. Wished the two of them were standing here now, although Rourke knew he couldn't have taken his grandfather's disappointment in him.

Not that his grandfather would have believed him capable of murder. Just guilty of letting himself be framed for murder. He'd played right into someone's hands. Whoever had killed Forrest had to have known how he was going to react. To Blaze dancing with Forrest. To the note on his windshield.

Two different instances. Two different women. That's why it had made no sense. For years it had just kept coming down to that damned note left on his pickup windshield that had sent him to the murder scene. It always came back to Cassidy.

Cassidy's scream shattered the silence.

He turned to see her scramble back from the open passenger-side door of the pickup, her eyes fixed on something inside, the scream dying on her lips as she tripped and fell.

He was running, fear knotting his stomach as he tried to imagine what had made her scream like that.

"What's wrong?" he called to her as he came around the front of the pickup. Cassidy had scrambled to her feet and was now backing up, her face bloodless as she pointed toward the pickup in sheer terror.

He heard it. The distinctive rattle. At first he didn't see it. Probably because he'd expected it to be curled under the pickup in the shade.

It wasn't. The huge greenish-colored rattlesnake was coiled on the floorboard of the truck, its ugly head raised, the beady eyes locking on him as it struck.

CHAPTER FIVE

ROURKE SWUNG THE DOOR closed just an instant before the snake could strike him. He heard the rattler hit the inside of the door with a soft thump, then there was silence.

"Did it bite you?" he asked Cassidy, unable to disguise the fear in his voice, his insides tightening at the thought of those fangs in flesh.

She shook her head, brown eyes huge.

"Stay here," he said, and walked across the narrow road to a stand of trees where he found what he needed. A long thick stick. Cassidy was still huddled where he'd left her, hugging herself as if it were a bitter-cold winter afternoon instead of a hot fall one.

On the other side of the pickup, he opened the door slowly. Just as he'd suspected, the snake had moved away from the slammed passenger-side door and was now lying under the driver's side on the floor mat.

The rattler coiled again at the sound of the door opening. Rourke had caught more than his share of snakes as a boy. He'd always been fascinated by them rather than repelled.

This rattler was huge and obviously hadn't liked captivity any more than Rourke had. It was mad and just looking for someone to take it out on.

Stepping to one side of the doorway, he used the thick stick to lift enough of the snake to urge it out. The rattler struck the stick, sinking its fangs into the wood and Rourke took that opportunity to pull the snake from the truck.

The rattler dropped to the ground next to the pickup, releasing the stick, looking for its next victim. Rourke didn't move a hair, keeping the stick ready. He'd met guys like this in prison. The snake seemed to eye him for a long moment, then turned and slithered across the road, disappearing into the deep grass down by the creek.

Rourke took a look around the inside of the pickup just to make sure there weren't any other surprises in there. He found a large burlap bag behind his seat, the kind snake hunters used, and swore under his breath.

He stuffed the empty bag back behind the seat and looked out at Cassidy. She was watching. From a safe distance.

"It's all right now," he said, going around the front of the pickup to where she stood. He could see that she was trembling, her face still white with fear. "The snake's long gone."

She glanced around the ground nervously and rubbed her bare arms as if rubbing down goose bumps.

He'd known a few people who were deathly afraid of snakes. The fear defied reason. His father had told him of a guy who jumped out of his pickup at more than forty miles an hour because some fool had put a dead rattler in his truck as a joke.

Rourke saw that kind of fear on Cassidy's face. "Aren't fond of snakes, huh?"

She shook her head, hugging herself again, as she kept an eye on the ground around her. "What was it doing in the truck?"

That was the sixty-four-million-dollar question, wasn't it? "It must have nested in there while I was gone."

She didn't look as if she believed that. "You're sure there aren't any more?"

He nodded, thinking about when someone would have had the opportunity to put the snake bag behind the seat. Probably while he was in the Longhorn. He hadn't locked the truck. Hell, it was Antelope Flats, Montana. Nobody locked their vehicles or even their houses.

And the snake wasn't some sort of joke.

It was a warning. As clear as any he'd ever had.

"I'll take you back to town," he said as he opened the passenger-side door for her.

She studied the floorboard. Looking relieved to find the space empty, she got in and he closed the door behind her.

He stood for a moment, thinking about the snake, then let out a long breath. Fury bubbled inside him like molten lava. But if he'd learned anything in prison, it was how to control his temper. But right now, if he could get his hands on the person who had put that snake in his truck...

He walked around the pickup and slid behind the wheel, angry with himself for bringing Cassidy out here. What had he hoped to accomplish anyway?

Whatever it was, he felt as if it had backfired. The damned woman had him feeling guilty for scaring her with a snake he didn't even know was in his pickup, guilty for hurting her even though he had no idea how she'd felt about him all those years ago.

No, he thought, what was really bothering him was that she had him doubting himself. He'd been so sure that she'd framed him. So sure that once he was free from prison he'd get the truth out of her.

Maybe he had, he thought glancing over at her. And then again, maybe there was a whole lot more to Cassidy Miller yet to be discovered. He knew one thing. He wasn't through with her. She'd be seeing him again. If she thought otherwise, she was sadly mistaken.

They rode in silence back to Antelope Flats. He couldn't quit thinking about what she'd said. What if he hadn't been framed—just used? The perfect patsy. That was certainly him eleven years ago.

But he wasn't ready to rule out Cassidy Miller and a frame job. Not yet. The woman had a jealous streak and had admitted a foolish crush on him. And if anyone did, he knew just how powerful jealousy could be.

He pulled up behind her car at the rear of the Longhorn and glanced over at her. She turned her head toward him, those big brown eyes swimming in tears. Behind them, something he couldn't put his finger on.

A well of emotions hit him like a sledgehammer. For eleven years all he'd felt was his own pain. That and bitter anger. He stared into her face and was filled with regret for hurting her all those years ago.

Cassidy started to say something but must have changed her mind. She opened the pickup door as if suddenly she wanted to get away from him as much as she had that rattlesnake.

"I didn't mean to hurt you when we were kids," he said, surprising himself as much as her.

She seemed embarrassed as she waved off his apology like a pesky fly. "I told you, I was young and stupid," she said as she slid out.

"We were all young and stupid," he said. "But you're wrong, Cassidy, I do remember the kiss in the barn."

His last words were lost as the pickup door slammed, Cassidy giving no indication that she'd heard him.

CASSIDY COULDN'T QUIT shaking. She rushed to her car, her legs weak as she dropped into the seat, closing the door, closing her eyes for a moment, trying desperately not to cry.

Could this day have been any worse? She thought she heard a soft rattle. Her eyelids flew open and she stared at the floorboard, expecting to see a rattlesnake coiled there just an instant before it sank its teeth into her bare leg.

The floorboard was empty. She glanced over the back of the seat. Also empty.

He'd lied about how the snake had gotten into his pickup. She'd seen his expression when he'd found the burlap bag. Someone had put that snake in the pickup. As what? A threat? A warning?

She shivered at the thought. Who would do such a thing?

She started the engine and was ready to pull away before she glanced in her side mirror and saw that Rourke's pickup was still behind her. He was leaning over the steering wheel, his hat hooding his eyes, watching her. How long would he continue to watch her? To follow her? To suspect her?

She met his gaze in the mirror and felt a chill. Putting the car into gear, she pulled away. She'd expected him to follow her, but when she looked in her rearview mirror, he wasn't there.

Still she couldn't quit trembling. He'd dug up all the old feelings. Pain and humiliation and resentment. But it was the old ache that hurt the most. An ache she'd always believed only Rourke McCall could fill.

She didn't know this man who had come home from prison. She let out a laugh. She hadn't known the other Rourke, the wild cowboy who'd made her heart flutter. Who still made her heart flutter.

Cassidy drove south of town and turned onto a short dirt road bordered on both sides by huge cottonwoods. As she drove down the lane, the fallen leaves floated up around her car, golden in the last of the day's light.

The house was small, an old farmhouse that suited her well. It came with twenty acres, corrals and a small barn for her horse and tack. She loved owning land even if it would take most of her lifetime to pay it off.

As she pulled into the yard and cut the engine, she expected to see Rourke's pickup pull in behind her. She sat for a moment, watching in her rearview mirror. No Rourke. Had he given up? She smiled ruefully to herself. Not a chance.

She didn't realize how tired she was as she climbed out of the car and went into the house. What would he do next? That was the question, wasn't it. Rourke McCall wasn't out of her life yet. She wondered if he would ever be out of her thoughts.

It was that carefree Rourke who inhabited her thoughts. The one who had been so full of life and possibilities. When he smiled, his blue eyes had shone like summer sunlight, and just as warm. But there'd always been that hint of mischief in them, too. You never knew what he was going to do next. He probably didn't, either.

She locked the front door behind her and, dropping her purse on the hall table, headed for her bedroom, anxious to get out of her uniform. The old Rourke. She smiled at the memory. Just being around him had made her feel part of something larger than her own life, something exciting and full of adventure.

But Forrest's murder had taken all that away from him. That Rourke McCall was gone. Injustice and prison had killed him.

She felt his bitterness as keenly as he did. Even if he found Forrest's real killer, it wouldn't bring back the old

Rourke McCall or eleven years of his life. How could he ever let go of the demons that consumed him?

As she started to undress, she glanced at the large trunk at the end of her bed. The letters. Her heart caught in her throat. Why hadn't she gotten rid of them? If Rourke found out about them—

She shook her head in disgust at her own foolishness.

In the bathroom, she turned on the water in the tub and poured in some of her favorite bubble bath. As she watched the tub fill, she was consumed with an emptiness born of longing. What a fool she'd been. Still was. The Rourke McCall she'd fallen for was gone. She'd waited eleven years for a ghost.

She looked away from the bubbles blooming in the tub and caught her reflection in the mirror. She looked like a woman, but she knew she was still that same lovesick girl, ever hopeful.

She wouldn't cry. She wouldn't. But even as she thought it, tears began to spill down her cheeks.

"Oh hell," she breathed on a sob, as she shed the last of her clothing and stepped into the tub, sinking into the bubbles and letting all the tears she'd never cried finally free.

Asa McCall looked for Rourke's old pickup when he returned to the ranch house just before dinner. He cursed under his breath when he saw it was gone. What had he expected? That maybe his son would stay? Would want to work the ranch his ancestors had fought for?

He knew he wasn't being fair. He'd done nothing to convince Rourke to stay. But Rourke was also without a doubt the most pigheaded of his children. If Rourke's mother Shelby were here she'd say Rourke was just like his father.

Asa scoffed at that. Rourke had always been the wild one and if anyone was to blame for that, it was Shelby. But then he blamed Shelby for most of his problems as well as those of their children.

Tonight he let himself wonder for a moment what their lives would have been like if Shelby had been here all these years and quickly pushed the thought away. He couldn't change the past, and thinking about Shelby only made him hurt.

Except lately, he'd been thinking about her more and more. And thinking about the mistakes he'd made, especially with his son Rourke.

"Are you all right?" his daughter asked as he walked into the house. "You've been gone all day. You look tired." Dusty took her father's arm and steered him to his chair, then went to the bar and made him a cold drink. "I'll bet you haven't eaten all day, either."

"Thank you," he said, taking the drink. He was glad she was talking to him again. He hated it when she gave him the silent treatment. He took a long swallow, pleased when she sat down in a chair across from him.

"You were avoiding Rourke, weren't you," she said. "That's why you were gone all day."

He didn't deny it.

"You know he didn't do it," she said, as if continuing a discussion they'd been having earlier. Except she hadn't been talking to him earlier.

"Rourke couldn't kill anyone."

He looked at his daughter. She was so young, so trusting. Maybe he'd lived too long, seen too much, become too jaded, but he knew that anyone could kill or do even worse—especially if he felt cornered or had become bewitched by a woman. And he feared Rourke had been both. Not only cornered that night up Wild Horse Gulch, but out of his mind because of a woman. The wrong woman. They were the ones who drove you to do something stupid.

"We need to help him," Dusty said.

He didn't want her to get mad at him again. But there was no way he was letting her get involved with this quest her brother was on. Asa had already heard from both J.T. and Cash about Rourke's plans to find Forrest's killer.

"I'll tell you what," he said, measuring his words carefully. "I'll help Rourke if you promise to stay clear of it."

She started to argue.

"That's my only offer," he said. "I can help him in ways you can't."

She pursed her lips, eyes narrowed, not happy with his terms but too smart not to see the value in his deal.

"You will ask him to come back to the ranch?"

He nodded. He'd offer but he knew his pigheaded son wouldn't take him up on it.

WHEN EASTON COULDN'T take Blaze's pacing and complaining any longer, he gathered up his papers and stuffed them into his briefcase. "I'm going to finish this at home."

She turned in obvious surprise from the window where she'd been looking out, waiting for Rourke McCall. "You're going home early?"

"It isn't that early, Blaze. Normally you are long gone by now." He gave her a pitying look. "If Rourke was going to drop by, he would have by now." In truth, it gave him no small amount of satisfaction that Rourke hadn't called or stopped in to see her. He could see it was driving her crazy. Her little scheme wasn't working and Blaze was used to getting her way.

Nor was Easton surprised his old friend hadn't come by to see him, either. He wondered what Rourke thought about him being with Blaze now.

Easton swore under his breath, remembering how badly he'd wanted Blaze when she was with Rourke. Had it been

Blaze or Rourke's life he wanted? Undeniably he had often wanted to be Rourke. To come from a big ranching family, to have the money and the power and the prestige that went with being a McCall.

Instead, Easton had gotten Blaze. It was little consolation. But then, Rourke had gotten eleven years in prison. Maybe, for once, Easton had gotten the better deal. But as he looked over at Blaze, he wouldn't have bet good money on it.

He dreaded seeing Rourke, but not as much as he dreaded seeing Blaze with Rourke. She would throw herself at him and Easton didn't need to see that. He'd seen enough of that eleven years ago.

"Good night," he said as he headed for the door.

"I thought we were going to have dinner?" she cried.

"Maybe some other night," he said, without turning to look at her. "I have a lot of work to do tonight and you were of no help today." He closed the door firmly behind him before she could argue.

"Rourke McCall," he said under his breath like a curse as he got into his ADC Suburban and drove out of town. "If she wants Rourke, she can have him. Her little plan to make me jealous isn't going to work. No matter what she does."

But that's what worried him as he turned off onto the road to his house on the edge of the bluffs. How far would Blaze go to get him to propose marriage?

Ahead, he saw his house as he came over a rise in the road, his prized possession. He'd had it built on a bluff overlooking the Tongue River and miles and miles of rich bottomland. It had a unique modern design with a long sloping roofline and lots of wood and stone.

He'd done all right for himself, he thought, as he hit the garage-door opener, parked the Suburban and, taking his briefcase, went inside. Even the furniture was modern, sculpted with clean lines. He liked that. Just as he liked the bank of windows that ran the entire width of the house overlooking the river.

It was an impressive view, the winding band of water reflecting the late-afternoon sun, the verdant green river bottom, the red bluffs on the opposite bank rimmed with dark, silken ponderosa pines.

If the house itself didn't relieve a bad day, the view always did. Except for today. He couldn't get Blaze off his mind.

He'd worked for years to accumulate nice things, to afford the comfortable life he knew he should have been born into. He'd made compromises, done things that were necessary at the time but that he now feared would come back to haunt him. His life was in jeopardy. Blaze knew too much about his business, too much about him and the past.

He'd seen it in her eyes. A quiet speculation as if deciding what to do with the information she'd come across. She'd never said anything, but sometimes he felt as if she had a gun to his head.

With Rourke McCall back in town and Blaze playing games, she had cocked the gun and had her finger on the trigger.

As he put down his briefcase and went to the bar to make himself a drink, he rued the day he'd hired Blaze. Sleeping with her was one thing. Working with her was a whole other ball game.

He'd only hired her as a favor to her father—and because John Logan was his silent business partner. Silent and secret. Not even Blaze knew about the exchange of money or the favors her father had demanded in return.

John thought working for ADC would straighten Blaze out. Right.

Easton had actually thought he could free himself of Blaze once he bought her father's share in the company and he tired of her. Except he hadn't bought out her father's share. Nor had he tired of Blaze even though she had always been a liability. Now, though, she was a loose cannon. Blaze thought she could use Rourke, play him for a fool. Again. All she was going to do was get them both into trouble.

Easton took a sip of his drink and looked out at his view, too anxious to enjoy it.

He knew Blaze would still be at the office, pretending to work late, waiting around for Rourke.

He closed his eyes. He could just imagine Blaze turning all her charms on Rourke. The image made him sick to his stomach. He downed the drink.

There had to be some way to stop her from ruining everything.

Returning to the bar, he poured himself another drink and had a thought, one that shocked him. Would he really consider something so drastic?

CHAPTER SIX

As the light started to fall over Antelope Flats, Rourke knew exactly where he wanted to spend his first night of freedom.

But as he drove down Main Street, he couldn't get Cassidy off his mind. Damn her. She'd taken him in with her sweet, innocent act and, fool that he was, he'd fallen for it. She probably thought he'd bought it. Wouldn't she be surprised when he showed up at her door tomorrow.

He couldn't believe that she'd made him feel guilty for hurting her all those years ago when she was the one who should be feeling guilty. He'd come home to get the truth out of her and she'd turned things around so that he felt he should be making *her* feel better.

Worse, for a while there, she'd had him thinking she might be right. That Forrest's murder *hadn't* been about him. That he was just the scapegoat.

He cursed himself as he pulled up in front of the sheriff's house. Hadn't he promised himself he would never trust another woman again?

Sheriff Cash McCall lived in an old Victorian two blocks from the Sheriff's Department. Antelope Flats was an unincorporated town, which meant the only law was the sheriff of what was also the smallest and most isolated county in Montana.

Cash had purchased the house right after college, right after he got the job as sheriff, the youngest sheriff ever in

Montana. He'd bought the house as a wedding present for his fiancée, a girl he'd met and fallen in love with at college. Jasmine Wolfe had been driving down from Bozeman to finally meet the rest of the McCalls but never made it. She'd disappeared, never to be seen again. Most people figured she got cold feet about being a sheriff's wife in a dinky little town like Antelope Flats and made a run for it before it was too late.

Cash had searched for her, but it was as if she'd dropped off the face of the earth. His brother had never gotten over her.

He and Cash had that in common. Falling for the wrong women.

"Rourke," Cash said when he opened the door. He'd obviously been expecting him and just as obviously hadn't been looking forward to it.

"No hard feelings, Cash," Rourke said. "I know you were just doing your job when you arrested me and sent me to prison." He smiled to soften his words.

Cash studied him openly for a few moments. Cash was six-four, big as their father, with the McCall blond hair and blue eyes. He was also solid as a tree stump and just as stubborn. Another trait they shared.

"That's real kindly of you, Rourke."

"You going to ask me in?"

"That depends," Cash said. "You going to give me any trouble?"

He shook his head and raised his palms up in supplication. He was just an inch shorter than his brother and in as good shape. "I've learned my lesson."

Cash shook his head but stepped aside. "You had dinner?"

"Ate over at the Longhorn."

His brother swung around, halfway into the living

room. "You aren't even thinking about bothering Cassidy Miller, are you?"

Rourke shook his head.

"Because if you are, I will have you back behind bars before you can blink," Cash said.

"I'm aware of that."

They eyed each other for another few moments, then Cash motioned toward a chair. "You want a drink?"

"I could take a beer if you have one," he said, thinking how protective his brother had sounded about Cassidy. Was something going on there?

Cash disappeared into the kitchen and came back with two bottles of beer.

"I thought I might be able to use the family cabin on the lake," Rourke said, twisting off the top of his beer. He took a long drink. Damn, that tasted good.

His brother looked at him suspiciously.

Rourke had to laugh. "I just need a place to stay and, well, I want to be alone and I don't want to have to watch my back."

"Any reason you would have to watch your back?" Cash asked.

"Damn straight. Whoever killed Forrest Danvers might be getting nervous with me back in town. Maybe start feeling a little guilty."

"Did something happen?" Cash asked, looking worried.

Rourke didn't see any reason to tell him about the snake and add to his worry. "Nothing I can't handle."

Cash was shaking his head. "You're going to cause trouble, aren't you?"

"I just served eleven years for a crime I didn't commit. I'd like to know who set me up, but at the same time, I have no desire to go back to prison."

Cash took a sip of his beer and sighed as he sat down

across from him. "I investigated the murder, Rourke, along with the state boys who were sent in because we're kin. They had you dead to rights."

Rourke nodded. "Oh, I know all about the evidence. My gun, my fingerprints on it, Forrest's blood on my shirt, the fact that I was found at the scene, the fight with Forrest earlier at the Mello Dee. I also know I didn't kill him." He held up a hand to still his brother as he continued. "Someone went to a lot of trouble to make sure I took the fall for the murder, though. I can't help but wonder why."

"We went over all this eleven years ago, Rourke."

He nodded. "That's why I'm not going to trouble you with any of it."

"If you think that eases my mind—"

"I'd forgotten how good a cold beer tasted," he said. It did feel good to be home.

"You should go fishing for a few days," Cash suggested.

Rourke did a little fishing of his own. "I hear you're not married yet." Of course that wasn't all he'd heard. He'd heard that Blaze had gone after J.T., then Cash and, in fact, hadn't necessarily given up on Cash.

"Have you seen her yet?" Cash asked.

"Blaze? Not yet."

"I meant Cassidy," Cash said, acting surprised Rourke hadn't known who he was talking about.

Rourke eyed his brother. "Saw Cassidy this afternoon. She waited on me at the café and then we went for a drive together."

Cash lifted a brow.

"It's cool. She's going to help me clear my name." One way or another. But he didn't tell his brother that.

"Dammit, Rourke, leave Cassidy out of this."

"Is there something between you and Cassidy I should

know about?" Rourke asked, surprised how upset his brother was getting at just the mention of Cassidy Miller.

"She's a nice woman. I don't want to see her hurt. That's all."

That wasn't all. Not by a long shot. He could see that in the way Cash avoided his gaze. Rourke was surprised that it bothered him.

"You know there is one thing that I could use, though," he said. "The file on Forrest Danvers's murder." Cash started to speak but Rourke cut him off. "A copy would do, big brother. Since I already served my time, what could it hurt?"

Cash groaned as he got up. He walked to a desk off the hall, opened a drawer and took out something. "Have you seen the rest of the family?"

"Yep. I can't believe the way Dusty has grown up," Rourke said, shaking his head. "She was just a kid when I left."

Of the McCalls, J.T. was the oldest at thirty-six, followed by Cash at thirty-five, Rourke at thirty-three and Brandon at thirty. They were all pretty evenly spaced except for the baby, Dusty.

Thirteen years after their mother Shelby died, Asa had gone off one day and came back with a baby. He'd told them that Dusty was orphaned, the child of a friend. He'd adopted her and stuck to his story, but the boys had been old enough to know better.

Dusty was the spitting image of the rest of the McCalls and obviously some love child of Asa's, although they'd never known who Dusty's mother was. They didn't blame the old man for being lonesome. They'd never understood why he hadn't remarried.

"After being married to Shelby, I would never dream

of marrying again," he'd said the one time Rourke had broached the subject.

Rourke couldn't even remember what his mother looked like. He'd only been three when she'd died, Brandon just a baby. There were no photos of her in the house. Asa said it was too hard on him having her photo around. But J.T. remembered her and maybe Cash. They'd both kept flowers on her grave all these years.

"You know Dad was hoping you'd come back and ranch," Cash said, turning from the desk.

Rourke gave his brother a give-me-a-break look. "He didn't mention that when I saw him earlier today. Maybe he didn't go through with legally disinheriting me but—"

"Who do you think put up the money for your appeal?" Cash said. "I'd hoped you'd come home a little smarter."

"Prison is such an educational place," Rourke quipped, trying to hide his surprise. The old man had paid for his appeal? "I thought Brandon and Dusty—"

"Dad paid for all of it. He just didn't want you to know," Cash said. "Stubborn pride. Obviously you inherited it from him."

He handed Rourke a key ring with two keys on it. "That's the key for the cabin. The other one's for the boathouse. Seriously, go fishing. Finding Forrest's killer can wait another few days. After all, you've waited eleven years, right? And I'll see what I can do about getting you a copy of your file."

"Thanks." He really meant it. He took the keys, suddenly exhausted. It had been a long emotional day and a damned surprising one. He knew he needed sleep more than anything else. The very last thing he should do was confront the *other* cowgirl he'd been thinking about for eleven years.

BLAZE WAITED AT the office until almost seven o'clock for Rourke. She'd worn her sexiest silk blouse, an expensive suit and her highest heels this morning, the ones that flattered her legs, legs encased in the finest silk hosiery money could buy.

And she knew she smelled and looked divine. She'd seen Easton's reaction every time he looked at her or came near her. It did her heart good that he'd been acting jealous all day. He knew she'd only dressed this way for Rourke and it had been killing him.

Except Rourke hadn't shown. Maybe he didn't know where she worked. Maybe he'd gone by her apartment.

But she knew that wasn't the case. Rourke would know where to find her. He just hadn't.

She considered that he might have gotten over her. After all it had been eleven years.

She quickly rejected the thought.

He had written her a letter right after his trial, asking her to write him and to wait for him. She'd written back that it wouldn't be fair to either of them for her to wait and that writing would only make it more painful, but that he would always have a place in her heart. He hadn't written her again. Nor she him.

She had thought about writing him just before he got out. But she hadn't wanted to give Rourke any ammunition in writing that he could use against her. She might want to make Easton jealous, but she didn't want to blow it entirely with him. He was still her best bet for an easy life.

She just hoped Rourke would be as simple to manipulate. She needed him to give Easton that little push he obviously had to have to ask her finally to marry him. She'd given up on using Cash to make Easton jealous. Cash was still hung up on some rich gal he'd met at college who'd disappeared. Even Blaze Logan couldn't compete with a ghost.

And J.T.... She didn't want to think about him. He'd made it very clear he wasn't looking for a wife unless she was interested in being a ranch wife, which meant she was to cook and clean and play mama not only to any children they would have, but also his little sister—and he hadn't minced words about it. He'd had a bad experience with some city girl who had soured him on city girls—and women with careers outside the home.

Blaze, who had no intention of being a career woman *or* a ranch wife, had informed J.T. that if he wanted her, he'd have to hire a cook, a nanny and a housekeeper, because he wouldn't be marrying one.

He hadn't given her the time of day after that. Not that he'd done the pursuing in the first place. All he cared about were his stupid cattle.

But Rourke... Well, Rourke should be flattered and grateful for her attention. Especially after all those years in prison. He'd boost her ego and make Easton delirious with jealousy. Rourke couldn't have gotten out of prison at a better time.

She glanced at her watch. Clearly Rourke wasn't coming by. She swore under her breath. As ridiculous as it was, it seemed she would have to do the pursuing. Turning out the lights and locking up the office, she walked out of the building and headed for her car.

That's when she saw him. He was just getting out of his pickup. He stopped and she saw his expression and realized this wasn't the man she used to keep curled around her little finger. Easton was right. Rourke had changed. It crossed her mind that she might be playing with a fire she could no longer control.

But that had never stopped her before, she thought, smiling as she walked toward him. Anyway, this wasn't about Rourke. This was about Easton and her goal to marry him come hell or high water.

"Rourke," she said in her most seductive tone as she stopped so close to him she could feel his body heat and smell the masculine scent of him. He was dressed in jeans and a shirt, boots and a straw cowboy hat. All looked new.

He was more muscular, his body a man's, no longer a boy's, and there was a hardness in his eyes. She couldn't imagine how he could be any sexier even if he tried. And Rourke never had to try.

"Blaze," he said, and gave her a slow, almost calculated smile.

She'd hoped for a little different reaction and felt disappointed that Rourke hadn't burst into her office earlier, swept her up in his arms, kissed her madly and told her that he'd thought about nothing but her all those years in prison. She'd hoped he would carry her off to ravage her as only Rourke could do.

Easton would have just died and word would have spread all over town faster than a wildfire.

Blaze wasn't merely disappointed, she was miffed at Rourke. There wasn't a soul here to see them together. His timing couldn't have been worse. Where had he been? She'd seen him go into the Longhorn Café earlier in the afternoon. If she hadn't decided to pretend to work late, she might not have seen him at all.

She was miffed enough that she decided she wouldn't go anywhere with him when he asked—especially to bed. Not tonight. It probably wouldn't hurt to play hard to get. Look what it did for Cassidy. Blaze had seen the way Cash McCall was always trying to strike up a conversation with her—and Cassidy not even noticing his interest.

"Working late?" Rourke asked, his tone almost mocking as if he knew she'd waited around for him.

"When did you get back?" she asked, changing the subject.

"Earlier." He leaned against the front of his pickup as if waiting for her to make the first move.

She glanced at her watch. This wasn't going anything like she'd hoped.

"You have someplace you need to be?" he asked. He did have a wonderful voice, deep and sexy. Hell, maybe she would let him take her to bed tonight after all.

"Just home. I have an apartment not far from here." How subtle was that?

"What are you driving?" he asked, looking around. She was driving another ADC Suburban parked next to his pickup.

"I walked to work today." A little white lie but one that might get her a ride home, and once Rourke walked her to her door—

"Nice evening for a walk," he said. "I should let you get going." He pushed himself off the front of the pickup, not even touching her as he started around to the driver's door.

"Did you stop by for something?" she asked plaintively.

He paused to look back at her. "Just wanted to see you. You're not married."

"No." She licked her lips.

"I hope you didn't wait for me," he said smoothly.

She bristled. "We agreed that was the best thing."

"Did we? Funny, I thought it was your decision." He shook his head. "I guess I forgot."

"I'm glad you're back," she called to him as he started to get into his pickup.

"Are you?" He was smiling over the top of the door,

then he ducked inside, closed the door and started the engine.

She stood on the sidewalk and watched him drive off. He hadn't offered to take her home. Hell, he hadn't even touched her. Was he angry that she'd broken it off eleven years ago? Like she was going to wait eleven years for him.

Or was he just plain not interested?

No way. He was interested. He was a man. He was Rourke McCall. He was just ticked at her for not writing him or visiting him while he was in prison. He'd be back. Probably later tonight. She wished she'd given him her address. Then she realized her own foolishness. He'd find her. He always had before.

She glanced at the dark green Suburban just feet away and then down at her high, high heels. No contest. She wasn't walking home. She pulled out the keys and headed for the Suburban.

Rourke would have to be punished for not falling all over himself to be with her. She would give him the cold shoulder for a while before she let him make love to her when he showed up at her door tonight. She'd make him park out front. That way Cassidy would see his truck when she drove to work in the morning. So would Easton.

That made Blaze feel better. It wasn't like Rourke had *rejected* her. He couldn't do that. Not as crazy as he'd been about her before he went to prison.

She was deciding what to wear after her shower as she drove to her apartment a few blocks down Main. It should have been a nicer apartment, but her father was still being a bastard and insisting she make her own way.

Which made marriage to Easton Wells look better all the time. But first she deserved one last wild fling with Rourke McCall.

OUT AT THE Sundown Ranch, Asa woke to darkness and the phone. The clock read 3:11 a.m. Nothing but bad news at this time of the morning. He fumbled for the receiver, already shaking, already scared. Rourke. It was his first thought. He hadn't had a call in the middle of the night since Forrest Danvers was murdered.

Heart hammering, he put the receiver to his ear. "Hello?" His voice sounded scratchy, tight. "Hello?" he said a little louder, and pushed himself up in the bed.

He could hear breathing. Not the heavy breathing of an obscene caller but definitely someone on the line. And there was music in the background. A song he recognized.

"Who is this?" he demanded, suddenly more worried. He listened to the soft breathing, holding his own breath. There was a click, then nothing.

He sat for a long moment holding the phone, trying to understand why his heart was racing. It hadn't been about one of the kids. It had been a wrong number.

He hung up the phone, fell back in the bed. Nothing to worry about. His heart pounded as he stared up at the dark ceiling and felt the world around him start to crumble. The soft breathing, the song in the background. He could almost smell her perfume. Shelby. If he didn't know better, he'd think he just had a call from a dead woman.

CHAPTER SEVEN

EARLY THE NEXT MORNING, Rourke heard a vehicle coming up the road to the cabin. One of the reasons he'd chosen this place to stay was because he could hear and see anyone coming. No surprises. He went to the back porch and watched Cash's patrol car wind its way up the mountainside.

The other reason he'd wanted to stay here was the solitude, the beauty, the stark difference between this country and a prison cell.

Having spent too many nights locked up, he'd slept under the stars last night in a bedroll on the beach in front of the cabin. The moon had been almost full. He'd watched it rise over the lake in a kind of breathless awe, feeling the night breeze against his face, feeling alive for the first time in more years than he could remember.

But it had proved to be a restless night, haunted with memories. He'd dreamed about Blaze. And worse, Cassidy. He regretted not taking Blaze up on her offer. He wouldn't make that mistake again.

"Morning," Rourke called in greeting to his brother as Cash climbed out of the patrol car. "Tell me you brought doughnuts."

Cash smiled as he pulled a large box out with him and headed up the steps. "You realize that's a cliché, cops and doughnuts." He handed Rourke the box.

"Right." Rourke could smell the doughnuts in the bag

perched on top of the stacks of papers in the heavy box. "Chocolate covered with sprinkles?" He let out an oath as Cash nodded. "I could kiss you."

"Don't," Cash warned as he pushed open the door for Rourke and followed him inside.

"I made coffee," Rourke said. "You have time for a cup?"

Cash shook his head. "There's a copy of the case file in the box, along with copies of the trial transcript."

Rourke shot him a look. There was no way Cash could have gotten his hands on a copy between last night and this morning. That meant he'd had it all along, had searched, as Rourke planned to, for the real killer.

"Listen," Cash was saying, "I've been doing some thinking."

Rourke put down the box on the table and turned to his brother. Cash and J.T. had always been the serious ones, the McCalls who worried and stewed, the responsible, sensible ones. "If you're going to tell me not to look into the murder—"

"No, that would be a waste of my breath," Cash said with a rueful smile. "Just…just be careful."

Rourke stared at his brother. "You think the killer is still around, don't you."

"I just know there were a lot of hard feelings over Forrest's death and some of what came out at the trial," Cash said. "Digging that all up again could be dangerous. You remember how Forrest's brother was? Well, Cecil's crazier now."

Rourke smiled. "Why can't you admit you don't believe I killed Forrest?"

"Because I'm a cop and I go by evidence, Rourke. Bring me some evidence to the contrary," Cash said, and turned to leave. "Enjoy the doughnuts."

And Rourke was the bad boy McCall.

After Cash left, Rourke ate the doughnuts as he considered the huge box full of paper. The doughnuts took him back to a time when he and his brothers would roughhouse in the mornings, having pillow fights and squirt-gun battles, which Martha, the ranch's longtime housekeeper, would break up with the promise of chocolate doughnuts.

He cherished the memory as he finished the last crumb, the smell, the taste, taking him back to his boyhood.

Finally he looked in the box on the table. It contained the reasons he'd gone to prison. Was it possible it also contained some missed fact that would clear his name and free him from the past? He knew the chances weren't good or Cash would have already found it.

For the better part of the day, Rourke went through every scrap of paper in the box. Head aching, he realized as he turned over the last sheet that he'd exhausted the possibility of finding a missed clue.

No wonder no one had believed his innocence.

He put everything back into the box and stared at it. The plan came out of nowhere and yet he knew it had probably been percolating for eleven years. He grabbed his jacket and headed for the door.

CASSIDY WENT INTO WORK as if it was just another day. Her eyes were puffy from crying and she felt horrible, but she put on a little makeup to try to cover it, and a smile. While she probably didn't fool anyone, she was glad she'd come in to work.

The café was packed, obviously with some who were hoping Rourke McCall was going to come in and threaten her again, only this time with a shotgun. What they didn't know was that Rourke's hold on her didn't require a gun.

Rourke didn't show up at all.

But Blaze did. Good old Blaze. She came in and sat at the counter.

"What can I get you?" Cassidy asked, dropping a menu in front of her cousin.

"Just coffee," Blaze said, eyeing her intently. "Are you wearing *makeup?*"

Cassidy didn't reply as she put a cup of black coffee in front of Blaze and left.

Blaze didn't even finish her coffee, Cassidy noticed when she came back by and found her cousin gone. Nor did Blaze leave a tip. Predictable.

As she glanced out the window, she saw Rourke pull up in front of the Antelope Development Corporation and get out. Jealousy raised its ugly head, making her sick to her stomach. This was how she used to feel when she'd see Rourke with Blaze. She turned away as he entered ADC, the door closing behind him. She wouldn't go through this again.

"Is everything all right?" Ellie asked.

"Fine," Cassidy lied.

The bell dinged over the door and she looked up to see the owner of the Mello Dee Lounge and Supper Club come through the door. Les Thurman brushed a lock of gray hair back from his forehead and headed straight for the counter and her.

"Good morning," he said cheerfully. "Place is busy this morning."

"Good morning." Cassidy could feel him seeing through the makeup and her own cheerful greeting.

"You all right?" he asked. He had a fatherly way about him and had always been kind to her, especially when it came to anything to do with Rourke McCall. Everyone in town must have known how she felt about Rourke—except Rourke. Les had been behind the bar that night at the Mello

Dee and no doubt overheard the guys at the bar giving her a hard time about Rourke before the fight broke out.

Now Les glanced toward the front window and Rourke's pickup parked in front of Blaze's office. "If you're dead set on a McCall, consider Cash. He's good and solid. He could make you happy."

She felt herself blush. "The only thing I'm dead set on is getting you some breakfast."

"Sorry. None of my business. I'll take the special," Les said, and picked up a copy of the newspaper lying on the counter. "Keep your nose out of other people's business, Thurman," he mumbled loud enough for her to hear.

She laughed as she hurried off to put in his order.

BLAZE LOOKED UP from behind her desk, unable to hide her surprise at finding Rourke McCall standing in her office doorway. She glanced to the street in time to see Easton drive away. Had Rourke purposely waited until Easton left the office, until he was sure she was alone? Blaze would bet money on it, she thought as she waited for Rourke to make his move.

"What exactly does Antelope Development Corporation develop?" he asked, coming into the office and closing the door.

She leaned back in her chair and watched him walk around the office. He picked up several pieces of paper from the edge of Easton's desk, glanced at them, then dropped them.

Although his movements didn't seem threatening, she felt a sudden stab of concern. The receptionist must not be at her desk. Otherwise, she would have announced Rourke. That meant Blaze was alone with him and no one knew he was here. Including Easton.

She realized Rourke was waiting for an answer. She

smiled, trying to hide the fact that she felt suddenly uneasy. Any sign of weakness could be seen as guilt, she reminded herself.

"Land development."

"Coal-bed methane gas leases," he countered.

She nodded, hearing the distaste in his voice. "Antelope Flats is growing," she said, sounding too perky, as if trying too hard. She could see that he'd noticed. "Methane gas is the future of this town."

"That's too bad," he said.

She smiled up at him as if to make it clear that she didn't care about all this business stuff. She'd worn a robin-egg-blue dress that clung to her curves today.

Easton's eyes had practically popped out of his head when he saw her. She'd flirted with him a little, just to make him feel better.

But it had been hard to hide her delight when he told her he had to go into Sheridan to meet with some coal-mining executives. She could tell he hated to leave her alone in the office. Too bad he hadn't seen Rourke come in.

"So what brings you out this early in the morning?" she asked. She hadn't been sure she would see him again after the way he'd acted yesterday evening. He hadn't called her apartment later last night. Nor had he stopped by. She'd started doubting her control over him. She should have known he couldn't stay away from her.

But what bothered her was the feeling that he hadn't come here to try to get her into bed. And that wasn't like the Rourke McCall she'd known. She feared she didn't know this one at all and that could be her downfall.

How would she know what was going on with him and Cassidy? With him and Forrest's murder? The more she thought about it, the more worried she was that Easton was somehow involved. He'd been acting…scared, and that wasn't like him. What else could it be but Rourke getting out of prison?

That's why she needed to be on the inside of things with Rourke, and there was only one way to get there. Was he going to make her seduce him? Just as she'd done when she was fifteen?

She had more experience now, she thought, and there was no doubt that he'd noticed the dress. But it worried her, Cassidy wearing makeup. Everyone knew what it meant when a woman started wearing makeup. She was after some man.

"I need your help," Rourke said, surprising her by settling down in the chair on the other side of her desk.

Her help? Now they were getting somewhere. She turned up the wattage on her smile. "Just name it."

Rourke would have had to have been dead not to hear the offer in her tone. Blaze definitely assumed they would take up where they'd left off eleven years ago. He'd always enjoyed Blaze. What man wouldn't? Especially when she turned on the seduction, and right now she had it cranked all the way up.

The blue dress hid nothing, making it clear that Blaze's body had only improved with age.

"I'm going to reconstruct the night Forrest was murdered," he told her.

She blinked. It obviously wasn't what she'd hoped for. He almost laughed at her strained expression.

"What?"

"I'm going to reenact that night."

All the color went out of her face. "You aren't serious."

He nodded and leaned back in the chair, meeting her gaze. "All the main players will be there, except Forrest, of course."

"That's the craziest thing I've ever— Rourke, why relive that awful night? I mean it's been eleven years. It isn't like you can uncover any evidence that might have been overlooked."

He shrugged. "You never know."

She took a breath and let it out slowly, making him think Blaze might have reasons of her own for not wanting to return to that night. Hadn't Cassidy insinuated that Blaze might be hiding something?

It irritated him that Cassidy had him second-guessing himself again. Blaze had nothing to gain by setting him up for murder. Did she?

He pushed himself up out of the chair. "So I'll see you at the Mello Dee Saturday night. Come by a little before midnight." He saw Blaze struggling to come up with a good reason she couldn't be there as he started to leave. "Oh yeah, and wear what you wore that night."

"What? You think I still have the same clothes I did eleven years ago?"

He turned to smile at her. "Then just wear something like that outfit you had on that night," he suggested.

"Those clothes have gone completely out of style."

He laughed. "I've missed you, Blaze."

She seemed to like that. "I can't believe *Cassidy* has agreed to this."

"It was her idea," he ad-libbed, and noticed the change in Blaze. She wasn't happy to hear this.

"Cassidy? Rourke, you aren't taking *her* advice, are you?" Blaze let out a pitying laugh. "My cousin would do anything to hurt me. You realize she only got you sent to prison to separate the two of us, don't you?"

He stared at Blaze, realizing just how blind he'd been when it came to her. Cassidy was right. He'd been a patsy and maybe in more ways than one.

"Cash has agreed to stand in for Forrest Saturday night," he said, anticipating Blaze's reaction and relishing in it.

"Cash?"

"Is that a problem?" Rourke asked innocently.

"No, it's just that…" She licked her lipsticked lips. "I suppose you heard about me and Cash?"

He smiled. "If I listened to rumors, Blaze, I'd think you'd slept with every eligible male in town." With that, he turned and walked out the door, closing it firmly behind him.

BLAZE SAT STARING after him, then picked up the first thing she could grab off her desk and hurled it across the room. The stapler hit the wall and clattered to the floor, leaving a gouge in the paneling.

"Bastard," she swore as she watched Rourke walk past his old pickup and cross the street, headed for the Longhorn Café—and Cassidy.

He hadn't even suggested that the two of them get together later, that they take up where they'd left off. Damn him. Worse, he was going over to see Cassidy.

Blaze couldn't believe this. Rourke should have been falling all over her.

She had to do something. Something drastic.

Easton drove up just then, got out of the Suburban, glared at Rourke's old pickup and then headed into the office. Wasn't he supposed to be at a meeting with coal-mining executives? Or had he just told her that's where he was going so he could double back and catch her with Rourke?

Only he hadn't caught her with Rourke. Easton had just missed him. Damn. She scrambled to come up with a way to salvage something from Rourke's visit. Easton had been in a foul mood earlier, had canceled their date last night, and seeing Rourke's truck outside didn't seem to improve his disposition.

She told herself she was getting to him. But she had to up the stakes.

She would pretend she'd left Rourke in her bed this morning and he'd stopped by to…to give her her apartment keys, she thought, hurriedly digging them out of her purse and dropping them on the edge of her desk. Let Easton think she'd spent the night with Rourke. What the hell. Easton wouldn't know the difference.

She pulled out the small makeup bag she kept in her desk drawer and opened her compact. The look in her eyes startled her. She looked scared and upset. That wouldn't do at all. Not if she hoped to convince Easton that everything was great between her and Rourke, the bastard. They were all bastards.

She heard Easton come in and stop at the receptionist's desk to pick up his phone messages. He would be coming into the office any moment.

Hurriedly she powdered her nose. *Pretend you spent a heavenly night in Rourke's arms,* she ordered herself. Her gaze softened a little at just the thought.

The door to the office opened and, still powdering her nose, she looked up at Easton and wondered how he was going to take the news about Rourke's plan. Not well, she thought, and realized she was scared, too.

"I'M GOING WITH YOU," Dusty said, her tone brooking no argument.

Asa looked up at his daughter as she came down the wide staircase toward the door where he stood. She looked so much like her mother that for a moment he was dumbstruck by her understated beauty—and her mule-headed determination.

"You're going to town to talk to Rourke, aren't you?" she said. "As you *promised.*"

"And pick up a load of grain," he said, his real reason for going into town. "Wouldn't you rather stay here? J.T. was talking about riding up into the Bighorns today on horseback."

She smiled and shook her head as if he couldn't fool her. She was *so* much like her mother. "You can buy me lunch in town. Cash told me that Rourke is staying at the lake cabin."

Asa nodded, not surprised by either the news that Rourke was staying at the cabin or that Dusty had wheedled the information out of Cash. "So what makes you think we can even find your brother?"

"It's a small town," she said, and headed for the door.

Asa could see that there was no getting out of this. The alternative was having her go back to refusing to talk to him, which in retrospect might not be so bad.

He followed her out to the truck, not surprised when she started to get in the driver's side. He was touched that Dusty tried to protect him, especially since his heart attack, but he was still the head of this family, dammit.

"I'll drive," he said, stepping past her. He could see she wanted to put up an argument, but he slid in behind the wheel and slammed the door before she could.

She chattered on the way into town about ranch business, the latest news about neighbors and old friends, the upcoming rodeo. He only half listened. He had other things on his mind. Like the phone call last night. He'd convinced himself that it had been a wrong number. Hell, he'd been half-asleep. It wasn't anything to worry about. Nothing at all.

"ROURKE JUST STOPPED BY to drop off my apartment keys," Blaze said, the moment Easton walked into the office. "You aren't going to believe what he's planning to do Saturday night."

"Nice to see you, too, Blaze," Easton said, closing the door firmly behind him. He'd gotten little sleep last night, tossing and turning, the night filled with horrible nightmares. He'd awakened in a cold sweat. And now he didn't give a damn what Rourke was planning for Saturday night. In fact, he didn't want to hear the man's name.

"He's restaging the murder."

Easton turned to look at her, her words chilling him to the bone. The woman was powdering her nose. Primping. And he didn't need to wonder for whom.

"What the hell did you do to cause this?" he demanded. Her cheeks were flushed and it wasn't from blush. She was enjoying this, he thought, wanting to strangle her.

"I didn't do anything," she protested. "He just came into the office this morning to give me my keys and announced that he wanted all of us to be at the Mello Dee Saturday night and, get this, to wear the same clothing— as if we still had it. What, we donated it to the museum for safekeeping? Can you imagine? Obviously time stood still for Rourke, but for the rest of us—"

"Blaze, forget about the damned clothes." He couldn't believe this. She was so worked up she was babbling and didn't even realize the consequences of her actions. "Don't you know how dangerous this is?"

She quieted for a moment to stare at him. "Dangerous?"

"Are you a complete ninny?" he snapped. "If Rourke isn't the killer, then who is? Someone we know?"

"That's crazy."

"Your cousin has said from the beginning that someone must have seen her put that note on Rourke's windshield and read it and saw a chance to set up McCall," Easton said in exasperation. "How else did the killer know that Rourke was going up Wild Horse Gulch, how else could the killer have framed Rourke for the murder?"

She was staring at him. "Assuming he *was* framed."

Easton stared back at her. She didn't really think Rourke was a killer, did she? Would she try to use a killer to make him jealous? Was she that stupid?

"Cassidy probably lied," she said.

He shook his head. "Let's not go there again." She'd been singing that song for eleven years, only no one had believed that Cassidy was behind the frame—or the killing. No one except Blaze and maybe Rourke.

"But if Rourke killed Forrest—"

Easton let out a curse. "If you believe that, then how in the hell can you agree to this reenactment? Hasn't it dawned on you that Rourke might be planning this merely to get even with us?"

"Us?" she echoed, her gaze honing in on him like radar. "What are you talking about?"

"This town, Blaze. We sent him to prison. Maybe for a crime he didn't commit. Either way, he's back and clearly he wants to even some score." He shook his head at her.

"If you're worried that Rourke will come after you because you're with me now…"

Easton gave a withering look. "He has already come after me. I found out today that he hired a private investigator who's been snooping around ADC, and I'm not the only one Rourke's been investigating."

"So what?" she demanded with obvious irritation. No doubt she was disappointed he hadn't made something of Rourke returning her apartment keys. She didn't have a clue.

He sighed. "So Rourke isn't going to rest until he gets vengeance. Rourke's going to take down as many of us as he can in that quest." He raised a brow. "Maybe you included, Blaze. I've never believed you went straight home that night and I would wager Rourke doesn't, either."

CHAPTER EIGHT

CASSIDY HATED THE bubble of euphoria she felt as Rourke walked into the café. She hadn't expected to see him, just assumed he would be spending the day—if he hadn't already spent the night—with Blaze.

He took a booth in her section rather than sit at the counter, meeting her surprised expression with a smile. He looked different today. More rested, less anxious, she thought as she grabbed a menu, a cup and a pot of coffee and headed toward the booth.

"Hi," he said. "I was hoping you could join me. If you're not too busy."

The afternoon coffee-break crowd had thinned out and it was still too early for supper. She couldn't really decline, even if she'd wanted to.

"Okay." Even with the obvious change in him, she couldn't help but be leery.

"Have you had lunch?"

She shook her head.

"Good. I hate eating alone."

She'd forgotten what his smile could do to her. "You know what you want?" He hadn't opened the menu.

"Chicken-fried steak, biscuits and gravy and whatever comes with it."

She couldn't help but smile as she wrote down the order. When she looked up, he was staring out the window.

"Is that all?" she asked.

He didn't respond and she followed his gaze to see Blaze pulling out in one of the ADC Suburbans. Cassidy had seen her earlier in a blue dress that left nothing to the imagination. Was it any wonder she attracted men like flies to honey?

Cassidy looked away to wipe at a spot on the table with the corner of her apron. She was determined to fight these feelings she had for Rourke. And she refused to be jealous of Blaze. If Rourke wanted Blaze, well, then that was just fine with her.

She hadn't realized he'd turned his attention back to her until she glanced up and saw that he was watching her and seemed to have been for some time.

"I should warn you," he said, as if he knew what she'd been thinking. "I had a talk with Blaze this morning."

"I don't need to—"

"I'm going to reenact the night Forrest was murdered Saturday at the Mello Dee Lounge and Supper Club."

She was speechless.

A sheepish grin moved across his face. "I told Blaze it was your idea."

She gasped. "Why would you do such a thing?"

He smiled and shrugged. "She was so damned sure that you wouldn't go along with it. I couldn't help myself."

"Blaze must be beside herself," she said, and glanced out as her cousin drove away. She caught Blaze's expression. The woman had fury in her eyes as she glared at Cassidy. "I'll put our orders in," she said, suddenly ravenous herself as the Suburban disappeared down the street.

When she returned to the booth, Rourke said, "Beautiful day, isn't it?"

Cassidy stared at him, wondering what had changed since yesterday. When he looked at her she'd didn't see the hard anger in his eyes or the brittle bitterness. Instead, she saw something that scared her even more. Hope.

She couldn't bear to see him hurt again and she feared he was setting himself up for a fall by staging the murder night. Worse, by crossing Blaze.

"Rourke, I have to warn you. Blaze can be a little mean-spirited when she doesn't get her way."

He threw back his head and laughed. "She's hell on wheels, but don't worry, I won't let her harm you."

"Me? I was thinking of you."

He shook his head. "You and your cousin couldn't be more different, you know that?"

She knew that. Eleven years ago she would have given anything for whatever it was about Blaze that had made Rourke want her.

"Seriously, are you sure this reenactment is a good idea?" she asked.

He was smiling. "It's a terrible idea. I hope we don't have to go through with it." He met her surprised gaze. "By Saturday, I'm banking on you and me having already found Forrest's killer."

"You and me?"

Was he serious? "Rourke—"

"You made me realize yesterday that I hadn't been paying a lot of attention to what was going on around me eleven years ago."

She felt herself blush and was grateful when she heard the bell announcing that their orders were up. She returned with his chicken-fried steak and a chicken sandwich for herself.

"Thanks," he said, and dug in. "This is great. So, will you help me?" he asked between bites.

Was he really offering her a chance to help him? To redeem herself for the part she'd played in his going to prison? She studied his handsome face. Or was he setting her up, still convinced she had something to hide?

It didn't matter. She would give anything to help him find even a little peace. She couldn't give him back the eleven years. But maybe she could put some of Rourke's ghosts to rest. And some of her own, as well.

"I'll do anything I can to help you," she said. "But, Rourke, I don't know anything. I can't imagine what help I would be."

"You've already helped," he said, and grinned. "By coming up with the reenactment plan." His expression warmed her to her toes.

They ate in silence for a few minutes.

"You've done a remarkable job with this place," he said, glancing around the café, his eyes coming back to her.

"Thank you." She felt shy under the intensity of his attention. This change in him reminded her of the old Rourke, but it also worried her.

"Last night, I thought a lot about what you said," Rourke remarked between bites. "If I really wasn't the intended victim, then that could change our entire approach to finding the killer."

"You're really serious about this, aren't you?" she asked. "I mean finding the killer. I thought after someone put that snake in your pickup yesterday…"

He smiled, his eyes dark. "Only a coward puts a rattler in a man's pickup to scare him. Or a fool. The person who killed Forrest doesn't want to kill again. That's why he's trying to warn me off."

She nodded, not so sure about that.

"I was thinking about your theory," he said as they finished eating.

"That's all it is, you realize," she said quickly.

He nodded. "The thing is, how did the killer know you

were going to write the note or that I was going to get into a fight with Forrest that night?"

She'd thought about this for years. "Well, the way I figure it, once he had the gun, all he had to do was wait for an opportunity to present itself—if his true intention was to get rid of Forrest and put the blame on you."

"My gun," Rourke said, and swore under his breath.

"You kept a gun on a shelf in your bedroom," she said, and hated her accusing tone.

"I know what you're going to say."

"Do you?"

"The gun was a…keepsake. I hadn't fired it since I was a boy and my grandfather used to take me out…." He shook his head. "Never mind. The point is anyone could have taken it the night of my birthday party."

She rolled her eyes. "What about in the weeks before the party? The truth is, you don't have any idea when it was taken—or by whom."

"Just for the sake of argument, let's forget about Blaze."

She raised a brow. "Is that wise?"

"I'm not having any trouble with it," he said, meeting her gaze.

"I don't care about your relationship with Blaze," she said, telling herself it was true. "I just think it is foolish to overlook a suspect out of…" She waved a hand through the air as if unable to find the words.

He grinned at her. "Because I'm so besotted with Blaze that I can't think rationally?"

"Yes."

He laughed. "Let me worry about Blaze. I might surprise you." He sobered. "As you were saying, my fight with Forrest that night gave the killer the opportunity he was looking for."

She nodded. "All he had to do was get Forrest to some

deserted spot and use your gun with your fingerprints on it."

His eyes narrowed as if he was wondering how her note to him played into her theory.

"Or," she continued, "the killer might have heard the same thing I did—Forrest on the phone setting up the meeting with Blaze."

"You're convinced it was Blaze, even though she denied it in court?"

Cassidy ticked off the reasons on her fingers. "Blaze left early. When was the last time she did that? Never. She used the fight, which she instigated, as her excuse not to see you later that night, right?" She nodded when he saw from his expression that she was right.

"Blaze liked to play hard to get sometimes," he said.

Cassidy wasn't about to touch that. "Also, when I saw Blaze and Forrest together a week before the murder, I heard him call her honey bun—just like he called whoever he told to meet him up Wild Horse Gulch the night of the murder."

Rourke's jaw muscle jumped. "Maybe he called all women honey bun. The guy wasn't very imaginative."

She gave him a pitying look. "Didn't it strike you as odd that Forrest stayed at the Mello Dee after the fight? After the beating you gave him, wouldn't he want to get the heck out of there? So he finishes his drink, glances at his watch, then goes to the phone as if he was waiting to call someone. Waiting for her to get home?"

Rourke was frowning.

"He calls a woman— We do agree on that, right?"

Rourke nodded.

"He says meet me and let's talk about it. What would you conclude from that?"

"Okay," he agreed. "I can see how you came to the conclusion you did."

"On top of that, Blaze has no alibi for the time of the murder."

"She lived alone in an apartment. That's not unusual," he said.

She wanted to slug him and he must have seen the fire in her eyes because he raised both hands in surrender and said, "Let's say you're right. So where does your note fit into this?"

Yes, her note. "If the killer didn't overhear Forrest on the phone like I did, then he or she had to either see me put the note on your truck or notice it under the windshield wiper—and read it," she said. "But if I hadn't written the note, the killer would have come up with some other way to get you to Wild Horse Gulch—or at least make sure you didn't have an alibi."

Rourke nodded slowly, but she couldn't tell if he agreed with her or was just going along with her theory for the moment.

She didn't point out that Blaze had purposely not given him an alibi by going home alone. "Remember, he already had your gun with your fingerprints on it and you had motive after the bar fight," she said. "I went back inside to the restroom, so I don't know what happened between the time I put the note under your pickup windshield wiper and came back out."

"Why did you go back inside?" he asked.

She looked out the window toward the street and saw that Blaze had returned from wherever she'd been. Cassidy watched her look at Rourke's pickup then glance across Main Street in the direction of the café. There was a glare on the window so Cassidy was pretty sure Blaze couldn't see them. Hoped that were true. There was something in Blaze's expression that chilled her.

"I was upset," Cassidy said, turning her attention back to him. "I'd been crying and I realized that I'd left my purse in the bathroom."

"Maybe you stuck around because you wanted to see what I did when I found the note," he said without rancor.

She dropped her eyes. "Maybe."

He said nothing for a moment. "Did you notice anyone in the parking lot when you went out—other than me?"

She shook her head. "I was too upset...." Her gaze came up to meet his. "Forrest's killer could have been waiting in the parking lot for him and saw me leave the note and read it. Or he could have followed him."

Rourke was shaking his head. "It would have been impossible for anyone to follow Forrest up that road in a vehicle without him knowing it. From where he was parked, he could have seen the car coming."

She nodded and saw the change in Rourke's expression.

"No wonder the jury was so convinced I killed him. So I guess we start with who was there that night. Who witnessed the fight. Who had been waiting for just this opportunity." He shook his head. "You and I, we really played right into the killer's hands, didn't we."

THE BELL OVER the door jangled and Rourke looked up to see his little brother coming in the café. Brandon was scowling. He looked as if he'd slept in his clothing—but not nearly long enough. He needed a shave and he was wearing the same clothing he'd had on yesterday when he'd picked Rourke up in Deer Lodge at the prison.

Rourke knew the look a little too well. At least he had eleven years ago.

Brandon caught his eye and motioned that he needed to talk to him.

"If you will excuse me," Rourke said to Cassidy who had seen Brandon, as well. "I need to talk to my brother." He reached into his wallet to pay his bill.

"Lunch is on me," she said.

"Thanks, but at least let me tip the waitress." He dropped more than enough for both their meals and a tip on the table. "No arguments," he said when she started to protest. Then he hesitated. "Thanks for helping me with this. Can we talk later?"

She nodded.

He stared down into her face for a long moment. He really did like her face. Then he touched her arm, squeezing it as he passed.

"You look like something the cat's dragged in," Rourke said as he let Brandon lead him outside. "What's up?"

Brandon smelled of alcohol and looked even worse up close. "I hate to ask you seeing as how you just got back to town—"

"You need money," Rourke said, and pulled his brother aside. Several people walked by. Rourke waited until they were out of earshot. "I thought you had a job, and what about the money Grandpa left you?"

"I'm in between jobs right now and Dad has my trust set up where I only get a stipend every month," Brandon said angrily. "I can't touch the bulk of it until I'm thirty-five." Five more years.

"How much do you need?" Rourke asked.

Brandon looked down at the sidewalk. "A couple grand."

Rourke let out a low whistle. "And this money is for what exactly?"

"Look, either lend me the money or forget it," Brandon snapped, and started to walk away.

"You're gambling," Rourke said, his voice low.

His little brother stopped and turned. "I'm in trouble."

Rourke swore. "Who is it you owe?"

Brandon shook his head.

"You tell me or I'm not going to help you."

"Kelly."

With an oath, Rourke raked a hand through his hair. "Burt Ace-up-his-sleeve friggin' Kelly? What the hell is wrong with you? Kelly has been fleecing ranch hands for years. Is he still with the VanHorn spread?"

Brandon nodded. "Look, don't go causing any trouble, all right? Just give me the money so I can pay him. You don't know what he's like. He'll kill me."

"*Kill* you?"

"He gets crazy sometimes. He told me last night that if I didn't come up with the money today I'd end up like Forrest Danvers," Brandon said.

Rourke froze. "You aren't making this up?"

"Do you think I'd lie about something like that?"

He hoped not as he studied his brother. Brandon had been nineteen when Forrest was murdered. "What do you know about Forrest's murder?"

"Nothing. Just what I told you," Brandon said.

"I'm going to pay your gambling debts," Rourke said carefully. "You're going to go back to the ranch and start helping the old man until you get a job."

Brandon started to argue but Rourke grabbed him by the collar.

"You are never going to gamble with Kelly again," Rourke continued, tightening his hold. "If I hear different, I'm going to kick your hide. Is that clear?"

"You sound like the old man," Brandon wheezed.

Rourke smiled. "Yeah, don't I? Too bad the old man didn't do the same to me. Maybe I wouldn't have gone to prison. But you and I, we're not having this discussion again." He let go of his brother. "We understand each other?"

Brandon rubbed his throat and nodded. "Let me pay Kelly. If you go out there—"

"I'll take care of it."

Brandon started to argue but wisely changed his mind.

"Go to the ranch, get cleaned up," Rourke said. "I won't mention this to J.T. when I call him to tell him you'll be working out there for a while."

"Look, can't I start tomorrow? I'm so hungover—"

"It will do you good," Rourke said. "I'll tell J.T. to put you on mending fence. You'd be amazed what the hot sun does to a hangover."

Brandon swore as he walked away. Rourke watched him drive out of town toward the ranch, thinking, damn if he hadn't become his father. The thought did nothing to improve his mood as he headed for his pickup.

ASA SPOTTED ROURKE'S pickup in front of the Longhorn just as Rourke started to climb behind the wheel. He should have bought his son a new truck, done something to let Rourke know he was glad he was out of prison, that he believed in his innocence, that he hadn't disinherited him and was sorry he'd ever threatened to.

But he'd done nothing, said nothing. He silently cursed himself for his stubborn pride or whatever it was that often made him act like an ass. Worse, that he couldn't even admit to acting like an ass to his own son.

"Rourke," Dusty called out the window, and motioned for him to wait.

Asa parked down the block from the café. "I'd just as soon do this on my own," he said as Dusty opened her door.

"I'm sure you would," she said, ignoring him as she got out and started toward her brother.

Her mother's genes again, Asa thought as he followed her. He hadn't gone far when he saw a familiar figure come out of a building down the street. He stumbled, nearly fell.

"Dad," Dusty said, grabbing his arm to steady him. "Are you all right?"

He didn't answer, his attention still on the woman getting into the dark sports car.

"What is it?" Dusty said. "Dad?"

A truck pulled out, blocking his view of the woman, of the car and the license plate. The car sped away, giving him only a glimpse of blond hair.

"Who was that?" Dusty asked.

"What? No one. It's nothing."

"You look as if you just saw a ghost," Rourke said joining them.

Asa shook his head. "I'm okay." His voice broke. "I just need to watch where I'm going, that's all."

Dusty was eyeing him suspiciously. She glanced down the street toward where he'd been staring and looked as if she were about to say something when Rourke asked, "Do you need to sit down?"

Asa felt light-headed and realized he was shaking like a leaf.

"Dad hasn't been feeling so hot," Dusty said, always covering for him.

"I'm fine," Asa snapped. "I want you to come stay at the ranch, Rourke, where you belong."

Rourke lifted a brow and Asa immediately regretted his tone. Even Dusty groaned beside him.

"Son..." Asa tried again.

"Thanks for the...invitation, if that's what it was, but I'm staying at the cabin right now," Rourke said.

"Well, if you change your mind…" Asa said, feeling helpless. He could see that he'd disappointed Dusty and angered Rourke.

But as much as that distressed him, he was more upset over the woman he'd seen down the street. Or thought he'd seen.

"See you later," Rourke said to his sister before heading to his pickup.

Dusty went after him and Asa overheard her say, "Dad's been under a lot of stress lately but he really does want you to come home."

Asa leaned against the side of the building next to the Longhorn and tried to calm his racing heart. Stress? Hell, isn't that what everyone blamed nowadays? But could stress make you imagine a face that you'd spent years trying to forget?

"You could have been nicer," Dusty said not unkindly as she returned to take Asa's arm. Rourke looked their way as he drove off, headed south out of town. "Are you sure you're all right?" She sounded worried about him.

"I'm fine. You're right, I didn't eat yesterday. Let's get a burger on the way to pick up the grain. I'll let you drive."

That seemed to satisfy her. At least for the moment. But as she drove the truck down the street, like him, she appeared to be looking for the black sports car the blond woman had gotten into just before she disappeared from view.

ROURKE STOPPED AT THE BANK, then drove south out of town. He couldn't believe that Kelly had the nerve to gamble with a McCall. Rourke's blood boiled at just the thought.

But it was the comment that Kelly had allegedly made about Forrest that had cooled Rourke down. Getting mad was one thing, but it took a cool head to get even. A lesson well learned at prison.

Just miles from the Wyoming border, he turned back up into the open country to the east through a huge log arch with the words *VanHorn Ranch* on a sign hanging from it.

Tacked on the post was a reward poster, the newer cardboard sign already weathered and worn but the lettering still readable: Reward For Any Information About The Vandalizing Of VanHorn Property.

VanHorn had been the first to allow coal-bed methane gas wells to be drilled on his property. The whole idea hadn't gone over well. In fact, someone had vandalized VanHorn's wells and drilling equipment. That had been before Rourke went to prison. Brandon had told him that VanHorn was still gunning for the culprit.

VanHorn had a long memory, never forgot a slight or a wrong. Mason was like Asa that way, Rourke thought, reminded of his own father.

The first VanHorn, Houston, had come to Montana with Rourke's great-grandfather, Jed McCall. Both men had been cattlemen, born and bred. Then the families had a falling out, with the feud continuing each generation.

Rourke wondered what Houston VanHorn would think of his descendants allowing coal-bed methane drilling to be done on his land. Maybe Houston's ghost had vandalized the gas wells. At the very least the old man must be rolling in his grave to see the drilling rigs on VanHorn land. In that regard, Houston VanHorn had been like Asa.

Dust churned up behind the pickup as Rourke raced up the road. There were drilling units all along the road to the ranch house. In the distance, Rourke spotted a new well going in.

"There is money in methane," Brandon had written him

in prison. "Dad's a fool to let it go to waste underground. It isn't like the wells hurt the land."

Good thing his brother wasn't here with him, Rourke thought. He'd have slugged him.

At the main ranch house, Rourke turned and drove down a short road to where a group of men were breaking a horse.

From the looks of the horse in question, it was a wild mustang from down in Wyoming. VanHorn had been rounding up the mustangs for years.

Rourke got out of his pickup. He didn't see Kelly in the group of men. He headed for the ranch office, cool and calm. At least on the surface.

He opened the door rather than knock. Burt Kelly looked up from behind a huge oak desk. The ranch foreman was tall and slim with a face like a ferret, eyes small and dark, his face pocked, his lips a thin mean line. He seemed surprised to see Rourke. It took something pretty big to get a McCall onto the VanHorn spread, given the long-running feud between the McCalls and VanHorns.

"Rourke McCall," Kelly said, and Rourke caught a flicker of worry in the older man's eyes. "I didn't think you'd have the guts to show your face around here again."

Rourke smiled. Kelly liked to goad people, make them angry, make them do something stupid. "You know why I'm here."

Kelly raised a brow. "I do?"

"I heard you're still a gambling man," Rourke said, his voice soft and deadly. "Want to make a wager as to why I'm here?"

Kelly laughed. "I'd win that one. Let me guess. Your little brother came whining to you. He's just like you, Rourke. A lousy poker player. Hotheaded and a poor loser."

Rourke smiled. "Some of us just don't play well with a liar and a cheat."

Kelly's face flushed. "Watch what you say, McCall, you're on VanHorn land now. If I pick up that phone, I can have a dozen men here within minutes. I don't think you want me to do that."

Rourke moved to the desk with such speed, Kelly rolled the chair back a few inches before he realized what Rourke had in mind.

Rourke picked up the phone and handed it to the foreman. "Better make that call, Kelly."

The older man just stared at him. "What is it you want, McCall?"

"You're never to deal another hand to any member of my family. If I hear you do, I'll be back and it will be the last hand you deal."

"Don't you come in here threatening—"

"Here." Rourke took out the roll of cash he'd picked up at the bank on his way out of town. He counted out twenty-five hundred dollars, five hundred more than Brandon said he owed, onto the edge of the desk and raised a brow at Kelly. "Will that cover it?"

Kelly nodded and reached for the money. Rourke grabbed his hand, bringing the man out of his chair with a cry of pain. As Rourke came around the end of the desk, Kelly took an awkward swing at him with his left. Rourke grabbed that hand as well in a little grip he'd learned while behind bars.

"Which hand is it you use to deal from the bottom of the deck?" he asked Kelly quietly, putting pressure on both sets of fingers, forcing the man to drop to his knees. "The extra five hundred is for information. Did Forrest Danvers owe you money?"

Kelly groaned in pain.

"Yes or no," Rourke demanded.

"None of your damned business."

Rourke increased the pressure.

"Yes. He owed me over a grand in gambling debts."

"How did Forrest get into you for a grand? That's not like you, Kelly. He was just a ranch hand. It would take him months to pay you off."

Kelly looked up at him with hatred. Rourke applied a little more pressure to his hands and Kelly howled before blurting out, "Forrest had something going on the side. He would show up with a fat roll of money. I took him for at least ten grand."

"What was Forrest into for that kind of money?"

"I don't know. I swear."

Rourke put more pressure on Kelly's fingers.

"Gavin Shaw. Forrest and Gavin had something going on the side. That's all I know."

Blaze's stepbrother Gavin? Rourke let go of the foreman's hands. Kelly fell back against the wall beside his chair, cradling his hands in his lap as he bent over them. "You had Forrest killed for a thousand lousy dollars?"

"Hell no," Kelly said, finding his voice as feeling came back into his hands. "I'd have had him beat up or his legs broke. You know how I operate."

Rourke nodded solemnly. "I remember it well. But maybe this time you'd already beaten him up and he wasn't cooperating."

"Forrest was too big of a sucker. He would have come up with the grand and a whole lot more," Kelly said.

That's why the card shark would never have had Forrest killed, Rourke realized. Not the goose laying the golden eggs. "Who else would want Forrest dead?"

Kelly glared at him. "Besides you? How would I know?" His eyes narrowed as if he were just catching up. "If you really didn't kill him—" Kelly sneered, his teeth dark from years of tobacco "—someone framed you and you thought it was *me*?" He laughed, his expression mean as the rattlesnake's. "I wish I *had* thought of it."

"Seen any rattlesnakes lately?" Rourke asked.

Kelly quit smiling, confusion taking its place. "Rattlesnakes?" He glanced around as if he thought Rourke might have let one loose in the office.

"Never mind. Where can I find Gavin?" Rourke asked, and thought for a moment that he'd have to use force again to get Kelly to cooperate. But all the fight seemed to have gone out of the man. At least temporarily.

"Palmer Ranch," Kelly said, as he got up from the floor, rubbing his sore fingers as he did and watching the floor. He didn't seem to like the idea of rattlesnakes. Definitely not the type to put one in a gunnysack behind someone's pickup seat.

As Rourke left, he half expected Kelly to put in that call, but the VanHorn Ranch foreman preferred an ambush, not face-to-face confrontation. Also Rourke suspected Kelly didn't want trouble on the ranch. He didn't want his boss to know. What Mason VanHorn didn't see, Mason Van-Horn let slide. There was no way Mason hadn't known for years about all the ranch hands Kelly had swindled. Van-Horn had just turned a blind eye to it.

But not even Mason VanHorn could turn a blind eye to murder. Assuming Rourke was right, and Kelly was too greedy to kill his golden goose over a thousand bucks, then Kelly hadn't killed Forrest. At least not for money. But Kelly also didn't have the patience or the brains to frame him. Nor any reason to. More and more, Rourke was beginning to think Cassidy was right, and this wasn't about framing him but about Forrest, and Rourke was just an easy scapegoat.

If Forrest was into Kelly for a grand, then he might have had other debts, other enemies who weren't as charitable. Also, how was a ranch hand with no education or much ambition coming into so much money? Not legally, Rourke was sure.

So what was Forrest up to? And why did it have to be Blaze's stepbrother Gavin he'd been up to it with?

HOLT VANHORN LOOKED around his almost empty apartment and began to throw a few things into a suitcase. He didn't have much to pack. Everything had already been pawned in Billings, a couple hours away. People didn't know him down there and didn't ask questions.

He had what clothing he would need in the suitcase when his cell phone rang. He thought about letting it ring. But maybe it was his father. Maybe the old son of a bitch had had a change of heart. Not likely, but Holt had to take the chance. He was broke and he knew he wouldn't get far on what little money and gas he had in his car.

"Hello?" he asked hopefully.

"Do you have my money?"

"I told you I can't get any more money." Holt glanced around the room. He was busted and there was no way he could get more money from his old man.

"Then I guess I'll have to pay a visit to the cops."

Holt closed his eyes tight. "Tomorrow." He'd be long gone by tomorrow. "I'll get your money by tomorrow."

"You wouldn't be thinking about skipping out on me, would you, VanHorn? Because if you do that, I will go to the sheriff and then I'll go to your father. I wonder which one of them would track you down the fastest. We both know which one would be the hardest on you, don't we?"

Holt slumped down on the edge of the bed. "I'll get your money."

"Damn straight you will. You can always rustle some more of your old man's cattle, right?"

"Give me until day after tomorrow," he said.

"Look out your window, Holt."

He froze for a moment, then moved slowly toward the window facing the street. As he pulled back the curtain, he heard laughter on the other end of the phone.

"I'm going to be your shadow until I get my money. Cross me and your father will be the first to know your secret." The line went dead.

Holt hung up the phone before he emptied out his suitcase. What was he going to do? He'd run out of places to get money and even if he got a job…

There was another way. At the mere thought, he began to shake. He closed his eyes and fought back the nausea that came with even the thought of blood.

CHAPTER NINE

CASSIDY COULDN'T IMAGINE how she could help Rourke find the person who had killed Forrest Danvers. It seemed impossible. The killer had remained hidden for eleven years.

And yet someone had put a rattlesnake in Rourke's pickup.

After the afternoon coffee-break crowd cleared out, she told Arthur she had to run an errand and drove south out of Antelope Flats toward the Wyoming border.

There was no road sign that marked the border between Montana and Wyoming. The only way she knew she was in Wyoming was when the narrow two-lane highway turned red abruptly. From there to Sheridan, the road had been built with red earth.

She followed the red highway a few miles to the old Danvers place. Cecil Danvers lived in a small, old log cabin down by the river. His rusted-out pickup was parked in front and smoke curled up from the stovepipe sticking out of the roof.

The late-summer air smelled of dried leaves and wood smoke as she walked to the front of the cabin and knocked on the weathered door. When there was no answer, she knocked again, a little harder.

The day was warm enough but she figured Cecil had built a fire in the woodstove because the cabin would be cold inside. She felt a sudden chill skitter up her spine and turned to find Cecil standing directly behind her.

Startled, she let out a cry of alarm.

He smiled, obviously pleased that he'd scared her. "What do *you* want?"

His brother Forrest hadn't been a bad-looking man, tall and slim with classic features. Cecil, though, was short and squat, thick-necked with a broad face, a predominant nose and thin lips stretched in a straight line across his stingy mouth.

"I was hoping to have a few words with you," she said, trying not to let him rattle her. Cecil had always made her a little nervous. She was questioning what had possessed her to come here by herself.

"I'm working," Cecil snapped. "I don't have time." He didn't look as if he'd been working, but she didn't argue the point.

"Maybe you could take a short break."

Cecil studied her a moment, then reached past her to open the cabin door. She could smell alcohol on his breath as he shoved the door open and moved past her. "Make it quick."

He went straight to the fridge and took out a beer. He didn't offer her one as she entered the dark cabin. Not that she would have taken it. The place was a mess, clothes strewn everywhere, dirty dishes on the counter and table and the smell of rotten food in the trash.

Cecil didn't offer her a chair, either. Even if there had been one that was cleared off enough to sit on, she wasn't staying that long. Now that she was here, she wasn't sure how to broach the subject of Forrest's murder.

"I know what you want," he said. "I heard you were helping Rourke try to pin my brother's murder on someone else." His laugh gave her a chill. "Good luck."

She wondered who would have told him, given that Rourke had only asked her to help him this morning.

Blaze? She must have told him about Saturday night. It surprised her, but who else knew about Rourke's plan?

"I just wanted to ask you about that night. You were standing at the bar with Holt VanHorn, Easton Wells and Gavin Shaw when I walked in. You said something like, 'Now's your chance with Rourke. Blaze is dancing with Forrest.'"

Cecil took a long drink of his beer, avoiding her gaze. "I don't remember saying anything to you. You weren't even old enough to be in the bar. Les had no business letting you stay."

"A few minutes later the fight broke out and you left."

"I left before that." Not according to his testimony at the trial and collaboration by witnesses.

Cassidy realized this had been a total waste of time. Cecil couldn't even remember what he'd said under oath.

"Did you see anyone in the parking lot when you left?"

"I didn't see nobody."

"The killer could have been hiding in the parking lot when Forrest left and followed him up Wild Horse Gulch."

He snorted.

"Why didn't you wait for Forrest to give you a ride home?" It was something she'd wondered about for years.

He took a drink of his beer and belched loudly. "I didn't feel like waiting around for him. You're wrong, there weren't nobody in the parking lot when we left."

We? "We? You just said when *we* left. I thought you hitchhiked home?"

He looked around the room as if something in it would help him out, then he made a resigned face and said, "Blaze gave me a ride as far as the turnoff to her daddy's ranch. So what of it?"

This isn't what he'd said at the trial. Was he lying now? Or eleven years ago?

"Blaze didn't leave until *after* the fight," she said.

"I was out in the parking lot smoking a cigarette," Cecil said defensively. "But I'd left the bar, all right?"

"You must have heard the ruckus inside." She hadn't meant to make her tone so accusatory.

His eyes narrowed. "It wasn't any of my business if Forrest wanted to get the piss kicked out of him. Didn't have nothing to do with me."

So much for brotherly love, she thought.

Cecil downed the last of his beer, smashed the beer can in his large paw of a hand and chucked it in the direction of the trash, missing. The can clattered to the dirty linoleum floor, not the first. Or the last.

He moved toward her and the door. "Time for you to go. McCall killed him and eleven years ain't near enough payment. If you were smart you'd mind your own business."

She backed up, slipping out the door. She could feel Cecil's cold, hateful glare drilling into her back like a steel bit as she walked to her car.

When she looked back over her shoulder, he was standing in the doorway, his eyes reminding her of the rattlesnake's in Rourke's pickup. As she got into her car, she hurriedly locked the doors and started the engine.

Cecil Danvers could have put the snake in Rourke's pickup. For that matter, Cecil could have killed his brother. Unless he had an alibi. Blaze. Was it possible she really had given him a ride as far as her father's ranch? But Blaze had been living in an apartment in town. Why had she gone out to the ranch? Maybe that hadn't been her destination. The next turnoff was Easton's family's place and the next—Cassidy felt a chill skitter across her skin. The next road past the ranch was Wild Horse Gulch.

BLAZE HEARD THE faint tap on the window and looked up to see Yvonne Ames peering into the ADC office.

Blaze groaned, wishing she could have hidden before Yvonne saw her, but the woman was already going around to the front door.

Blaze had gone to school with Yvonne, but they'd never been friends, not that Blaze had had girl-type friends. Yvonne was one of those girls who'd always been chubby and unpopular with boys unless she put out.

"Hi," Yvonne said shyly as she opened the door to Blaze's office. "Got a minute?"

No. "What's up?" Blaze asked, motioning her in. She glanced at her watch to let Yvonne know she didn't have a lot of time.

Yvonne nervously took a chair across from Blaze's desk, dropping her purse, spilling the contents, then frantically trying to get everything back inside.

Blaze sighed and waited impatiently. "If this is about business, Easton will be back—"

"No," Yvonne said. "I wanted to see you." She got everything back inside her purse, clutching it to her, fingers nervously kneading the soft leather. "I heard Rourke McCall was back? I knew you'd see him when he got back." Yvonne swallowed. "I wondered if he said anything about me."

Was the woman serious? "Why would he say anything about *you?*"

She gave a slight shrug of one shoulder. "I just wondered."

"No, he didn't mention you at all." Yvonne must be losing her mind. Rourke wouldn't look twice at her.

Yvonne got to her feet. "I heard he was looking for the person who really killed Forrest," she said, still kneading her purse with nervous fingers.

"Of course, that's what he would say," Blaze snapped. "He has to make a show of proving his innocence." Rourke had lost her loyalty.

Yvonne's eyes widened. "You think he killed Forrest?"

Blaze shrugged. "I hate to think that any man I ever dated could be a killer...."

"Rourke wouldn't kill anyone," Yvonne said.

As if anyone cared what Yvonne thought. "Why would you think Rourke might be asking about you?" Blaze asked, unable to let that go. "It wasn't like you were even at the Mello Dee the night of the murder."

Yvonne nodded and stepped toward the door. "I wrote him a couple of letters while he was in prison and sent him some cookies a few times, that's all."

Blaze stared at her. Why was Yvonne lying?

"Gotta go," Yvonne said, and made a hasty departure.

What was that about? Why would Rourke ask about *her?*

Blaze frowned as she watched Yvonne walk by the window. Yvonne shot a look back at the office. Yvonne looked as if she'd just put one over on her.

Blaze let out a curse. Cassidy had sworn on the witness stand during the trial that she'd overheard Forrest on the pay phone at the Mello Dee talking to a *woman* after his fight with Rourke, after Blaze had left, right before he left and was later murdered up Wild Horse Gulch.

The prosecutor had argued that Cassidy had no way of knowing if Forrest had been talking to a man or a woman. Cassidy had said Forrest called the person on the line "honey bun."

Blaze swore again. Forrest always called *her* honey bun, so she'd just assumed Cassidy had been lying to try to implicate her in the murder.

Now Blaze realized there *had* been another woman.

What other reason would Yvonne have to stop by to ask if Rourke had inquired about her? Forrest had been two-timing her the night he was murdered? With Yvonne Ames? "You sorry bastard."

ON THE WAY through town, Rourke stopped at the sheriff's office to see his brother.

"Dad just called," Cash said when Rourke walked in. "He wants everyone at dinner tonight. No arguments," he added before Rourke could decline. "And no I don't know what it's about, just that it must be a big deal or he wouldn't insist on having us all together in the same room."

Rourke knew the truth in that. He remembered too many meals that had turned into near knock-down, drag-out fights. Funny, but he almost missed them. He thought about how strangely his father had been acting today when he'd seen him and Dusty. His sister had said Asa hadn't been feeling well. "I'll be there. What time?"

"Six," Cash said, and looked relieved. "I heard Brandon is back out at the ranch. You know anything about that?"

Rourke shook his head.

"Yeah? You probably don't know anything about why Burt Kelly is acting oddly, either."

"Kelly?" Rourke echoed.

"I already heard that you were at the VanHorn Ranch this morning. Mason saw your pickup at the office and thought there might be a problem. He said Kelly was un-usually subdued after you left."

"Really?"

Cash leaned his elbows on the desk and rubbed his temples with his fingers. "Want to tell me about it?"

Rourke knew he had to give his brother something. "Forrest owed Kelly money, a grand in gambling debts."

Cash sat up and let out a low whistle. "You thinking Kelly might have killed him over it?"

Rourke shook his head slowly. "But it makes me wonder if Forrest might have had other debts, other creditors who weren't so understanding. It also makes me wonder where Forrest got the money to start with. Kelly said he'd taken Forrest for ten big ones. Any idea where someone like Forrest Danvers would get that kind of money?"

Cash shook his head. The Danverses had been dirt poor for as far back as Rourke could remember. They were also uneducated and often in trouble with the law.

"I hope you're wrong about Kelly," Cash said. "I'd love to bust that bastard for murder."

Rourke nodded, knowing the feeling.

"So you didn't tear up the place? Kick Kelly's butt?" Cash sounded surprised.

"Prison taught me a few things," he said.

"I hate to think," Cash said and sighed. "But obviously prison didn't make you any smarter. Easton was just here. He's afraid you're going to get someone killed."

Blaze had told Easton about the Saturday-night plan. Dear Blaze.

"He told me some fool story about you reenacting the night Forrest was murdered. Someone could get killed."

"They did the last time. I was hoping you'd play Forrest," Rourke said.

"You can kiss my—"

"Don't worry." Rourke wondered why Easton had come whining to the sheriff. "Cassidy and I are going to find the killer before Saturday night."

"Cassidy? Dammit, Rourke, you aren't involving her in this, are you?"

"She's already involved, bro. And she's a big girl, she can make up her own mind about whether or not to keep helping me, all right?" He got to his feet. "By the way, those doughnuts you brought me this morning were wonderful."

Cash looked like he had a whole lot more to say but was biting his tongue. Obviously it was painful for him.

"Who do you think Easton was worried about getting killed?" Rourke asked, thinking of something the private investigator he'd hired had told him.

"You know Easton's been seeing Blaze."

Rourke smiled. He knew a whole lot about Easton. And Blaze. "Hasn't everyone been seeing Blaze?" He started for the door. "Even you, I hear."

"It wasn't a date," Cash called after him. "She asked for a ride home when her car didn't start."

Rourke was laughing as he left. It felt good. "See you at dinner."

"WHAT'S WRONG?" EASTON said from the doorway. All he'd heard was Blaze utter the words "You sorry bastard!" but he knew that look on her face only too well as she swung around from the window.

He would normally assume he was that bastard. Except something in her expression told him it wasn't him this time.

"Was that Yvonne Ames I saw leaving just now?" he asked. "What did she want?"

Blaze stared right through him for a moment. She shook her head as if trying to clear it. "She just stopped in to say hi."

He raised a brow. He could tell when Blaze was lying, without any effort, anymore.

"She invited me to lunch, wanted my advice. Man problems."

Blaze should have quit while she was ahead. He knew

there was no way Yvonne would ask for her advice on anything. Maybe Blaze couldn't see it, but Yvonne hated her guts. He wondered what Blaze had done to her. Yvonne didn't seem the malicious type. He'd bet Blaze had taken some man from Yvonne that she was interested in. That was usually the case with the women who hated Blaze.

He walked over to his desk and put down his briefcase. "I think Yvonne is nice," he said, knowing it would set Blaze off.

"You would," she said under her breath but plenty loud enough for him to hear. "You should date her. If you haven't already."

He turned to look at her, unable not to smile. Blaze was so transparent sometimes. He noticed she'd changed out of that sexy blue dress she'd been wearing earlier. He wondered what that meant. Rourke must not be coming around. Is that what had put Blaze in this mood? Or was it Yvonne's real reason for stopping by that had set Blaze off? And what real reason had that been?

"Is everything all right?" he asked.

"Fine." She smiled but didn't put much effort into it.

"You seem a little on edge. I hope it isn't Rourke who's causing it," he said.

A flash of anger sparked in her eyes. "Rourke?" She let out a laugh. "Rourke has never caused me any trouble."

Uh-huh. Easton nodded, his mood picking right up until he remembered the trouble Rourke was causing him.

ROURKE DROVE OUT to the Palmer Ranch only to find that Blaze's stepbrother Gavin had taken the day off. He got the impression that Gavin had left that morning after getting a phone call warning him that Rourke was looking for him. Good old Kelly, no doubt.

On the way back to town, Rourke took the old road,

slowing at the Mello Dee Supper Club and Lounge on the outskirts of town. The place looked just as it had eleven years ago. A roadhouse with a gravel parking lot, faded-paint building and blinking neon sign out front.

Rourke hoped to hell he and Cassidy found the killer before Saturday night as he pulled into the parking lot. He didn't want to come back here. There was only one other vehicle in the lot, a new blue pickup, so new it didn't even have plates yet.

He sat for a moment, just staring at the place, reliving memories that had haunted him for years. If he had just let Blaze dance with Forrest…or never gone up Wild Horse Gulch. But Cassidy was probably right. It wouldn't have made any difference once the killer had Rourke's gun with his fingerprints on it.

The place even smelled the way he remembered it. The supper club section was closed until five, but the bar was open. He glanced past the pool table. The place was dark. Except for the lit screen of a video poker machine in the corner. The single patron, a gray-haired man, sat on a stool in front of the machine, his back to him. The man didn't turn as Rourke took a stool at the bar.

Les Thurman was filling the beer cooler. He'd been behind the bar the night Forrest was murdered. Rourke had heard that he was still bartending even though he owned the place—just as he'd been the night Forrest was killed.

Les had always been cool, letting underage teens in to play pool or dance to the jukebox if the place wasn't busy. Which it often wasn't.

Les turned and blinked as if not sure he believed his eyes. He closed the cooler. "Rourke," he said warmly as he came over and shook his hand. "It's great to see you."

It was the most sincere greeting Rourke had had from

locals and it warmed his heart more than he wanted to admit.

"What can I get you to drink?" Les asked. He was pushing sixty, his thick gray hair, his skin worn and wrinkled from years of ranching, before he sold the place to Van-Horn and bought the Mello Dee some twelve or thirteen years ago.

"A beer would be great." Rourke watched Les pull a cold one out of the cooler, twist off the cap and place the bottle on a napkin in front of him.

Les leaned toward him, keeping his voice down as he glanced every so often at the man playing video poker. "I've thought about that night a million times over the years," he said before Rourke could bring up the subject. "I've regretted the hell out of not breaking up that fight sooner."

Rourke shook his head. "Nothing you did or didn't do that night had any bearing on what happened."

Les didn't look comforted by that.

"I've come to realize I brought a lot of it on myself."

Les didn't seem to hear him; he appeared lost in reliving the night. "I remember I was trying to close up. There were only a few of you kids hanging around. I started to shut down the jukebox at midnight but Blaze—"

"Wanted one last dance."

Les wagged his head. "I didn't see the harm in one more dance. She can be damned convincing when she wants to be."

Rourke nodded. Didn't he know it. "She was trying to make me jealous and, me being the fool I was, I let it get to me."

Les said nothing, clearly in agreement on all counts.

The guy at the poker machine got up, his back still to

Rourke and the bar. Rourke watched him disappear down the hall to the men's room.

"I remember little about the fight, but Cassidy said she thought some of the guys at the bar were goading me on," he said, turning his attention back to the bar.

Les raised a brow at Cassidy's name. "Yep, Easton. Cecil." He dropped his voice even lower. "Holt VanHorn. They were giving you a hard time, that's for sure. They even gave Cassidy a hard time when she came in. They were trying to stir up anyone they could that night." He shook his head. "I'm sorry as hell about what happened."

Rourke drank his beer in the silence that fell between them. Everything about the place reminded him of that night eleven years go. He doubted Les had changed a thing. It was as if time had stood still here.

The sound of the video poker machine in the corner broke the long silence.

Rourke looked toward the man seemingly intent again on his game. "He must be winning."

Les shook his head. "Losing," he whispered. "Usually plays a lot better. Must be distracted trying to hear what we're saying."

The man turned as if on cue.

Rourke was stunned to see that it was Mason VanHorn. Mason had changed drastically in the past eleven years, his dark hair now completely white, his face lined. He looked much older than his contemporary, Rourke's father, Asa.

Mason didn't seem all that surprised to see him. Obviously Les had been right about VanHorn trying to hear their discussion.

"Welcome home," Mason said, sliding off his stool to walk over to him. "Les, give Rourke another beer. Put it on my tab."

"Thanks just the same," Rourke said, and downed some

of his beer, suddenly just wanting to get out of there. He could feel the hotheaded younger Rourke bubbling under his skin, the one who used to make scenes and get into barroom brawls.

Mason VanHorn pulled up the stool next to him at the bar and motioned to Les to make him another drink. Rourke saw Les's expression. He didn't like VanHorn any better than Rourke did. But then Les might have even more reason to hate VanHorn. There'd been talk years ago that VanHorn had cheated Les out of his ranch, forced him to sell.

"I'll have to go get another bottle of Scotch," Les said, making it clear he was put out.

Mason didn't seem to notice. "So how is your father?" he asked Rourke, as if he and Asa were old friends instead of lifelong adversaries. "Probably pretty much semi-retired like me, I guess."

"He's fine," Rourke said, not looking at him.

"I haven't seen him in town much," Mason said, and turned his empty drink glass in his fingers as he waited for Les to come back. "I heard he had a heart attack a while back. I hope he's feeling all right."

Rourke could feel the heat, the anger like a second skin just beneath his. "How is Holt these days?"

Mason bristled. "Fine."

Brandon had told him that Mason and Holt had had a falling-out and Holt had moved into town. Right after Rourke went to prison. "Some kind of bad blood there," Brandon had said. "No one seems to know what it was about."

Les came from the back with a bottle of Scotch and took his time mixing Mason a drink.

"Holt's just fine," Mason repeated and took a swallow

of his old drink, all water by now. "I'll tell him you asked about him."

"You do that," Rourke said, finishing his beer. Les motioned that his beer was on the house as he set Mason's mixed drink in front of him.

Rourke nodded his thanks and left a tip as he slid off the stool.

"It was good seeing you," Les said.

"You, too," Rourke said.

"Again, I'm sorry the way things turned out," Les said, sounding like he meant it.

Rourke tried not to look at Mason VanHorn. He knew he should just walk away before he said or did something he would regret. Mason knew damned well that his foreman fleeced every cowhand in the county when he got the chance. But Rourke knew that was only part of the reason he despised the man. His dislike was inherited—a family grudge that went back to his grandfather's time but had continued with his own father and Mason.

Rourke wasn't even sure what all the VanHorns had done to start the feud between the two families. Whatever it was it ran deep. Probably a battle over land. Wasn't that usually the case? That or a woman.

He glanced over at Mason. "On second thought, don't bother to give Holt my regards. I'll be looking him up myself."

He noted Mason's uneasy look, then turned and walked out. He was almost to his pickup, when he saw the piece of white folded paper stuck under his windshield wiper.

A sense of déjà vu made him sick to his stomach. Like a sleepwalker, he moved toward the pickup and plucked the note from under the windshield, unfolding the paper just as he had the night of Forrest's murder.

He thought he could feel someone watching him from inside the bar. Mason.

He stared down at the words scrawled on the note: *Leave well enough alone or join Forrest.* He balled up the note, turning to look back at the bar. The late-afternoon sun glinted off the windows, making it impossible to see inside. Mason had left the video poker machine supposedly to go to the men's room. He could have slipped out the back door easy enough and put the note under the wiper.

Rourke realized he could also have been followed to the bar. He hadn't been watching for a tail, hadn't even thought he needed to. He wouldn't make that mistake again.

Rourke got into his truck, tossed the note to the floor and started the engine, shaking inside from anger.

Did someone really think he could be scared off by a rattlesnake or a stupid note?

CHAPTER TEN

EVERYONE WAS ALREADY in the family dining room standing around waiting when Rourke walked in just before six.

He took his old spot across from J.T., and for a moment he felt as if he hadn't been gone eleven years, as if he'd never been to prison, as if it had all been a bad dream.

"You want to tell us what this is about?" J.T. asked his father after they were all seated.

"Can't a father have his family to dinner without there being some big announcement?" Dusty asked.

They all ignored her, instead waiting for Asa to tell them what was going on.

Rourke looked down the table at his father. Asa had been acting strangely, but Rourke figured it had something to do with him getting out of prison. He just hoped to hell that wasn't what this dinner was about as he watched Martha and several new cook's assistants serve the food.

"Come on, what's going on?" J.T. demanded. "You practically jump out of your skin every time the phone rings."

Asa was pushing his food around on his plate and didn't seem to hear.

"Dad?" Cash said.

His father looked up in surprise. "I'm sorry, you want the roast?" he asked, reaching for the large platter.

"No," J.T said. "I asked what the hell is bothering you. If something's going on we should know about—"

The doorbell rang. Asa knocked over his water glass as he stumbled to his feet.

"Martha's got it," J.T. said.

Rourke, like all the others, was staring at his father. Asa had gone pale and, even from where Rourke sat, he could see that his father was shaking.

Martha appeared in the doorway. Like Asa, she seemed upset.

Rourke was on his feet. "Martha, what is it?" He'd barely gotten the words out of his mouth when a woman appeared in the doorway. She was blonde, somewhere in her late fifties although she could have passed for much younger. She had the palest, clearest blue eyes he'd ever seen—even paler than his own.

Although he'd been too young to remember his mother, he knew that's who she was. Just as he realized in that instant of absolute silence before all hell broke loose that his father had lied about her death.

"What the hell is going on?" J.T. demanded.

Asa didn't seem to hear him. "As usual, Shelby, your timing is horrendous."

Her laugh was magnificent and Rourke thought he remembered it, that wonderful joyous tinkle of laughter that seemed to light up the entire house.

"Oh, Asa, you old goat, you know you love surprises," she said, looking around the table, her blue eyes seeming hungry as if she couldn't get enough of each of them.

Asa was looking at Shelby, a mixture of anger and awe, Rourke thought. He could practically feel the chemistry between them.

He looked over at his sister. The resemblance was uncanny between Dusty and Shelby and he could see that Dusty hadn't missed it. He let out a low oath and shook his head. He'd always suspected Dusty was his half sister but now it was clear who her mother had been.

Everyone was talking at once, just like the old days before the knock-down, drag-out fights began.

Shelby walked over to Asa, her eyes tearing as she kissed his old weathered cheek. "Something tells me this is going to be some story," Rourke said under his breath.

"Everyone settle down," Asa ordered loudly. "Martha, break out the good bourbon. Now you know the truth. Your mother is alive."

"No kidding," J.T. snapped.

"*Our* mother?" Dusty demanded.

Asa nodded, turning his attention to her, his expression softening. "You're a McCall in every sense of the word."

Rourke could see that Dusty was as angry as her brothers now. "You lied to me all these years?"

"I need to speak with your mother alone." Asa looked to Shelby, his expression as close to a plea as Rourke had ever seen.

"If you'll excuse us," Shelby said.

J.T. and Cash started to argue.

"We'll only be a moment," she said. "Then I want to talk to all of you."

Asa closed the dining-room door firmly behind them.

J.T. was the first to speak. "What the hell? Did any of you…" He broke off, seeing that none of them had a clue. "Someone please tell me why we've been putting flowers on her grave for the past thirty years?"

"You think they are still married?" Dusty asked Rourke.

"Must be."

"Where has she been?" Brandon asked into the stunned silence. "Why didn't she let us know she was alive?"

"Amnesia," Dusty said. "I read about this woman who

was on her way to the grocery store and bumped her head and they found her years later in Alaska or someplace."

"Our mother didn't have amnesia," Cash said. "Unless it comes and goes. Dad just said you were his daughter with her."

Dusty frowned. "Why did he let me believe that he adopted me?"

"Who knows what else the old man has been hiding from us," Rourke said, and chuckled to himself. Just when he thought his father couldn't surprise him.

"How could he keep a secret like this?" J.T. said. "I've seen our mother's obituary from the newspaper. There's an elaborate tombstone on her grave."

"*Everyone* thought she was dead, not just us," Rourke agreed.

J.T. shook his head. In the silence that fell between them, they could hear raised voices in the den.

"She is beautiful, isn't she?" Brandon said.

Rourke nodded and looked at Dusty, who was fuming at her end of the table. "Just like her daughter."

Tears welled in Dusty's eyes as she looked at him, then quickly excused herself and disappeared into the hall powder room.

"I could kill the son of a bitch for hurting *her*," Rourke said.

"You've killed enough people," J.T. snapped.

"It's just an expression," Cash said.

"Not one Rourke should be using," J.T. said.

"Okay, let's not argue," Brandon said. "This is stressful enough as it is. Let's not turn on each other."

"Brandon's right," Cash said. "If anything, we need to pull together."

"You're right," J.T. said. "Can you imagine what will happen when the news hits town?"

They all groaned.

"What if she isn't staying?" Dusty said from the doorway. They hadn't noticed that she'd returned.

"What if she is?" J.T. said.

They fell silent as they heard the den door open and close, then footfalls.

Asa appeared in the doorway. Shelby wasn't with him. "Your mother wants to talk to you all in the den, but first there is something I need to tell you." He cleared his throat. He was visibly shaking and his voice broke as he said, "Your mother is back."

They all let out a nervous laugh.

"No kidding," Rourke said.

"Back from the dead?" J.T. asked.

"Back?" Dusty echoed. "You mean she's going to be living with us? Where has she been?"

"Shouldn't this have come up years ago?" J.T. joined in.

Asa raised one hand and picked up his glass of bourbon with the other. He drained his glass. "I think I'd better explain."

BLAZE WAS WORKING late again when she looked up to see her brother Gavin pass by the window. He slowed, looked in, saw her and quickened his step.

Blaze heard the front door open and braced herself, curious and yet dreading seeing her brother. She'd heard that Gavin had left the VanHorn Ranch and was now working on the Palmer Ranch. She wondered how that had happened. Knowing her brother, she had a pretty good idea.

"Hey," he said, coming into her office and closing the door behind him. He wore old jeans and boots, a soiled shirt and hat.

"Why are you so dirty?" she asked, hoping no one had seen him come in.

"I've been *working*," he said, sounding irritated with her, but quickly added in a more civil tone, "How are you?"

As if he cared. "Fine." If he wanted money, he was out of luck. She used all that she made and then some—and didn't even live that well.

He looked around the office. "Not bad."

"Not mine," she said.

He turned to grin at her. "You think I came by to bum you for money?" He laughed as if the idea were ludicrous. They both knew better. "Can't a brother stop in to see his sister?"

*Step*brother. She hadn't been all that thrilled when her mother died and her father had remarried a woman named Kitten—who named their child Kitten, anyway?—and Kitten had a son who was two years younger than Blaze.

"What do you want, Gavin?" she asked, cutting to the chase.

"Have you seen Rourke?"

Rourke? "Of course."

He looked relieved. "I figured you two would get back together."

She didn't correct him. "What do you want with Rourke?"

"I heard he was looking for me." Gavin didn't sound happy about that. Was there some reason he shouldn't be?

First Yvonne and now her brother? "Why would he want to see you?"

He shrugged. "I thought he might have told you what he wanted."

She stared at her brother. "You never told me why you left VanHorn."

He glanced toward the street. "That's old news."

"He fired you."

Gavin swung his head around to glare at her. "Why would you say that?"

"What did you do?" she demanded impatiently.

"There was a misunderstanding," he said, looking away again. "Over a couple of his cattle."

"You were rustling his cattle?" She hated the admiration she heard in her tone.

He grinned. "I got a hundred head before I was caught."

"I'm surprised VanHorn didn't kill you."

"It was close," he admitted.

"And you still got on at the Palmer Ranch?" This surprised her. Under normal circumstances, his actions would have him blacklisted from every ranch around.

He shrugged again. "VanHorn gave me a good recommendation. How do you beat that?" He glanced again to the street.

This time she followed his gaze and saw Holt VanHorn sitting in a pickup across the street.

"Do you need to go out the back way?" she asked.

Her stepbrother laughed. "Naw, Holt's waiting for me. I gotta go."

Her brother was running with Holt VanHorn? This could explain why VanHorn had let the cattle rustling go. He must have thought his son was involved.

"When will you see Rourke?" he asked.

She had worked late again tonight hoping he'd come by. He'd disappointed her for a second time. "He's tied up tonight." She just hoped it wasn't with Cassidy. "Did you want me to give him a message?"

"See if you can find out what he wants."

She eyed him. "Why would he want to talk to you?"

Gavin shrugged. "Not a clue."

"You know he's determined to find out who killed Forrest," she said.

"I know." He met her gaze then and she saw fear, but she couldn't be sure if it was for her or for himself.

"I ADMIT IT. I LIED," Asa said, the words like stones in his mouth. He looked around the table, hoping to find one of his offspring who might show him some compassion, some understanding. He saw nothing but anger, confusion, suspicion. Not even Dusty gave him the least bit of encouragement.

He reached for the bottle of bourbon to pour himself another drink, but J.T. moved it out of his reach.

"Shelby and I were wrong for each other from the very beginning," he said.

There was a burst of laughter around the table. "What? You didn't notice until after your fourth son was born?" Rourke said.

"It was a love-hate relationship," Asa said, realizing how ill-equipped he was to explain this to them. He'd had trouble explaining it to himself for years.

Maybe he should throw himself on their mercy. He looked around the table. It would be like throwing himself to wolves.

"We realized we couldn't live together. She would have to leave, but I didn't want you kids thinking your mother had just left you—"

"She *did* just leave us," Cash said.

"—so I faked her death."

"Unbelievable," J.T. said.

"And illegal," Cash added.

"You don't understand," Asa said, and groaned. "I wanted to protect you kids."

"Protect us from our mother?" Brandon asked.

Asa looked at his youngest son, the one most like Shelby. "Protect you from divorce, a divided family."

"And how do you explain me?" Dusty said, sounding close to tears.

Asa looked down the table at her, wanting to shelter her but there was no holding back now. If he didn't tell them, Shelby would.

"You were a love child, just as I told you," he said quietly. "Shelby and I...got together to talk and—"

"When was this?" J.T. demanded.

"Seventeen years ago, give or take nine months," Rourke said.

"That trip down south you took," J.T. said, as if suddenly remembering. He shook his head. "Has anything you've ever told us been the truth?"

Asa sighed and pinched the bridge of his nose. He straightened to his full height. "I did what I had to do. Someday when you're a parent—"

"Bull," Brandon said, and got to his feet. "I want to hear what my mother has to say about all this."

The rest were on their feet. As Rourke passed him, Asa saw that at least one son expected there was more to the story.

The moment they were gone, Asa grabbed the bourbon and poured himself a stiff drink. He was going to need it. Shelby was back. God help them all. At least the truth was out. He told himself it couldn't get any worse than this, but he knew better. When the past came back to haunt you, you never knew what other ghosts it brought with it.

SHELBY LOOKED UP as Rourke and his siblings entered the den. She'd been standing by the fireplace, obviously waiting for them.

Rourke closed the door firmly and, as the others moved deeper into the room, he stayed by the door.

His first impression of her hadn't done her justice. She

was beautiful. He'd always wondered where their looks had come from. Obviously from their mother.

"Dad just told us how he faked your death to protect us from the truth," J.T. said to her. "Now we'd like to hear the truth."

She studied her children one by one, her gaze locking with Rourke's as if she was acknowledging he would be the hardest one to sell her story to. Her smile slipped away.

"Your father and I couldn't get along. One of us had to go."

"Why didn't you send *him* packing?" Cash asked.

"Asa would never leave his ranch. I had no idea how to run a ranch and you were his sons. Sons need a father."

"And daughters?" Dusty asked.

"So you just agreed to leave?" J.T. said.

"It was a sacrifice I felt I had to make," she said softly, her attention on Dusty. "As hard as it was for me. I felt your lives would be better without me than with me in town. I didn't want you torn between two quarreling parents like in so many divorces."

"So you're divorced?" Cash asked.

"No," she said. "That was another stigma we didn't want you to have to live with, and I knew I would never remarry."

"Marriage to Asa was that bad?" Rourke said from his spot by the door.

She smiled at him. "I knew I would never love anyone the way I loved your father."

"Uh-huh," Rourke said.

"So you went along with his plan to fake your death, right down to the memorial service and the gravestone at the cemetery?" Cash demanded.

She straightened. "It seemed like a way to put an end to it at the time."

"What about me?" Dusty demanded. Rourke could hear the anger and hurt in her voice. She sounded close to tears.

"Oh, honey," Shelby said, and took a step toward her but stopped as if seeing something in Dusty's eyes that warned her not to come any closer. "Your father and I got together to discuss a financial matter and…" She waved a hand through the air. "I know you're all angry and think we acted irresponsibly."

There were sounds of agreement around the room.

"Not to mention illegally," Cash piped up.

"But we love each other. You were all born of that love," Shelby said. "We just couldn't live together and that's why I went away, planning never to return."

"But you have returned," Rourke said.

"Yes." She looked across the room to him again. "I had to come home."

"Why now?" J.T. asked.

"Why not years ago, when we needed you?" Brandon said.

She shook her head, tears welling in her blue eyes. "I wanted to, desperately. But I never knew how long Asa and I would be able to stay together without killing each other. I couldn't do that to young children."

"So you waited until we were old enough to understand?" Rourke suggested, knowing there was a whole lot more to this story.

"That's partly it," she said, as if choosing her words carefully. "Your father and I need to work out some things."

"Financial things?" Rourke asked.

"It isn't what you think," she said. "It's between your father and I."

He'd heard enough. He turned and opened the door. If he hurried, he could catch Cassidy before the café closed.

"Are you staying?" he heard Dusty ask her mother as he

headed down the hall toward the front door. He caught a glimpse of his father still at the dining-room table, steadily depleting the bottle of bourbon in front of him.

Rourke didn't catch his mother's answer. He didn't need to. Shelby wouldn't be staying. She was the kind of person whose first instinct when things went bad was to run away from it. Rourke knew now who he'd inherited it from.

ASA HEARD THE front door open and close five times, heard several vehicles start up, heard angry voices in deep discussion out on the porch and figured Rourke and Cash had left. The other three were tearing him to shreds on the porch.

He poured himself another drink. Not even the alcohol was going to work tonight.

At the sound of her soft footfalls, he looked up. "How did it go?" he asked, already knowing the answer.

Shelby sat down heavily in a chair next to him. He pushed the bottle of bourbon toward her.

She had never been a drinker, so he was surprised when she poured a shot into the glass and downed it. She shuddered, eyes closed, tears beading her lashes.

When she opened her pale blue eyes, he felt a start, just as he had the first time he'd seen her. His heart ached just looking at her. He'd loved this woman all of his life, and not even the bad years or the long time apart could dull that all-enveloping love.

Nor could they have been more wrong for each other.

"You think they'll ever forgive me?" she asked.

"Yes," he said without hesitation. "They're just angry right now. They think you abandoned them."

"I did."

He shook his head. "You and I know that isn't true."

"I could have put up more of a fight."

Again he shook his head. "It wouldn't have done any good. You and I would have ended up killing each other. And imagine how many more children we would have had."

She smiled at that. "They are all so wonderful, aren't they?"

He started to tell her that *wonderful* wouldn't be the word he would choose for their pigheaded, contrary offspring, but he said, "Yes, they're wonderful. Dusty is the spitting image of you."

Tears welled again in her eyes. She discreetly wiped at them. "There will be an uproar when word gets out."

He nodded. "Why are you back, Shelby? I thought we had a deal," he asked, even though he feared he already knew, had known, the moment he saw her in town.

She reached silently to cover his hand with her own. As she squeezed his hand, tears spilled down both her cheeks. "You know why, Asa."

He nodded. Some secrets were impossible to keep.

CHAPTER ELEVEN

As ROURKE PULLED UP in front of the Longhorn Café, he felt a rush of relief at the mere sight of Cassidy inside the café. He'd made it just in time. She was putting up the Closed sign as he got out of his pickup.

The rush of feeling surprised him and he realized it wasn't just his temper he'd learned to control in prison. He'd put a lid on a lot of other emotions, as well.

Cassidy spotted him, seeming surprised, as she opened the door. After everything that had happened today, she was like a breath of fresh air.

"Is everything all right?" she asked, studying his face.

He smiled at her. "Could we maybe—" he glanced at one of the booths "—talk?" It surprised him how much he was hoping she'd say yes. He couldn't think of any other place he wanted to be right now than here with Cassidy.

She didn't hesitate. "Sure. Want something to eat or drink?"

"Coffee would be nice if you still have any or I could make some."

"You?" she asked with a laugh.

"I worked in the prison cafeteria before I got on at the ranch," he said. "You'd be surprised at all my talents."

Did she blush? She pointed him toward the coffeepot while she went to close the blinds. As she was closing the last one, he saw her hesitate and looked past her to see

Blaze sitting in her office across the street obviously waiting for someone. Guess who.

Task completed, Cassidy turned back to him.

"Where do you want to sit?"

She pointed to a booth, waited as he slid in, then sat down across from him. Their knees bumped. She jerked as if hit with a cattle prod. Or maybe she was just startled and he'd imagined the electrical current that shot through him.

"Did something happen today since I've seen you?" she asked, sounding worried.

"It's been quite the day," he said. He recounted what his brother Brandon had said about Forrest's gambling. He told her about his visit to the VanHorn Ranch and Kelly, leaving out how he'd gotten Kelly to talk to him. And finished up with his visit to Les Thurman at the Mello Dee.

"He told me you were right about the guys at the bar egging me on during the fight."

Cassidy nodded. Was that what he'd wanted to tell her? That she'd been right?

He looked at her across the table. "Cassidy—" The coffee machine shut off noisily.

It was a knee-jerk reaction. She started to slide out of the booth to go get the coffee.

"Let me," he said, and got up.

Slowly she lowered herself into the booth again. Her heart was hammering in her chest. What had he been about to say?

"Here," he said, returning with the pot and two cups. He filled hers, then his, and took the pot back.

She cupped her hands around the cup, needing the warmth. She was staring down at the coffee when he returned. She didn't look up until the silence was too much for her. "You were saying?"

He shook his head as if he couldn't remember or it didn't

matter anymore. She felt her heart drop. She had a feeling it did matter. A lot.

"Mason VanHorn was at the Mello Dee," he said.

She knew about the bad blood between the families. Not what had caused it, just that Asa and Mason couldn't be in the same room together.

Rourke seemed to hesitate. "My father called a family dinner tonight to make an announcement." He drew away to stare down into his coffee but not before she'd seen that instant of vulnerability in his blue eyes.

So unlike Rourke, she told herself she must have imagined it. "What was the announcement?"

"He didn't get to it before my mother walked in."

She stared at him, not sure if it was some kind of morbid joke or she just wasn't getting it.

"You heard me right. My mother. Shelby Ward McCall. It seems her death was exaggerated."

Cassidy gasped. "But your brothers put flowers on her grave every Sunday."

He nodded. "I guess she and my father cooked up her death thinking it would be better for us kids to believe her dead than divorced."

"That's screwball thinking if I've ever heard any," she said, then wished she could bite her tongue.

He laughed. "My thought exactly." He shook his head, his gaze moving gently over her face. "I would suspect my father paid her to go, threatening to take us kids and leave her penniless. That sounds more like him. You want to hear the real kicker? Dusty is theirs. She's our biological sister. It seems at some clandestine meeting to discuss finances, Dusty was the result."

Cassidy wouldn't have believed it if it hadn't been Asa McCall. *"Amazing."*

Rourke nodded in agreement.

"Why did she come back if they had an arrangement?"

"That is the question, isn't it," he said with a shrug. He looked worried.

"Didn't she say?" Cassidy asked.

"Not really, but my father didn't seem all that surprised to see her."

"Maybe they're getting back together," she suggested.

Rourke let out an oath. "I hope not. I was pretty young when she supposedly died, but I remember how the two of them fought. I could barely remember what my mother looked like, but I remember their infamous arguments. My father said they had a love-hate relationship. I doubt that has changed."

She sipped her coffee. "Good." She motioned to the coffee when he seemed confused.

He nodded and they fell into an uneasy silence.

Had he just wanted to tell her about his mother coming back from the dead? Or was there something else on his mind?

"I'm sorry," he said after a few minutes.

She looked up in surprise.

"I was so quick to blame you for what happened eleven years ago," he said. "I'm sorry."

She waved off his apology. "I would have thought the same thing. I did some investigating on my own today," she said. He seemed surprised. "I went out to see Cecil."

"Cassidy, you shouldn't have—"

"I figured it might be safer for me to talk to Cecil Danvers than for you," she said. "He was the one who'd goaded me about you and Blaze that night at the bar. He left when the fight broke out, which is odd in itself, but today he told me that he got a ride partway home."

Rourke put down his coffee cup.

"Cecil says he caught a ride with Blaze," Cassidy said.

Rourke stared at her. "That's not what he said in court. Not what Blaze said, either."

She nodded. "He could be lying. But I thought it was interesting because he said she dropped him off on the highway at the turnoff to her father's ranch—just up the road from Wild Horse Gulch."

Rourke let out an oath.

"There is just one problem. If Cecil is telling the truth, then the woman Forrest was talking to on the pay phone at the Mello Dee after your fight couldn't have been Blaze."

"He was meeting someone else," Rourke said, and let out a laugh.

She nodded. "It could explain why Cecil didn't wait around for a ride home with him."

"You think Cecil knew who his brother was meeting?" he asked.

She shrugged. "I wonder why Blaze lied about going straight home."

Rourke let out a low whistle. "If Cecil is telling the truth, this puts a whole new spin on things."

"You believed, the past eleven years, that Forrest was meeting Blaze, too," she said in surprise.

"Knowing Blaze, it was definitely a possibility. Especially after I heard that Forrest had come into some money."

Cassidy laughed. "Maybe you know Blaze better than I thought."

"You think Blaze could have killed Forrest?" he asked.

"I think she's capable of it. Aren't we all?"

He raised a brow. "I can't imagine you hurting a fly."

"You think I couldn't kill someone who was hurting someone I loved, well you're just wrong, Rourke McCall."

"Whoa," he said, holding up his hands in surrender. "Sorry for even insinuating you weren't a killer."

She took a breath, regretting her outburst. "It's just that people in this town think I'm a Goody Two-shoes without any of the normal feelings that everyone else has."

He laughed. It was a wonderful sound that she realized she had missed desperately. "I don't think of you as a Goody Two-shoes."

She eyed him suspiciously. "You're just saying that to make me feel better."

He laughed again. "You are one strange woman, Cassidy Miller. Strange and quite…unique and wonderful."

Her cheeks flamed. She lowered her eyes then felt his fingers, warm under her chin as he raised her face again.

"I mean it," he said. "There is no one like you."

Not exactly what she'd hoped to hear him say all these years. She returned to their discussion. "What makes you so sure Blaze didn't kill him?"

"What was her motive?" he asked, making her realize he'd already considered Blaze a suspect. Maybe he wasn't so clueless when it came to Blaze after all.

"Does Blaze need a reason?"

He smiled at that. "Believe me, if Blaze killed him, she had her reasons."

"Maybe he was threatening to tell you about the two of them," she suggested.

"Then why dance with him at the Mello Dee?" Rourke said, shaking his head. "Blaze loves to make men jealous."

He had a good point. "You suspected Forrest and Blaze were sneaking around, didn't you?"

His eyes narrowed, a muscle in his jaw tightening. "I know you think I'm a complete fool, but I'm not so dumb that I didn't suspect she was seeing Forrest behind my back."

She shook her head. "That's why you were just spoiling for a fight when you tried to cut in on the dance floor."

"I'm not that man anymore," Rourke said, realizing it was true. The man he was now wouldn't fight over Blaze or go chasing after her up Wild Horse Gulch or any other place. He got up to refill their coffee cups. "I need you to tell me everything you can remember about the days leading up to the murder and that night, and I need you to be honest with me."

"I thought I've been painfully honest with you."

He smiled. "Very painful. You've made me take a hard look at the person I used to be."

"But you still aren't sure I didn't frame you," she said, her voice sounding small.

He shook his head. "I wanted to believe it, because it made things easy. I don't anymore."

"What changed your mind?"

"You." His gaze locked with hers. "I never knew you, Cassidy. If I had…" He waved a hand through the air. "I was obviously oblivious to a great deal. I can't help but wonder what else I missed, you know?"

She nodded slowly. She had a great face, big brown eyes and a smile that had a stunning effect.

"So where do we start?" he asked her.

"I guess with what we know. Whoever killed Forrest didn't do it on the spur of the moment," she said. "The killer planned it maybe even before he or she took your gun."

"Planned for me to take the blame—if not get even with me," he said.

She nodded. "It would help if you knew when your gun went missing."

"The night of my birthday party, everyone who was at the Mello Dee the night Forrest was killed, was also in the house." Not to mention that Blaze had access to it in the weeks before the murder since he'd kept the gun on a shelf in his bedroom. How stupid that he hadn't realized the gun could be more than a sentimental souvenir to someone with murder on his mind. Or her mind.

"Didn't Blaze throw that party for you at your ranch?"

"You make a good argument," he admitted. Maybe he had been blind when it came to Blaze.

"The party was a week before the murder," Cassidy said. "Let's say that was when the gun disappeared. So our suspects are those same people who were at the Mello Dee the night of the murder, because no one else could have known about Forrest's plans to go up Wild Horse Gulch." Cassidy frowned. "I take that back. Blaze's stepbrother Gavin wasn't at the party now that I think about it."

"You're right. I vaguely remember something about a fight?"

Cassidy nodded. "At the bunkhouse out on the VanHorn ranch where Forrest and Gavin had both been working."

"So Gavin Shaw couldn't have taken the gun at the party."

"But he was at the Mello Dee that night," she said.

"The only other person we can't be sure about is whomever Forrest called from the Mello Dee pay phone and asked to meet him up the gulch," Rourke pointed out.

"So the people who were at the party and the bar were Blaze Logan, Easton Wells, Cecil Danvers and Holt Van-Horn," Cassidy said.

"What we don't have is motive."

"But we do know that the killer is patient," he said. "He stole the gun, waited at least a week until he saw his chance. He doesn't do things on impulse. Or *she*," he added. "Doesn't sound like Blaze, does it?"

"No. But I really am worried about you, Rourke. If that rattlesnake had come out while you were driving, you could have wrecked the truck and been killed."

He shook his head. "It was just a warning. The killer is waiting to see what we come up with. I'm not sure he has the stomach to kill again. Remember, he has to find someone to blame it on again."

"How do you know the killer hasn't been planning this for eleven years?"

"I don't know what I would do without your help. I mean it. For eleven years, I couldn't even imagine that Forrest's death was about anyone but me, because it sent me to prison. But I was the perfect scapegoat, wasn't I?"

"The wild McCall?" she asked with a laugh. "Every father in this county warned his daughters about you and your brothers."

"You didn't listen, did you?"

She sat back down and dropped her gaze to her lap. He'd embarrassed her. It surprised him the way her cheeks flushed, and when she looked up, her eyes were bright. He felt his breath come a little quicker.

She looked away and bit her lower lip.

"Anyway, thanks to you, I feel like we're making progress," he said into the tense silence that stretched between them.

"Just be careful," she said, finally looking at him again.

"Don't worry." He reached across the table to cover her hand with his, then pulled it back as if he thought better of it. The gesture lasted only an instant, making Cassidy not sure she'd imagined the shock that made her hand tingle and her heart race.

He got up. "It's late," he said, leaning down to peer through the blinds out into the night.

It was dark, the street empty except for an occasional car that passed.

"Why don't I help you close up and walk you to your car," he said.

"Really, that's not necessary—"

"I insist."

THE MOON WAS just coming up as they stepped outside the café. Cassidy breathed in the night air, too aware of Rourke's presence next to her.

It suddenly felt awkward between them. As if they'd been on a date and she wasn't sure if he was going to kiss her or not.

She fumbled for her car keys, dropped them. They both leaned down at the same time to pick them up. He got to them first and looked up at her, both still squatting down, so close she could smell his faint aftershave, feel the heat of his body warming the already warm night.

In the moonlight his face seemed softer, almost tender, and she was reminded of the boy who'd kissed her in the barn all those years ago.

At that moment, she couldn't have denied him anything.

He started to hand her the keys. His smile set her heart to pounding. So did the look in his eyes.

As their fingers met, he grasped her hand and pulled her toward him. His lips unerringly found hers, his mouth covering hers and, for a few fleeting seconds, she was lost in his kiss—just as she'd been in the barn.

And then as if history were destined to repeat itself, he pulled back. "Sorry." He pressed her keys into her hand before she could tell him he had nothing to be sorry about.

But she could see that, like her, he didn't want to break her heart again. He wasn't through with Blaze and they both knew it.

She nodded, unconsciously touching her tongue to her lower lip. It still tasted of him. Turning, she practically ran to her car.

She had opened the car door and started to get in, when

she spotted the piece of folded paper stuck under the windshield.

Rourke must have been watching her because, in two long strides, he was at the car and plucking the note from under the wiper.

Cassidy watched him unfold the paper. He leaned toward the open car door to read it in the glow of the interior light.

She read over his shoulder, "'Stay out of this if you know what's good for you or you will end up like Forrest.'"

The handwriting looked scribbled as if someone was purposely trying to disguise the penmanship.

Cassidy felt the blood rush from her head. She looked at Rourke. He didn't seem surprised and she knew at once why. "You've already gotten one of these, haven't you."

He looked from the note to her and nodded. "One. Pretty much the same message. Same handwriting."

He carefully folded the note and put it in his shirt pocket. "I'll take this note to Cash. Maybe you shouldn't go home tonight."

"I'll be fine."

"I don't like the idea of you staying at your place alone tonight."

What was he suggesting? Whatever it was, it was with obvious hesitation.

"Why don't you come with me?" he suggested, not sounding thrilled by the idea. "I'm staying out at the family cabin on the lake. There are two bedrooms but I don't use either—"

"Don't be ridiculous. It was just a silly note. Like you said, whoever is doing this isn't serious." There was no way she was going to his cabin. She'd promised herself she wouldn't fall for Rourke all over again. Ultimately, he would break her heart. Look how he kept defending Blaze.

No matter what he said, he wasn't over her. And Cassidy wasn't going to let the two of them break her heart again.

"I'm quite capable of taking care of myself," she said. "Anyway," she added, glancing toward Antelope Development Corporation, "I have a pretty good idea who is behind this."

"You aren't suggesting that this is Blaze's doing?"

"No, I'm not suggesting. I'm telling you this has Blaze's style written all over it," Cassidy snapped. She felt her temper rise, angry at Blaze, at him. "You still have illusions about her." Cassidy shook her head and looked away, wanting to shake him. "Men." She got in and started her car.

He hadn't moved. He seemed unsure what to do next. He motioned for her to roll down her window.

She sighed and did, telling herself she was damned glad the kiss hadn't gone any further than it had. The man was an idiot. Why had she thought, when Rourke got out of prison, he might have matured, might finally see Blaze for what she was?

"Here's my cell-phone number in case you need me." He reached in and plucked the pen and pad from her uniform pocket and scribbled down his number. He handed the pen and pad back to her. "Be careful."

"Good night, Rourke," she said. "When you see Blaze, tell her to butt out of my life. I'll do anything I damned well please—including helping you." She drove off before he could say anything more. Probably because she had the feeling he was going to tell her he didn't want her help anymore.

When she glanced back in the rearview mirror, he was still standing there, looking after her. She thought of the kiss. It had been so tender, so… Her body demanded to know why she hadn't taken Rourke up on his offer.

Maybe he really was just offering you his bedroom. Or

maybe he was offering you a night of pleasure beyond your wildest dreams. Good thing you aren't the kind of girl who is interested in a one-night stand.

Right.

"YOU SHOULDN'T HAVE touched it," Cash said as he bent over the piece of plain white paper and dusted it for prints.

"I wasn't thinking," Rourke said, and realized he'd been too upset both times he'd found the notes. This time, he'd been too shaken by the kiss.

Cash looked up at Rourke as if to say, *When are you ever thinking?*

He paced as he watched Cash dust the paper and check it against his own prints, which of course were on file. "Well?"

"It appears there is only one set of prints on the note, yours. The paper is white copier paper, the most common paper around."

"What about the handwriting?"

Cash shook his head. "Obviously disguised. Could have been written by a right-handed person using his left hand."

Rourke let out a sigh. "But it proves that I'm on to something."

Cash shook his head. "It proves someone doesn't want you bringing all this back up."

"Someone put a live rattler in a burlap bag behind my pickup seat my first day back in town," Rourke said.

Cash looked startled, then upset. "Dammit, Rourke, this is exactly what I was afraid of."

"Who do we know who sells rattlers?"

Cash chewed at his cheek for a moment. "Cecil Danvers for one."

"Easton Wells used to have a fondness for snakes," Rourke said.

"Have you seen him since you've been back?"

"No, but I'm thinking about paying him a visit."

Cash shook his head but saved his breath.

"Forrest had a wad of cash on him that night at the bar," Rourke said. He'd forgotten all about it until he'd talked to Kelly.

"It wasn't on him when he was found dead," Cash said.

"Exactly. And you didn't find it on me. So if he had it when he left the bar but didn't when he was found, then the killer had to have taken it."

Cash nodded. "You're wondering where he got it and if anyone was a little richer after his murder."

"You know me so well," Rourke said with a grin.

"Sorry, bro. I have no idea what happened to the money. Nor did the state guys come up with anything. As for after his murder—" Cash was shaking his head "—there was a lot going on around here, but I don't remember anyone flashing any money around. Would have been a fool to."

Rourke knew he was just grasping at straws, but now that Cassidy was getting the notes, he felt pressure to find the killer before the threats possibly escalated.

Cash sighed and looked at his watch. "It's late. Why don't you let me talk to Cecil and Easton about the rattle-snake tomorrow?"

Rourke stood to leave. "No, I'd rather not let them know that I'm suspicious of them at this point. Easton used to be my best friend. We'll run into each other sooner or later." He didn't mention to Cash that he'd had him investigated and come up with something interesting. Cash would find out soon enough. The whole town would.

CASSIDY WAS SURPRISED by how exhausted she felt. She didn't even bother to turn on a light as she followed the path of moonlight streaming in the old farmhouse windows to her bedroom.

She couldn't believe how late it was. She shrugged out of her uniform, so tired she just tossed it aside. The blouse landed on the old trunk by the window and fell to the floor.

She stared at it for a moment, then tiredly went to pick it up. The letters. Now, more than ever, she didn't want Rourke finding out about them. She would build a fire in the fireplace and destroy them tonight.

She shoved aside the uniform blouse and opened the trunk. It was nearly full of the carefully addressed envelopes. She picked up one and stumbled back to sit on the edge of her bed. What had she been thinking?

She started to open the envelope. A thud outside the window startled her. She froze as she saw a shape move past, skulking along the side of the house. An instant later, she heard someone jiggle the back doorknob.

Her heart in her throat, she rose as if sleepwalking and inched her way toward the phone as she heard the lock on the back door break in the sharp splinter of wood.

She hurriedly dialed 9-1-1 and locked the bedroom door. She was surprised when Cash answered the phone instead of the night dispatcher.

"Cash, it's Cassidy. Someone is breaking into my house."

"Where are you, Cassidy?"

"In my bedroom at the house."

"Lock the door, push whatever you can against it and the windows, we're on our way."

We're? She could hear someone moving through the house. She hung up and got behind the large bureau and pushed with all her strength. For a moment, it didn't move. She could hear the intruder on the other side of the door, trying the lock.

The bureau slid with a lurch. She shoved it across the worn wooden floor to block the doorway, then looked toward the window. It was large and paned. Anyone who wanted to get to her could come through it without any trouble.

She grabbed the mattress off the bed and pulled it over to the window, then did the same with the box spring, standing it up, shutting out the moonlight.

She could hear the intruder trying to break down her bedroom door, angrily slamming against it again and again.

Then silence.

The silence terrified her. Where had he gone? She stood in the middle of the room, then rushed to the trunk and began to shove it toward the window. She stumbled over the mattress and almost fell, hitting her head on the box spring frame. Stars glittered in the darkness and she felt light-headed. She touched her forehead, her fingers coming away wet and sticky with her own blood.

The sound of shattering glass brought her out of her stupor. She pushed the trunk against the mattress and box spring, then she leaned against it, putting her weight into it, but she could tell it was a losing battle.

He was stronger than she was. She felt the mattress being forced into the room. She could hear his ragged breathing now, smell his sweat.

Then his hand found her hair. She let out a scream as he grabbed a handful of it and said her name.

CHAPTER TWELVE

As the wail of the siren died off in Cassidy's yard, Rourke leaped from the patrol car and ran toward the house. He could hear Cash calling after him to wait.

The front door was locked. He ran around to the back.

The first thing he saw was the broken bedroom window and the crushed bush outside. From inside the house, he heard soft sobbing.

"Cassidy?" It was half call, half cry. He practically dove through the window.

She was slumped on the floor in the shaft of moonlight coming in through the window. She looked up at the sound of his voice. And the next thing he knew, he had her in his arms.

"He would have killed me if the siren hadn't scared him away," she whispered.

"Who?"

"Cecil Danvers."

Rourke held her in his arms, telling himself this was all his fault. He'd gotten her into this. She pressed her face into his chest for a moment, but when she heard Cash at the bedroom door, she stepped away, gathering a strength that he couldn't help but admire.

He shoved the bureau away from the door, unlocked the door and turned on the bedroom light. She stood, hugging herself, looking away from the window. There was a small cut on her forehead, but she was all right, he told himself. But he still wasn't leaving her alone again. He'd take her back to the cabin. He wouldn't let her out of his sight until Forrest's killer was caught.

He'd hesitated earlier because he'd been afraid of what people in town would think, her staying with a known criminal. Now he didn't give a damn. And while he was being honest with himself, he'd been afraid to take her to the cabin, unable to trust himself around her, and it had nothing to do with the fact that he hadn't been with anyone in eleven years. He was determined not to hurt her again.

"Are you all right?" Cash asked as he went to Cassidy.

Rourke stood back, watching the two of them for a moment. Did Cassidy care for his brother? It was obvious Cash cared for her. But not like a lover. More like a sister. Cash was still hung up on that woman from college.

She was telling Cash that it had been Cecil Danvers. Rourke started to turn away when he spotted something on the floor. A cream-colored envelope. What caught his attention was the name and address on the envelope. Rourke McCall #804376, 700 Conley Lake Road, Deer Lodge State Prison, Deer Lodge, Montana.

He leaned down and picked it up. His gaze shot up to the left-hand corner. The return address was Cassidy's.

He stared at it in confusion. He'd never received a letter from Cassidy while he was in prison. Obviously she had never mailed it.

He glanced back toward her and saw the large old trunk she'd pushed up against the mattress and box spring. The lid on the trunk was partially open, an envelope the same color as the one in his hand was sticking out of the opening.

Another letter? He stepped to the trunk and lifted the lid. He caught his breath, never expecting to find the trunk full of letters. Dozens and dozens of them. All addressed to him. All never mailed.

He heard the soft gasp and turned to find Cassidy staring at him, one hand over her mouth, her eyes wide with a different kind of fear than what he'd witnessed earlier.

"I didn't mean to pry. It was lying on the floor."

She closed her eyes and nodded.

He stared at her. "What is this?"

Cash glanced at the trunk full of letters.

"I can explain," Cassidy said.

"I'll be outside if you need me," Cash said to her, then shot Rourke a warning look as he walked out of the bedroom. "I'll call in an APB on Cecil. He couldn't have gone far."

"What are these?" Rourke asked again after Cash was gone.

"Letters." Obviously. "I wrote you every Sunday for eleven years," she said, tears shining like jewels in her eyes.

He was flabbergasted. "Why didn't you mail them?"

She shook her head and looked away. "It's hard to explain." He waited. "I wanted to tell you how I felt. I guess I thought it would make a difference."

He couldn't believe this.

"I also wrote you about things that were going on in town, the weather, funny things that had happened at the café." She seemed to choke back a sob.

"Oh, Cassidy," he said, closing his eyes as he stepped to her and pulled her back into his arms. "I wish you'd mailed the letters."

He heard Cash come into the room, hesitate then clear his throat. Rourke let go of Cassidy and turned to face his brother. He didn't need to look far to see the disapproval on Cash's face.

"The highway patrol just picked up Cecil Danvers about a quarter mile from here in the ditch," Cash said, turning his attention to Cassidy. "He's drunk and bleeding from cuts on his hands. He admitted to coming after you, Cassidy. Any idea why?"

"I went out there this morning and asked him questions about his brother's murder," she said as if that explained it.

Cash shot Rourke a look. "This is your doing."

Rourke nodded and cursed himself. "I should never have gotten her involved."

"I *am* involved," she said.

Cash, to Rourke's surprise, nodded in agreement. "Well, Cecil is in jail so you won't have to worry about him. I doubt there is any chance he could make bail even if the judge allowed it. But you can't stay here. I was thinking I have that big, old house—"

"I'm taking her with me," Rourke said. "I'll see that nothing happens to her out at the cabin."

Cash motioned Rourke outside. "We'll just be a moment, Cassidy."

"What?" Rourke demanded, once they were out of earshot, although he knew what.

"Cassidy."

"Are you in love with her?"

"No, I just don't want to see her hurt."

"I don't, either," Rourke said. "I thought we already had this discussion?"

Cash sighed. "You know how you are with women."

"Actually, I don't. I was twenty-two when I went to prison."

"I would have thought you would hook up with Blaze as soon as you got out," Cash said.

Rourke nodded. "I would have thought so, too."

"Don't tell me she's not interested in you."

"Don't spread it around town, but it seems that my taste in women has changed." Rourke hadn't known how much.

It was still hard for him to believe that Blaze no longer appealed to him and Cassidy did but not in the same way. With Blaze it was fun and games, nothing serious. With Cassidy...he felt shy, he thought with a laugh.

"What?" Cash demanded.

"I think I might finally be growing up. Don't look so surprised. I've got a ways to go."

Cash just shook his head. Back inside, Cash asked Cassidy what she wanted to do. Before she could answer, Rourke said, "She's coming with me." Then he added quietly to Cassidy, "Let me do this."

Cassidy seemed to hesitate, then nodded slowly.

Cash sighed. "I'll see about getting a sample of Cecil's handwriting when he sobers up so we can compare it to the threats you both received. I wouldn't be surprised if the handwriting matches."

Rourke glanced at Cassidy. She didn't believe that any more than he did. Cecil did things like break into a house with his bull head and no plan. He didn't write notes to scare someone. He came after the person with a sawed-off shotgun or his fists.

"I'll call Simon at the lumberyard and have him secure your house for you until he can put in a new window," Cash said to Cassidy.

"Thank you, Cash."

He nodded, looking worried. "We don't know yet if Cecil killed Forrest. So, be careful, okay?"

"I wouldn't be surprised if he breaks down and confesses," Rourke said. "It would definitely explain why he was acting odder than usual the night Forrest was murdered." He told Cash about what Cassidy had learned.

"Cecil caught a ride with Blaze?" Cash said. "Then he was there during the fight and even for a while afterward. He could have known where Forrest was headed, could have gone up there easily enough after he got a ride home—or even been waiting for Forrest when Forrest got there."

"Looks like Cecil just pushed himself to the head of the suspect list," Rourke said.

CASSIDY HAD HEARD about the McCall cabin on the lake but she'd never been there before.

"It's pretty rustic," Rourke said as he parked behind it. He sounded as if he was worried she wouldn't like the place. Was it possible she was the first woman he'd ever brought here?

The inside of the cabin was small but neat, everything in miniature.

"This is your bedroom," he said pointing into a room with four bunk beds and a large chest of drawers. "It's the big one," he said with a laugh. "This is the master bedroom."

She walked the few feet to the next room and peeked inside. He was right. It was just large enough for a double bed. "This must have been your parents' room."

"Way back when. It's funny but Asa never slept in there after her alleged death. He always opted for the porch cot and let us boys fight over who got the big bed." He smiled. "I thought it was because he missed my mother and couldn't deal with her death. Now I'm not so sure."

"Couldn't it just be that he loved her and the room reminded him of everything he'd given up?"

Rourke looked down at her for a long moment. She practically squirmed under his intensity.

"Maybe you're right," he said quietly. "Want to see the rest of the cabin?" He led her through a small living-room area with rustic furniture and a bookshelf filled with classics and board games. No TV.

"It's wonderful," she cried, then blushed.

"I'm glad you like it," he said. "I don't have much in the fridge, but I do have beer," he said as he stepped into the kitchen. He turned and held up a bottle of beer.

To her surprise, she nodded, not wanting to call it a night yet. Earlier she'd been so exhausted, she thought as she walked to the wide expanse of windows that looked out on a screened-in porch and, beyond that, the lake.

The moon had scaled the mountains and now hovered over the lake, huge and buttery-yellow, the water shimmering like liquid gold.

"Let's go out on the porch," Rourke suggested as he uncapped her beer and handed it to her.

On the screened-in porch, he pushed open the door and she joined him as he sat on the top step and looked out at the lake. Only a slight breeze whispered in the pines above the shoreline. The night was still, warm and scented with the last days of summer.

"Pretty, isn't it?" he said, beside her, and took a sip of his beer.

"Breathtaking."

"See that spot right over there?" he asked, pointing to an outcrop of rocks at the edge of the water. "I was fishing there once when I was about six and I hooked into a huge bass. I'm telling you, it was the biggest fish I've ever seen in my life. Cash and J.T. were cheering me on, although it was clear they thought I couldn't possibly land it." He was lost in memory for a few moments.

"Did you?"

"Hmm? Oh, I landed it all right. J.T. thought it was a state record. He'd run to get something to weigh it. Cash was yelling at Dad that we were going to have bass for dinner."

She was watching him, recognized his wry expression and knew. "You let it go."

His smile broadened as he looked over at her. "Yeah. I never heard the end of it." Their eyes met, making her heart compress. Cassidy could feel the heat, almost see the sparks flying back and forth between them.

Rourke glanced away and took a drink of his beer.

Since the day he'd come back, he had talked to her about nothing but Forrest's murder. Tonight he wasn't that embittered man who'd come out of prison seeking vengeance. Nor was he the wild boy. He was someone in between, someone who made her feel warm and safe and alive sitting next to him. She wished this night would never end.

They finished their beers in a companionable silence, but she was never more aware of a man as she was Rourke. As he shifted to point out one thing or another, their thighs would brush and heat would spread through her. Her flesh felt on fire. She hugged herself, suddenly wondering if she'd made a mistake coming out here with him.

She wanted him to kiss her. No, not just kiss her. She wanted him to make love to her. To hell with tomorrow. She would have given anything to lie in Rourke's arms tonight.

Her heart pounded a little harder at just the thought of waking up tomorrow in his arms. Uh-huh. And having him tell you that last night was a mistake? And it would be a mistake. She knew that. Not that it made it any easier to push the fantasy away and rise to her feet. "I should get some sleep."

He rose with her. "Cassidy, I'm sorry I got you involved in this."

She shook her head. "I was already involved and I volunteered to help you."

"With a little arm-twisting," he said.

"I can take a lot of arm-twisting if I don't want to do something," she said and turned to go inside but he caught her hand—and just as quickly let go of it.

"Thanks," he said, and nodded as if that was all he wanted to say. Or do. But his gaze went to her lips. Her pulse quickened and she knew all she had to do was lean a little toward him, her face lifted to his and he would kiss her.

"CASSIDY." HE HADN'T even realized he'd said her name. Nor that he'd moved to her. He looked into her face and wondered how he could not have noticed her eleven years ago. She was so appealing, from her understated beauty and warm brown eyes to her golden mane of hair that tumbled around her shoulders and the soft cadence of her voice.

But it was the tenderness he saw in her eyes, the shyness that tugged at his cynical heart and made him feel weak in the knees around her.

There was something about her that made it easy to talk to her, easy to be around her. There was an intelligence and a determination that exemplified why she had done so well with the Longhorn Café. Not to mention, a kindness, a goodness that seemed to radiate from her face.

He admired the hell out of her.

But what he was feeling now went beyond admiration.

She was frowning at him, her head cocked a little to one side, her eyes bright as sunlight.

Kissing her right then was as natural as breathing. And yet he hesitated. He didn't want to mess this up, and he feared kissing her might ruin something good. He liked her, felt they were becoming friends. He didn't want to lose that.

But he only hesitated a moment. His desire to kiss her

overpowered everything. Throwing caution to the wind, he leaned toward her.

She didn't pull back. Her eyes widened, her lips parted. He dropped his mouth to hers. A soft, gentle brush of a kiss.

She seemed to hold her breath, eyes wide. Then she giggled. "Sorry," she said.

He shook his head, pulling back to smile at her.

"I'm a little—" she hiccuped "—nervous."

His smile broadened. She had the hiccups? "Can I get you a glass of water?"

She nodded and hiccuped again, her face reddening. "Oh, I am so embarrassed," he heard her say under her breath, which only made him smile more as he went into the kitchen and got her a glass of water.

"Here," he said, when he came back out.

She took the water and gulped it down, holding her head back. "I get the hiccups when I'm...nervous."

"I'm sorry I make you nervous."

She swallowed the rest of the water, then they both waited to see if the water did the trick.

She laughed in relief and he laughed with her, but as their laughter died, the atmosphere between them seemed to change as if the molecules themselves had become charged with electricity.

"I should..." She made a motion toward her bedroom.

He looked at her and smiled. He wasn't going to mess this up. No way. "Good night."

She nodded, seeming disappointed. Not half as much as he was. But the more he was around Cassidy, the more he liked her. The more he was determined not to hurt her.

As the door closed, he stood on the steps and silently cursed himself. So much for his pledge not to get too close to her. He couldn't believe he'd kissed her. If she hadn't gotten the hiccups...

He smiled to himself, remembering. He liked Cassidy. She seemed to bring out something good and strong in him, something he liked.

He let out a long breath and stared up at the moon. It felt as if he'd never seen it before, as if his life really was beginning all over again. How about that?

He went onto the porch and sprawled on the cot, the moonlight filtering in through the screens. For the first time in a long while, he felt at peace.

CHAPTER THIRTEEN

THE NEXT MORNING Rourke woke to the sound of a vehicle coming up the road. He rose, surprised how well he'd slept last night.

Cassidy's bedroom door was closed as he padded to the back porch. He suspected it would be Cash coming out to check on Cassidy.

But as the vehicle drew closer, he saw that it wasn't the sheriff's patrol car but one of the green Suburbans from Antelope Development Corporation. Easton? He'd been expecting a visit from him. The Suburban pulled up, morning sun glaring off the windshield. The door opened.

He groaned as Blaze stepped out. What did she want?

"You're a hard man to find," Blaze said, coming to a halt at the bottom of the steps. She looked up at him as if waiting for an invitation.

"What can I do for you, Blaze?" he asked, leaning against the railing, not inviting her inside.

She seemed to take in his rumpled T-shirt and jeans, his bare feet.

"I have something important I wanted to tell you," she said. "About the night Forrest was killed." She looked pointedly at the door to the cabin. "Well?"

He knew it was probably just a ruse. "Okay." He motioned her in, leaving the door open as he walked back into the cabin to the kitchen where he started a pot of coffee.

When he turned, she was right behind him. He swore

under his breath, angry with himself for the shot of desire that bulleted through him at just the familiar scent of her perfume. It brought back a wave of sexual memories that reminded him how long it had been.

With Blaze it would be so easy. Hadn't he promised himself that the next time he got a chance, he'd sleep with her? Well, this wasn't that chance given that Cassidy was in the next room. But the idea definitely had its appeal.

He'd noticed the last couple of days that his libido was starting to resurface. He didn't trust himself with Cassidy. Maybe if he took Blaze up on her offer, it would make it easier to be around Cassidy.

He took a breath. "There was something you wanted to tell me?"

"A cup of coffee would be nice."

"It's brewing."

She stepped closer. "It's been a long time," she whispered. "I never forgot you, Rourke." And then her mouth was on his.

He closed his eyes, lost in the kiss, in the familiar. But then he opened his eyes and saw Blaze and pulled back.

She blinked in surprise. "What?"

He shook his head. He could no more explain it than speak at the moment. Blaze was a sexy woman and the offer was clear, but he wasn't interested even if Cassidy hadn't been in the next room. It surprised him more than it did even her.

He looked past Blaze and saw Cassidy and knew she'd witnessed the kiss. Damn. She was wearing his robe. She met his eyes for only an instant, then hurried into the bathroom, closing the door silently behind her.

Blaze hadn't seen Cassidy or heard her pad quietly to the bathroom. "Come on, stop playing hard to get. You know you want me."

"Sorry, Blaze, but I don't want you."

She glared at him with a mixture of anger and contempt in her eyes. "This is a one-time offer, Rourke."

Surprisingly he was glad to hear that. He heard the shower come on. Blaze didn't seem to notice. "What is it you wanted to tell me about Forrest's murder?"

She shook her head and he figured it would be a cold day in hell before he ever found out.

"Unless you were lying about having something you wanted to tell me," he added.

She bristled at that. "Yvonne Ames." She practically spit the words at him. "She's the woman who was meeting Forrest the night he was murdered."

He couldn't have been more surprised. "How do you know that?"

"She told me. In so many words. She came by to see me because she thought I'd be seeing you." Blaze glared at him. "She was afraid you were going to find out. She asked me if you'd said anything about her since you'd been back. She said she sent you letters and cookies at prison. I knew she was lying."

Yvonne had never been overly bright. Going to Blaze was one of her dumber moves. She was lucky Blaze hadn't strangled her on the spot. Blaze had to be beside herself at even the thought that Forrest was seeing her and Yvonne Ames. It definitely put Blaze in a category she didn't want to be.

"What's so funny?" she demanded.

He shook his head. The shower stopped. "It must have ticked you off royally to find out Forrest was running around with you and Yvonne."

"I didn't see a ring on my finger," she snapped. "I could date anyone I wanted."

"Seems Forrest felt the same way."

She whipped around angrily and he thought she was going to stomp out right then. Instead her expression softened. "Rourke, don't do this." She pressed her palms against his T-shirt and gave him the come-hither look that used to draw him to her like a bear to honey. *Now or never,* her look said.

Never, he thought, surprising the hell out of himself.

"I know you're angry with me," she purred. "But if you could just forgive me, you and I could—"

"Blaze, that's not it. I'm not angry. I'm just not... interested."

She reared back as if he'd slapped her.

Just then, Cassidy came out of the bathroom, wearing his robe, her hair wet and clinging to her flushed skin.

Blaze turned and let out a curse before swinging back around to face him, her face hardening to stone. "You just made the biggest mistake of your life." Then she stormed out, slamming the door behind her.

Cassidy was also giving him a look. "You have lipstick on your cheek," she said, and walked down the hall to the bedroom, closing the door behind her.

BLAZE DROVE LIKE a demon back into Antelope Flats. Rourke didn't know who he was dealing with. She'd show him. He would rue this day, so help her, God.

She pushed open the door to ADC ignoring the receptionist's cheery "good morning," and stormed into the office, dropping her purse and keys onto her desk before turning, surprised to see Easton at his desk.

He looked so good this morning she almost poured her heart out to him. "Something wrong?" he asked.

Everything was wrong. Nothing was going the way she'd planned it. And worst of all, Cassidy was with Rourke. She felt tears flood her eyes and realized what was killing her. She didn't care about Rourke, she never had. She just didn't want Cassidy to have him. And she wanted Easton to be so jealous that he'd break down and finally ask her to marry him.

As she stared at Easton, she realized what a fool she'd been. "Oh, Easton." She threw herself into his lap.

He caught her, obviously surprised by her outburst. "Let me guess. Rourke."

"This isn't about Rourke. It never was. You're the only man I love." She wiped her eyes and he reached into his pocket for his handkerchief. He handed it to her. It was true, she realized with a start. She loved him.

Easton laughed. "Blaze, you really are something. Love? You might want to marry me. Or at least think you do right now."

She blinked. "I'm serious. The past few days have made me realize just what you mean to me."

His eyes narrowed and he stood, forcing her off his lap. He walked around the end of his desk, putting distance between them. "What's going on with Rourke?"

"Nothing!"

"So that's it."

"No, I don't care about Rourke. He didn't even come back the same man I knew."

"What a surprise after eleven years in prison."

Blaze stared at him. Easton had never been this snide to her, never this cold. A chasm of fear opened up inside her. "East, I never wanted Rourke. I just wanted to make you jealous, make you realize that you couldn't live without me."

He let out a startled laugh. "Did I just hear the truth come out of your mouth? This is a first."

She lowered herself into the chair he'd vacated feeling suddenly too weak to stand. She dropped her head, crying in front of him, no longer worrying about what it would do to her makeup. "You have to believe me. I love you."

"Really, Blaze? What if I had no money?"

She looked up at him in surprise.

"What if I lost everything? What if we had to live the rest of our lives in that dinky apartment of yours? Would you still love me then, Blaze?"

She was trying to imagine why he would lose everything.

"That's what I thought." He strode to the door, his face hard with anger. "I can see the answer in your face. Don't even try to deny it."

"No," she said, stumbling out of the chair. "I…would love you. I would. I do. Easton, please."

But it was too late. He stormed out, slamming the door, leaving her alone. She dropped back into the chair and buried her face in her hands.

Why would Easton lose everything? It must have something to do with Rourke. That would explain why Easton had been acting strangely lately. He and Rourke had been best friends. Was it possible Easton really did have something to do with Forrest's murder?

She felt strangely protective of Easton as she forced the sobs to recede, dried her eyes and picked up her purse. She would help Easton any way she could.

ROURKE WAS UNUSUALLY quiet on the drive into town. Cassidy suspected it was because he was regretting having turned down Blaze.

"I'm sorry I complicated things for you this morning at the cabin," she said, glancing over at him.

"I assume you heard everything."

"Not *everything*," she said, trying to sound indignant. "I've already told you. I could care less about you and

Blaze. That was all in the past." She could feel his eyes on her. Did he suspect she let the shower run while she listened with her ear to the door and then took a speedy shower? "Blaze is obviously still interested in you. I'm surprised you don't take her up on her...offers."

Rourke laughed. "Me, too. Did you hear what she told me?"

Cassidy couldn't remember if she was supposed to be in the shower during that discussion. "What was that?"

He eyed her suspiciously. "That she believes Yvonne Ames was meeting Forrest the night he was murdered."

Cassidy widened her eyes at him.

He smiled and shook his head. "I thought maybe you and I could stop by and talk to Yvonne. She might be more likely to talk to a woman about it than me." He glanced over at her again. "What do you say?"

"I need to get changed and go to work." What she needed to do was distance herself from Rourke. It was just a matter of time before Blaze got to him and he gave in to her. Cassidy had to remember that.

"Sure." He sounded disappointed that she wasn't coming with him.

True to his word, Cash had seen that a large sheet of plywood had been placed where the window had been in her bedroom. The house looked fine. Rourke offered to check the outside while she changed.

She thought about the kiss last night at the cabin. Hurriedly brushed it from her thoughts as she heard Rourke come back into the house. Blaze would do whatever it took to get back at him.

"Mind if I use your phone to call Yvonne?" he called.

"Help yourself." She heard him dial.

"No answer. What do you say to a change of plans?" She could hear him just outside the bedroom door. She didn't trust her voice. "I was thinking we could go for a horseback ride this morning. I can get Martha to make us a brunch basket."

She opened the bedroom door and looked at him. Was he serious? Hadn't she just said she had to go to work? "I own a business, Rourke—"

"I know. I was just hoping you could take off the morning so we could ride up Wild Horse Gulch. The back way," he said.

She stared at him. "You think the killer went by horseback?"

"It crossed my mind after what Cecil told you," he said. "Four landowners have the property in that area, my family, Blaze's father, the Forest Service and Mason VanHorn. I didn't see anyone else on the road that night or any other car parked at the end of the road."

"Cecil is in jail," she said. "You still want to keep investigating?"

"I want to spend the day with you and I know this spot that is perfect for a picnic. Say you'll come with me."

She thought about him and Blaze and what she'd witnessed this morning and warned herself not to get involved with Rourke McCall. He wasn't over Blaze. No matter what he said. "I really need to get to work."

"Okay, I don't think Cecil killed his brother. The truth is I'm still investigating and you promised to help me," he said, and grinned.

"You're that determined to get me to go with you?"

"Yes."

"Did you mean it about Cecil?" she asked.

He shrugged, still grinning. "Maybe."

"This isn't about keeping an eye on me, is it?"

He pretended to be offended. "Would I be that transparent?"

She knew she shouldn't but in truth, she wanted to go riding with him. She felt herself weaken. "I'll call the café and see if they can get by without me for a few hours."

He grinned from ear to ear. "Thanks. I really appreciate this."

WHEN SHE CALLED the Longhorn, Arthur said he and Ellie could handle it. She promised to be in later to help with the dinner rolls and bread. Then she changed into jeans, a snap-button Western shirt, boots and her jean jacket and cowboy hat.

When she came back into the living room, Rourke looked up, his gaze caressing her as it moved slowly over her body, lighting on her face.

"What?" she asked, feeling embarrassed by his scrutiny. She turned to peer into the hall mirror.

He laughed and shook his head, his smile broadening. "I was just admiring your face. It's a wonderful face. You don't even need makeup."

"Thank you. I think."

"Come on, I can't wait to get back in the saddle," he said, and winked at her.

She walked past him to the pickup and could almost feel him watching her behind. She hid a smile as he hurried to open her door. This felt like a date. She warned herself to be careful.

She hadn't been out to the McCall Ranch in years. She was glad to see that it hadn't changed. Rourke gazed out at the landscape as if he couldn't get enough of it.

"When this is all over," he said, "I think I'm going to help my brothers with the ranch." He glanced over at her. "You don't seem surprised."

"I always knew you would," she said, and looked away from him. "You love the ranch. It's a part of you."

Rourke laughed. "Maybe you know me better than I know myself."

Maybe, she thought.

He parked the pickup and they walked down the hillside to the barn. The same barn where Rourke had kissed her when she was thirteen. She followed him inside, fighting the memories.

The day Rourke had kissed her she'd come out to the ranch with her father to deliver a load of oats to Asa. While they unloaded it, Asa suggested J.T. show her the horses. But Rourke had volunteered.

She had thought her heart might stop. It had been the happiest moment of her life as he'd led her out to the horse barn.

Inside, she had watched him with the horses, heartened to see that he obviously loved horses as much as she did. She'd thought then that she and Rourke were perfect for each other.

"Would you like to ride sometime?" he'd asked just when she thought the day couldn't get any better.

She nodded, unable to trust her voice, and he'd smiled at her in his sweet, tender way, and that's when she'd realized he was going to kiss her.

Her breath had caught in her throat as he'd cupped her cheek and dropped his head. And then his lips were on hers, sealing her fate. That fate being unrequited love.

"You all right?" Rourke asked now.

She blinked, focusing on the present. From the look on his face, he'd been studying her.

"I thought you could use one of my sister's saddles and ride Sunshine," he said, still eyeing her closely.

She took the saddle he handed her and nodded, unable to trust her voice just as she had so many years ago. That kiss had started her heart along this path. And the kisses since then had only made her more sure that she'd fallen in love with a man who might never really see her for one reason or another.

She saddled Sunshine, practically hiding behind the horse. Even if he'd forgotten about her kiss, he had to have seen her feelings so clearly on her face.

They led the horses out of the barn, Cassidy intently aware of Rourke beside her, glad when they'd left the cool darkness of the barn, so full of memory and young-girl hopes, for the warmth and clarity of the morning sunshine.

The air was still cool from the night before as they rode across to the foothills, then climbed up over the mountains to drop into the gulch.

"I didn't realize how much I've missed this," Rourke said, breathing in deeply. He glanced over at her as if she was the one person he knew understood.

The McCall ranch ran over several drainages ending in a stretch of Forest Service land that connected with Wild Horse Gulch. Beyond the gulch was a section of Logan land that Blaze's father owned. The rest was VanHorn land. VanHorn had been buying up everything he could get his hands on ever since he'd discovered there was coalbed methane.

They stopped on a mountain ridge overlooking the gulch. Rourke carried the brunch basket Martha had made to a cluster of magnificent ponderosa pines and spread out the blanket on the dried pine needles. A breeze whispered softly in the boughs overhead.

They ate, talking about everything under the sun expect for murder and Blaze Logan. He seemed to like listening to her and encouraged her to talk about herself, something she felt awkward doing.

"I never forgot our kiss in the barn," he said after a while. "I'm sorry I never followed up on it."

She felt her face flush as he reached over to brush her hair back from her cheek.

He stared into her face, her lovely face. Her scent mixed with the scents of the land he'd always loved and he felt weak with a need to kiss her again.

Her mouth was wide and generous, her lips full and heart-shaped. And when she smiled—

She was smiling at him now, her head cocked a little to one side, her eyes bright as sunlight.

He'd known he would kiss her again. It was all he'd thought about since last night. He leaned toward her, brushing his lips over that wonderful mouth.

He pulled back to look into her eyes. She was beautiful! The thought hit him like a brick. It wasn't just her face or her eyes or her smile. Everything about this woman was like sunshine.

He'd never wanted anything more than to be with her right now. Not even his freedom from prison. He leaned toward her again, cupping her cheek with his palm. With Cassidy, he felt like he'd really come home.

"Cassidy." It was as if all of his feelings were wrapped up in that one word.

Her eyes darkened with desire and her lips parted as he dropped his mouth to hers. He pressed her back into the blanket, the scent of pine and her filling his nostrils.

He heard her catch her breath and thought he could hear her heart pounding and realized it was his own. He pulled back. "Cassidy?"

The look in her eyes was answer enough. He kissed her again, deepening the kiss, burying his hand in her hair.

His pulse was pounding so hard he didn't hear the first shot.

But the horses did. They started, rearing back from

where he'd tied them a few yards away, their heads coming up in startled surprise.

The second shot came on the heels of the first, this one closer. Rourke threw himself on top of Cassidy, rolling them both across the blanket to the cover of the thick trunks of the pines. The shots had come from the gulch. He heard an engine crank up.

"Stay here," he ordered Cassidy as he scrambled out from the pines and ran to the edge of the ridge. A green Suburban with ADC on the side disappeared in a cloud of dust over a rise and was gone.

But in the sunlight, he spotted one gold spent casing lying in the dust not far from where he'd found Forrest in his pickup.

"It was just another warning," Cassidy said beside him. "Just like the notes."

"Except Cecil is in jail."

She nodded. "This wasn't Cecil."

"No," he said. "I caught a glimpse of the vehicle as it was racing away. It was one of the green Antelope Development Corporation Suburbans."

"Blaze," Cassidy said on a breath.

He didn't bother to argue it could have easily been Easton. He dropped down, carefully retrieving the casing from the dust. "Let's get back to town," he said, looking up to see Cassidy watching him closely. "I'll take you to the café where you'll be safe, then I'll drop off the shell with Cash."

As Cassidy walked in the back door of the Longhorn Café a couple of customers called to her. Les Thurman from the Mello Dee was sitting at the counter. He gave her a nod. Past him, she saw Holt VanHorn. He looked like he was waiting for someone. Cassidy glimpsed a pickup outside the café. There was a person sitting in it. Cecil? Was it possible he'd somehow made bail?

Cassidy was so angry with Blaze, it was all she could do not to storm over there and accost her. Blaze seemed hell-bent on keeping Cassidy away from Rourke and had since Cassidy was thirteen.

The worst part was, Blaze's plan was working. Cassidy wondered if Rourke regretted that they hadn't made love under the pines as much as she did.

He hadn't said much on the way back to town, insisting he follow her from her house to the café to make sure she was safe. She wanted desperately to know what he was thinking, then decided it might be best not to.

The phone rang. Ellie picked it up before Cassidy had a chance and, turning, covered the receiver to say, "It's Yvonne Ames."

Cassidy couldn't imagine why Yvonne would be calling her. She stepped into her office to take it, leaving the door open. "Hello?" Silence. "Hello?"

"Cassidy?" Yvonne sounded upset. "I have to talk to you." She sounded as if she'd been crying. "I heard you were helping Rourke look for Forrest's murderer?"

"Yes. What's wrong, Yvonne?"

"I know I should have come forward eleven years ago, but I couldn't. You have to understand. If my father had found out that I was meeting Forrest—and then after what happened, I couldn't tell anyone."

"You saw Forrest that night up Wild Horse Gulch?" Cassidy said, and realized her voice had probably carried out into the café. She hurriedly closed the office door. "Yvonne, did you see the killer?"

Yvonne was crying, sobbing, her words indistinguishable. Then "I have to blow my nose." She dropped the phone.

Cassidy waited impatiently. Was it possible Yvonne really had been the woman Forrest was meeting and not Blaze? And had Yvonne seen something?

"Sorry," Yvonne said, finally picking up the phone again.

"You were there that night?"

"I didn't see the killer," she said.

Cassidy's hopes sank.

"When I got there, Forrest was still alive. The killer had just left. I don't think he saw me. He took off on a horse."

Just as Rourke had suspected.

"Forrest had something in his hand. It was a St. Christopher medal on a chain. It had blood all over it."

"Forrest's?" Cassidy asked.

"No. The chain was broken. I think Forrest must have reached for his killer and grabbed the chain."

"Yvonne, you've had something of the killer's all these years and you've never said anything?"

"I couldn't." She began to cry again. "I didn't know who killed Forrest. It's just a medal. If I told the police all it would do was let the killer know I was there that night. I didn't see anything, but he wouldn't know that for sure. He'd kill me, too."

The medal might have cleared Rourke, might have helped find the real killer eleven years ago. "Yvonne, why are you telling me this now?"

"I'm afraid. I think he's found out somehow that I was the one there that night."

"Where is this medal?" Cassidy heard a sound in the background at Yvonne's. "What was that?"

"Someone is at the door again."

Again? "Don't answer it," Cassidy cried, suddenly afraid.

Yvonne choked back a sob just before she dropped the

phone again. Cassidy heard a voice. It sounded like Blaze's stepbrother Gavin.

"Yvonne? Yvonne?!" Cassidy fumbled her cell phone out of her purse and dialed 9-1-1, keeping both phones to her ear. She could hear nothing on Yvonne's end.

The dispatcher said Cash was unavailable at the moment.

"Tell him to go to Yvonne Ames's house," Cassidy said. "I'll meet him there. It's urgent."

"Yvonne? Yvonne?" Cassidy listened for a few moments, thought she heard a scuffing sound but Yvonne didn't come back on the line. She left the phone off the hook, grabbed her purse and left. What had she done with Rourke's cell phone number? She'd left it on the table by the door at her house.

She couldn't wait for Cash. Maybe the person at the door had been a beauty supplies salesman. Cassidy told herself she was overreacting. But she thought she'd heard Gavin's voice. What if someone *had* found out that Yvonne was the woman meeting Forrest up Wild Horse Gulch that night and had kept it to herself all these years?

What was Cassidy thinking? If Blaze knew, then the whole town could know by now—let alone her stepbrother Gavin.

"WHERE HAVE YOU BEEN?" Easton asked as Blaze came into the office. She looked scared and upset and her clothing was a mess, dusty and dirty.

She seemed surprised to see him, and at the same time, relieved. "I have to tell you something."

He nodded. "And I have something to tell you, too, something I think you already know, or at least suspect. I'm in trouble. I did some creative bookkeeping when I first started this business. Rourke hired a private investigator and now the auditors are coming to go over my books—the real books. I'll probably be going to jail for a while." He waited for her to say something.

She stared at him, then began to laugh and cry at the same time.

"You're taking it better than I expected," he said. "I figured you were only interested in marrying me for my money and once you realized there was no money..."

"I thought you killed Forrest," she managed to get out between sobs.

"Oh, Blaze," he said, and opened his arms as he moved to her.

She stepped into his arms. "I did something really stupid eleven years ago and again today, East."

"Did you kill anyone?" he asked, holding his breath.

She shook her head. "But I lied about where I was the night Forrest died. I tried to follow Forrest. I thought he was meeting someone else. I lost him, but Cecil knew because I gave him a ride as far as my dad's ranch."

"Has Cecil been blackmailing you?" Easton asked, wondering how Cecil had made bail. He'd just seen him on the street outside.

"Cecil isn't that smart," she said.

Easton watched as Rourke's pickup pulled up out front, then the sheriff's patrol car. The two men got out and looked into the Suburban Blaze had just returned in. His heart caught in his throat. He hadn't realized how much he didn't want to lose Blaze until that moment. "Blaze, I think you'd better tell me what you did today."

THE SUN WAS HOT coming in the car windows as Cassidy drove to the outskirts of town. Yvonne lived in a small house that she'd bought after beauty school. The front of the building housed her beauty shop, Hair For You.

As Cassidy drove up, she saw that the Closed sign was still in the window of the shop. She climbed out of her car and went to pound on the door. Locked. Peering in the window, she could see the place was empty, the door that went into the apartment part of the house closed.

The lot next door was waist-high weeds. On the other side, there was a flower shop that had gone broke, the windows soaped, a For Lease sign out front.

Across the street were more empty lots and several old houses that were in the process of being torn down for a minimall that she'd heard Easton was building.

Cassidy hurried down the narrow sidewalk along the side of the house. Yvonne's small blue car was parked at the back next to a shed.

Grasshoppers rustled in the tall weeds, the air back here hot and rank. She caught a whiff of the garbage cans along the dirt alley as she stepped up to the back door and knocked. No answer.

"Yvonne!" she called, and pounded on the door. Through a crack in the curtain, she peered into the house but could see nothing beyond the small kitchen and breakfast nook.

She tried the knob. To her surprise and concern, the door swung open. She stood for a moment, wishing Rourke was here with her. Wishing she heard the sound of Cash's siren.

Silence. Except for the chirp of the grasshoppers.

She peered in and saw two dirty plates on a small breakfast-nook table, a half-eaten slice of bacon sitting in the congealed egg yolk on one. Yvonne had had company.

"Yvonne?" She stepped in and had to stifle a gasp. The house had been ransacked, everything pulled out of drawers and cabinets.

She stood looking at the mess. Wait for Cash. A noise

came from upstairs. Like the scuff of a shoe on the wood floor, the same sound she'd heard earlier on the phone. "Yvonne?"

The living room was also ransacked. A floorboard creaked overhead. Cassidy looked up the narrow stairway against the wall. She could see nothing at the top of the stairs but shadowy darkness.

Wait for Cash, her instincts told her. *Don't go up there alone.*

But as she started up the steps, Cassidy knew she had to go up. She had to see if Yvonne was up there, maybe hurt. Another creak of a floorboard.

"Yvonne?" No answer. Just the old house creaking like old houses tended to do.

Cassidy ascended the steps coming out on a short dark landing with three doors, two closed, one partially open. She started toward the door that was open a crack.

"Yvonne?" she called as she pushed the door slowly open.

"THERE'S A .22 RIFLE under the backseat of this one and the engine is still warm," Rourke said as he and Cash moved along the side of the green ADC Suburbans.

"I'll go down the street and get a warrant from Judge McGowan," Cash said. "You think you can keep Blaze and Easton from leaving until I get back?"

Rourke just laughed and headed for the front door of ADC. He tipped his hat to the receptionist, not bothering to stop, going straight to Blaze and Easton's office. He wasn't in the mood to wait for anything. Cash had told him that Cecil Danvers had made bail. The good news was that there was a decent print on the casing they'd found up Wild Horse Gulch.

Rourke still couldn't believe either Blaze or Easton had

taken a potshot at him and Cassidy. He knew the reason he was so angry was because of what the shooter had interrupted. He was kicking himself for taking Cassidy up there and yet, at the same time, he couldn't remember a morning ride he'd enjoyed more. He knew it was probably for the best that he and Cassidy hadn't made love up there. But it didn't help his mood any.

He'd followed Cassidy to the café, making sure she was safe before going by the sheriff's office. Cassidy hadn't said much on the way to her place to change her clothing or on the trip into town. He couldn't wait to see her again. He had to know what she was thinking, what she was feeling.

Easton and Blaze both turned in surprise as the door opened and he walked in.

"Rourke," Blaze said. She'd obviously been crying. She shot a glance at Easton.

He had stepped forward as if to protect her. It surprised Rourke. He'd just assumed Easton didn't care that much about Blaze since he hadn't married her.

"Which one of you just got back from Wild Horse Gulch?" Rourke asked, unable to miss the look Easton shot Blaze.

"I did," he said, and Blaze couldn't seem to hide her surprise. "What's the problem?"

"Someone driving a green ADC Suburban just took a couple potshots at Cassidy and me."

Easton was shaking his head. "Can you prove that?" He stole a glance at Blaze, obvious worry on his face. "I'm sure this is just a misunderstanding."

Rourke smiled. "Just like Forrest's murder?"

"I didn't have anything to do with that," Easton said. "Look, Rourke, could we talk about this?" He shot a glance at Blaze, who'd sat back down behind her desk. She looked scared.

"Why don't we step outside," Rourke said.

Easton raised a brow. "Okay."

As they left the office, Rourke told the receptionist to make sure Blaze didn't leave.

"I'm sorry I didn't make an effort to come see you in prison," Easton said. "I feel bad about that."

Rourke nodded. "But you started dating Blaze the second I left town, so that probably would have made it awkward during your visit."

"Well, you're here now. There's nothing keeping you from taking Blaze back."

Rourke smiled at that. "Actually there is, but it's not you. I'm interested in someone else." The admission surprised him. "Blaze and I were never serious about each other anyway. At least Blaze wasn't."

Easton raised a brow and glanced toward the office as if things were clearer now. "Blaze and I are going to be getting married."

Rourke couldn't hide his surprise. "Why now? It's been eleven years."

"I guess I wanted to be sure she was over you. She loves me and I love her." He seemed to challenge Rourke to say otherwise.

Something passed between them, a remnant of the friendship they'd once shared.

"Congratulations," Rourke said, and meant it. "Too bad one of you will be behind bars. I know Blaze took the shots at us, not you. You're willing to go to prison for her?"

Easton let out a soft, amused chuckle. It reminded Rourke of all the good times they'd shared. Gone, just like the past eleven years. But not forgotten. "I think we both know that I'm headed in that direction already and, like I said, we love each other. We're two of a kind, as it turns out."

Cash came up the street with the warrant. Easton took it and nodded, watching while Cash searched the Suburban and found the rifle.

"I'm the person you're looking for," Easton lied. "I did it."

"Why?" Cash asked. He could have meant why did you do it. But Rourke suspected, like him, Cash knew Easton was covering for Blaze.

Easton directed his answer at Rourke. "Sometimes we do stupid things to protect the people we love." He turned back to Cash. "Before I say anything else I'd like to speak to my lawyer."

"I won't be pressing charges," Rourke said.

"What?" Cash demanded.

"Consider it a wedding present," Rourke said to Easton. "I hope the two of you will be happy."

Easton nodded, eyes shiny. "I'm glad you're back, Rourke. You'll have to give me some tips on staying alive in the Big House."

"For a white-collar crime like cooking your own books?" Rourke said. "A good lawyer can get you off. Now that you're marrying his daughter, I'm sure John Logan knows of a good attorney or two."

Easton smiled and held out his hand. Rourke looked at it for a moment, then shook it.

Cash started to say something but the two-way radio in his patrol car squawked. "Don't move. I'm not finished with you," he said to Rourke and went to answer it.

Through the window, Rourke watched Easton go back inside the office. Blaze looked up, her expression filled with fear. Rourke couldn't hear what was being said but he could guess. Blaze's expression turned to one of disbelief, then shock, then she was crying and Easton was on his knees proposing. Blaze must have said yes, because the next moment, she was in his arms.

"Get in!" Cash called from the patrol car and flipped on his siren.

The car was already rolling as Rourke closed the door.

"It's Cassidy. She got a call from Yvonne. She's gone out there. The dispatcher said Cassidy heard a sound on the line, then the phone was dropped."

Rourke swore and watched the highway as it blurred past. For the first time in years, he prayed for someone other than himself.

As CASSIDY PUSHED on the bathroom door she saw the sink, the mirror over it fogged with condensation. Had Yvonne dropped the phone because she'd forgotten she'd left the water running in the tub?

But then where was she now?

Cassidy caught an acrid wet scent as the door creaked all the way open.

The red shower curtain was drawn across the tub. No water on the floor, but the room was humid as if someone had just taken a bath. Odd. Odd, too, that smell. Like burnt electrical wiring.

She glanced at the red shower curtain, her imagination creeping her out. *Don't. Don't even consider it.*

She'd seen too many horror movies as a teenager. She reached for the curtain to pull it back. That's when she heard it. A siren in the distance. Cash. She breathed a sigh of relief and thought about going downstairs to wait for him.

But her fingers were already on the shower curtain. She drew it back, telling herself later she'd laugh about how scared she was because the tub would be empty, a faint ring around the edge from where the sudsy water had been earlier.

She heard something behind her. A sound like a soft jingle. But her gaze was on the tub.

It wasn't empty.

Cassidy screamed, the sound ricocheting off the walls as the sight branded itself on her brain. Yvonne fully clothed lying in the tub of water. Her face blue and floating just under the surface, legs splayed, knees up. The still-plugged-in hair dryer resting on her chest.

Cassidy swung around, half falling, half lurching back through the bathroom door onto the landing. She heard a sound, a door creaking open. She turned her head.

At first she thought it was Cash, that somehow he'd gotten there quicker than she'd expected. But she could still hear the siren drawing closer and the dark figure came from a now partially opened doorway that had been closed earlier.

She couldn't make out the features in the shadowy darkness of the landing until the figure was almost on top of her. And then it was too late. She didn't have time to react. Didn't even have time to get her arm up.

The blow caught her in the temple, the force knocking her backward. She felt the air rush from her lungs as she fell, then saw nothing but darkness.

CHAPTER FOURTEEN

"CASSIDY!" ROURKE TOOK the stairs three at a time with Cash yelling for him to wait as he ran through the ransacked house.

She was slumped against the wall on the landing, her head tilted to one side. His heart caught in his throat. No! Oh, God no.

But the moment he touched her, he knew she was alive. She stirred and let out a soft moan, her hand going to the bump on her head. Her eyes came open. She focused on him, a smile turning up the corners of her mouth.

"Rourke."

He thought his heart would burst from his chest as he drew her to him. "Are you all right?" he whispered against her hair.

She nodded and rubbed her temple. "He hit me."

"Who?" Cash asked as he reached the landing, his weapon drawn.

Cassidy drew back a little from Rourke's embrace, her eyes widening. "Yvonne." The word came out on a sob as she motioned toward the open bathroom door.

Rourke exchanged a look with Cash, then Cash stepped into the bathroom, his weapon still drawn. Rourke heard a curse, then Cash checked the other rooms and called for the coroner and forensics crew out of Billings.

"Yvonne's dead," he said, then knelt down close to Cassidy and checked her pupils. "Who hit you, Cassidy?"

"A man. I think I saw his face...." She frowned, then held her head.

"I don't think you have a concussion," Cash said. "How do you feel?"

Rourke was still holding her, never wanting to let her go.

"Woozy but all right. Yvonne said she was at Wild Horse Gulch the night Forrest was killed. She said she went up there to meet him. She saw the murderer leaving on horseback, but didn't recognize him. She was scared because she thought he'd found out about her." Cassidy let out a sob. "Forrest was still alive when she found him that night. He had a medal in his hand, a Saint Christopher medal, the chain broken. He gave it to her."

"The killer's?" Rourke said on a breath.

Cassidy nodded. "That's why she was so afraid. She feared the killer would get her before you found out who he was if he knew she had the medal and had been the woman Forrest was meeting that night."

"Yvonne has been sitting on this for eleven years?" Rourke couldn't believe it.

"She was scared he'd come after her."

"It seems that's exactly what he did," Cash said. "Is anything coming back? Something you might have seen or heard or smelled...?"

She shook her head.

"Do you think you can stand?" Rourke asked her. He couldn't remember ever being that frightened. He held Cassidy tightly to him as he helped her up.

"Wait a minute, there was something. I heard a jingle, like change in a pocket or a lot of keys on a ring." She shook her head. "That's all I can remember and I can't even be sure about that. I thought I saw his face, but it's gone now."

"You were hit pretty hard from the size of the knot on your head," Cash said.

"Gavin," she said suddenly. "I thought I heard Gavin's voice when Yvonne left the line before I came out to check on her."

Cash looked startled. "I passed Holt's car as I was coming out. It looked like Gavin behind the wheel. You take Cassidy back to the cabin. I'm going to have a talk with Gavin." Cash took off.

He glanced back at the bathroom. "If only Yvonne had come forward eleven years ago."

A set of dual sirens grew louder and louder as the state boys arrived.

Rourke told them where the sheriff had gone and left word for Cash to call him when he heard something.

Cassidy was quiet on the drive to the cabin. He turned up the heater and wrapped his coat around her, but he could see that she was still shaking.

He drew her to him and she snuggled into him.

"I can't believe this is happening," she whispered against his chest. "I can't believe this."

He wished he couldn't, but he'd known for eleven years that the killer was still out there.

At the cabin, Rourke dug out his father's stash of good bourbon from where Asa kept it hidden for his fishing trips with Cash.

He poured Cassidy a little in a glass. "Here, drink this."

She downed it, coughed and looked up at him. "What was that?" she said on a single breath.

"The best bourbon money can buy. Asa's good stuff. He swears it will put hair on your chest."

"I hope not."

CASSIDY DIDN'T REALIZE how tense she was until Rourke's cell phone rang and she practically jumped out of her skin. She watched as he answered it, listening to his side of the conversation.

"Yeah? Thanks, Cash. Yeah, I'll tell her. No, she's fine. I will. Okay." He clicked off.

She watched her face. "It's bad, isn't it?"

"Gavin was driving Holt's car. Cash tried to pull him over. Gavin made a run for it and missed that corner down by the coal mine. He's dead."

Cassidy took a breath and let it out as Rourke sat down beside her.

"Gavin had a nasty scratch on his face. The forensics tech found skin and blood under Yvonne's fingernails. Cash is waiting for the results but it looks like Gavin killed Yvonne." He hesitated. "There's more. The forensics tech found a Saint Christopher medal in Gavin's car. The chain had been broken and the silver was tarnished."

Cassidy felt tears burn her eyes. "The one Yvonne told me about."

"Looks that way. It's over, Cassidy. You're safe. And I'm…I'm free."

"Oh, Rourke," she whispered, and began to cry, so filled with emotion. She had prayed for this day. She looked into his wonderful pale blue eyes and felt her heart soar.

He kissed her softly on the lips, then pulled back. "No hiccups?" he asked, smiling at her.

She shook her head, waiting for a moment, then smiled. "Not a one."

He slipped his hand around her waist and drew her to him. His mouth dropped to hers and her lips parted not in surprise but in response to his ardor. Her arms came around his neck, she sighed against his mouth, a satisfied sigh as he wrapped her in his arms.

Cassidy felt as if she'd come home. It was the oddest feeling. Especially given her response to the first kiss. Actually their second. The barn kiss had been quick, a brush of dry lips, but it had jump-started her heart.

Their second kiss had been better, no doubt about that. Her racing heart and her hiccups could attest to that.

But this kiss. Oh, this latest kiss… It was all that she'd dreamed of. Just like being wrapped in Rourke's arms.

She told herself she was dreaming as she listened to the thump-thump of his heart. This couldn't be happening. Dreams like this didn't come true.

He drew back and she thought, well, that was that. He would apologize, promise never to do that again and she would hang on to the memory of the kiss for another fifteen years.

But when he looked into her eyes, she felt her heart jackhammer in her chest.

"Cassidy?" he asked in a whisper.

She nodded, not sure what the question was but darn sure of her answer.

He seemed to hesitate, but only for a moment before his mouth lowered to hers again, the kiss slow and sensual. His tongue parted her lips and, as he entered her, she couldn't stop the moan that escaped.

He drew her to him, pressing his body to hers as the kiss deepened. This kiss she could live on the rest of her life.

"Cassidy," he whispered against her mouth as if her name were a prayer.

She locked her arms around his waist as his mouth devoured hers. Her knees seemed to melt and the next thing she knew, he was sweeping her into his arms.

He kicked open the bedroom door and strode in with her. And then they were on the bed and he was kissing her senseless again.

His fingers worked the buttons of her uniform top. She felt the cool breeze caress her skin, then his warm palm. She sucked in a breath as his fingers skimmed over the hard tip of one nipple then the other.

She'd squeezed her eyes closed tight but didn't realize

it until he stopped touching her and she opened her eyes, startled to find him above her, looking intently down at her.

"Are you sure about this?" he asked.

Just as sure as she was about taking her next breath. She nodded, wanting to plead with him not to stop. Not now. Not after she'd dreamed of nothing else for years.

His gaze held hers for a long, long moment, then his mouth dropped to her left breast. She groaned, arching against the warm wetness. *Don't stop. Don't ever stop.*

He didn't. It was everything she had ever dreamed— and so, so much more.

IT RAINED THAT NIGHT. A soft *tap, tap, tap* on the metal roof that lulled them both to sleep in each other's arms.

It was the first night Rourke had slept in a real bedroom since he'd gotten out of prison or without waking with a start in the middle of the night and feeling disoriented, scared and alone.

He awoke to find Cassidy's face inches from his own, her brown eyes open. Clearly she had been watching him sleep. Something about that seemed more intimate than even their lovemaking the night before.

She smiled at him shyly, tentatively. "Good morning."

"Good morning." He returned her smile. She looked dewy-eyed fresh, uninhibited. He remembered how Blaze had gotten up before him in the mornings, rushing to re-fresh her makeup as if afraid for him to see her without it.

Cassidy wore no makeup. She always looked fresh and clean, smelling of soap.

This morning she looked as delectable as she had last night, maybe even more so given their new intimacy.

He leaned nearer to gently kiss her. His cell phone rang. He groaned and fished through the pocket of his jacket tossed carelessly on the floor the night before.

"Hello?"

"Rourke, it's Easton. I just heard the news. I'm so glad that your name is going to be cleared." News traveled faster than the speed of light in Antelope Flats.

"How is Blaze taking the news about Gavin?"

"You know Blaze. She and Gavin were never close. He's always been in some sort of trouble or another. She was surprised that he was capable of killing anyone, though. It's too bad but we're just glad it's over."

"Me, too."

"I don't know if you've heard but Les Thurman is throwing a party tonight at the Mello Dee to celebrate your freedom and announce Blaze's and my engagement. I hope you and Cassidy will come. It would mean a lot to me. And to Blaze. New beginnings?"

Rourke glanced over at Cassidy. They would have all day together before the party tonight. "I'll ask Cassidy." He told her what Easton had said.

"They're engaged?" she whispered. "This I have to see."

"We'll be there." He clicked off.

"It won't bother you to go back to the Mello Dee? It is Saturday night," she said. "Or did you forget about *my* plan?"

He smiled. "That was the worst plan you ever came up with," he joked. It seemed like a million years ago that he'd come up with that crazy idea.

"Rourke, I can't help but wonder why Gavin killed Forrest."

"He and Forrest were involved in something illegal, we know that much, and they had a falling-out," Rourke said. "We might never know. I've wondered too how Gavin got my gun." He met Cassidy's gaze. "Blaze. You think she stole it for her stepbrother?"

"Anything is possible, I suppose," Cassidy said slowly. "But they were never close. I find it hard to believe even Blaze would do that."

"Remember this is the same woman who took pot-shots at us just yesterday," Rourke reminded her as he leaned down to kiss her. "I think Blaze is trying to change, though."

"Right." Men could be so naive sometimes, Cassidy thought.

"I feel like an incredible weight has been lifted from my shoulders. It's over, Cassidy. Now I can start thinking about the future. Speaking of the future…" She smiled and he drew her to him. "We have all day before the party."

"Hmm," she whispered. "All day, huh?"

THE PARKING LOT at the Mello Dee Lounge and Supper Club was packed when Rourke and Cassidy arrived. Rourke spotted his brother's patrol car in the lot. Cash wasn't much of a partygoer so it surprised him.

As they walked in the front door, Cash met them as if he'd been waiting for them. "Cassidy, could you give us a minute?" he asked.

"Cassidy!" Les called. "I heard what happened. The drinks are on the house. What will you have?"

"Go ahead," she said to Rourke. "I'll be fine." She slid onto the barstool and ordered a light beer.

"You sure you wouldn't like something stronger?" Les asked with a smile.

She shook her head, smiling. She was already intoxicated on life. On Rourke.

"Well, at least let me pour it in a glass for you." Les laughed as he went down the bar to get her beer. Several other bartenders were behind the long bar, serving up drinks to the lively crowd. Music blared from the jukebox and voices tried to talk over the music.

Everyone in town seemed to be here. The tables were full and people were spilling in and out of the larger rooms at the back.

She noticed Blaze and Easton were at the center of it all. Blaze saw her, whispered something to Easton and headed her way.

Cassidy groaned inwardly. It was one thing to celebrate her cousin's engagement, it was another to actually be forced to talk to her. Was that why Cash had wanted to talk to Rourke, because he'd discovered that Blaze had stolen Rourke's gun, which her stepbrother used to kill Forrest?

"Cassidy, I'm so glad you came tonight," Blaze said. "There is something I need to say to you."

Cassidy braced herself.

"I'm sorry."

Sorry? Cassidy couldn't help her surprise.

"I've always resented the hell out of you," Blaze said with a laugh. "In truth, I wanted to be you." She laughed again. "That's not going to happen so I'm just trying to deal with being me."

Cassidy was speechless.

"I'm really happy about you and Rourke. That's the way it should have always been. If I hadn't messed things up for you years ago…"

Cassidy was shaking her head. "Rourke and I aren't—"

"Maybe things worked out for the best, you know? Rourke has changed and that's good." Someone began to make a toast to the lucky couple. "Anyway, I'm sorry. I'd better get back to Easton."

"Congratulations," Cassidy managed to say before Blaze left. She stared after her in shock. Had Blaze really said she'd always wanted to be her and that she was sorry?

Les put her beer down in front of her at the end of the bar and she took a drink. "How is it?" he asked.

"Great. Thanks."

"So Gavin killed Yvonne and Forrest?" Les asked, shaking his head in disbelief.

"Looks that way. I'm just glad that it's over."

"You all right? I heard Yvonne Ames's place was ran-sacked and you were the one to find her."

She nodded, not letting herself remember what she'd found behind the shower curtain.

"Any idea what Gavin was looking for?"

She hesitated, not sure how much of what she knew was public knowledge. She shook her head and took a sip of beer.

Les was watching her closely, as if he knew she wasn't telling him everything. Les was worse than a hairdresser when it came to wanting all the good gossip.

"So Yvonne saw Gavin kill Forrest?" he asked.

"We may never know."

"Too bad all this didn't come out eleven years ago at the trial," he said. "Could have saved Rourke a lot of heart-ache."

She nodded.

"I wonder why Yvonne called you? I didn't realize the two of you were friends," Les said.

"She'd heard that I was helping Rourke look for the real killer."

Les was shaking his head. "All these years she never said a word. Who would have known? How's your head? I heard you got hit pretty hard. You didn't see Gavin hit you?"

"No, I…" Again she hesitated. She could see the dark hallway, someone coming toward her, remembered thinking it was Cash, then realizing it couldn't be Cash.

"You remember something?" he asked.

She shook her head and smiled. "I feel like it's just right there, like on the tip of my brain."

He glanced at her beer glass. "Drink up. I'll make you something special that's bound to help you remember."

Cassidy took another sip of her beer as Les went down

to the other end of the bar to make her drink. She wondered what was keeping Rourke and Cash.

ROURKE DIDN'T LIKE leaving Cassidy alone. Not because he was worried about her anymore. He just liked being with her. "What's so important we have to do this now?"

"Forensics found something that doesn't make any sense," Cash said, once he and Rourke were outside the bar and away from earshot. "Yvonne had had sex right before she was killed."

Rourke stared at him in shock. "You aren't going to tell me—"

"Gavin's DNA was found inside her."

"Was she raped?"

Cash was shaking his head.

"What the hell?" Rourke said, pacing in a tight circle. "She had sex with him and then he put her clothes back on and drowned her in the tub?"

"They could have had a lovers' quarrel afterward, after they were both dressed," Cash suggested.

"A man who's worried that she's going to talk and get him sent to prison for murder isn't going to make love to her first," Rourke snapped. "You're telling me he might not be the killer."

"I talked to one neighbor," Cash said. "This wasn't the first time Gavin spent time at Yvonne's. It seems they were lovers. The neighbor also heard them fighting a lot. One time, Yvonne had a black eye the next day. That could explain the scratches this time."

Rourke swore and looked toward the Mello Dee. "Gavin didn't kill her."

"Then why did he run when I tried to pull him over?" Cash said.

"Guilty conscience over something else maybe."

Cash nodded. "I talked to Holt VanHorn, asked him

why Gavin was driving his car. He broke down and told me that Gavin had been blackmailing him." He sighed. "Holt admitted to stealing the murder weapon from your bedroom the night of your birthday party."

Rourke swore.

"Holt swears the gun was stolen out of his car and he doesn't know who killed Forrest," Cash said. "It looks like the killer is still out there."

LES RETURNED TO Cassidy at the end of the bar, laughing at some joke someone had told him. He had a drink for her in his hand. "Come here," he said, motioning for her to follow him.

She took a quick glance toward the room full of people. Everyone was gathered around Easton and Blaze. She looked toward the door. Rourke and Cash must still be outside talking.

"You've got to hear this," Les said, motioning her toward the hallway to the back door.

She slid off the stool, feeling woozy. She hardly ever drank. The beer had gone to her head. Or she was still unsteady from the blow she'd taken yesterday. She started down the short narrow hallway toward the back of the Mello Dee.

"Easy," Les said, suddenly at her side.

"I just need a little air."

"Here, let me help you. You don't look so good." He led her down the hallway, the music and voices growing dimmer. As he walked beside her, his keys jingled softly. She tried to remember where she'd heard that sound, but her brain seemed fuzzy and she could barely lift her feet.

"Where are you taking…"

"Just need to cool you off," he said, and opened the large walk-in beer cooler. He shoved her in before she could react. She stumbled and fell to her knees. The door closed with a soft whoosh.

She turned as she grabbed a shelf and pulled herself up to her feet. Her legs felt like water. She had to lean against the shelf full of cases of beer and wine. Her mouth felt cottony and she could see her breath when she breathed. Les seemed to waver in front of her like heat waves on pavement in the hot summer sun.

"What are you doing?" Her voice sounded funny. But her brain was still working, just too slowly. "You put something in my beer." She opened her mouth to scream.

"Don't bother screaming. The walls are too thick. Even if the music wasn't so loud, no one would hear you."

Her scream died before it made it to her throat. She swallowed, her mouth so dry she could barely talk let alone scream.

"You saw me, didn't you," Les said.

She tried to focus on him, focus on his words.

"You looked right at me. I knew I should have finished you right then, but I could hear that damned siren." He was shaking his head.

"It was *you* in the hallway at Yvonne's?"

"Right on the tip of your brain, huh? At the café, I heard you on the phone with Yvonne, heard what you said about Wild Horse Gulch and the mystery woman Forrest had called. Everyone thought it was Blaze."

Cassidy shivered as his words registered. The cold air in the cooler was already working its way to her bones and she felt sick and weak.

"The back door of Yvonne's house was open," Les continued as if talking more to himself. "I heard Gavin upstairs with her, the radio blaring, the two of them fighting, then making love. I knew Yvonne had no imagination if she was doing Gavin, so it was easy to figure out where she would hide my Saint Christopher medal. I knew I had to tie up all of the loose ends." He took a breath. "I put the medal in the car Gavin was driving, then I waited for him to leave. The problem was he came back a second time. He'd forgotten his hat. He saw Yvonne in the tub and freaked." Les laughed. "Serves the worthless puke right. Beating up women."

He abhorred beating up women, but he'd killed Yvonne? And Forrest?

He rubbed a hand over his face. His words came out in puffs of white. "I thought Forrest was dead, then he made a grab for me. I could hear the car coming up the road. Any moment I'd be caught in the headlights. I tried to pry his fingers loose from the chain, but there wasn't time."

Cassidy fought to stay awake. She could feel the effects of the drug coursing through her system. If she fell asleep in here, she'd die of hypothermia.

"I didn't stick around. That property used to be mine before Mason VanHorn cheated me out of it. I knew every inch of it. Forrest couldn't have picked a better spot. He never expected anyone to come by horseback."

Les seemed lost in his story, as if he'd needed to tell someone and now he had a captive audience. She couldn't move. Feared if she tried to take a step her legs would fail her.

"I just assumed the vehicle coming up the road was Rourke's. Or Blaze. I'd hoped my Saint Christopher medal was lost in the rain that night when it didn't turn up."

She mouthed one word. "Why?"

He seemed surprised she could still talk. "Why? That bastard Forrest was blackmailing me. He'd seen me vandalize Mason VanHorn's coal-bed methane wells. He was bleeding me dry. Mason knew about the methane on my land. He knew I was losing the place, he offered me pennies on the dollar for my land, then made a fortune. So I destroyed a few of his precious wells out of spite and I knew it was just a matter of time before Forrest gave me up and collected the reward Mason was offering. I had no choice but to kill him."

The words she muttered were almost indistinguishable. "Rourke's gun."

Les must have been anticipating the question. "I stole it out of the back of Holt VanHorn's rig, thinking I'd get back at Mason when his son was arrested for murder. I had no idea it wasn't Holt's gun. I was sick when it turned out to be Rourke's. I could have killed Holt."

Les looked at his watch as if worried he'd been gone too long. Surely he wouldn't leave her here to die. He stripped off his belt and came toward her.

She tried to dodge him, but her legs gave way. Her fingers clasped the front of his shirt as she fell. She heard the tinkle of buttons hitting the cold floor, heard him let out an oath.

He was on her at once, using the belt to tie her to a metal shelf. Her teeth chattered. She licked her lips, tried to form the words, "Don't...Les."

"I'm sorry, Cassidy. If Gavin hadn't come back, I wouldn't have been trapped in the bedroom, I wouldn't have had to hit you, you wouldn't have seen me." He shook his head. "I never wanted any of this. But I couldn't take the chance you would remember seeing me."

She pulled against the restraints as he rose to his feet. She was too weak to pull free. She watched him push open the door. She tried to scream, but nothing came out, then Les was gone, taking a case of beer with him. The door closed and she was alone, freezing cold and scared she would never see Rourke again.

ROURKE RUSHED BACK into the Mello Dee, fear tightening his insides the moment he saw the empty stool at the end of the bar where Cassidy had been sitting.

"Have you seen Cassidy?" he asked as he moved through the bar. No one had.

He got Les's attention.

"Cassidy?" Les asked over the din. "Ladies' restroom?"

Rourke started to head for the opposite end of the bar where the restrooms were found when he noticed that Les's shirt was open, the buttons missing. He frowned. A memory from a night Rourke had spent eleven years trying to forget. Les breaking up the fight between him and Forrest. A flicker of light, something cool swinging down and touching his cheek as Les bent over him and separated him and Forrest.

"You used to wear a Saint Christopher medal."

Les met his gaze. "What?"

"What happened to the buttons on your shirt, Les?"

Les reached down and Rourke knew before he lifted his hand that the bartender was going for the baseball bat he kept behind the bar.

Before Les could swing it, Rourke grabbed Les by the arm and dragged him over the bar.

"Kill the jukebox," Rourke yelled as Cash appeared next to him.

In the next instant, the music stopped and Cash was yelling for everyone to be quiet.

"Where is Cassidy?" Rourke was yelling down at Les. "Tell me where she is. If you hurt one hair on her head—"

"I saw her follow Les down the hallway toward the back of the bar," someone called from the crowd.

Rourke released Les and ran down the hallway. There were only two doors. A storage room. He jerked open the door. No Cassidy. And the beer cooler. He pulled open the heavy door, a gust of cold coming out.

He saw her huddled against one of the shelves. "Cassidy, oh God, Cassidy."

Her eyes fluttered open and her lips formed a lopsided smile. "My hero," she mouthed.

He hurriedly untied the belt and swept her up in his arms, rushing her from the cooler.

"Blankets," Easton yelled.

"There's one in my car," Blaze said, and ran outside.

Moments later Rourke had Cassidy wrapped in a blanket, in his arms. All the years he'd repressed his anger, he'd also repressed his emotions. But one emotion threatened to drown him as he looked down at her.

"I love you, Cassidy," he whispered as he pressed his cheek against hers, then pulled back to look into her eyes. "I came home bitter and angry. All I wanted was revenge. Against you. But once I got to know you..." He shook his head. "You are an amazing woman, Ms. Miller. I can't imagine life without you in it."

Cash took Les into custody and searched the bar, finding the drug he'd used to dope Cassidy. "She's going to be all right. Doc says it will just wear off. But if you hadn't found her when you did, she would have died of hypothermia."

Rourke took her to the closest place he knew of—the Siesta Motel—and got her into the shower with him. It didn't take long to warm her up. He seemed to have a talent for it.

"I love you, Rourke McCall," she whispered. "Do you realize how many years I've waited to say that?"

EPILOGUE

CASSIDY WOKE TO the smell of bacon. She opened her eyes. Rourke stood over her holding a tray.

"Hungry?"

She was, she realized, as she sat up and he placed the tray on her lap and sat down on the side of the bed.

He'd taken her to his family ranch. Rourke's mother had insisted the guest room be prepared for her.

"I was going to put her in my room," Rourke said.

Shelby had given him a look. "Cassidy doesn't want to be in any bed you've shared with another woman, no matter how many years ago it was. Don't you know anything about women?"

"No, but I'm trying to learn," Rourke said.

Cassidy had laughed.

"Now get," Shelby had said to her son last night. "The girl needs her rest."

Rourke left and Shelby smiled down at her. "I know we've never met, but I've heard wonderful things about you," the older woman said. "I couldn't be happier about having you here. Now, you get some rest. If you need anything, you just press that button, all right?"

"Thank you," Cassidy said. She'd closed her eyes, wondering if she'd only dreamed the part where Rourke had said he loved her and she'd said she loved him.

"How did you sleep?" he asked now. Sunlight streamed in the windows, the day bright.

"Good," she said, and realized it was true.

"Eat up, you'll need your strength. The rest of the family is anxious to see you." He handed her a piece of toast with a strip of bacon on top.

She took a bite and looked at Rourke. She felt shy around him. Did he regret telling her he'd loved her? If he really had. "I don't remember much from last night."

"You remember Les drugging you?" he asked.

She nodded. "And I remember most of what he told me in the cooler about Forrest blackmailing him over the coal-bed methane wells Les had sabotaged on the Van-Horn Ranch. Les took the gun out of Holt's car, thinking it was Holt's, and killed Forrest."

Rourke nodded, and picked up a piece of bacon, eating it before saying, "He's made a full confession to Cash. He killed Yvonne once he realized she had his Saint Christopher medal. He was afraid she'd seen him as he was leaving, after killing Forrest. It was like a house of cards, once it began to fall. Cash arrested Holt. He's confessed to stealing my gun at the birthday party. I'm sure he'll get off. Mason will hire the best lawyers money can buy."

"Is it really over?" she asked.

"Yes." He touched her cheek with his fingertips and gazed into her eyes. "It's really over." He moved the tray and pulled her into his arms.

"Ahem," came a familiar voice from the doorway. "Let her eat and get a shower. We're all waiting downstairs," Shelby ordered, then left.

Rourke laughed. "Looks like she's not only staying, she'd ordering everyone around, even Asa, but amazingly he's taking it." He shook his head as if he didn't understand it at all. He rose from the bed and smiled down at her. "See you downstairs?"

Cassidy nodded.

She showered, finding everything she needed along with some of her own clothing, which Rourke had brought from her house. After brushing her hair, she dressed and went down the wide stairway to find Rourke was right. The entire family was waiting.

They all greeted her, but it was Rourke who got to his feet and met her on the bottom step. He looked a little nervous and she wondered why he'd been so insistent about her staying at the ranch for a while.

"Cassidy," he said, and dug into his jacket pocket. "There's something I want to ask you."

She glanced toward his mother. Shelby was nodding, her eyes brimming with tears.

"Will you marry me? I promise to make you a good husband. I'll love you and cherish you and take care of you—"

"Give her a chance to answer," Asa said. Everyone laughed.

Rourke produced a small jewelry box from his pocket. "I love you, Cassidy."

She stared at him. It hadn't been a dream.

"Help me out here, Cassidy," he whispered. "Please, say you'll marry me. I know it's sudden but—"

"Yes. Oh yes," she said, and threw her arms around him, then she opened the small dark velvet box. A beautiful diamond ring twinkled up at her.

Rourke took it out and slipped it on her finger. She stared down at it, then at him. She'd imagined this since the age of thirteen and she couldn't have imagined it being more wonderful.

The family rushed to the two of them with congratulations and hugs and tears. Asa offered Rourke land up the road to build a house on and asked him to come back to the ranch. When Rourke looked to her, Cassidy nodded her approval.

He kept his arm around her, his gaze often meeting hers, as they all talked about the future.

Maybe someday she'd even let him read the letters she'd written him while he was in prison.

ROURKE HAD NEVER appreciated his family as much as he did at that moment. He loved them. And, he realized just how much he'd missed them, warts and all. That's why he'd brought Cassidy here, that's why he wanted to ask her to marry him with his family around them.

"I've decided to go to law school," Brandon announced. "I wasn't cut out for ranch work. I want to be a lawyer."

There were groans all around.

"This family could use a good lawyer," Brandon argued. "One of us is always in trouble."

Asa patted his son on the back. "If that's what you want, then do it."

They all looked at Asa as if they'd never seen him before. He'd been a different man since Shelby had returned. Rourke still suspected there was more to the story, but Asa and Shelby weren't telling it.

"*I* could use some help around the ranch," J.T. said disagreeably.

"Well, Asa isn't going to be helping," Shelby said, coming to stand by her husband's side. She took his hand. "He and I need to spend some time together and he's worked this ranch long enough."

"Don't look at *me*. Cassidy and I are going on a long honeymoon," Rourke said. "I'm thinking something tropical."

Cassidy smiled and nodded. "Sounds heavenly."

"You have to get married first," Dusty spoke up. She'd been pretty quiet since Shelby's return. Of all the kids, she was the one who hadn't forgiven her mother or father.

"Will you help me plan my wedding?" Cassidy asked her. Dusty's eyes lit up. "Really?"

"I'm going to need a lot of help," Cassidy said. "And I'm going to need a maid of honor."

"*Really?* I have some magazines," Dusty said, then flushed when everyone looked at her. "I was just *looking* at them." As far as Rourke knew, Dusty wasn't dating. But the neighbor boy, Ty Coltrane, had been coming around a lot, making excuses, always looking for Dusty and trying to get her attention when he found her. She didn't seem to notice.

"I suppose you heard that my camp cook broke his leg trying to ride some mechanical bull down in Cheyenne," J.T. complained. He really did need a woman, Rourke thought.

"Buck'll find you a cook before you go up to bring the cattle down from summer pasture," Asa said.

"I hate to imagine what Buck will come up with," J.T. grumbled. Buck Brannigan had been the ranch foreman since Rourke was a boy. He was a crusty old character who grumbled more than J.T. A loner, he stayed up the road in the original homestead cabin and wasn't much help anymore, but a definite permanent fixture at the Sundown Ranch.

"When is this wedding going to be?" Shelby asked.

Rourke looked at Cassidy. "As soon as possible."

She laughed and nodded. "Can we put together a wedding in the next two weeks?" she asked Dusty.

Dusty's eyes were as big as saucers. "There is so much to do. Flowers, food for the reception, everyone in town will want to come, and a cake and a dress…"

Cassidy looked to Shelby. "Will you help, too?"

Shelby glanced at her daughter. "Would you mind?"

Dusty shrugged. "I guess not."

"Great," Cassidy said. She couldn't wait to be Rourke's wife.

"J.T., can you wait to go up into the high country until after the wedding?" Rourke asked. "I want to see you in a tux as one of my three best men."

Rourke pulled his wife-to-be closer and wondered what he'd done in life to deserve this woman. Nothing, he thought. He'd just gotten lucky. And he would never forget it.

* * * * *